Forgiveness

By Jefferson R. Blackburn-Smith

Also by Jefferson R. Blackburn-Smith

The Ogre Prince

Retribution

Dedication

For Denise, without whose belief and support nothing would be possible.

This book is dedicated to all the men, women, and children whose lives have been disrupted by the violent actions of others. I am especially inspired by those who put the safety of others ahead of their own, and by the angels among us who find it in their hearts to forgive what has been done to them.

Chapter One

The distant crump, crump, crump of artillery created a faint bass line that reverberated against the tin roofs of the barracks. A brilliant cloudless blue sky, the March sun bright but not warming, was marred only by the ragged columns of black smoke that rose from the city twenty miles to the southeast. Walter Krang glanced across the parade ground towards the pit, an open scar at the edge of the concentration camp. The woman was right; someone had failed to show up for duty and the pit was unguarded. Was it a trap? Was someone waiting to shoot him the moment he ran? Krang looked quickly around the camp. The four guard towers were staffed, but the men were focused on the mass of people milling about on the other side of the parade ground. The pit would be at the edge of their field of vision. Trying to escape was a risk, but he knew he was dead if he didn't.

The battle for Mountain City had been raging for a week. They had heard tanks maneuvering in the woods outside the camp last night, meaning the camp would be liberated any day, but Krang knew that neither he nor any of his friends would be alive by the time the Corabian soldiers reached the camp. He was sure that the four trucks that had been pulled up to the edge of the parade ground had machine guns mounted on their beds. He was just surprised they hadn't been killed already.

Krang looked at the woman standing before him. Sarah Jezek. The camp had stolen her youth, her vitality, her beauty. And her husband and son. He still didn't understand, but he couldn't just wait to die. Krang nodded at her and turned away, walking slowly towards the pit. He resisted the urge to run, even though his back itched with the thought a thousand guns were trained on him at that very moment. Would he hear the shot that killed him?

The pit was a football pitch size abomination on the edge of the camp where the bodies of dead prisoners were thrown, covered in lime and eventually burned. The bulldozer that pushed the bodies around like so much refuse was idle today, parked on the far side of the pit. Krang stopped at the edge. Fifty or sixty bodies lay in a haphazard pile below him. They were the dead from the last few days. They lay on the accumulated misery of four years of death in the concentration camp. Thousands of bodies had been burned in this pit, and hundreds were rotting there now, coated in lime, awaiting their turn to be burn to ash. If the war hadn't interrupted, the pit would be burning right now.

Krang took a deep breath and pitched himself forward into the land of the dead.

The stench of the pit enveloped Krang like a damp blanket before he landed onto the mass of decaying bodies. Fresh bodies lay randomly across the pit where they had been thrown; the Corabians had buried no one since they took over. Krang hit hard, a head driving into his ribs, knocking his breath away. Krang gasped for breath, the air fetid and thick with the stink of rot. He fought the urge to retch, feeling the nausea boiling in his stomach and throat, and finally gave in and vomited where he lay, heaving until his belly was empty. The vomit was hot on his face and chest.

Krang scrabbled to find some purchase among the bodies. He was sinking below the dead bodies like a man drowning in a bottomless lake. As he struggled, he listened for the sounds of his betrayal.

No one shouted at him from the camp. No prisoners were screaming for help. No shots rang out. Was he safe? A quick glance at the late afternoon sky convinced Krang that he would be seen easily if he tried to cross the pit now. Krang crawled forward away from his vomit, trying to move slowly enough that he wouldn't call attention to himself. He stopped a few feet forward, and then lay still. Could he just be another dead body until night fell? If someone looked in the pit he might be recognized. Especially if they noticed he was missing. That meant he couldn't just lay there motionless and pretend to be dead. He needed to be hidden or be gone.

Taking a deep breath, he pushed his arms under the body in front of him, dipping his head like a swimmer slipping below the surface of a lake, and pulled himself under the body. He fought for purchase among the strangeness of the bodies, seeking to get deeper below the surface of the pit. His legs wriggled and pushed as he propelled himself down, trying to get at least two bodies above him. When he thought he was hidden, Krang froze.

Something skittered across his neck, reminding Krang that the pit was alive with all manner of vermin, from flies and roaches to rats and even wild dogs. At night, the guards would turn a spotlight on the pit and use the rats and dogs gnawing at the bodies for target practice. Krang felt vulnerable and exposed. He couldn't tell if he was really hidden or if some part of him was still visible.

Which would be worse, Krang wondered: Someone taking potshots at him from the edge of the pit or a rat gnawing on his fingers or toes? Or on his cock? The thought made him want to run for the far side of the pit. Krang bit his lip to calm himself. It was death to move before dark. He would wait.

Something, blood or body fluid, was dripping from the bodies above him into his hair and along his neck. His face was pressed against a corpse. He turned his head slightly, just enough to move his mouth and nose free of the body below

2

him. The buzzing of flies was incessant. His whole body itched and trembled. He could feel the pressure building up inside, like a kettle set on the fire to boil. He was going to lose everything if he didn't find a way to calm himself.

Krang drew in a slow, deep breath. And then a second. He forced his mind away from the pit. What the fuck had she been thinking, to let him go? Who was Sarah Jezek? Krang had no reason to doubt her, but he didn't remember her. He had been shocked when she told him her story. Not because he didn't believe her, he did, but he couldn't believe that he had forgotten her. She was just one of many, nothing special. He had been even more shocked when she had said she forgave him, and kissed him on the cheek and then told him the pit was unguarded. Was she his Judas? He still thought she would be back, bringing gunners with her, telling them he was in the pit. He wondered if they could open fire on the bodies of their fellow prisoners in hopes of hitting him, Walter Krang, the one they called *the Guard*. Had he burrowed deeply enough to be safe?

Krang smiled. Prisoners he had tormented, and maybe even killed, were now protecting him. Sarah's husband Abraham and son Capek had to be somewhere underneath him, nothing more than skeletons being pulverized by the weight of the death piled above them. They would have been burned, fifteen or twenty times, so they weren't even bone, just ash and dust. A small laugh escaped before Krang could stop it. All three of Sarah's men are in the pit now, but only one will be reborn.

Krang relaxed. As long as he remembered that he still was in control, everything was fine. Sarah had let him go because he still held power over her, not because she forgave him. That was simply her rationalization, the story she would tell herself. He owned her, as he owned every Corabian who had walked through the gates of this camp. He would terrorize their dreams for decades. They would never be free of him.

Krang promised himself that for Sarah things would be different. It wasn't enough to haunt her memories. Some night after she had put her life back together, a year or two from now, he would show up at her door and teach her what her forgiveness really cost.

Krang fought the urge to curl up in a tight ball. The stench of the pit was suffocating, even when he breathed through his mouth. It was as if he had wiped a dead animal across his face. A giddy laugh forced its way up, almost like vomit, as Krang felt the body pressed against his face and realized how close to truth his thought had been. But not dead animals, not road kill. Dead people. Krang-kill.

Krang felt himself hyperventilating, and he knew he was on the verge of jumping up and running for the far side of the pit. Running was certain death. He bit his tongue, hard, the pain giving him something on which to focus. Krang slowed his breathing again. Keep it together, he thought. Think about anything, he told himself. A great fuck. Emma. The kids.

Krang wondered how little Walter would feel, seeing his father lying in this pile of dead bodies. Would he even recognize me? I haven't been home often enough the last two years, none of the kids really know me. He had four kids. Emma had birthed the youngest just six weeks ago. Krang hadn't seen the infant yet, hadn't heard what name she had picked. Walter was the oldest. He was seven…, no, eight. Krang's last leave had been hard on the boy, who had clearly been scared of his father, a stranger upsetting the equilibrium of the household. Emma had spoiled the boy, he wasn't a fighter. He had been unwilling to challenge this man he did not know. Or did know, but hated. It made Krang question once again whether Emma had other men over to the flat. What if the boy was used to waking up in the middle of the night to the sound of his mother and a stranger fucking? What if Krang was only one in a succession of men in his own bed? Emma had always liked to fuck. It wasn't her infidelity that would hurt him, but the idea that she wouldn't hide it from the children. She could fuck around all she wanted to, Krang thought, as long as she didn't flaunt it to his children and friends.

And what of the boy? What if I rose up out of the pit? Would he shit his pants? Would he run for his mother, cursing this resurrection of his father? Or would he finally find the courage to stand up to me? Krang smiled to himself, realizing how much like his own father he had become. That man tortured me to within my last breath before I would fight back, he thought. He would have loved to drag me out to the edge of this pit on a night as black as death and rise corpse-like before me and demand a kiss to show my love of him. And I would have done it. I would have done anything for that man who deserved nothing more than to end up in a pit just like this one. It's a pity he didn't end up at the camp. How I would have laughed at him then. I would have kissed him then, just to smell the fear on him. But wouldn't every son love to have his father in his camp?

Walter should be tougher than he is, Krang thought. Emma certainly didn't prepare him to survive. If he was still alive by the time the tanks rolled into the city, I am sure he was hiding behind his mother's skirts wailing for help. Emma was too easy on him, and it cost him his life. At least my father prepared me for this. He prepared me for the pit.

The young woman stood at the window of her fifth floor apartment, wearing only a silk camisole, and watched the city falling apart. The Citizen's army had broken from their positions outside the city earlier in the day. The soldiers had flooded chaotically back into the city, running pell-mell in groups of five or ten, a contrast to the manner in which they had marched into the city weeks ago, in long precise columns. Black smoke, like angry storm clouds, rose from the eastern edge of the city where bombers had been pounding the army fortifications.

The steady rain of artillery shells falling on the edge of the city rattled the windows of the building constantly. The heavy bombers came in waves, making the entire building shake when they unloaded their destruction. The pressure from the explosions buffeted through the city like mini cyclones, blowing dust and debris everywhere. Stray bombs had been falling within the city all week. Just a few blocks away, a building was engulfed in flames, the upper two stories collapsed. Katie could see soldiers running through the streets a few blocks away, not sure, in the failing light, if they were Montrovian Citizens or Corabians invaders.

She was seventeen, coming into her womanhood, but thin from too many missed meals. Katie looked at her faint reflection in the window. Her long brown hair curled down onto her shoulders. She liked to keep her hair up, but Captain Stojespahl preferred it loose. He had returned early in the morning, while the fighting outside the city was at its worst, a half-empty bottle of vodka in his hand, a tinned ham under his arm, and demanded that she put on the camisole. He had taken her from behind, roughly, whispering in her ear that she was his Corabian whore, that he hated her and loved her, and that he would trade her to the Corabians for his freedom. He slept now, sated, in an alcoholic stupor.

Katie stared out at the city that she had once loved and now hated. She had grown up in a Corabian village a few miles outside the city, her father a respected religious teacher and village elder. She had come to the city with her mother on market days ever since she had been old enough to help with the shopping, and it had seemed such a magical place. Katie had loved the city center, with its big square and fountain that became the Saturday market. She would walk among the stalls, looking at bolts of cloth, fresh vegetables, and handmade crafts and dream of the day she would be shopping for her own family, each week a different boy in her head as her imagined husband. There would be no husband now.

Katie had especially loved to walk through the Corabian quarter, with its tight streets and family run businesses. If Katie had been good her mother would stop at the sweet shop for a bag of hard candies, or one of the many bakeries for an iced cinnamon bun. Every week they went to the dry grocer.

The dry grocer was located in an old stone building, and you had to walk down three steps to enter. The most delightful aroma hit you the minute you walked in the door. Cinnamon, cloves, basil, and a thousand other spices created a unique aroma that was the store's alone. The first floor was lined with shelves of spices, flours, sugars and other goods, and there was a counter at the back where the grocer waited on you. Mr. Rohlecek and his wife lived above the shop, and whenever Katie met either of them outside the store, she would swear she could smell the aroma of the store on them. Katie had loved to guess which of Mr. Rohlecek's sons would run the store after him: she hoped it would be the younger, with his broad shoulders and gentle smile.

If mother wanted a ham or some specialty item for a holiday meal, Mr. Rohlecek would lead them down a narrow stair under a trapdoor in the shop's floor, to his basement pantry. The hams hung from the basement ceiling, and shelves lined the walls. She could recall the tins of goose liver and other delicacies, and the small boxes of chocolates, her favorites. Life had seemed a blessing back then. When a new, modern grocery store opened a few blocks away, mother never wavered. She never even went inside to see what it looked like.

When the Corabian war started, the outdoor market had closed. The square was used for demonstrations, for troop assemblies, and then became the deportation center. This was where Corabian families gathered to board buses that would take them to the rail depot and put them on a train to the camp. Katie could still remember, as if it were yesterday, watching as her parents and sister climbed on the bus that took them away. She had been fourteen, and had pleaded with her father to run away. She could still remember how angry he had been with her. He didn't believe that his Montrovian neighbors and colleagues meant him harm. He was Corabian, he said, but also a Citizen. The rumors about the camps were just rumors, started by troublemakers.

Her father had believed that as a leader of his people he had to make a good example, and that cooperation was the key to safety. The deportations started among the Corabians living in the city proper, but once the Montrovian authorities began sending families from their village, her father had volunteered for his family to be transported, to prepare a place for the others at the camp. He had hired a carriage to bring them from the village to the city, saying that it was important to act as someone of their station should. Katie had argued and cried the entire trip. It had been a sunny day, so they rode with the top down, their luggage tied to a rack behind them. As they entered the city, the streets had become clogged with Corabians and Citizens moving towards the square. They sat for minutes at a time. Katie had grown more and more agitated, sure that her father was making a mistake. She stepped down from the buggy as they approached the square, trying to pull her sister Bela down with her. Bela was only eleven and had refused to go. Katie pulled her harder, tugging her from her seat as if Bela had been her own child. Katie's father grabbed Bela and pulled her from Katie's grasp. He held her tight.

"What are you doing?" he shouted at Katie. "Now is not the time for games. Do as you're told."

Katie looked at him, at the anger and fear on his face, and understood he couldn't save her. She shook her head at him, and without saying a word, or taking any of her belongings, she turned and ran into the crowd. She had disappeared into the crowd, fighting tears. How could he be so blind? And why had her mother had been silent? Didn't she care? Katie wormed her way through the crowd until she was on the far side of the square from her family. She watched the caravan of buses arrive. She was afraid she was making a mistake, and several times almost rejoined her parents. She was also afraid someone in the crowd would recognize her, but they were too focused on the Corabians in the center of the square to pay attention to one girl.

The crowd frightened her. She had never seen a deportation, and had expected it to be an orderly process, like the first day of school each year. The crowd was pushing and shoving trying to get close to the families that were being deported. They cursed and taunted the deportees. Once the buses were full and they pulled out for the rail depot, a huge cheer went up from the crowd. They surged forward to the center of the square, the men and boys doing a bizarre dance where the families had stood, like boys on a soccer team who had won a match, standing on the center of their opponent's field and jumping up and down.

Katie had slipped from the crowded square and wandered the city in a daze. She had not planned her escape, and had no idea how she was going to survive.

From her window above the city, Katie could just make out the entrance to the alley where she had been caught. A policeman had recognized her. He knew her father, knew she should have been on the train. It had only been two hours since the buses had left the square, so the trains were still at the rail depot. The policeman could still make sure she was deported with her family.

The choice the policeman had given her was easy. She followed him deeper into the alley, and had knelt before him on the cobblestone street. Her only fear, as she watched him unbutton his trousers, was that he would still turn her in when he had finished. Katie could still remember gagging and choking, and spitting his seed from her mouth. He had laughed at her discomfort while he buttoned his trousers, but had given her enough money to buy dinner. She cried as he walked away, her knees hurting from the cobblestones. Katie remembered trying to wash her mouth out later, trying to get rid of the salty taste of his sperm. Even today, as she remembered, she felt like she could still taste his bile. But she had learned a way to survive.

Katie glanced at Stojespahl snoring on the bed. He was the logical outcome of her first encounter. She had lived on the streets for two years, selling herself to anyone who wanted her. Her price had been a place to stay for the night, or the cost of a meal, and far too often all she received for her efforts was a beating. She had been picked up by the police several times, but had always been able to use her body in exchange for her freedom. For a few months she had found a patron, and had regular meals and a place to stay, until Stojespahl had arrested her.

7

Katie had no papers and knew that he could have her sent to the camp, but Stojespahl had no intention of deporting her. He told her she reminded him of his daughter. He had claimed it was a kindness, to bring her here, and demand his take of her body and her earnings. Katie hated herself for not running away from him, but she had just been too weary and scared to consider returning to the streets and losing a guaranteed place to stay and food to eat. So she had accepted his demands in return for being allowed to live in the apartment with him.

A shot rang out in the building below her, and someone screamed. A second shot and the screaming stopped. There were people in the building, going from apartment to apartment, rounding up the families that hadn't fled the bombardment and shooting them. Katie had heard the screams and shots all afternoon. Stojespahl was too drunk to hear anything. Katie didn't think it was Corabian soldiers going through the building. They hadn't advanced far enough into the city. And she didn't think they were Corabians who had been hiding out in the city. There had been no meaningful resistance against Montrovia during the war. So that meant, maybe, that some Corabian prisoners had escaped from the camp and reached the city as the Corabian army was advancing. Katie shivered with delight. If anyone had escaped, that meant there were survivors. Maybe her parents and sister had survived. She felt no sadness at the thought that she wouldn't see them again. When she had run from the square that day, it hadn't been because she had thought she could survive on her own. It had simply been an act of defiance, a refusal to go quietly. She had never expected to survive the war. It was enough to know that maybe her family had.

Whoever was in the building would be here soon. Katie turned away from the window and looked at Stojespahl. She walked to the chair that held his clothes and pulled his 9mm pistol from its holster. She slipped the safety off and jacked a shell into the chamber, as she had seen him do so many times when he threatened to shoot her, or turn her in. She wanted to be ready when they broke into the apartment. She stood beside the bed for a moment, watching him sleep. Bile rose in the back of her throat and she gagged, fearing she was going to vomit. She was so afraid, but she had become used to fear. She took a deep breath and regained control. She climbed onto the bed and straddled his chest, kneeling with her knees on his arms. She pressed the pistol hard against the bottom of his jaw.

"Wake up, darling," she hissed, kissing him violently on the mouth.

Benjamin Woerful sat outside the motor pool building, furtively smoking a cigarette. The large overhead garage doors on the building were all raised to accommodate the crowd of newly freed Corabians who wished to watch the tribunal. Even now, with the tribunal on recess, the building was full. From where he leaned against the back of the building the incessant chatter from the crowd

8

reminded Woerful of the endless buzzing of flies over the pit. Woerful took another drag on his cigarette, turning his head so he could see the body of Commandant Bitmeyer hanging from the flag pole on the parade ground.

Bitmeyer had been the first man to come before the tribunal, sentenced to death in less than ten minutes. Woerful felt no guilt about the man's death, even though he knew that Bitmeyer had thought he was negotiating his own freedom when he turned control of the camp over to the Corabians. The camp's Chaplain, a Montrovian priest, was also dead, having been burned to death in his little chapel when he refused to come out and face justice. The tribunal hadn't ordered his death, but it would have. What kind of man provides religious succor to the men who perpetrated the horror of this camp?

Woerful glanced again at Bitmeyer's body, hanging lifelessly from the flag pole. How he had shrieked and cried when he realized he wouldn't escape! At least the priest had suffered his fiery death in silence. The other guards were all on the parade ground, tried en masse and in abstentia, unaware of the death sentence hanging over their heads. Only one man had escaped justice; the one man who deserved it more than anyone else: Walter Krang, aka *the Guard.*

Krang, more than any other person, had epitomized the horror and brutality of the camp. He didn't brutalize inmates because he got off on their pain and fear like some of the guards, rather he was coldly impersonal. Every inmate had been touched by his random brutality and willingness to kill for the slightest infraction. And now he was gone. The moment it had been reported that he was missing, Woerful had sent teams of men into the woods surrounding the camp, but there had been no sign of him.

The murmuring in the room behind him rose to a crescendo and Woerful knew the woman had been brought in. He flicked the cigarette butt to the ground and shook his head. He had lost two daughters to the camp and now he was going to lose his wife. He hadn't known if their marriage would survive the strain of the camp and the loss of their daughters, but he knew it couldn't survive this. Katerina had already said as much. The young woman accused of collaborating with Krang was one of Katerina's favorites. Katerina had already come to see him privately to argue for Sarah's life, but what could he do? Woerful sighed. Maybe the tribunal had been a bad idea. After the triumph of Bitmeyer, it had turned into something toxic, with neighbor accusing neighbor of collaboration and the crowd demanding death. What could he do? He didn't disagree with what most of them felt. His soul cried out for justice for all of those lost to this miserable place. Whether they had been killed, died from disease or the physical strain of the work they were assigned or even had broken down and killed themselves when the pain of this place became too much, they all deserved justice.

9

But is it justice the tribunal is delivering? Or is it something else? Woerful had a fear so secret he couldn't share it with any of the men on the tribunal, but Katerina had seen it somehow and accused him.

"Your ego is driving this charade," she had said to him, when she was arguing for Sarah's life. "You are no more about justice than they were. You are no different that *the Guard!*"

Could it be true? He had come out here to pray, but had smoked instead. He couldn't find that quiet spot in his mind to pray, hadn't really found it for months. Maybe not even since they arrived here three years ago. Had God abandoned him? Or had he abandoned God? That was more likely, Woerful knew. He had never believed that God abandoned anyone until he had arrived here. God was absent in this camp. He had fought so hard to find God here, in a spring flower, in the birth of a baby, or the camaraderie of community. But when they made you pull up the flower and took the newborn and tore apart your community by killing every third person sitting with you at dinner that night, you soon learned that God was not here.

God was not here. So any justice served was not God's justice, but man's. And men without God had no compassion and so Sarah would die. If she was guilty, Woerful reminded himself. The trial must come before the sentence. But of course she was guilty or she wouldn't be here. Someone had accused her of freeing *the Guard* and Krang was gone, so of course she was guilty.

Woerful wished he had another cigarette. He wished he had some guidance. He had just over one thousand Corabian prisoners to save. Maybe ten thousand had passed through the camp during the war, most of them gone, most fed into the gaping maw of the camp. A few hundred had been sent to other camps, a handful, less than ten, had escaped, perhaps a hundred had fled the camp since Bitmeyer's death, and the rest were dead, thrown in the pit, burned and bulldozed like so much trash. How can God exist in the face of the pit? But the people need their God, and they need to know that God brings justice. Life will have no meaning if God doesn't bring justice. And my life, my hurt, can't stand in the way of that.

"I'm sorry, Katerina," he whispered, knowing it didn't matter that she couldn't hear him. He was sorry, but that wouldn't change the outcome of this case, and it wouldn't save what was left of his marriage. God was a harsh master.

The tribunal was led by the camp's Council of Elders, all men acknowledged as strong spiritual leaders in their community. They had worked with Woerful to provide leadership to the Corabians in the camp, and to blunt the worst of the oppression of their jailers. Benes Marek was from the same village as the accused woman, and had known her husband and infant son before their deaths. Tomas Slezak had been a butcher in the city, who had retired to pursue his passion, teaching the word of Christ. He had passed his butcher shop onto his son, who had been murdered in the city when the butcher shop was burned to the ground by an angry mob in the early days of the war. Jan Sobek was the oldest man on the Council and he preferred to spend his days reading the bible, as if the Word of God could erect a fence between him and the horrors of the camp.

Woeful banged the wooden mallet he used as a gavel on the table, calling for quiet. The crowd was restless, but after a few moments, came to order.

"I don't need to tell anyone here," Woerful began, "about the calamity that befell our people in this war. I don't need to say a word about the historic hatred that the Citizens of Montrovia have held for our people. To be Corabian, in this land, in the last twenty years, has meant to be a second-class citizen, to be denied your basic rights to gather, to commerce, to education. To be a Corabian, in this land, in the last five years has meant surrendering your right to be a human being. For all too many of our brothers and sisters, our mothers and fathers, and our children, it has meant surrendering your very life.

"That is why the crime of collaboration is so heinous, and today we must decide the case of a woman charged with collaboration..."

The room erupted in a chaotic symphony of hatred. The girl stood alone, between the Elders and the crowd, and seemed to shrink in the face of all that rage. She trembled from head to toe, and Woerful thought she would collapse, but she didn't. She caught herself, lifted her eyes from the floor to stare at the council, and smiled. Woerful was taken aback. He saw no despair in her eyes, only peace. It was as if she knew something he didn't. He trembled then, and beat the room into silence with his mallet.

"You are accused of freeing *the Guard*" Woerful said.

The woman nodded.

"You don't deny this?"

She shook her head.

The crowd surged forward a few feet, as if to engulf her, and then stopped and backed away. An angry current ran through the room, bitterness and pain voiced underneath it.

"Stone her!" someone shouted and Woerful knew he was about to lose control of the crowd and she would be killed now, in front of them all. He beat on the table for silence but it did not calm the crowd. Woerful glanced at the men sitting behind the table with him. He could see their own fear of the crowd, and their agreement with her death. The tribunal would lose all meaning if Woerful allowed the crowd to take her. They had to maintain control, they had to pass judgment, or they would lose the tenuous authority they had and the survivors would die.

11

Woerful stood, pounding on the table with the mallet. "Quiet," he shouted, pointing at a man in the front of the crowd, forcing him with his will to freeze. He stared down the crowd until the room was quiet and order had been restored. Then he sat.

"I find the defendant, Sarah Jezek, guilty of the crime of collaboration..."

"Husband!" Katerina Woerful had forced her way to the front of the room and was standing next to the girl.

"Go away, Katerina," Woerful said, sadly. "You cannot save this woman from her fate."

"Why don't you ask her why she freed him?" Katerina stared at him and Woerful wondered once again how he had lost his wife to this camp.

"There is no purpose to that question since she admits that she is guilty."

"I would like to hear what she has to say," Benes Marek said from his seat next to Woerful.

Woerful looked at the other men at the table. They nodded or shrugged.

"Go ahead," Katerina was saying to the young woman. "Tell them what you told me. Why did you free Krang?"

"God told me to free him," she said. She spoke so softly Woerful wasn't sure he had heard her correctly.

"God told you to free him?" Woerful asked, incredulous. Someone in the crowd laughed.

"I wanted to kill him," she said. "I have hated him for so long it was tearing my soul apart, and I went out on the parade ground where all the guards were to kill him..."

"You were going to kill him? How?" Marek demanded.

Sarah reached into the pocket of her worn uniform and pulled out a shiv, a thin blade with a wrapped cloth handle. An inmate would die for carrying a shiv.

"Where did you get it?" Woerful asked, as shocked as anyone in the room to see this slight woman with a weapon.

"I worked in the laundry. Last year one of the inmates working there collapsed and died. I found this hidden in his pocket. I was afraid the guards would kill us all if they found it, so I hid it in my undergarments until the end of the shift. I was going to throw it away, but I couldn't. It was the answer to my prayers. So I hid it in my barrack and I retrieved it today."

"So you wanted to kill *the Guard*, but God stopped you?" Marek asked, gently now.

Sarah nodded. "As I sat and watched him, I saw Abraham in my mind. He smiled at me and forbid me act against the laws of Christ who taught us to love our enemies. He told me I was to forgive the man who killed him and my son. That God wanted forgiveness."

12

The room was silent.

"So it was not God, but your dead husband that spoke to you?" Woerful asked. He hadn't believed it could have been God. God had not spoken to him since the day he set foot in this camp. God was not welcome here.

"Abraham speaking for God?" Marek clarified.

Sarah nodded.

"Did God tell you to free him? Why didn't you offer him your forgiveness and leave him to his fate?"

"Is that truly forgiving? To send a man to his death? I understood that if you killed him and threw his body in the pit that the weight of his evil would trap the souls of our dead here forever. For my son and my husband to be free of this place, *the Guard* had to be free. Anything else was a lie before God."

Marek leaned over to whisper in Woerful's ear. "What she says makes sense. She lost so much, on her first day here, that I am inclined to believe her, even if I disagree with what she has done. He cannot get away. The camp is surrounded and he will be caught. I think we should release her. If the others carry her away in the night, it is not on our souls."

Woerful nodded. He looked at Katerina, standing next to the girl and saw the glimmer of hope on her face. Could he win her back by releasing the girl? Was it that simple, to take life from all of the death of this camp and find love again?

Woerful raised the mallet, ready to pass judgment. The crowd had quieted, uncomfortable with Sarah's profession of divine intention. The beast had been tamed, at least for a moment.

"She kissed him!" a man shouted from the back of the room. "I saw it. She kissed *the Guard.*"

A slight young man pushed his way to the front of the room. "She is lying. She was his mistress, I am sure of it."

The crowd erupted into a maelstrom of shouts and curses. Sarah looked bewildered. Woerful thought Katerina was going to strike the man.

"Who are you?" Woerful demanded after beating the table until the room had subsided.

"I am Rybar Vrba, Abraham's cousin. I saw her kiss *the Guard* and when I looked for him again, he was gone. I sounded the alarm. I knew she was sleeping with someone, but I never thought it was him."

"What do you mean?"

"After Abraham died, I asked Sarah to be my wife and she refused. For two years she refused. What adult can go two years without love? I just never knew it was him."

In the end, it was the kiss that convicted her. The kiss was the symbol of her bargain with the devil. Other witnesses had suddenly come forward with tales of

Sarah getting special treatment or being spared from some odious task or another. Death had fallen on those around her, but never on Sarah. The council convinced itself they would have freed her, but for the kiss. Before night had fallen completely, Sarah Jezek had taken Krang's place on the parade ground awaiting death.

Benjamin Woerful sat in the darkened motor pool and cried. The trials of the day were over. The crowd and the other elders had left. Someone had turned off the lights, but he had stayed, seated at the long table. He cried silently, with few tears.

The sight of Katerina in a rage, being held by two men, screaming and spitting, her hair escaped from her head scarf and wild around her head, had torn at his heart. And Sarah, walking away so calmly, as Woerful imagined the Christ must have when he heard the verdict of the crucifixion. No other prisoner had been at peace. They had begged and pleaded for their lives, but Sarah hadn't.

Could Sarah be right? Woerful knew that if he had heard Sarah's story five years ago, he would have turned it into a great sermon, just as she told it. He would have said forgiveness was the highest virtue of all, and the hardest thing that God asks of us. How many times had he counseled forgiveness for a straying spouse, a cheating business partner, or misguided youthful behaviors?

Woerful shook his head. To forgive what had happened in this camp, to forgive someone like Krang, was to dishonor all who had died here. God cannot ask us to forgive so much. Our souls cannot bear the price of it. Was all that I believed before the camp wrong? Is an eye for an eye the highest virtue in the bible? David was a child, an innocent, when he smote Goliath and he became King. Is the true lesson of the bible that righteous violence is our destiny?

Woerful wiped his face on his arm. He could not let the others see his doubts. He must be strong for them. God did not want to be understood, that much was certain. He wanted to be feared, like the neighborhood bully. Woerful had learned to fear in the camp, and he was never going to forget that lesson. Katerina was lost to him, and Sarah would die, but his people could now recover. It was a hard bargain.

Katie lay on the bed next to Stojespahl and stared into his eyes. She was on her left side and Stojespahl on his right, face-to-face. She held his pistol under his chin. His eyes were big with fear and anger. Even though she could still smell vodka on his breath, Stojespahl didn't seem drunk any longer. They had been laying like this for two hours, listening to the sounds of people dying. It was a strange kind of intimacy as they lay so close and Stojespahl begged and pleaded with her to let him go. Like the lovers they had never been. When the intruders broke into the apartment next door, he had started again.

"We still have time to escape," he said.

"They're next door," she replied. "We can't get past them."

"We can go down the fire escape at the end of the hall."

"I don't want to leave. I want them to find us."

Voices were yelling next door, dulled by the apartment walls, and a woman was crying.

"Doesn't our love mean anything to you?" Stojespahl looked desperate.

Katie looked at him in disbelief. "What love? You arrested me so you could fuck me."

"You'd be dead if it wasn't for me."

Katie knew that was likely true. Since she had no papers, she was at risk every time she was on the streets. Sooner or later someone would have stopped her who wouldn't let her fuck her way out of the camp. "I survived before I met you. I didn't need you to be my pimp."

A shot rang out next door and a woman began to wail hysterically.

"I rescued you from the streets. I gave you a safe place to live and food to eat."

"I already had a place to stay when you arrested me." Katie hoped the intruders would get here soon. Her arm was getting tired from holding the gun.

"I saved you from that woman!"

Katie shrugged, staring at the captain. Stojespahl was talking about Matilde. Katie had lived with Matilde for three months before Stojespahl had arrested her. Matilde had been in her late thirties, a smaller woman with short blonde hair, who worked as an illustrator at a magazine. She had been full of nervous energy, always in motion, like the kid who hadn't done her homework and was afraid the teacher would call on her in class. Matilde lived in one of the neighborhoods Katie frequented and had seen her on the streets. She had followed Katie into an alley one evening and stood in the shadows and watched Katie give a man head. When the man had left the ally Matilde had approached her. Katie had been afraid she was the man's wife, but couldn't have been more wrong.

"I'll let you stay at my place as long as you want," Matilde promised.

"In return for what?"

Matilde laughed. "I want what they all want. I'm just willing to give you a safe place to stay, and enough food to eat. What you do with your spare time is your own business. Have you ever been with a woman?"

Katie shook her head.

"Are you willing to try it once?"

Katie thought for a minute. Would it be any worse to fuck a woman? She couldn't image it so. She nodded, and followed Matilde back to her apartment. Matilde had instructed her on exactly what she wanted and Katie had complied. It was less imposing than being with many of the men she serviced. When Matilde had tried to reciprocate, Katie had pushed her away. She wanted no illusions. She wasn't in love with this woman, and didn't want to be her girlfriend. Katie still had hopes that someday she might get married and have a family. Until then, she wasn't making love, she was fucking people. She wanted no pleasure out of it. Matilde pouted for several days, but finally quit trying to make their business agreement into a relationship. The one concession Katie had granted her was that she slept each night in Matilde's bed, wrapped in her arms. She missed that some times.

"Saved me from what?" Katie had asked. "She didn't make me work the streets and give her my money. She didn't bring her friends over for me to fuck."

"I saved you from her."

"Do you think I care who I fuck? I'm not doing it for love."

"But..."

"You told me I reminded you of your daughter. And you think you saved me from a woman?"

Several shots were fired in the apartment next door and the woman's wailing was cut-off midstream. Then everything was quiet.

Katie pushed Stojespahl onto his back on the bed and straddled him again. She let her hair cascade around his face, blocking out the room. All she could see were his dark eyes. It was like looking in a mirror and seeing the stain on her soul through his eyes.

"They're going to kill you too," Stojespahl said.

"I can't wait," she whispered. Katie realized suddenly that was true. She could no longer defend what she had done to survive and was just waiting for them to kill her. She hoped her family would understand.

"We still have time to escape," he said. His eyes flared with panic like the horse she had seen last summer that had been struck by a truck. The horse's owner had had to shoot it to stop it from hurting.

Stojespahl began to struggle. He was much bigger than Katie, and tried to flip her from his chest by rocking his hips. She jammed the pistol hard against the bottom of his jaw, pressing into his throat with all her might. Stojespahl stared at her, his dark eyes narrowed and hard. Katie could see the moment that his anger was replaced by the realization that she wasn't going to let him go. For the first time since she had met him, he didn't own her.

Someone pounded on the door to the apartment. Katie grinned, knowing she had won. Stojespahl stared at her, a look of hatred in his eyes. She leaned forward

16

and gave him a quick kiss. A Judas kiss, she hoped. The door to the apartment burst open. Katie looked over her shoulder at the intruders. There were seven of them, gaunt stick people, three men and four who might have been women because of their longer hair. None of the women had breasts or hips to speak of. They all carried guns they must have taken from dead soldiers in the streets.

Stojespahl reached up and grabbed Katie's hand, slipping his thumb past the trigger guard. She looked down at him, at the fear and defiance on his face. He pressed his thumb against her finger, hard, pushing on the trigger. The pistol roared and Stojespahl's head exploded, showering Katie in blood and brain matter. The top of his head was a bloody mess.

Time stopped for her. Katie was too dazed to move. She hadn't thought she would be the one to kill him. The gunshot had deafened her, making her ears ring tinnily. She let the gun drop from her hand. Someone grabbed her by the legs and dragged her from the bed. Katie hit the floor hard, face down, the impact knocking her breath away. She rolled onto her back, gasping for air.

A scarecrow-like woman squatted over her and spit into her face. The woman grabbed Katie by the hair, and Katie looked into her pinched face. The look of hatred on the woman's face was as absolute as the look on Stojespahl's face had been. Her eyes were dark and lifeless, as if the only force animating her was her rage. Most of her teeth were missing. The woman raised her hand and hit Katie across the face, knocking her head back against the floor. Katie tried to raise her arms and cover her face, but the woman knelt on her right arm, keeping Katie from fully protecting herself. The blows continued. Katie rolled towards the woman and curled into a ball, trying to make herself as small as possible.

As the woman continued to beat her, Katie felt a sense of disconnect, almost as if she were standing in the room and watching, rather than actually being beaten. It was much the same way she felt when she was having sex with Stojespahl, or some man on the street, as if she were an observer and all of the pain, hurt and anger was being felt by someone else. She had been expecting this beating ever since she ran from the square three years earlier. Katie had always known she would be punished for disobeying her father.

She couldn't catch her breath. The blows landed on her side and back now, instead of her face, pounding her kidneys. The more she struggled to catch her breath, the more she was sucked back into her own body and into the beating. Katie lay on the floor and cried silently. She didn't know if she was crying from fear or relief. Finally the beating stopped.

Katie was pulled to her feet by her hair. The others had been watching the beating, doing nothing to stop it. She stared at her attackers, trying to find the anger to save herself, but nothing was there. What right did she have to want to live? She could tell that the intruders had been through hell already, so what

17

mercy could she expect from them? They were so emaciated they looked like walking skeletons. The flesh of their faces was pulled taut over their skulls, stretched so tight that it appeared transparent, like old parchment. They didn't even look like real people, so thin and ragged that Katie thought about the stories of the walking dead that had scared her as a child. They had been stealing clothes as they went through the apartment building, so they were dressed in an odd collection of unmatched finery making them look like ghoulish clowns. One of the women had on an evening dress and wore a soldier's helmet on her head. Another wore a man's tuxedo coat over the remains of her prison uniform.

Her tormentors gathered around her, shouting and poking. Her ears were still ringing; she couldn't hear them, couldn't understand what they were screaming at her. She wanted to tell them she was Corabian, but she couldn't speak. And she knew that being Corabian might be worse right now than being a Citizen. Katie stood before them, flinching, feeling their rage. She wanted to ask about her parents, her sister, did anyone know them? Were they still alive? But she couldn't find the words. Even after she caught her breath, she didn't feel like she had the right to ask them anything, or try to save herself from their anger. She knew she deserved this.

A short woman, wearing a scarf over her thinning hair, knocked the floor lamp on its side and used a serrated knife to cut the electrical cord that ran from the bottom of the lamp. The cord sparked when she cut it, until she pulled it roughly from the electrical outlet. She looped the cord around Katie's neck and dragged her to the apartment window. Katie looked out and saw a building several blocks away in flames, and hoped the city would burn to the ground. This was not her city any longer. She hoped the advancing army would level it. She didn't care if everyone died.

The woman hit Katie in the back of the neck, knocking her to the ground. She laughed as she retied the electrical cord around Katie's neck, pulling it so tight it was choking her. Katie saw the blue-green numbers tattooed on the woman's left forearm. It should have been Katie's tattoo. Katie felt a sense of horror that this woman, or someone like her, had gotten the tattoo that should have been Katie's. She felt sick, realizing that someone else had paid for Katie running away with his or her life. She was no different from the Citizens after all.

The woman opened the window as far as it would go, and then pulled Katie up from the floor by the cord wrapped around her neck. The woman pushed her roughly, knocking Katie's head against the bottom pane of the open window. The blow hurt, and Katie knew she would have a bruise. She started to laugh, finding it funny that even though she was about to die she was worried about a bruise on her face. The woman pushed Katie's head down enough to slip below the window pane.

Katie stared at the street five stories below, full of people scurrying one way or another, and then caught her breath as the woman shoved her out. Katie plummeted for a foot or two before the electrical cord tightened around her neck and she somersaulted, slamming against the building. The pain exploded as brilliantly as the gun had, and then hands were in her hair and on her arms, pulling her back into the building. Her neck was on fire.

The woman who had thrown her out the window was pushed up against the wall yelling ferociously at one of the men. The other women in the room were also yelling. Katie didn't understand what was happening. She sank to her knees on the floor, gasping for air, trying to get the cord loose from her neck. The two men who had pulled her inside stood behind her, keeping the women away. After a minute, the four women stormed from the room. The men pulled Katie to her feet and led her to the bed, pushing Stojespahl's body to the floor before throwing Katie on the blood soaked bed.

Now she understood. Katie caught her breath and worked the cord loose from her neck. She knelt on the bed, reaching for the first man's belt. This was what everyone wanted from her. Death could wait.

The women returned before the men were done with her. Katie crawled from the bloody bed feeling embarrassed and exposed having been watched. The four women were making angry comments that she couldn't quite hear, but the looks they shot her told everything.

A younger woman, the one wearing the tuxedo jacket, spit at the feet of one of the men. The man shrugged, and looked away, but did not respond.

"The bitch needs to die. We need to kill every one of them," Tuxedo said.

Katie shook her head slowly. "I'm not..." She stopped. There was no point.

"Not what?" the younger woman hissed.

"Not a Citizen..."

"Bullshit!" This was the woman who tried to hang her. She was carrying the serrated knife she had used to cut the electrical cord. "They all say that." Katie tried to blink back the tears she felt welling up in her eyes. She didn't want to cry in front of them.

"I ran away. From the transports. I left my parents and ran away."

"You're lying, not that it matters, since you were living with him." Tuxedo pointed to Stojespahl's body, before balling up her fist and punching Katie below her right ear.

The blow to her face caught Katie off guard and she staggered, almost falling down. The younger woman hit her again and again, forcing Katie to her knees. The blows were systematic and brutal. Katie could tell her lip had split. She was bleeding from her mouth and nose. She didn't even raise her arms to protect

19

herself. She knew she had brought this on. She just had never thought it would be her own people who killed her.

"Enough!" one of the men stepped between Katie and her assailant, pushing the woman away.

The woman with the knife stepped up and grabbed Katie by the hair. She pulled a handful of hair tight, and then used the knife to cut it off. She cut again and again, until the floor was covered in Katie's hair.

"This is what we did in the camps to woman who fucked the enemy so everyone would see their shame before we drowned them in the toilets," she whispered into Katie's ear. "You have given up your right to be Corabian. Your family is dead because you deserted them. God spits on you."

Katie looked at her hair covering the floor and began to cry. She tried to hold back, but couldn't. She was almost hysterical, fighting to catch her breath. Tuxedo hit her again. Katie looked up at her, catching the woman's eyes. They were pure hatred. She took a deep breath, calming herself. They would kill her soon, and all of this would be done. She could accept that. She nodded to the tuxedo woman standing over her, encouraging her to continue.

"Finish it," she said. Tuxedo smiled grimly, nodding.

The room disappeared in a roar of fire and brick as the apartment walls imploded, knocking everyone to the floor. Katie had her breath knocked away by Tuxedo woman who landed on top of her. As the smoke and dust cleared, Katie could now see out a massive hole in her apartment where the window had been to the building across the street that was burning furiously, having been hit by an artillery shell or bomb. Choking on the dust, her ears buzzing and ringing, Katie pushed Tuxedo off, rolling her body away. The woman weighed almost nothing, her body as insubstantial as a ghost. The younger woman in the tuxedo was dead, a fist-sized piece of glass stuck like a knife in the back of her head.

Katie lay on the floor for a long time. She felt herself carefully. No broken bones, except maybe her ribs. She was terribly hurt, however. She couldn't stand to be beaten like that again. It would kill her. She wondered if she could expect the same from every Corabian she met? What about from her family? Her father had cursed her as she ran from the square. Would he curse her now, if she found him? Was he even alive?

Katie stood up, swaying unsteadily on her feet. The Corabians were dead or unconscious, covered by brick and shards of glass. She had been on the floor when the room exploded, shielded from the deadly debris by her attackers.

"I should be the one who is dead," she whispered, looking at the dead tuxedo woman. The back of the tuxedo had been shredded by flying glass. The look of rage on the woman's face was gone, but Katie would never say she looked at peace. She tried to be angry at the Corabians for beating her, but she couldn't. She knew they were right and she deserved it. She looked out the gaping hole in her wall at the city. The building across the street was engulfed in flames. Thick black smoke made the twilight seem as dark as night. At some point, the approaching Corabian forces had turned their bombs from the army trapped in front of the city to the city itself. Many buildings were burning, and several were just piles of rubble. The beating she had endured had been so severe she hadn't noticed the shelling. She spit blood from her mouth again. She could see people running down below, and flashes from guns being fired. She could see bodies lying in the streets. Katie knew she would die if she stayed in the apartment. For a moment she thought about curling up on the bed and letting go, but she couldn't. She was still alive.

She thought about running to Matilde's apartment, but looking out from the building she could see the entire west side of the city was in flames. Matilde was either gone or dead.

Katie stumbled across the room to get dressed. It hurt to move. She passed a mirror on the wall and was shocked by her reflection. Her left eye was swelling up, her face covered in bruises. An angry red welt circled her neck, already turning purple on the edges. Her face was speckled with blood, her own and Stojespahl's. Her hair was just stubble in some places and as long as two inches in others. It was short enough, however, that she thought she could pass as a boy. That might be best for now. She didn't need men wanting to fuck her right now. She just needed to get away. She rolled up the cuffs on a pair of Stojespahl's trousers, tightening them with one of her own belts, and put on one of his undershirts and a sweatshirt. She went to his closet for a jacket and hat, tucking her loose hair underneath.

Katie looked around the apartment. The kitchen area had been untouched by the explosion. The empty bottle of vodka was still upright on the table next to the remains of a small ham. Stojespahl had told her he wanted to celebrate the end of the war. Katie sighed. He had eaten his last meal, that was all. If he had truly wanted to escape he would have tried to slip away from the city, not fuck her one last time. The food had come from the Rohlecek's grocery shop. When the Rohleceks were carted off to the camp, Stojespahl somehow got the keys to their shop and had treated the place as his own stocked larder. There was enough food in the basement pantry to feed Katie for a year.

The key was on a chain around Stojespahl's neck. Katie rolled his body over, staring for a moment at the mess that was his head. The bullet had ripped a fist-sized hole in the top of his head. She pulled the key from his neck, fighting the urge to cry. She didn't understand why all this had happened. Why had her parents gone meekly to the camp? She blamed her father for not keeping her safe. That's what fathers were supposed to do. And yet, how could he? Katie sighed, wiping her face on her sleeve. These were old questions, ones she had asked a million times. They didn't mean anything.

Stojespahl's pistol lay on the floor. Katie took the gun and slipped it into the pocket of the jacket she wore.

Another explosion rattled the building. Katie stood and ran from the room. The apartment next door stood open, and Katie glanced in the door, and then stopped. The mother was tied to a chair, shot through the head. Her four children, none of them older than six, were crumpled against the room's far wall. Four red, bloody smears on the wall told her the children had been executed in front of their mother, before she was killed. Katie leaned over and vomited. She threw up all of the ham Stojespahl had forced her to eat earlier, until her stomach was empty. She had passed this woman and her children in the halls every day. The woman's husband had been killed during the invasion of Corabia, before Katie even moved into the building. She hadn't oppressed anyone. Her babies hadn't done anything wrong.

Katie stumbled down the stairs, her tears blurring her vision. She hadn't prayed since she had run away from the square, when in the middle of her prayer the policeman had found her and used her, but now she found words bubbling up.

"I hate you, God," she mumbled. "How can you let us hate each other so? My father said you're only love. How could you lie to us so?" She stopped at the entrance to the building, wiping her tears away. She pushed her mind off of what she had seen and began to plan the best route to the dry grocer's.

Katie ran through the burning city, shells falling more quickly around her. She had come to learn the city intimately in the last three years: she knew which alleys were safe for a quick fuck or a blowjob, which parks were the best place to find a willing customer, which neighborhoods wouldn't tolerate her presence. None of that helped her tonight. The streets were an angry maze of death and destruction. Bodies lay everywhere. People darted frantically from building to building trying to find someplace safe. She saw an old woman knocked to the ground by a man running down the street. No one helped the woman to her feet. To her shame, Katie didn't stop to help either. She simply ran past. Some streets were packed with people trying to get away. She began to fear she wouldn't make it to the grocer.

Katie turned into an alley that cut several blocks from her journey and ran into a blockade halfway down the block. A truck had been pulled sideways across the alley. A group of bodies, twenty or thirty, lay in front of the truck. They had been herded into the alley and then gunned down. Katie turned to run back the other way, but someone stood at the end of the street. All she could see was a silhouette. She didn't know if it was someone fleeing the soldiers or a soldier, or if it was the person who had killed all these men. Taking a deep breath, Katie moved

22

along the shadows of the ally, stepping on the mass of bodies to reach the truck. She dropped to her knees and crawled under the truck, holding her breath. She kept waiting to hear a shout, or the sound of a gun, but nothing happened. Once she was free of the truck, she climbed to her feet and ran.

The artillery shells began to fall faster. They landed randomly, throughout the city, sometimes close and sometimes far. The concussion of one explosion knocked Katie to the ground. A flying pebble struck her forehead, opening a cut. She could feel the blood running down her face. She had to wipe it away with the sleeve of her jacket to keep it from getting in her eyes. Her left eye had now closed from the beating; the entire left side of her face was bruised and painful.

Katie could hear the drone of planes overhead, and then the heavy bombing began. The first strike wasn't near her, but she could feel the heat wash across the city as the flames rose majestically above her like a giant bonfire, glazing everything in an orange glow. The flames were so bright they illuminated the underbellies of the bombers flying over head.

Katie found the shop as more formations of bombers flew over the city. She glanced over her shoulder, but no one was in the little side street. She fumbled with the key, struggling to make the lock turn. The door finally opened. More explosions rocked the city as she pushed her way inside. Katie slammed the door and ran for the grocer's cellar. An explosion knocked her to the ground. Bags of flour, knocked from a shelf on the wall, exploded on the floor, covering Katie and the room in flour dust. The whole building seemed to be shaking. Bright flashes from the street lit up the room.

Katie pulled up the trapdoor to the cellar just far enough to slip her head and shoulders through. She wriggled into the darkness of the cellar like a kitten burrowing past its litter mates to find the teat, the trapdoor snapping shut behind her. Katie sat on the steps in the cellar, her arms around her knees, rocking back and forth. There were no windows in the basement, but the explosions outside were so brilliant that light strobed through the cracks in the floor boards above her head, lighting the room like a photographer's flash.

The explosions came closer together. They grew louder and louder. The floor above her, the wooden steps underneath her, the stone walls of the basement, all were rocked with each explosion. The noise became deafening. Katie began to scream, a long, high pitched note that was lost in the carnage that was going on above her. She stumbled off the steps, crawling desperately into a corner, thinking the world had surely come to an end.

Krang lay in the pit waiting for the moment he could escape. Night had fallen but the camp had not quieted. Gunfire echoed through the camp every few minutes, every shot followed by peals of laughter. Underneath the sounds of the camp were the thunderous rumblings of the massive bombardment of the city. He fought the urge to break free of the bodies and run. To run too soon was to die.

He still couldn't believe the woman had helped him escape. The guards had been moved to the parade ground early in the day, and Krang was sure they were to be gunned down. They had been joined by any family members living at the camp, as well as local farmers and their families who had supplied the camp with food. Sometime early in the afternoon a group of Corabians had found the courage to approach one of the guards and accost him, spitting and punching him. The guard had cowered before them, still hoping he could survive. Soon a stream of prisoners flowed through the parade grounds, heaping vindictive on the guards, but no one approached Krang. Not *the Guard.* They still feared him. Krang had laughed to see how they avoided him, avoided even seeing him there, and walked carefully around where he stood. He still had his power, even unarmed and awaiting death.

The woman approached him slowly, as if unsure of herself. Krang watched her walking through the soldiers, looking from face to face soberly, and then moving on. She moved painfully slowly, as if each step hurt her body. Like all of the prisoners, she was emaciated, her skin stretched tautly over her skull, giving her the look of a walking skeleton. Krang wondered if she had been pretty before. She stopped before him, looked briefly into his eyes, and left. He fumbled in his pocket for another cigarette. Might as well smoke them all, he thought. I doubt I'll need them tomorrow.

Ten minutes later the woman returned. Krang watched her as she marched across the parade ground directly toward him. The purposefulness of her stride made him uneasy. She did not wander as the others did. The look of pain that had been on her face earlier had been shoved down. It wasn't altogether gone, but you could see she had something in her head that pushed the pain away. She did not appear to be carrying a weapon, but he was uncertain what she could hide in her rags. Krang drew himself up stiffly as she approached. I will take whatever she brings, he thought. I owe myself that much, to admit that I deserve whatever she chooses to do.

"You're Krang." Her voice was soft, almost inaudible.

He nodded, looking her in the eye. She looked back steadily, unafraid.

"The one we call *the guard.*"

Krang smiled in spite of himself, and nodded again.

"I always thought, before I came here, that you could look at a bad person and know they were bad. I look at you and wonder how someone so evil could look so normal. More than normal, even. How can you look so beautiful? I could have taken you home to my mother, or to make my girlfriends jealous."

Krang shrugged, suddenly uncomfortable. He had always thought that his evil, his moral corruption, was clearly visible. Hadn't he been told that all his life?

"You don't know me?"

"No," Krang replied, as softly as she had asked. "There are too many of you Corabians. I cannot remember you all."

"I remember you. You will remember me from this day on, until you die."

"And how long will that be?" He nodded towards the trucks parked at the edge of the parade ground. The trucks he was sure had machine guns mounted on their beds to kill them all.

Sarah smiled, her teeth yellowed and broken against her sunken cheeks. She pushed thin strands of hair from her face. "Long enough to understand what I have to do, I guess."

Krang squared himself, ready for the blow. Was it to be a slap, or did she have a blade?

"I am Sarah Jezek. I am the widow of Abraham Jezek. My son was named Capek. You must repeat the names to me."

Krang smiled, humoring her. "You are Sarah Jezek, mother of Capek and wife of Abraham. A fine family, I am sure." Sarcasm had always been one of his weapons of choice when dealing with an angry woman.

Sarah looked at him coldly. "You will remember us, I promise you that."

Krang nodded. It wasn't often he felt the power of others, but he could tell this woman had some inner strength empowering her. It flowed off her in waves. Why had he not noticed her before? "Why will I remember you?"

"I want to tell you about my first day here."

Krang nodded. What harm could come from humoring her? Like so many of her people she thought words were more powerful than actions. She was to be pitied for that. "Go ahead. I am not going anywhere, unless they decide to shoot me."

She smiled when he said that, brushing the hair from her face again and shivering in the breeze. Clouds were blocking the setting sun, and it was becoming uncomfortably cool on the parade ground.

"I came to this camp two years ago, more or less. It was a hard trip on the train, and many people died before we even got here. We were locked in a car with no seats or windows. There were so many of us that there was no room to lie down. Abraham smuggled a small water skin onto the train, strictly for Capek, our boy. We had to fight to keep it, others wanted to take it for themselves, but Abraham wouldn't let them have it. It was hard to know that we had water and not drink it, because we were both suffering terribly, but the water was for Capek. Abraham held me while I cried. He was my strength.

25

"When we got here, and were ordered off the train, it was night. I carried Capek in my arms; he was only 9 months old. The depot was awash in the glare spotlights, like a night soccer game. They were so bright, after days of being locked in the train, that I could barely see anything. It was hot, and so humid, but after the train the air seemed sweet and full of promise. The first person I saw when I came off the train was a guard who wanted to take Capek from me. All the small children were being taken from their parents. We were told it was to go the hospital for a check-up. I refused to let the guard take Capek. What mother would? To be asked to give up my boy, before I had been five minutes in this place?

"Then I saw you, striding across the depot towards us, clearly a man with some authority. Even when you were still far away, you were calling to the guard about the hold up. It seems we were blocking the way. You looked so forceful in your uniform. You looked like you were in charge of all of us. I walked up to you, my boy in my arms, my husband at my side, needing your help and you changed my life forever. You carried a pistol in one hand, but it seemed to fit you so well, I didn't even feel scared by it. I was still pretending this was a normal place.

"I said I needed help, the guard wanted to take my baby. I remember that you never put your gun down. You moved it to your left hand, and reached out gently for Capek with your right. I was going to give him to you. I thought you wanted to hold him for a minute. You smiled at me as I held him towards you and then grabbed him roughly by his leg and pulled him from my grasp. He squealed in fear. You swung Capek by his heel and smashed his head upon the ground. You looked up at Abraham and me and said 'Problem solved.'"

Sarah stared at Krang. Her voice never changed, never wavered. She was lost inside the memory.

"Abraham stepped forward, a cry of anguish on his lips and you shot him in the face. And then you left me there, sitting on the ground, with my dead husband and my dead son in my lap as the others walked past us.

"I don't know which of the woman helped me to the barracks that night. I think, perhaps, it was my sister-in-law, Abraham's sister, but I was never sure. She blamed me, you know, for Abraham's death. She thought I should have sacrificed Capek for my husband.

"Sometime that first night, you came into the barracks. You wanted a woman for sex, to appease you for what had happened earlier. The other women were all afraid. I was so numb I didn't care what happened to me. I thought maybe you would kill me then. You took me into a room and you raped me. I still had my husband's blood on my face from when you shot him, and you raped me."

Krang waited for her to continue. He wished her words meant something to him, but they didn't. He was *the guard* and he acted as he saw fit. After a moment he spoke. "I'm sorry, I don't remember."

Sarah shook her head vehemently. "I remember..."

"Wait," Krang interrupted, touching her gently on the shoulder to calm her. "I am not denying what you said. I am sure it happened. I am simply saying that I don't remember you, or your husband, or your boy. There were too many just like you that came through those gates for me to remember one night. If it makes you feel any better, I didn't do that to you personally, I did it to all of you. Interchangeably. This camp was about destroying your spirit and I was the best at it."

Sarah looked at him coldly, a tear trickling down her right cheek. "No," she said softly, "that doesn't make me feel any better, but this will."

Krang stiffened slightly as she stepped forward. He steeled himself against the blow he expected. Sarah grabbed him tightly by the shoulders, pulling him down towards her, and then kissed him on both cheeks. "I forgive you," she whispered in his ear.

Krang reeled back from her as if he had been punched. He couldn't understand what she had said, or why it made him feel so off-balance. "What?"

"I forgive you."

Krang had looked her over. She had lost the look of coldness and reserve. Tears were running freely down her face, but she wasn't sobbing. She still looked like she had something inside her, pushing her on, but it was no longer pushing away her pain. Something else was going on. "I don't understand."

"I don't want Abraham and Capek to be trapped here, in this place of death, for eternity. If I hate you, that is what will happen. So I choose to forgive you."

Krang had been stung by her sincerity. He hadn't known what to say. He still didn't believe it. How could she forgive him? What right did she even have to forgive him? He was *the Guard*, the man who had terrorized this camp, who single-handedly kept the Corabians cowed. At the height of the war the camp had held over four thousand Corabians and maybe one hundred guards. If the Corabians had ever tried to revolt, as they had at one or two other camps, it would have been a massacre. He had stopped that. The death he brought had been so random, so pervasive, that every Corabian in the camp expected to die every time they saw Walter Krang.

The camp quieted as night marched towards dawn. The bombardment of the city, a roiling, sizzling thunderstorm, dominated the night. Krang could see flashes of light strobing through the bodies above him and thought briefly of Emma and the kids. They were dead by now, he was sure. Emma wouldn't have been capable of saving herself, let alone four children. Not that he was sure the baby was his.

Emma liked to fuck and he had been at the camp most of the time. If the baby wasn't his, he was sure that one or two if the infants in the camp were. Life always balanced out in the end.

Chapter Two

Krang awoke with a start, a fly biting at his lip. The fly crawled along his face, and something, blood?, ran into his eyes. He could not see. A moment of panicked thought, my God they've eaten my eyes, gave way to incredulity. How could I have fallen asleep? Am I more of a beast than even I recognize? Krang blinked one eye open, then the other, and slowly the horror of the pit focused before him. The buzzing of the flies, white noise like a radio still playing after sign-off, enveloped him. The face next to him, mouth gaping toothlessly, eyes gone, stared up towards the sky like a beacon or sign. Krang twisted his head upward, trying to catch a glimpse of what the corpse would be seeing. He could make out the faintest light, and realized that he had almost slept the night through.

Taking a deep breath, Krang began to work the blood into his numb limbs. He was not worried at the moment that he would be seen. By the morning light it couldn't be any later than five am and no one was alert at that time of day. It was too late into the shift for the overnighters, and too early for a day shift to have come on. He knew that if he didn't make good his escape now, he would soon rejoin his fellows on the parade ground. Dead is dead, whether they shoot me here or up there, he thought.

He began to struggle, trying to break free of the hold the dead had on him. He pushed against the bodies below him, but barely moved. Krang bunched his shoulders for strength and used his head to push against the flesh that held him down. His head slowly pushed the body above him to one side, and he began to twist and turn to free himself. Wriggling his way free of the bodies seemed much more difficult that slipping beneath them, but Krang's head finally broke free into the cool dawn air.

He listened intently, but the camp was quiet. He could not hear any sounds of the battle for the city, nor even the howling of a hungry dog. He slipped his left shoulder upward, free of the muck, and slid his arm free and out. Twisting, he fought his right arm to the surface, and with his hand, wiped the blood and sweat from his face. He coughed violently, the mucus covering his face gagging him. The high pitch whine of gnats rang in his ears as they swarmed his head, the metallic taste of blood on his tongue. He drew in a deep breath, his first as a free man. Krang pushed against the mass of bodies, slowly freeing his chest and stomach. It was like escaping from a tunnel of flesh that grasped and squeezed him. He continued to work his hips upward, and with a groan of exertion broke free of the bodies as the muck and slime fell away from him. He rolled onto his side, gasping for breath.

Krang struggled to his feet. He looked at the camp and saw no one in the dim morning light. He took a tentative step, his balance uncertain. He moved slowly, stripping as he made his way across the pit. He dropped shirt and undershirt, kicked off his boots, pants and underclothes piece by piece as he stripped, not caring that someone might see them in the light of day. After a step or two he turned around and grabbed his bloody boots and carried them in his hand. He was covered from head to toe in gore, the passing remnants of those who died before him. Struggling across the pit, his steps sinking into the bloody quagmire as if he were walking through knee deep snow, Krang had to suppress a laugh.

Walter Krang had entered the pit, but would not leave it. Abraham Jezek would leave the pit, to roam the earth once more, reborn. Sarah has provided the means of my escape from this place, he thought. I can move among them, searching for the wife and son I've lost, and none will be the wiser. Until the day I find her again, and teach her that forgiveness is a weakness, and weakness is a sin.

Krang pulled himself naked from the far side of the pit and ran into the tall grass surrounding the camp, his boots in his hand. He stopped, a few hundred yards from the camp, and bent over to catch his breath. He slipped his feet into the boots and quickly tied them. The sun had just broken the horizon, not yet having the strength to melt the frost that covered the grass. Krang drew in ragged breaths, struggling to calm his breathing. He was beginning to think he might make it. He fought the urge to run blindly through the fields to the woods. He was sure the prisoners would have patrols out looking for him. Crouching in the grass, he surveyed the land around him. When he was sure no one was near he began his slow patient escape.

Krang was a half mile from the camp when a short burst of machine gun fire split the air behind him. Krang winced involuntarily as terrified screams followed the gunfire, then more concentrated gun fire silenced the screams. He had heard that death shriek so many times in the past few years. Funny how it felt different, he thought, when it was your friends being killed.

"Gerri, you poor fuck," Krang whispered, shaking his head. Gerri had been his best friend since the first day of school almost thirty years ago and had gotten Krang the job at the camp when his only other choice had been to join the army. "I told you they would kill us. You're dead, you son-of-a-bitch."

And I'm not, he thought. He grinned in spite of himself. Sarah Jezek was right, he wouldn't forget her.

30

Krang began to move again. He needed to get as far away from the camp as possible, and find a place to hide to wait out the end of the war. And he needed to clean the blood and gore from his body. He scratched as he scuttled from tree to tree, his skin crawling from the memory of lying in the pit. I must look like I'm a crazed killer, he thought with a grin. How often do you see a naked man scurrying through the fields, covered in blood and gore? Krang laughed, he couldn't help it. He was feeling almost euphoric, and the image of what he would look like to some family walking home from church was too much. The laughter kept him from catching his breath, so he stopped and doubled over. When he calmed himself and caught his breath, he stood up and looked around to orient himself. He didn't even know where he was. To his right, fifty yards away, he saw a creek. He went to look.

The creek was deep but very clear. The current was slow, so he could see the sand and pebble bottom. Schools of minnows darted along the bottom in organized chaos, never breaking apart even when they swam through another school. Krang thought of all the summer days he and Gerri had swum in creeks like this one, turning over rocks to catch crawfish, dunking each other, and as they go older, spying on girls in their private swim holes. They had loved to watch the girls undress.

"Damn it, Gerri." Krang shook his head.

Krang jumped in without thinking, his boots still on his feet, and the cold took his breath way. The water was bone numbing. Grabbing handfuls of gravel from the stream bottom, Krang savaged his skin, trying to wash away the touch of death. He rubbed the gravel so furiously into his scalp that some of his hair came out. He scrubbed and scrubbed until he couldn't see any blood on his body. By the time he left the water, he couldn't feel his feet and hands. Krang rolled himself in the tall grass until he was somewhat dry. He stripped his wet boots from his feet and left them in the grass. They were regulation issue and might give him away.

Krang looked around. The cold of the water had cleared his mind, stripping away the euphoria that threatened his safety. He knew exactly where he was. An old couple that had been brought in to the camp two days ago had a small farm less than a mile from here. A couple that would be dead now, gunned down with the guards in the camp behind him. He began to jog, slowly, to protect his bare feet.

The running breathed life into him. The air on his body invigorated him. Every muscle felt alive, the blood pumping through his body with an energy that was almost frightening. Every stride separated him from his death and celebrated his escape. I could wrestle a deer down, Krang thought, and kill it with my bare teeth. I am a savage; a God inspired savage, living in this world to take what I need, and proving my own invincibility. I should be dead like the others, except that I cannot die. Like a God. As long as I live, my people live. I will populate the world with my likeness. I will be a God.

Krang laughed. Do I hear myself? If I believe that bullshit, I'll be dead before the day is over. The only thing God has to do with my being free is that He seduced Sarah into making a terrible mistake. Typical. Like He seduced my mother into believing that heaven would make up for the hell she lived through on earth.

Krang came upon the deserted farm twenty minutes later. He couldn't understand the idea of the prisoners killing off the men and women whose food had help to keep them alive. Even though the farmers were only after money, they had saved more lives than Krang had taken. And some of them hadn't been after the profit at all. They knew their friends and neighbors were in the camp and hoped to keep them alive. But they were all dead now, whether profiteers or not.

The farm consisted of a ramshackle cottage, paint peeling from the badly weathered cedar shingles, and several small out buildings. A small stone smokehouse was the only structure that didn't appear to be on the verge of collapse. Krang checked the outbuildings first to be sure no one was hiding in any of them. Several hams hung undisturbed inside the smokehouse, but all the livestock had been run off from the small barn. An old two bottom horse drawn plow rested against one wall of the bigger barn, which was stacked full of sacks of seed. Someone would soon be farming here again, just not the old couple that, by now, lay rotting in the pit.

Krang broke a small pane of glass in the kitchen door, reached in, unlatched the lock and entered the home. The prisoners had been polite, not damaging anything in the home, and locking it as if the old man and his wife were going to be allowed to return. Krang had a moment of fear: what if the old couple had just been forced to witness the executions of the guards, and were even now on their way home? Or more likely, what if one of the prisoners were claiming this place as his own? He guessed it did not matter, for he knew he could fight the old couple or the Corabians off if need be. No fire was banked in the hearth, but the cottage still felt warm compared to running naked through the chill March air.

A pie sat on the round kitchen table, under a glass pie cover. Only one piece had been served. Krang lifted the cover and sniffed. Apple. Krang reached out and broke off a piece and shoved it into his mouth, savoring the sweetness. Picking up the pie plate, Krang walked to the kitchen window, and stood gazing out at the fields, naked, wolfing down handfuls of apple pie, until there was nothing left.

He laughed again, hysterically, on and on, until he slowly sank to the cold kitchen floor, exhausted. My God, he thought, why me? How did I come to be freed of death, among all those people? Why not Willi? Willi, eighteen, had only joined the camp guards in October after finishing his schooling. There was a boy who truly had only been following orders. He had hated the camp, had hated every act of violence that he had witnessed. Willi used to vomit every time a train came into the depot, because he hated the culling of the weak that happened at unloading. He would go out of his way to be nice to them.

Krang shook his head, tears rolling down his cheeks. The boy had never acted on his convictions; that was why he was dead. He should have quit the camp and joined the army, but he was a coward and afraid of dying. *None of them acted on their convictions, except me. I became* the guard, *but they were just guards. Even Gerri. I am a man of purpose, so I live.*

The house had no running water, only a hand pump in the large kitchen sink. As tempted as Krang was to take a real bath, he feared that lighting a fire might bring someone to investigate, so he contented himself with washing the pie filling off his face and hands. He went into the couple's bedroom and searched through the old man's closet and dresser. Krang took a pair of boxer shorts, a pair of blue work pants and a heavy wool shirt. He put on two pair of socks and was delighted that the old man's work boots fit him reasonable well.

The pantry proved to be full, and Krang was excited about the prospect of having several days' food supply to take with him. The farm house yielded a few treasures: a blanket, a water skin, and a warm jacket. The prisoners must have taken any guns the old man had, but Krang did find a hunting knife, and the old man's razor. He also found a small set of tools, already in a satchel bag, and an old oil lamp he found in the barn. He knew a cave not far from the farm where he could hide out for a week or two until the fighting for the city was done.

Krang sat at the kitchen, his treasures laid out before him. *How do I explain to the world who I am once it's all over? I cannot be Walter Krang, that's for sure. There are records of my service, and the testimony of all those survivors. Walter Krang must disappear forever. I like the sweet irony of masquerading as Abraham Jezek, but what if I run into his family? What if I see Sarah on the road?* Krang shook his head. *What could she do? She was a stupid bitch, letting him go. I would never for a minute have let me get away. I know enough about the camp that I could pass for an inmate, but I am much too fat. The clothes won't be a problem; they will all be discarding their uniforms as soon as they find something else to wear. Will it be a problem I know next to nothing about their religion?* Krang snorted. *Knowing nothing about his own religion had never been a problem. He was sure there were Corabians who had strayed as far from the church as he had. It's not like it was a secret religion. They were also Christians; they believed in God and Jesus too.*

Krang saw the empty pie plate lying on the kitchen counter. *I better not eat any more, at least for several days. I'll come out of the cave after Mountain City has fallen and the fighting is over, claiming to be a freed prisoner, and I'll go back* to where ever the hell Sarah is from. I should have asked her, so I would know where to look for her. Won't Sarah be surprised to see me, once I find her? Would any of the Corabians want to settle in Mountain City? Krang couldn't imagine any of them would stay anywhere near the camp. I had better wait long enough for anyone from the camp to be gone from the city, so that I won't be recognized. Krang laughed. And I can tell stories about *the guard*, and about the crazy bitch who set him free.

The war was on again when he left the house, the sound of heavy armor in the air, and a flight of fighters streaking towards the city. Krang couldn't imagine why it was taking so long to capture the city. No one there would bother fighting. They would quickly surrender, happy to be still making money. Vojacek, the commander-in-chief, must have made a decision to make a final stand there, of all places. Mountain City could never earn a break.

The bombardment ended as abruptly as it began. One moment Katie could feel the concussions of the bombs rocking the city and the next nothing. The air was as charged as at the end of a thunderstorm, and thick with anticipation. An eerie silence echoed in the room. Katie had screamed herself hoarse. She was astounded that she had survived, and couldn't believe any of the city could be left standing. Katie wasn't sure what to do now. She was afraid to leave the cellar. What if the Corabian soldiers had overrun the city and were just killing everyone they saw? Or if they hadn't entered the city yet, what if the Citizens knew she was Corabian, or even saw her leaving a Corabian shop, and took their revenge on her? She was too afraid to move and just sat in her corner, in the dark, and eventually fell asleep.

Katie awoke with a start. She was curled in the dark, and for a moment all she was aware of was pain. Her neck was on fire; she could barely move her head. Her face, breasts and lower back ached so badly she began to cry. It hurt to breathe. The pain was so intense it took several minutes just to sit up. The pantry was black. Faint light filtered in from tiny cracks in the ceiling, but all Katie could see were dust motes shimmering like ghosts in the darkness. She took a deep breath to calm herself. She was alive. That was a start.

She sat stoically in the corner, measuring her bruises in the dark, using the tenderness of her skin under her fingers to judge by. Her left eye had opened up again, but her face was deeply bruised and had several small, stinging cuts. As badly as her ribs and breasts hurt, she still didn't think she had any broken ribs. Her neck was a world of pain unto itself. Last night she had been too terrified to really notice how anything felt, but today she had time to contemplate the pain. Katie could barely turn her head from side to side or move it from front to back. She was scared that something was wrong, but who could she go to? There were

34

no doctors for her in Mountain City. She could not trust anyone, Citizen or Corabian, at this point. She could only hope that in a few days she would feel better and be able to begin searching for her family.

She wondered if she should have defended herself from the beating. She was sure that she was stronger than any of them had been, and she'd had Stojespahl's pistol. Katie reached down and brushed her hand over it in the dark basement. She could have killed them. Or at least refused the men. Katie hated the truth: sex was currency to her now. It was easier to fuck or blow someone than even to talk something over with them. She remembered her first boyfriend, who kissed her out behind the shed in her parent's backyard. One afternoon he had touched her breast and she had slapped him, indignant that he would think she would allow it. And today she would allow anyone her body for nothing more than a scrap of bread. Or nothing at all, if it came down to it. It was simply too easy to close her eyes and be somewhere else, so what did she care if they used her body?

Katie shook her head. She couldn't have killed them. And she wouldn't have cared if they had killed her. She had been taught all her life that God doesn't judge, that God doesn't punish, but she didn't believe that anymore. Katie knew that she had to pay a price for what she had done, so willingly, to survive. She had known that from the first instant she had knelt in the alley before the policeman. It was written so clearly on his face. He had despised her for giving in to his lust. They all had. It was like they hated her because they wanted her. She had thought she was surviving, but now she could see that wasn't true. She had been buying time, but nothing else. Maybe it wasn't God judging her, but simply the law of cause and effect. She had valued her life more than her family, and now she was alone. And they were together, alive, safe outside the city.

Katie shook her head. Sitting in the dark feeling sorry for herself wasn't helping. She had done what she had done, so there was no point in throwing it all away now, in a moment of regret. She didn't have time to worry about whether or not God, or anyone else, cared about what she had done. If she didn't take care of herself she would die, and she wasn't ready to die yet. Not today. She realized that she was hungry and sitting in a room full of food. Katie laughed. The low chuckle surprised her in the silence of the pantry. It sounded mischievous, not terrified. She tried to remember the last time she had been down in the pantry before the war. There was a lantern down here that the grocer would light when he came down the steps.

Katie crawled across the cobblestone floor to the stairs. She felt her way up, on hands and knees, until her head bumped against the trapdoor. She turned around and sat, facing into the dark void below. She used her hands to search the walls on either side of the step. When she found nothing, she scooted down one step and began again. On the third step, she found the lantern, hanging on a nail.

The matches were next to it. Katie fumbled with the matchbox, dropping it in her lap. She took a deep breath to calm herself, and started over, pulling a match from the box and striking it.

The flaring match let her adjust the wick on the lantern and light it. The lantern burned slowly at first, but brightened over time. Katie stared at it for several minutes, before raising her eyes to the pantry. She laughed in delight when she saw the almost fully stocked pantry. Stojespahl had used it sparingly. Hanging the burning lantern on the nail, Katie explored the pantry. Several sausages and one ham hung from the ceiling. Tins of sardines and pates were stacked on the shelves. Blocks of baker's chocolate sat wrapped in foil. Katie couldn't help herself. She grabbed a piece of chocolate from the shelf and tore the foil away. The chocolate was divided into blocks for cooking. Katie broke three of the smaller blocks from the piece and ate them, one after the other. She closed her eyes as she savored the flavor. The bitter sweetness of the chocolate flooded her mouth. It reminded her of afternoons with her mother, baking in the kitchen. Katie would steal bits of chocolate from the counter, and her mother would laugh and shoo her away. She had always liked the baker's chocolate better than milk chocolate. She stuck the rest of the chocolate in her pocket.

The tinned meats were neatly stacked on several shelves along one wall. The tins shined merrily in the glow of the lantern. They had always been considered delicacies in Katie's home, only being purchased at Easter or Christmas, although when Katie was eleven her mother had bought her a tin of sardines for her birthday. Katie went for the sardines now, breaking the metal key from the lid of the tin and twisting it round the tin until the oil soaked her fingers. She laughed, momentarily forgetting her pain, and licked her fingers clean, one hand at a time. She climbed the steps and sat at the very top, her head pressed against the trapdoor and wolfed them down.

Katie let the weight of the trapdoor push down against the back of her head and neck. It felt solid, substantial, as if it was the only real thing in the room. She had been surprised to be alive when the bombing stopped, and even now was afraid to try to open the trapdoor. What if the building had caved in around her? She could be sitting in her own luxurious grave, with enough food to last her for months, but little water. Would she even know if the building took a direct hit? Maybe she was already dead, and this little room was her heaven or hell. How would she know the difference? To have everything you needed but be forever separated from the world was hell wasn't it? Or was it simply peace and the opportunity to no longer have to abase herself for food and a room to sleep in? Would God be so cruel as to give her everything and nothing at the same time?

Katie realized with a start that she needed to pee. She looked around the basement for a suitable spot. There was an open drain in one corner, but she didn't know where it ran. She didn't want to create odors that would ruin her little haven. And she couldn't imagine squatting over the drain unless it was her only choice. She had never been fastidious as a child, but had always struggled when she had to squat in a corner of some alley to relive herself. Part of it was a fear of being caught with her dress up and her panties down, and unable to run away if she needed, and part of it was simply the sense that it was improper to pee anywhere but in a toilet. She smiled. Her mother had certainly done a good job of impressing that on her. She remembered one time, when she was four or five years old and had been playing in the garden, when she waited too long to make it to the privy, and had squatted behind the barn. She had been caught, of course, and had cried with mortification. Her mother hadn't even punished her because Katie had been so ashamed at being caught. Katie couldn't understand how that little girl had ever grown up to run away from her parents or sell herself to strangers.

She sighed. She would have to find out if the trapdoor would open or not. She squirmed around on the step so she was partially facing upward, and placed her hands against the door, tensing her legs and buttocks. As she started to push, the door and steps vibrated roughly with the first rumblings of a new bombardment. A second vibration shook the steps beneath her and she heard a dim explosion. Katie scuttled down the steps, her need to pee forgotten. She set the lantern under the steps where it might be protected if things fell, and blew it out, and then scrambled back into her corner. Within minutes the bombardment was in full swing, the darkness of the basement broken by jagged strobes of light.

Katie didn't scream this time, even though she realized these bombs were falling even closer than before. The entire basement was moving, and she could hear things crashing to the floor in the store above her. She couldn't scream this time, her throat was raw. But for the first time in three years, she found that she could pray. Everything that she had kept bottled up from that first moment in the alley came out in an unintelligible rush of words and emotions. All of her anguish and anger, and her guilt, and the secret joy that she had hidden away, even from herself, that she was alive and not in the camps. And her prayer became her refuge, more solid than the cobblestone floor and walls of her cellar, until she slept, unaware of the carnage around her.

It was late in the day before Krang reached the cave. The crisp March morning had transformed into a glorious spring afternoon. The sun was bright and it was at least sixty degrees. Except for the distant sounds of the city's bombardment and the patrols of Corabian soldiers filtering through the woods, Krang could have pretended he was on holiday. He moved slowly, his eyes constantly scanning the landscape, looking for any signs of the enemy. When he reached the cave Krang settled into the heavy brush around it and studied the area for more than an hour to be sure no one would see him enter the cave.

At first glance, the cave was nothing more than a deep depression in the mountainside, a twenty foot deep hollow that might provide cover from the rain as long as the wind was blowing from the right direction. If a person looked closer, as Krang had done as a boy, he would see an opening in the upper right corner of the depression that ran back even further into the mountain. This opening was small, maybe a meter square, and appeared to dead-end about two meters deep. If a person looked closer still, as Krang did as a boy, he would find an opening at the rear of the narrow tunnel that dropped down into a surprisingly large cavern.

Krang had spent hours in the cave as a child, exploring the one big room until he knew it front to back. It was the perfect place to wait out the war. A small snow-melt fed spring trickled along a back wall until well into the summer. It was hard enough to find that it wouldn't be an obvious place for soldiers to look, and hard enough to get into that Krang would know well in advance if someone else tried to enter.

When he was convinced no one was nearby, Krang scrambled the last hundred yards to the depression. He shoved all his possessions into the tunnel and climbed up, then lay on his belly in the narrow tunnel and lit the old lantern, and gently lowered it into the cavern on a piece of twine. Krang dropped his meager bundle of possessions into the cave and squirmed, head first, into his new home, grabbing a stone shelf with both hands and swinging his feet out of the tunnel to drop into the cave. The cavern had the same mildewy smell he remembered as a child. Krang quickly checked the cave to make sure that no bobcat had made its home there, and satisfied that he was alone, blew out the lantern.

Blackness sprang up around him, but in a moment he could see the faint glow that marked the entrance to the tunnel. He sat and watched as the meager light faded away, until he was left in pitch dark, that total blackness that prevented him from seeing his own hand held just inches in front of his face. Krang had forgotten how dark the true black of the cave was at night, and he felt a wave of nausea and panic wash over him. The blackness was so thick that he felt his chest constrict, as if the air itself was solid and unbreatheable. He fought the immediate temptation to relight the lantern. He had a very limited supply of oil, and knew that he might need to hide out for several weeks, so he could not afford to burn up all the oil his first day in the cave. Taking deep breaths to calm himself, Krang sat on the cave floor and stared into darkness, alone with his thoughts. I will have no way to know how much time has passed at night, he thought, but then maybe I don't really need to know. I'll be able to count days by the faint light in the tunnel during the day. He knew that he could climb out of the cave as often as he needed to, and just by listening for the guttural roar of the war, he would know when the worst of the

38

fighting was over. As soon as actual combat was over, Krang felt he would be safe. And by looking at the phases of the moon, he could have some confirmation of how many days had passed.

He felt elated. He had actually made it. All day he had been expecting to be discovered, but he had escaped detection. He was free, now. His one risk would be when he eventually rejoined people, but he thought he could pull off the role of a freed Corabian from the camp. Who would know, unless they already knew him? That meant he couldn't stay in Mountain City, but once he was twenty miles from the city, he was home free. And he knew enough about the camp to tell believable stories. Hell, he could tell only the truth, except about his own identity. He could tell about what he had done, as long as he told it from a prisoner's point of view. They won't know I wasn't a prisoner if I don't give it away, he thought. They simply won't know.

He sat in the blackness of the cave, his back against a rock wall and waited. The pit came back to him slowly. Krang never figured out afterwards if he had been hallucinating, or merely dreaming, or if indeed the dead had been talking with him. It started simply enough. Krang felt an itch on his left shoulder, a simple crawling of the skin as if a fly had landed there or perhaps even an ant dropping from a tree into his shirt. The muscle trembled, a little involuntary quiver to dislodge the unwanted guest, but the itch did not stop. A bigger bug, he thought, a cockroach, or some kind of beetle. Maybe like the grossly huge beetles and roaches that he saw every day all around the pit, grown large on an unending supply of human tissue. Krang shuddered as he remembered the insects crawling across his body as he lay immobile in the pit. He began to scratch frantically, to brush them away as he couldn't do when he lay in the pit.

Krang groaned, and shook his head. Jesus Christ, he thought, I'm going nuts. He squeezed his eyes shut against the blackness until he saw sparks of color. Opening his eyes, the green and red rings floated in the blackness before him. The blackness shimmered and twisted, turning in upon itself again and again, gradually lightening as if dawn had found its way into the cave. Sarah materialized before him, slowly pulling herself together from the faint colors swirling around Krang's head, so insubstantial that he didn't believe what he was seeing until suddenly she was there. She smiled at him, her face thin beyond reason. She had lost most of her teeth, he realized with a start.

Sarah saw Krang draw back when she smiled. "I had a beautiful smile," she whispered. "I flirted with that smile. It helped me win Abraham, you know. He told me he was intoxicated by it, from the first moment he saw me at University. We never saw you at University, but you must be close to the same age as we? Do you remember Abraham?'

Krang shook his head. "I'm sorry," he said, "I'm older, and I was never at University. At the camp there were too many. I don't know him."

She smiled. "But you must. You shot him in the face. Did you shoot so many men in the face that you can't remember them?"

Krang shrugged.

"Surely you remember our boy, then? You beat him to death against the ground? Just before you shot my husband?"

The train had come in very late that night, he suddenly remembered. It had been so very hot, all day, and the humidity was hovering around ninety percent. He had thought that he was going to die, standing on that platform, waiting for that damn train to come in. And he had been hung over! There had been a party the night before. One of the other guards was getting married and they had celebrated in the barracks. Krang had gotten so drunk that he was still hung over, even though it was close to midnight. He had been sipping vodka from a flask he kept hidden in his pocket, hoping to dull the effects of the hangover.

The train had come in, miserably slow, the steam engine huffing and clanging like a roaring dragon, the damn engineer blowing the whistle in the long blasts as if anyone cared if one or two of the prisoners were crushed by the train. He had been miserable, just trying to keep from throwing up. Krang had fantasized about shooting the engineer; in fact he had pulled his pistol from the holster to make his point. Then, when the cattle car doors were finally opened, the Corabians had spilled out onto the platform in a wave, straining desperately to get away from the dead and dying on the trains. He had been at one end of the platform supervising as the guards were sorting the healthy workers from those who couldn't work, when she had stepped from the train, the boy in her arms.

All children were forbidden in the camps. They were just a distraction to parents, so they were taken and disposed of as soon as the train arrived. It was the one humane thing they did in the camp: the children were never killed in front of their parents, and their bodies were never thrown into the pit.

Krang had heard her arguing with one of the other guards. She held the boy on her hip, her body twisted so he was out of reach of the guard, her husband at her side. She argued with passion. The nerve of her! Prisoners never argued, not fresh off the train. They were all so afraid at that moment that they would do anything to avoid attention. Krang shook his head, and walked down the platform to solve the problem. She was creating a logjam, keeping the prisoners from getting off the platform. He smiled when he reached them. She was beautiful in her anger. He transferred his pistol to his left hand and raised his arm gently to her, asking for the boy. She acquiesced, and he pulled the boy from her arms by his legs. It was her fault. She should have hidden the boy. Enough children did make it past the guards during unloading that Krang could claim a clear

40

conscience for the ones who didn't. Krang remembered the look of fear that ran over her face when he grabbed the boy, and then the man stepping forward, not pleading, but angry, acting to save his boy.

He had been brave, Krang had to allow for that. He had no fear when he stepped up to pull the boy from Kang's arms. Krang had already grabbed the boy's foot and was beginning to swing him about, even as he raised the pistol in his left hand and brought it up into the man's face. Those eyes stared at him fearlessly, hands still reaching for the boy. Strong eyes, clear. He never knew his son was dead, Krang realized. The bullet tore apart his brain at the same time I smashed the boy against the loading dock. They both died of massive brain trauma.

"He had blue eyes," Krang said, quietly, "and he was brave. I remember him now."

Sarah treated him to another smile, more brilliant than the first. It was a smile made for flirting. "Thank you for remembering."

Krang wondered if he would have made the same sacrifice for any of his children. He shook his head, laughing derisively. Fuck, no. It wasn't that he was a coward and was afraid of dying. He just never cared that much about any of them. Kids were what happened when he and Emma fucked, that was all. They were just part of the package.

Krang felt the bodies of the dead, lying beneath him and above him and around him, struggling to move. They churned against him, the mass writhing like a stocking pond in a fishery when you threw bread into the water. He wondered if they would fight over his carcass the way the fish fought for the bread crumbs. He laughed, realizing that he was now in their dominion, as they had once been in his. I always knew I would have to pay for this at sometime he thought. Just never in the pit. I thought I'd be run up the flag pole like Bitmeyer, or shot like Willi and Gerri. Suddenly Krang was free again, out of the pit, watching the bodies twisting and turning from a vantage point on the edge of the pit.

They unfolded themselves from the pit for what seemed like hours. The bodies gently unlocked, slithering over and under each other to pull free. Each apparition came out of the pit whole, even though Krang knew that they hadn't all gone into the pit whole, and that they had moldered and been burned again and again. Each one stopped to look him in the face, before moving slowly away. Krang fought the urge to flinch, or to back down in any way. He saw the first man he had killed; Krang had shot him in the back as the man ran from the depot. He had never learned the man's name. There was the butcher, Polkin, still dressed in the tattered nightshirt he had worn every day in the camp, who Krang had killed for taking an unauthorized break while on work duty, and Bela Myska, who Krang had hated for the entire year of fifth grade and had been killed for reminding him of that year. For every Corabian he recognized, two or three more who climbed from the pit struck no memory, but he knew they were all his. Krang-kill.

One old man, sporting a long, thin beard, with wisps of hair stretching across his scalp from ear to ear shook his head gently when he faced Krang. Krang reached out and grabbed him, surprised by the mass behind the apparition and the rough texture of the uniform. Krang shook him roughly.

"I remember you," Krang whispered bitterly. "Why are you here? You were executed for killing another prisoner. A boy you accused of stealing your food, although I always thought you were the thief and killed the boy to cover up your crime. Bitmeyer ordered you killed for the murder, his only virtuous act ever."

Krang shook his head, and pushed the old man away. "Get away from me, old man. You are ruining their righteousness. Look at them! They stare at you as if you were me."

The old man faded away and the slow procession began again. Krang looked each of them in the face, marveling that he could see them so clearly now, so many years after their deaths, when he wouldn't have noticed a thing about them alive. He saw the blush on a cheek, light glistening on hair, the beauty of crow's feet gracing a woman's eyes. He noticed the tattoos on their wrists, the blue-green marker that chained the prisoners to the camp the way ear notches identified a pig to a farm, and felt a voyeuristic sense of indignity. They never stopped coming, slowly unfolding themselves from the pit, puffing up what should have been nothing more than mold-covered detritus into yet another human being. Krang sat through it all, self-consciously watching himself watch them, awed by his ability to believe that anything could be moving around him in the cave. They filled the cave with their accusing stares, packed in so tightly they didn't have room to move. Even though the old man, the one Krang had thrown out, had seemed so solid to his touch, at the same time they all seemed insubstantial. He could see them all, even those at the very edges of the cave, as if they were in front of the group, not behind. How could they be so real, yet transparent? It was as if Krang's looking in someone's direction suddenly made that phantom solid and the others insubstantial, as if each phantom needed Krang's eyes on them to give them meaning and form.

Laughter broke the spell. Loud, raucous laughter. It took Krang a moment to realize that he was the one laughing, and several minutes to work feeling back into his legs so he could crawl out of the cave. Dawn had not yet broken, but the morning stars were high overhead. It would be morning in another hour.

What an impossible dream, he thought, as he sat in the shallow cave, breathing the fresh night air. Why did I not force them to maim me, or kill me, if I though guilt was necessary? Why dream of them today, when I never dreamt once in all the years that I worked in the camp? Nothing I did, not even swinging

42

Sarah's boy against the loading dock gave me a bad dream, and then tonight, safe and warm, I dream of this. I could feel their anger, he thought. In the camp, I knew only their fear. I suppose they were angry then, too. I knew they hated me, but the fear overwhelmed everything. Not a single prisoner ever challenged me, or attacked me. I felt their anger tonight, but they still did not attack me. Even two hundred to one, they didn't have the balls to attack me. Krang smiled at the thought that the dream was truly about his power, and their inability to act against him, their fear of him, no matter how many of them stood against him. Unless it wasn't a dream, he thought with a soft laugh. If those ghosts were real and I am haunted, then even the spirit world cannot touch me. What about you, God? Can you punish me?

Katie sat on the top step of the cellar, preparing to open the trap door. The lantern hung on its nail, and she quickly leaned over and blew it out. She didn't know what she would do if the door wouldn't open. She would have been willing to let it go for another day or two, and not find out if she was trapped in her own tomb, but the small pantry was beginning to stink from her makeshift toilet.

The bombing had stopped sometime during the second day. The eerie silence was quickly shattered by the sounds of war as trucks and tanks had poured into the city. Katie sat in the cellar and listened, and prayed they would overlook the store. She could hear rifle and machine gun fire, and feel shells, she guessed from tanks, exploding one after another. The fighting went on for several hours, and then it was quiet. It was quiet for several hours, and just when Katie thought everything might be over, she felt the deep vibrations of the heavy bombs. The final onslaught was the worst of all, and Katie sat in her corner and prayed, unsure to whom she was praying.

It had finally stopped three days ago. Katie would have preferred to stay in the cellar forever, but the bucket she had found to use as a toilet was full to the point of overflowing, and she had to empty it. She could only hope that three days was enough, and that they wouldn't start bombing again. She reached up and gave the trapdoor a hard push and it swung open easily, crashing against the floor with a loud bang! Katie feared the noise might bring someone to investigate. She crouched on the first step and raised her head into the darkened, much fresher smelling room.

Knife-sharp shards of light illuminated the grocery. At first, all Katie could see were the columns of dust glowing in the light, the bright particles dancing crazily in the air. Her eyes gradually adjusted to the streaks of light and dimness. The first floor of the grocer had been destroyed. The wall shelves behind the counter had been knocked from the walls. The free standing shelving units had toppled to the ground. One of the huge wooden units lay less than thirty centimeters from the trapdoor, and Katie realized she would have been trapped if it had blocked the door. Bags of flour, sugar, coffee and other dry goods had burst open and scattered their contents everywhere. Glass shards were scattered throughout the debris, shining in the light. Nothing remained undamaged.

The room was so dim it could have been evening, but when Katie glanced up at the windows that ringed the top of the first floor she could see a bright sky. Katie walked across the store, leaving footprints in the powdery mess on the floor. She stopped at the bottom of the steps that lead up to the street. The frosted glass in the front door was still intact, and Katie couldn't see what was beyond it, but something was blocking the entrance to the building. Katie unlocked the front door open and pulled it open. A concrete slab had landed against the front stoop of the store, effectively blocking the entrance. Light flooded in along a narrow gap on the left side of the slab. Katie crouched down and peered through the gap. She could see nothing in the street, but the gap was big enough that she could slip out of the building, and narrow enough that most people wouldn't be able to get in. Katie smiled. This was the first good thing that had happened to her in days.

Katie went back into the store and locked the door behind her. She found a broom and began sweeping up the mess near the trapdoor. She didn't want to track stuff into her pantry. She carried her bucket up the narrow steps and dumped it into a floor drain in the small room behind the counter. She turned on the water faucet, but nothing happened. A third room served as washroom and led up to the living quarters above the store. The stairs to the second floor had collapsed, blocking the stairwell. When she had cleaned up as much as she could, Katie went back out the front door.

Katie crouched on the protected stoop, trying to get a look at the street through the gap in the slab. She could see no movement on the street, nor hear anything. She sat for more than an hour before trying to slip through the gap. It was getting late, and the light in the street had taken on the golden hue of late afternoon. She carried Stojespahl's pistol in her pocket. Katie was able to slip through the gap in a crouch, her back against the brick exterior of the building, her breasts pressing against the concrete slab. She found herself standing in a tall narrow alley of rubble that blocked her view of the city. She turned to her right and made her way towards the thoroughfare.

When she came to the intersection of the alley and the thoroughfare, she still couldn't get her bearings. All she could see were mounds of rubble, fifteen, twenty, thirty feet high. A building on one corner of the intersection had pancaked down upon itself, the top floor in perfect condition but sitting on the street, as if a giant hand had pressed the building into the ground. The building that had been next to it, Katie remembered it was a bank with granite columns, was just rubble. Turning in a slow circle to survey her surroundings, she saw no people, and no intact buildings. Katie turned to her left and looked for Stojespahl's apartment building. It was five or six blocks from the grocer's, but she couldn't see it. She couldn't see any buildings, just rubble and smoke. The city was gone.

Katie felt a guilty stab of pleasure. It was as if every person who had abused her, every place where she had been pushed down to her knees and forced to blow someone, had been wiped away. She remembered wishing for this just as the camp woman pushed her out of the window. And yet it was so wrong, what had happened. Katie couldn't get her mind around the devastation she saw. So many landmarks were gone that she couldn't place herself in the city that she had known so well. So many people must have died.

She couldn't really make this destruction equal to her own pain. It was too much. She hoped that her thoughts of rage hadn't somehow brought all of this into being. No one deserved this, no matter what they had done to her. Not even Stojespahl. People had been kind to her, too. An old man used to give her food when he saw her on the street, and he never asked her for anything. And there was a woman who had been living in the park, Jana, who shared her hiding place when Katie had nowhere to go, and taught Katie about living on the streets, who had wanted nothing more than someone to talk to. What happened to them?

Katie walked numbly down the street, her head swiveling back and forth warily. It was like walking on the moon. After a block, she climbed one pile of rubble that looked safe, hoping to get a sense of what had happened. To the west, under huge columns of black, oily smoke, she could see that blocks and blocks of the city were burning. That was the part of town with all the factories and smelting operations, and the artisan area where Matilde had lived, and it was apparent from the blazes that nothing was left. The rest of the city was gone. A lone building stood, maybe a mile away. She could see a clock tower rising above the rubble, but the building underneath it was gone. From her vantage point, the city around her looked like a maze of junk and rubble. Many streets were impassable, but the others cut deep channels through the brick and concrete landscape. She didn't see anyone alive, just bodies in the streets.

Katie imagined there must be other hidden treasures like her pantry. She would have to find them. She skittered down the rubble and started to walk, feeling a little more comfortable than before. She was halfway down the block when she came across the first body. A man. He had been crushed by a collapsing building, and his lower half was buried under rubble. Katie wondered if he had been killed instantly. She studied the body, but then walked on. What could she do?

The next street was littered with dead bodies. Many lay clear of the buildings, killed by the advancing army, not the bombing afterward. The body of a dead horse lay before the cart it had been pulling. The horse's bloated belly was taut, so

45

swollen it looked like it might explode at any moment. The overwhelmingly sweet smell of rot made Katie gag and she hurried past.

A sound broke the incessant buzzing of the flies. Katie stopped, unsure if she had heard anything. She listened intently for several minutes, until she heard it again. A soft sob, the sound of someone crying. Katie looked around her, but there was no place for anyone to be hiding. She wondered if her ears where playing tricks on her, but the sobbing continued. Katie realized with a start that it had to be coming from under one of the piles of rubble. She went to the closest building, but in moving lost the sound. Was someone under the building?

Katie began to toss loose bricks from the pile. She worked frantically, but after several minutes had made no real headway. And she couldn't hear the crying any more, couldn't tell which building it was really coming from. She stepped back from the rubble, feeling her own tears running down her face. She was leaving someone to die, and it felt even worse than shooting Stojespahl.

The sun had fallen to the edge of the city, and Katie decided she had better get back to her pantry. As she turned to head back, she caught a glimpse of someone, alive, in the distance. The person was too far away to tell if it was a man or a woman. In the failing light, all Katie could tell was that they walked towards her. She shrank against the rubble, suddenly having no desire to meet anyone. How could she tell if they were safe? And who was safe for her anyway? Her own people considered her a collaborator and the Citizens considered her the enemy. Katie skittered away, running as quickly as she could, trying to stay as close to the rubble piles as possible in the hopes that she wouldn't be seen. At the intersection of the main thoroughfare with her alley, she saw another person, this one clearly a man. He was standing in the street, less than a block from her. He had his back turned to her, so she took a chance to dart across the street. She glanced over her shoulder as she ran, but didn't see anyone behind her.

She was numb when she returned to the grocer's. She had almost given herself away. Katie understood she couldn't relax her vigilance for even a moment if she hoped to stay alive.

She studied the alley for a long time, making sure no one would see her enter her home. She darted up to the concrete slab that blocked her door and turned around, her back to the grocer's. No one was in sight. She slipped past the concrete barrier and allowed her eyes to adjust to the darkness. Katie opened the door to the store and studied the footprints on the messy floor. Only her prints were visible. She locked the door behind her.

She walked across the room and opened the cellar trapdoor, stopping to light the lantern. She pulled the trapdoor shut as she slid down the steps. Katie stopped about halfway down the steps and began to cry. She didn't know how she was going to manage her life. All the rules had changed again, just like three years ago. How would she ever be able to find her family? Katie had killed the one man who might have protected her. Could she have trusted Stojespahl to get her out of the city?

Katie surveyed the food around her and laughed bitterly. It seemed like one of those lessons her father preached, about having everything and nothing. About how the world wasn't enough to live on, you needed faith as well. She wished she still had her faith. But her faith had been lost three years ago, in an alley on her knees before a policeman she had thought was a family friend.

One detail of the dream kept coming back to Krang over the next few days: the serial numbers tattooed onto the prisoner's left forearm. How many times had he seen those blue-green numbers showing so starkly against the pale skin of the prisoners? Every inmate who ever escaped had mutilated their forearm, literally trying to cut the tattoo out of their arm, as if it was the tattoo that was the agent of their oppression, rather than the Citizens.

How they had fought the tattoo. Mothers would give up their children, accepting the slimmest chance that they would meet again, and yet balk at the tattoo. Men who showed no emotion at the death of their spouses would weep before the needle. The tattoo was what symbolized the permanence of their state. It was what made them grieve for the children who were now dead, for the older relatives who were being "cleansed." The tattoo became the source of their hopelessness, more than the camp, more than the death that surrounded them. In that way, the tattoo and *the guard* were one and the same. They were the confirmation that the system was too strong, that resistance was meaningless.

Krang needed the tattoo. It would serve as his talisman, as protection against any accusation that might find its way to his doorstep. The tattoo would serve as his travel pass through Montrovia, as his status as one of the oppressed, the proof of his innocence. It would be the symbol of his struggle, of his journey through hell, of his triumph. He smiled at the brilliance of it.

Krang spent the next five days fasting, climbing up to the entrance of the cave once or twice each day to relieve himself. He could no longer hear any sounds of war.

He made a small fire each day in the mouth of the cave, burning it just hot enough to turn the blade of his knife red hot. He slowly burned the number into his forearm above the wrist, grinding charcoal into the fresh wound to blacken it. The pain was a worthy price to pay. He gritted his teeth and suffered, knowing the pain made his freedom belong to him and not to the crazy bitch that had let him go. He would make her pay for the pain, and then they would be even.

After several days he had a reasonable facsimile of the tattoo. It wouldn't pass a close examination, but it would do at a glance. Then he defaced it slightly,

47

so it became part scar and part number, an indication of his escape, a badge of his courage. Krang was ready to return to the world.

Chapter Three

The crescent moon glowed ghost-like in the western sky, chased away by the half-light of approaching dawn. Katie made her way through the city's rubble, back towards the cellar she now called home. In the two weeks that had passed since she had first left her hideaway she had developed something of a routine. Katie had discovered that soldiers patrolled the city during the day. She assumed they were Corabian soldiers, but wasn't willing to find out. Once it was dark, the soldiers disappeared and the rubble came alive. Katie guessed there were hundreds of survivors like her, hiding from the occupying soldiers during the day, who came out of the rubble after dark like rats to scavenge for food and supplies. Every night full dark brought sounds of running feet, shouts of anger, gunshots. Katie limited her excursions to the twilight of early evening and the half-light of early morning, when the streets seemed to be empty.

A refugee camp had sprung up in the fields on the eastern edge of the city. White canvas tents, in orderly rows, housed a few thousand refugees. She could tell from a distance that the camp housed Citizens, not Corabians. No one had the stick-like appearance of the prisoners who had beaten her. It didn't matter to Katie who was living in the camp. She was a collaborator; to enter probably meant jail or worse. She had hoped she would see an influx of Corabians from the camp, but it never happened. She realized it wouldn't be safe to house the Corabians with the Citizens since the war had just ended, but was secretly afraid that it meant no one else had survived the camp. Her rational mind told her the prisoners were either still being cared for out at the camp or they had been taken away, maybe to Corabia. Her parents had always talked about visiting the Homeland, so why wouldn't they take the freed prisoners there? Katie knew that if she had seen the caravan of freed Corabians she would never have joined them. How could she? They would despise her. They had suffered so much at the hands of the Citizens while she had been fed and housed by them. Who would ever forgive her? All she wanted was a chance to see her family. It would be enough to know that they were alive.

Katie stopped at the end of the alley that ran to her cellar. She stepped into the shadows of the rubble, crouched down and waited. She had Stojespahl's pistol in her hand. She wouldn't approach the cellar until she was sure that no one would see her. The cellar was her refuge and she couldn't risk giving it away. When she was sure no one was near, she walked quickly down the alley to the wreckage of the shop. She slipped behind the slab of concrete, blessing the shell that made this cover for her hideaway. She stepped down and through the door into the shop, locking the door behind her. She studied the footprints on the messy floor and saw only hers, and knew that she was safe.

Katie had told herself she left the mess on the floor so she could see if anyone had entered the shop, but today that didn't feel true. She had left the mess because her life was as chaotic as the floor, and just as dirty. She thought of the boy and felt tears begin to flow down her face. In a minute she was crying uncontrollably, her body shaking as she sank to the floor against the door.

She had been surprised by the boy. Man. He was her age, or perhaps a year or two older, and had come upon her while she was in a narrow corridor flanked by tall piles of rubble. He had come from a side alley and suddenly they were face to face.

"Hello," he had said, and smiled at her.

Katie smiled back nervously, her heart suddenly in her throat..

"Do you have any food?" he asked. "I've been looking all night."

Katie shook her head, but didn't say a word.

"Do you have a safe place to stay? I've never come this far east. I'll trade you some water for a place to stay." He lifted a water skin and held it out to her. Katie could see he had two more hanging from his shoulder.

Katie shook her head and saw his smile turn into a frown. He looked angry, his big eyes accusing her of lying. She grabbed him by the hand and pulled him back down the narrow channel of rubble, to a small clearing, almost like a room, that she had passed a few minutes earlier. The boy had been surprised when she offered herself, surprised but more than willing. He had been quick, and had called out to her quietly when she left him in the dark, his pants around his ankles.

She wanted to bathe, to wash him away, but that wouldn't clean away her own filthiness. She didn't understand it. She had the pistol and more food than she could eat, but still found herself offering her body to those who wanted it. She had fucked another man four days ago. She hated herself. Hated the weakness that made her sell herself. Not even for food or a place to sleep anymore. Just for the transaction. She was afraid of everyone she saw, except when she was offering herself. That was why she didn't want to go to the Homeland. What would her parent's think? Had they already heard stories about their daughter, the whore?

Katie stayed crouched by the door until her tears stopped. She was stupid to even think about it. This was her life, and it was the only life she had. She didn't have time to cry. She walked over to the trapdoor for the cellar. It was time to sleep.

*   *   *

An incessant chatter had arisen from the trees at the edge of the woods as the starlings and blackbirds anticipated morning. Krang wanted to wring their collective necks just to shut them up. He hadn't waited twenty days in the cave, with only the sound of his own breathing to break the monotony, to go deaf from a flock of starlings.

"Fuck," he whispered, and stared at the remains of the camp. He had come back to the camp hoping to destroy his service records, but he hadn't considered the Corabians might try to obliterate the camp. The guard towers and flag pole still rose into the sky, but overlooked nothing. The double fence was intact, but there was nothing left to be fenced-in. Every building in the compound had been burned to the ground. All Krang could see were dozens of piles of charred lumber. No trucks had been left at the camp, but the burned out remains of the bulldozer sat near the muddy scar that had been the pit.

The pit was the worst of all. They had filled it in. Dirt and rocks and the burned wreckage of barracks had been bulldozed into the pit, until it was a muddy mess. They hadn't been able to smooth it over, to make it invisible. Thousands of people were buried in the pit and the Corabians had turned it into a junk heap. They had created a garbage dump at the edge of the camp.

Krang spat on the ground, a righteous sense of anger burning in his chest. Didn't the Corabians see the futility and disrespect in what they had done? The elders must have thought that with a simple bulldozer and several gallons of diesel fuel they could undo everything that had been done here. He imagined the prisoners standing outside the camp, cheering as the burning buildings collapsed one by one. As if burning down the barracks wiped out all the misery and pain of those who lived and died here. Krang shook his head. He was disappointed that anyone felt that the work that he had done here could be dismissed so easily. He wished that one of the Corabian prisoners were here, so he could show them that the buildings hadn't been what had oppressed them. He wanted to beat the shit out of someone, until there was no life left in them, so they would understand. You couldn't change what had happened here by burning the place to the ground. This place deserved a great monument. Some granite or marble obelisk towering into the sky like a giant prick. Not to celebrate the deaths, not to mourn them, but to account for them. To account for the work Krang had done to take those lives. It should be seen as hallowed ground.

Didn't they understand the horror of it? The evil? Had they already forgotten that Krang was still alive, that he could hunt each of them down and resurrect the horror of this place simply by saying hello?

Krang laughed. He didn't believe in evil. At least not as the opposite of good. Evil was an everyday condition, not something special. It was good, whatever the fuck that was, that was the outlier. Good people, truly good people, didn't really exist. Was anyone truly selfless? Krang tried to think of anyone he had met who would qualify, but couldn't.

All of his life he had been told he was bad. He was always in trouble, from the day he started school. His mother, his teachers, the priests had all tried to beat his spirit out of him, but they hadn't been able to do so. Krang now understood, however, that nothing that he had done before the camp had been evil. He had been a fuck up, but not evil. But the camp had changed all of that. He had finally come to understand that his life couldn't be lived in safe mode. That wasn't living at all. Call Krang evil if you liked, the camp had been more about declaring to the world who the fuck he was than about being evil. You couldn't have an identity if you didn't transgress everything. Did his mother count? His father? Fuck no. They had lived by the rules and died by them, with God watching on with amused contempt. Krang wouldn't suffer that ignoble ending. He had become. No one could deny that he existed.

He hadn't become *the guard* because he was evil. Or at least not because he was more evil than anyone else. He had succeeded where the others had failed because he had been able to wall himself off from the world. All of his cruelty and violence had erected a wall that freed Krang from the tentacles of other human beings. Everyone else had moments of weakness in which they believed they were connected to other people and that connection left them vulnerable. Abraham had died because he had felt he had to save his son. Sarah had freed Krang because she thought she was doing something to save the soul of her dead husband. Stupid.

Krang felt outraged when he thought of Sarah. His power couldn't be undone by her simple action. What had happened in this camp was unforgivable, and Sarah needed to understand that. They all needed to understand that. His crimes transgressed all the boundaries that men had ever established and no one but God could ever release Krang from what he had done. Krang wasn't even sure about God. If God had the power to forgive what Krang had done, then he would have had the power to stop Krang from doing it, but he hadn't. Just as God had never acted on the prayers of Krang's mother, had never lifted her above the pain of her life, God had never stepped in here to save anyone. The truth was He had been Krang's partner, had been the whimsy and capriciousness behind Krang's violence, had been the chance that saved one man's life but took another's. Wasn't that worse than God being absent from the camp entirely?

It had been a mistake to come here to destroy his records, he realized. He needed them intact. That was how the world would know who he was. It wasn't enough simply to be hated by the men and women from the camp. His life deserved more than that. Krang needed his own Nuremburg like the Nazis had gotten. That would be a fitting end to his life, with the whole of the world watching and reading about him, shivering in their beds at night, thankful they had never crossed his path.

The moon glowed faintly behind the clouds but did not illuminate the city. Krang sat on the trunk of a felled maple, a half mile above the city. His mind struggled to make sense of what lay before him. The plains were covered in a heavy fog and nothing was visible, as if the city were not where he had left it. Krang rolled a cigarette to clear his mind and get his bearings. He had hiked hard all afternoon and through the early part of the night. He was just too tired to make sense of it all. Maybe he hiked over the wrong pass and was in the wrong valley.

The clouds began to clear as Krang smoked and he breathed a sigh of relief: the city was covered in a blanket of fog. Krang could make out the top of the city clock tower in the moonlight, just breaking the plane of the fog. He shook his head at the tricks of memory - it seemed the clock tower had been moved. Was it stress he wondered, or did I really create memories with the clock tower in a different place? Krang laughed to himself, wondering if Emma had done the same thing when he came home on leave. Did she say to herself, 'I remembered your cock was bigger than this measly thing?'

The clouds continued to clear, the moonlight growing brighter by the minute. And with each passing minute Krang struggled to reconcile what he saw with what he knew to be true. The city was coming into focus wrong. City landmarks weren't where they belonged.

In the final clarity of the night, the sky now perfectly clear and the moonlight bright, Krang wept. The clock tower he thought had been breaking through a sea of fog was actually breaking from mist only a meter or so deep, thrown some hundreds of meters from where it should have been. It was only ten or fifteen meters tall. And it was still the tallest thing in town. The city was nothing more than smoldering piles of rubble. Krang couldn't see a single building that remained in pristine condition. It was as if a giant scythe had cut the city off at seven meters tall. Mountain City had been a town of fifty thousand people. Had the prisoners done this?

Krang shook his head at the stupidity of that thought, and wiped his tears away. What the fuck did he care what happened here? He could see no sign of his apartment building, but that didn't matter. He hadn't expected Emma to be able to keep the kids alive and wasn't coming back for them anyway.

Krang could make out a sea of white canvas tents on the east side of the city. Some kind of refugee camp had been set up. It wasn't big enough. At best, it might house a few thousand people. Krang knew that even if Emma had survived, and she and the kids were among the lucky ones in the refugee camp, he couldn't risk showing his face there. The camp would be under someone's control; the kind of someone that would arrest Krang if he were recognized by friends or family.

Krang let his cigarette burn out in his finger and then rolled and lit another. What had possessed the Corabians to devastate the city so completely? Mountain City hadn't been an important place in Montrovia. It wasn't the home of the government, or a center of cultural pride, or even home of the largest of the death camps. Even if Vojacek had made his last stand here, was that cause for such destruction?

This city had benefitted from the war, Krang knew. Hell, they had celebrated the war, and the prosperity that it had brought them. The boys who died on far off battle fields were a reasonable sacrifice for the good of the community. Even their families understood that. After centuries of neglect and terrible fortune, we deserved the good luck the war brought us, Krang reasoned. We were forgotten for so long, we deserved every penny of profit that came our way. But how could we deserve this? No one ever thought the war would come here.

Krang couldn't imagine there were other cities across the Balkans that looked like this. He had believed in the war as a pristine exercise in violence among soldiers. He had figured that the camps were built as an outlet for that darker need to destroy the spirit of a people, and that they kept the war pristine. He knew that some Montrovian Citizens, living in the occupied territories, must have suffered as he had caused the prisoners to suffer. He accepted that. People in the camps were sacrifices, just as the boys from the city had been. They were the price that you paid for going to war. A fair price, he reasoned. There had to be some cost, beyond the soldiers themselves, or we would be at war all the time. But this was obscene. Was it payback for similar destruction done by our soldiers? Or simply blood lust?

Looking at the rubble of the city, Krang estimated that at least thirty thousand people must have died there. Thirty thousand killed in just a week or two. Had this happened in all the cities across Montrovia and Corabia? Could it be possible? Krang couldn't figure out what the point was. He had been happy before the war, fucking his way through clubs and bars and working when he had to. Who the fuck would give that up for this?

He hiked slowly down the hill, hesitating when he reached the edge of the city, then walking past the first mounds of rubble, stopping when he stood in front of the clock tower. The clock looked perfect, the glass face unblemished. Krang could see the gargoyles jutting from the top of the tower. He could remember trips to look at the clock tower, both as a boy and with his own son. His father had told him about the gargoyles, as he had told his son, but he had never seen them clearly. They were the faces of men, distorted by rage, lust, avarice, sloth. They were, allegedly, the faces of the Corabians, displaying their inherent weaknesses. Krang laughed, seeing them up close. They were the faces he had looked at in the mirror every morning when he was younger, hung over from another night on the town.

The tower only stood because it was supported by the rubble of another building behind it. Krang saw the cornerstone of the northwest city gate, and knew where he was in relation to the city in his memory. His stomach growled and he realized he needed to find something to eat. He hadn't eaten a real meal since he had escaped from the camp. Part of his confusion was hunger, he was sure. He remembered that a supermarket had stood not far from this place. It was a modern store, and had been built about the time he and Emma had married. He walked past the tower, past the remains of the gate, past piles of still smoldering debris, and began looking for food.

The devastation was overwhelming. The stench of decay was everywhere, reminding Krang of the smells of the pit. Bodies and pieces of bodies lay everywhere. It was impossible to align the piles of rubble with his memories of the city, but every few minutes, Krang would see some piece of a building, or a sign or some other recognizable land mark and have some idea of where he was. Some streets were impassible; the remains of buildings crumpled into the street, blocking passage, while other streets were open, the buildings having collapsed within themselves. Krang wondered what made one building explode outward over the street and the next to have folded up into itself like it was trying to shrink away from the bombardment. It was baffling.

He looked at the decomposing bodies that lay where they had fallen and wondered why so many people had been caught in the final onslaught. Did they just cower in their homes until the very end? He imagined that his fellow Citizens were no different than his Corabian prisoners had been: paralyzed by the fear of death to the point of not being willing to risk death to save their own lives. And too stupid to see what was coming early enough to get out when it was easy. Maybe we all deserved this, he thought. Maybe this is the best humanity can aspire towards.

Krang walked past the remains of the supermarket, its big electric sign lying undamaged in the street. The store was gone, only a shallow crater in its place. It must have taken a direct hit. More than one, even, for it had been a large store. Krang stared at the crater and cursed. Krang had known it was unlikely he would find food there, but he was still disappointed. He had let himself go too long without food. He could only stare at the crater and feel angry. He was having trouble putting his thoughts together cohesively. The city was too fucked up to make sense to him. Where else could he find food? There was another place Emma had shopped near the supermarket. Krang closed his eyes for a minute, imagining the city as it had been. Krang nodded, knowing where to go. He turned a corner into what had once been a narrow alley, and that now seemed more like a deep trench between two stone walls.

Ahead, to his left, Krang saw a concrete slab covering the stoop of the building he wanted. Emma had hated the supermarket. She found it to be much too sterile and unfriendly. She had continued to come here, to a basement dry goods store run by a Corabian family that also owned a share in a butcher store and worked closely with the dairy. Krang shook his head. He couldn't remember their name. Each week they would deliver Emma's purchases directly to the apartment, and she would tip the delivery boy and give him a kiss on the cheek. Krang had loved to watch her flirt with the boy, who was overwhelmed by Emma's flagrant sexuality. Krang wondered briefly if the boy could have become Emma's lover, and then shook his head with a laugh. The family had come through the camp just in the last year. One of the boys, what was his name? survived, Krang thought. The parents were dead, in the lime pit, but the boy had been transferred to a factory in the south. He should be alive, Krang told himself. The other son had hung himself, just a few weeks after coming to the camp.

The concrete slab lay at an odd angle, sealing the stoop as tightly as a tomb.

"Fuck," Krang said savagely, his hunger flaring at the sight before him. Krang tried to remember if there was another way into the shop. He could remember no rear door, no alley entrance. The top floors of the building, where the family had lived, were gone. The first floor looked sound and undisturbed since the bombing. A row of windows, near the top of the first floor, had lost all of their glass. That might be the way in. The windows were too high above the street for Krang to reach from the alley. He walked around the building, looking for a way to get up to the top. The concrete slab that blocked the entrance had a slight angle to it that might work. It was smooth near the street, but pitted and cracked at the top, enough to provide finger holds.

Krang ran from across the street as far as he could up the concrete slab. He reached upward, his hands grabbing the top edge of the slab, and pulled himself up onto the top of the building. He lay on his back in what must have been a sitting room. The remains of a shattered easy chair crumpled on the floor next to him. Krang crawled across the building to the edge facing the alley, where the windows were located and peered over the side. The windows were less than a foot below him. It was too dark inside the store to see anything. Krang slithered feet first over the edge of the building and into the window. His butt rested on the window frame for a moment before he pushed himself inside, the window frame scratching at his back. He dropped seven feet into the shop. Once inside, Krang knelt where he landed and waited for his eyes to adjust to the darkness.

He wished he'd brought the old man's lantern, rather than leaving it in the cave. Krang's stomach was growling excitedly at the thought of finding something to eat. Krang fished a match from his pocket and struck it on his thumb nail. He was near a stone hearth at the rear of the shop, behind what had once been the counter. The room had been trashed, shelves overturned, bags of flour and corn meal dumped over the floor.

"Fuck," Krang muttered again, looking at the devastation before him. He lit a second match and walked across the room to the door and tried the handle. The door opened perfectly to reveal the concrete slab blocking the stoop. Krang shut the door. He blew the match out, dropped it on the mess, and sat down hard, his back against the door. When would he find food? He could smell a faint trace of kerosene, and wondered if someone had spoiled the goods in the shop like they had the food in a cabin he had seen on the way into town.

Krang admired what the Corabians were doing. Beat the people down, starve them, and make them so hungry that they will do whatever you demand of them. It had been a favorite tool of his at the camp, to put someone in isolation, starve them beyond the almost non-existent rations, and then degrade them even further. How many blow jobs had he gotten for a raw potato?

And how close was he to that state now? What would he do for food, today, tomorrow, the day after? Was he ready to give his power to someone else for a fucking raw potato? Krang laughed. What would my benefactors have done, he wondered? He didn't know about Abraham, but he thought knew Sarah. Her weakness was others, that was clear. He thought she would accept any indignity for the sake of another person, and would resist to her death if it were only her. Krang almost admired her for that, although she had gotten it backward. Save yourself and let the others take care of themselves. Krang smiled. Of course, if Sarah had been like me, I wouldn't be sitting here now, so I guess maybe you did have it right, at least when it came to me.

What would Emma do? Krang shook his head. She wouldn't wait to be starved. She would degrade herself right from the start. That was her weakness and her strength. You could never do anything to hurt Emma, because she had already done it to herself. He remembered coming in here with her. She would tell Krang that you could never trust a shop keeper, especially a Corabian shop keeper. She was convinced they would steal from her, so she always beat them to the punch and overpaid for at least one item every week. "It keeps them honest," she had sworn to Krang. He remembered one visit when she paid for a ham, and had then sent the old man back down into the cellar to get her a smaller one, because she said they wouldn't eat all of the bigger one. Emma was convinced that she got a better price from him on everything else.

The cellar! There was a pantry under the floor. The old man had stored most of the goods down there, especially anything perishable, because it had been naturally cool.

Pulling another match from his pocket and lighting it, Krang looked towards the rear of the shop, where he remembered seeing steps. There was a spot in all the chaos of the store that had been swept clean, no flour on the floor. Krang waved the match out, walking to the corner of the room. Dropping gently to his knees, Krang ran careful fingers along the floor until he found a crack between two boards. Using his knife as a pry bar, Krang was able to lift the trapdoor. Lighting another match, Krang stared down into a fully stocked pantry.

A lantern stood on the top step. Krang lit the wick, descended into the pantry and pulled the trapdoor closed behind him. The smell alone made his mouth water. Cinnamon, ginger, and other spices overwhelmed him. A small ham hung from the ceiling. Krang used his knife to cut off a thick chunk and stuffed it in his mouth. It was almost too big a piece to chew and he worked at it mechanically. He barely tasted the first bite, but grinned uncontrollably. Sometimes life was just too good.

Krang ate his fill, cutting off great hunks from the smoked ham, and in between bites of the ham, he washed everything down with a dry white wine. Krang belched loudly, a self-satisfied congratulation on his find, and wondered happily what meager scraps of food Sarah had downed in the last several days.

Thinking about her made him angry. Who was she to forgive him? Krang could feel a rage rise within him every time he thought of her. How could she even think that what he had done *could* be forgiven? His acts were unforgivable. It was like Sarah was somehow demeaning him, trying to erase the enormity of what he had done. Krang knew he had crossed every boundary imaginable, and no gesture by Sarah could change that.

Krang explored his new domain. The pantry appeared undamaged. The trap door could be rigged to not open. There was enough food to last the better part of a year if he were careful, or perhaps a month or two if he continued to gorge. Sitting on the steps, surveying his bounty, Krang grinned. This was the perfect base of operations: well stocked and easily defended. Now he could take as long as he wanted to figure out what his next steps would be. He went back upstairs to explore what was left of the store itself.

The store front had been heavily damaged in the bombing. Flour, rice and other goods, everything that had been stored on a shelf, had been dumped on the floor. Krang saw where the kerosene smell came from: a lantern had been knocked to the floor and had leaked kerosene. Nothing up here was salvageable. The store was a disaster.

Except for the area of the room by the trap door. Someone had swept up the flour, rice and other crap in a ten foot radius around the trap door. A pail sat in the corner. Someone's toilet. So Krang had a competitor. Where was he? If the authorities that were running the refugee camp outside of town were in charge of the city as well, then night might be the only safe time to scout out the city.

Morning would be arriving soon, within the next hour. Krang needed to prepare a special homecoming.

He knew the direct approach would be the best: surprise him and kill him. Krang wasn't sure how the man was getting in and out of the shop. He didn't think the man came in through the windows like Krang had. There must be another entrance. Krang found a spot near the front of the building that gave him good sight lines. He crouched uneasily in the darkened corner near the door, his back resting against the wall for support, his knife resting gently on his lap, drifting in and out of sleep.

The door creaked slightly as it pushed gently open. Krang was instantly awake. It must still have been early morning, for very little light entered the room as the door opened. Krang was puzzled how the intruder had gotten past the concrete slab. Someone stopped in the doorway, holding the door open, and surveyed the scene. Krang noticed his own footprints criss-crossing the room in the spilled flour.

"Damn." The voice was soft, barely more than a whisper.

The intruder stepped into the room, slowly closing the door. Krang tensed, but did not move. The intruder took one step, then another, towards the trap door. Krang tightened his grip on the knife. The intruder sighed and Krang sprang forward, driving his shoulder into the man's slight body, knocking him to the floor. Krang quickly wrapped an arm around the man's neck, pulling it taut, bringing the knife up for the death blow.

"Don't... don't hurt me," the intruder gasped in a soft voice.

Krang brought the knife blade up against the taut neck. "Why the fuck not?" he grunted.

A hand grasped his thigh, and then rubbed insistently against his crotch. "I'll fuck you," the intruder gasped.

Krang shifted his arm down, running his hand over the intruder's chest, discovering her breasts.

"Fuck, you're a girl," he said. "Not that it makes any difference." He pushed the blade against her throat.

She squeezed his cock through his pants. "Please," she begged him. "Don't hurt me."

Krang let her undo the buttons on his fly. She snaked her hand into his pants. He let the knife drop and released his arm from her head, reaching down to pull her pants down below her knees. She let go of his cock long enough to push down her underpants, then grabbed him again. He slid down to find the right angle. His cock was in her instantly. She groaned, her face pushing against the wood floor with each thrust. His climax was almost painful, more business than pleasure.

Chapter Four

Krang studied the girl as she lay on the floor beside him. In the hour that had elapsed since their coupling, the room had lightened enough for Krang to see clearly. He lay on his right side, a handful of her hair held tightly in his hand. She was slight, a little more than five foot tall, her breasts effectively hidden by the bulky shirt she wore. Her pants were still pushed down around her knees. Fading yellow and purple bruises were evident everywhere: on her face, her arms, her thighs and pelvis. A bruise ran over the protruding bone of her hip and disappeared into her dark pubic hair. The girl's brown hair had been unevenly hacked off, leaving it two or three inches long in places, with just a short stubble on the left side of her head. A bald patch was evident along her temple.

She stared at him, her head pulled away from the floor at an uncomfortable angle. Her face was thin, but not pinched. Her eyes seemed just a touch too big for her face, giving her an inquisitive, curious look. Her eyes were green, with a look of intelligence and wit that would have made Krang uncomfortable if he had met her at a party or a bar. He hadn't often dated women he thought were smarter than he was. She looked directly at him, searching his face for some sign of what he was going to do. She was not cowed by him, even after the violence of their meeting. She was indifferent to his menace without being arrogant or dismissive. It was as if she knew he could kill her, and that she could do nothing about it, so she wasn't wasting any time worrying about it.

She was pretty, in spite of the beating she had endured. Something sparkled about her, a sense of confidence perhaps, even in these conditions.

"Why are you here?" Krang asked.

"This is my store," she said softly.

Krang banged the girl's head on the floor. She winced but didn't cry out. "Don't lie to me. I know the old couple who own this store."

"The Rohleceks, they're dead. It's mine now."

Krang laughed softly. "How can you be so sure they're dead? Did you kill them?"

"They went to the camps. They neatly locked up like they were going on holiday, and climbed onto the bus to go to the camps. That means they're dead.

Captain Stojespahl took the key to this place from them when they were deported and now he's dead too. So after he died, I claimed this place as mine."

"It's mine now."

"You're just lucky I was out when you came. I have a gun. I'd have killed you if I had been here."

Krang laughed at her defiance. No one had spoken to him like that in years. She was very different from the camp. He liked her fearlessness, like a kitten going after a big dog.

Her eyes came across the tattoo scar on his forearm and widened slightly. "You were in the camps," she whispered.

Krang nodded absently. He couldn't decide if he should kill her or not. Could she be valuable to him in the future?

"Do you know my parents?"

Krang flinched as he understood what she was asking. "You're Corabian?"

She nodded.

"I'm sure I don't. I came to the camp late. I didn't get a chance to know anyone."

"But..."

"I don't know anyone," Krang said, tightening his grip on her hair. He didn't want to know who her parents were. He was through with the camp.

"Why didn't you go to the camp?" he asked. "What happened to you?" He nodded at her fading bruises.

She stiffened, and then shook her head slightly. Krang could feel her hair pulling against his hand. He banged her head on the floor again.

"I'll kill you," he whispered.

"Go ahead. You're going to anyhow."

Krang nodded. "Most likely I am. Give me a reason not to."

"I don't have any reason, other than I don't want to die, and I doubt that's enough."

Krang laughed. The girl had balls. "Tell me anyhow."

She sighed, looking like she was going to break down and cry, but began to tell her story. The words were hesitant at first, until she had run away, but she spoke with more confidence about her life on the streets. She ended with Stojespahl claiming her as his own.

The girl was very different from the Corabians at the camp, Krang thought. So few of them had resisted in any meaningful way. Even men like Abraham just ended up getting themselves killed. This girl had found a way to survive.

Krang nodded absently at the bruises on her body. "Your Captain did this to you?"

"No, he's dead. That's how I got my gun. I shot him in his sleep, the night before the city fell. I think he wanted me to do it. He showed me how to shoot the gun that night."

"So what happened to you?"

"The survivors from the camp did this. They came through the city the first day of the bombardment. They killed soldiers and their families." She pulled the top of her shirt down from her neck. An angry purple bruise encircled her neck. Krang imagined that Bitermyer had one just like it. Not many people survived being hung. This girl had balls.

"They wanted to kill me. They called me a collaborator and beat me."

"Why didn't you use the gun to stop them?"

She smiled in the half light. "Because they were right."

Krang shook his head vigorously. "You're not a collaborator, you're a survivor."

Katie shook her head, tears forming at the corner of her eye. "What's the difference?"

Krang sat in the rubble that had been the second floor of the grocery and studied the street before him. The city had seemed empty when he had walked through it just before dawn, but it didn't seem empty now. It was nearing midnight. The clouds were patchy tonight, alternately obscuring and revealing the City. Sometimes alone, sometimes in small groups, people made their way cautiously down the street, pulling on doors and checking windows. None of them tried to move the concrete slab from the storefront, although enough of them stopped and studied it for Krang to realize that many people knew what was inside. He would not be able to stay here long.

The Corabian army seemed content to leave what was left of the city to the few thousand survivors who combed through the wreckage every night. There was no food, no water, no electricity. Thousands more would die here soon if someone didn't step in with help.

He climbed back inside the store. The girl sat on the floor, her arms around her knees, watching him.

"Why haven't they left?" Krang asked her.

"More do every day, but in truth, where are they going to go? The country has been destroyed by war. Their war. No other land will welcome them."

"What happened to the Corabians from the camp?"

"I never saw anyone except the ones who beat me. I assume the army took them all home."

"Home? To the Homeland? This is their home."

"Are you going to stay here, after the camp?"

"And what about you? Why didn't you go with them?"

"I can't leave. The women have named me a collaborator. The Corabians will kill me if they see me."

"You can't stay here," Krang said. "Someone will find their way inside, just like I did. Even if they don't, the food won't last forever."

Katie shrugged. "My family is dead. I can't travel alone. I'm as good as dead now. I'm just postponing the inevitable."

Krang walked over to her, shaking his head. "You're a whore. You have all the tools you need to travel alone."

The apartment building was nothing more than a huge pile of rubble, unrecognizable as the place that he and Emma had called home. They had lived on the fourth floor of the six story building, living in a much larger apartment than Krang could have ever paid for, thanks to the largess of Emma's father. He had despised Krang, but hadn't wanted his daughter and grandchildren to live in some tenement. The building was compressed into a pile of brick and wood no more than twenty feet tall. Unlike Rohlecek's grocery, nothing was intact. It must have suffered a direct hit in one of the bombing raids. What had happened to Emma and the kids? Had all the families died, or did they have time to escape the bombardment?

Krang scaled the rubble, cautiously making his way up the shifting slope to the summit. He saw pots and pans, bits of furniture, even the broken head of a porcelain doll scattered in the rubble. At the top, Krang sat gently, his legs stretched before him, and watched the night sky. The moon had set some time ago, the stars spilling across the black sky like diamonds on cloth.

He felt devoid of emotion. No sense of loss, or anger, or relief. No sense of anything. Did my brats die here? Am I sitting on their tomb? And Emma? Was she with them when the bombs fell, or drinking her life away in some club, or sucking someone's cock in the men's room? Did she comfort them? Tell them stories about why their father wasn't there to save them? Or did she curse my name with her last breath? Krang shook his head.

"I don't care," he said softly, shocked. He had said it before, but had never understood that he really meant it. Krang wondered what was wrong with him. He thought about Sarah and Abraham. Suddenly, he could feel their son's leg in his right hand again, could feel the pistol in his left, could see the rage on Abraham's face. He saw the shot that tore Abraham's head apart, felt the weight of the boy's body as he crushed it against the loading dock.

Krang stiffened. I wouldn't have done what Abraham did, he thought. I would not have so eagerly thrown away my life to save my son. I don't think I ever felt anything for him, other than a slight sense of pride that I was man enough to have a boy rather than a girl. I never really cared for any of them. I didn't even care for

Emma. I liked fucking her, she was good in bed and liked to drink and was wild enough to blow me in front of room full of our friends, but I only married her because of the baby. Hell, I don't know if any of them were mine, and I never cared.

Krang thought of Abraham again. He was a brave man. And he loved that child more than he loved his life. The very thought of it left Krang feeling puzzled. And then he thought of Sarah.

Why did that bitch forgive me? Why not Willi? Willi never understood the camp. He was sick every time something happened. Literally. The boy would vomit whenever something happened in front of him. He could never have hurt any of them. Or why not forgive Gerri? I may have said I took the job to provide for Emma, but Gerri really was there to feed his family. Why not forgive him? No matter why I went out there that first day, I stayed because I liked it. Because I was good at it. I belonged there.

Krang looked up into the night sky. The blackness seemed to go on forever, limitless. He felt a sense of vertigo, like he might fall up into the sky and be swallowed up forever. It reminded him of the feeling he had had in church, as a small child, sitting next to his Mother for hours as she knelt and prayed, staring up into the eyes of the Christ on the cross. He had been afraid of Jesus. Afraid of what Jesus meant. Even as a small child, Krang had known he would never sacrifice himself for another. How could God be so cruel to his only son?

"God, have you blessed me? Have you anointed me as your child, instead of those more deserving? Or am I free because I rejected you so completely?"

Krang sat on the rubble, his chest heaving. He raised his hand in an obscene gesture to the sky. Fuck you, God. I will find Sarah Jezek and teach her the lesson that she so deeply needs to learn, that she has no power to forgive in this world. She confused her sense of powerlessness before me with pity. In order to forgive me, she would have had to have the power to punish me. What ego she must have had, to think that she had that power. I am so far outside the limits of God that I am unpunishable. And unforgivable. No one has the right to offer me absolution. I am a creature of hell as completely as the devil himself, and I will exact the same pain and suffering from those around me as if I were still in the camp. I'm going to hunt you down Sarah. I'll give you a chance to regret your act, and then I'm going to kill you.

Krang wiped his face furiously, feeling his rage slip away, once again able to think. It was time to plan his departure for the Homeland.

The peddler's cart was just the kind of thing for which Krang had been looking. The cart was wooden, about two feet wide and three feet long, with a canvas shade that sheltered the top. There was storage on the bottom, it had been

64

made out of an old cabinet, and it had a fold up table leaf that doubled the size of the work surface. Two bicycle wheels were set at one end, opposite the handles the peddler had used to push it. It lay on its side, one wheel bent slightly out of shape. A stone sharpening wheel had fallen from its apparatus, but appeared to be unchipped. Krang righted the cart, lifted the sharpening stone back into place, and tried pushing it. He could move it, but the bent wheel was going to need to be repaired. He opened the doors on the cabinet and saw most of the tools were missing. He had a hammer, a pair of pliers and two small screwdrivers. Krang liked the idea of masquerading as a peddler. The cart would disarm people and give him a reason for being.

Krang hid the cart in a burned out building around the corner from the store front. He approached the grocery cautiously, looking for any sign that someone had found it during his time away. The sky was beginning to lighten when he climbed the rubble to the roof. Krang slipped his head over the side of the building and looked inside and listened. Nothing. He wriggled inside.

As soon as he left the big hearth, the girl stepped out into the faint light.

"Why the fuck are you still here?" Krang demanded.

She smiled hesitantly, then pointed a pistol at him. "I told you I had a gun," she said softly.

Krang watched her, wondering why he hadn't taken the gun from her earlier. That was the problem when you fucked someone, he thought. It made you careless. The girl's hand shook gently, the gun barrel wavering.

Krang gambled and took a step toward her. "Then use it."

Her eyes widened in surprise.

He stared at her, his eyes locked on hers, until she couldn't stand the intensity of his look and glanced away. Krang moved quickly. He caught her with an open-handed blow to the cheek, knocking her to the ground. He stepped over her and pulled the gun from her hand. Krang then bent down until his face was just a foot over hers and pressed the gun against her forehead.

"Don't ever forget that I can kill you whenever I want," he hissed, and then straightened. Her cheek was blotchy red from his slap, and the gun had left a reddish pressure mark on her forehead. She stared up at him angrily, looking more defiant without the gun than she had with it.

"Kill me," she whispered. "Do it now and get it over with."

Krang reached down and grabbed a handful of her hair. "You'll die when it's convenient for me, not before." He pushed her away. "Get down in the cellar, we need to pack."

Katie carried several sausages up the pantry steps into the storeroom. Her cheek hurt where she'd been hit. His blow had landed on top of a bruise from the other night. She didn't want to cry and kept blinking away the tears. It wasn't the pain that was making her cry, it was him. At least she hadn't begged him not to hurt her like the other day when he broke in. She hated how scared she had sounded when she begged him not to hurt her. Her voice had trembled like a little girl's. She'd rather be dead than afraid. She glanced at him when she set the food on the floor. He was fixing a wheel for some cart he had found when he was out.

She couldn't remember seeing him around the city before the war. He was tall and slender, but without the gauntness of the other prisoners she had seen. He was much stronger than they had been. Katie shook her head. That wasn't right. The prisoners who'd beaten her had been strong. He was more powerful. He wore his power like a uniform, or maybe like a lion, ready to spring into action. He was comfortable in the midst of all this destruction.

Katie had hoped that he would just disappear, but had thought she could kill him if he returned. She hated that she hadn't been able to shoot him. She had felt a moment of confusion as she stood there with the gun. It was still wrong to kill, even if it meant he might kill her. She didn't understand how that thought had suddenly been in her mind. She thought she had left all of those beliefs on the streets, but suddenly everything she had been taught as a child was alive in her again. And she had just been too tired to pull the trigger. She didn't want the noise. She didn't want to see him dead like Stojespahl. She just wanted to be safe. She went back down into the pantry for more supplies.

Krang watched the girl as she brought food up from the pantry. Who was she? He realized that he didn't even know her name, not that it mattered. Maybe he would call her Sarah. He wasn't surprised that she hadn't been able to kill him. As easy as killing someone was, it was still harder than most people thought. He didn't mean crimes of passion. Those happened without thought. But to stand in front of someone, to look into their eyes and see the fear, to know that they have a family, and then raise that gun to their head and shoot them, that wasn't easy. Not everyone could be a Krang. The girl didn't have that kind of strength, but she was clearly strong. He just couldn't figure out what her power was. Not yet.

She must have been very pretty before the beating. He could see how she managed to live through the war. Men would be more than willing to pay for her. Her beauty and her youth would have made her rich if there had been no war. Maybe she would be useful along the way. Krang could be the world's first peddler/pimp. The thought made him grin. After nearly an hour, Krang broke the silence.

"If you couldn't kill me, how did you manage to kill your pimp?"

She set down the tins she had brought from the basement and turned to face Krang.

"Everyone sleeps, you know. It's easy to kill a man when he's asleep."

Krang laughed at her implied threat.

The girl was silent for a minute. "I didn't really kill him, you know. I wanted to, but I couldn't do it. I don't know if I wanted them, you know... the Corabians who were going through the building, to kill him for me, or if I was just too scared to pull the trigger. I mean I was right on top of him, sitting on his chest."

She stepped over to Krang and lifted her hand to the soft spot under his jaw. He felt her fingers trembling as they touched his neck. "I held the gun right here and stared into his eyes. And then they broke into the apartment and he reached up and pulled the trigger. I had his blood and brains all over me...." She paused again.

"So he was a coward and left you at their mercy?"

"Maybe," Katie shrugged. "I think he was trying to save me, to make it look like I killed him, but it didn't work. The women still tried to hang me. I would have died if the men hadn't wanted to fuck."

Krang nodded. He bet they wanted to fuck her. He could feel her energy next to him, radiating sex. His cock twitched. He pushed her back a step and pointed to a pair of scissors in the pile of supplies she had made. "Cut your hair," he said, "I can't have you looking like that. By the way, what's your name?"

"Why?"

Krang laughed. "I have to call you something, and I'm not partial to whore."

She shook her head. "Why are you doing this? Why do you want to take me with you?"

Krang shrugged. "I'm not really sure. Part of me thinks I'll regret it immediately, but part of me thinks I may need you. I'm looking for someone, and you can help me find her. And if you do, I'll be your witness that you weren't a collaborator." He pointed to his partial tattoo. "This is like gold, you know."

"And what I told you..."

"That you're a survivor? I admire that, believe it or not. I don't care if you fuck for money or food or protection or fun. That seems like a fine idea to me, if that's what it takes to get what you need."

She nodded. "So now you're my pimp?"

Krang grasped her chin in his hand. He squeezed, but not too hard. He needed the bruises to heal. "You'll do whatever I tell you to do, because that's what it will take to survive. I'm not in this for money, I'm in it for myself. Understand this: if you prove to be more trouble than you're worth, I'll take you out and put a bullet in your brain. I won't lose any sleep over it, either. But I think I need you, just the way you need me. So for now, we're cousins, or brother and sister, hell, we could almost be father and daughter. I don't care. I'll tell what ever story seems to be the best for the situation." He let her go.

She looked at him intently. "I don't think I can trust you," she whispered.

"You can't," Krang replied.

"Katrina. My name is Katrina"

Krang smiled. "Katrina. Very traditional. I'll call you Katie."

Katie shrugged. "That's what they all call me."

Krang reached out and grabbed her by the hair, pulling her head back tightly. He leaned in and whispered in her ear. "Katie, don't ever point that gun at me again. I won't just knock you down next time, I'll kill you. And I won't waste a bullet on you. I'll beat you to death. I'll break your ribs, and your cheeks and jaw, and your arms and legs, and you'll take hours, or even days to die."

Katie shuddered. Krang saw the look of anger that crossed her face and understood that she hated feeling weak. That would be useful. She reached up and pushed him away. Krang let go of her hair and returned to his wheel.

Krang laughed the next time she came up from the cellar. "You can call me Abraham," he said with a grin.

Chapter Five

They left the city sometime after midnight, when the scavengers had finally settled down, but the night was still dark enough to hide their passage from prying eyes. The sky was cloudy, hiding the moon and the blackness of night settled around them like a comfortable blanket. Krang worried the peddler's cart would be a magnet for thieves. An assault within the narrow, winding maze of the city, even just one or two attackers, could be deadly. Rather than risk being overwhelmed by an ambush, Krang gave Katie back her pistol. He hoped her survival instincts would kick in if they were attacked. Even if the girl just pulled the trigger without aiming, the shots could help drive away an attack. His knife was sheathed at his waist.

Krang knew the cart, stuffed with food from the store's hidden pantry, could be a death sentence for them. People were so desperate to find food that they would kill for the food that was in the cart.

The journey out of the city proved to be uneventful. The cart's repaired wheel rolled smoothly, and soon they were outside the towering piles of rubble. Walking through the deserted city gates was like breaking free of a deep pool of water. Krang could breathe again. The claustrophobia of not being able to see more than a few feet in any one direction was gone. They headed east, towards the mountains and the camp. The clouds overhead were breaking up, allowing a gentle light to guide them. A few hundred yards outside the city, Krang wheeled the cart off the road and onto an old cow path that looped around the city. The path was worn bare and hard by decades of animal traffic being driven from surrounding farms to the city market. Within minutes the path entered an old woods and the city was lost from sight.

"Look for a good place that we can wait out the rest of the night," Krang whispered to the girl. She nodded absently, her eyes searching the woods along the path. He took the gun from her now that they were outside the city and slipped it into his waistband.

"Don't bother running," he said softly. "I'll kill you before you get three steps away."

Katie turned and looked at him, her eyes alive, but not scared. "Why would I run? I'm dead if I stay in the city, so I might as well go where you take me. I remember hearing stories of bandits in these woods, that's all."

Krang nodded. He had carried contraband through these woods as a young man. "Yeah, there were bandits out here when I was a kid. Well, they were smugglers more than bandits. Most of them were rounded up during the war. I don't think we need to worry about them now, but it is good to be vigilant."

Katie's eyes widened, but she said nothing.

"What?"

"You grew up around here?"

Fuck. Krang had almost revealed himself. If she ever guessed that he was *the Guard*, she held his life in her hands. How far would she go to save herself? He had to be more careful.

"I grew up in Mountain City," he said and nodded for her to go on ahead of him. "My father knew several men who live out here. They made liquor, mostly. He was too cheap to go to a bar to drink."

He pushed the cart forward, trying to read her expression from the corner of his eye. He wasn't sure if she believed him.

After an hour, he stopped near a stand of small trees and shrubs. The sky was already lightening in subtle ways that suggested dawn was near.

"We'll stay here until morning," he said. "Be ready to leave in two hours."

Katie shrugged. "I thought you were afraid of traveling by day?"

"I didn't want to risk losing the cart to soldiers or end up getting killed by some hungry kid with a gun. Most of the Citizens who are leaving the city don't trust the Corabian army enough to join the refugee camp, so they're walking south. As much as I hate the idea, we need to join the refugees making their way to the south. We can lose ourselves among them, and try to catch up the Corabians from the camp."

"What if someone recognizes you?"

Krang didn't say anything, just looked at the girl. He wasn't really afraid any old acquaintances would recognize him, but he didn't know if the Corabians had offered a reward for the capture of *the Guard*. If they had, and someone recognized him, it wouldn't be long before the authorities arrested him. "If they recognize me, they'll kill me," he said softly. "And if they kill me, they kill you."

Katie nodded slowly, looking more bored than afraid. Krang manhandled the cart off the path and into the woods.

"Stay here," he told the girl. "I want to make sure we're really alone here."

Katie sat with her back against a tree and watched him leave. He moved with a grace that belied his violence. It wasn't just athletic. She was reminded again of the big cats in the zoo that paced back and forth in their cages. They were so graceful, but you could never ignore the threat of violence that underlay their every move.

The camp survivors hadn't been graceful in any way, just walking rage. He wasn't like that. The rage was there, she was sure of it, but it was pushed down inside of him, deep enough to fool a passerby, but never so far down that you weren't in danger. She thought he was handsome in a very physical way, with broad shoulders, a narrow waist and a tautness that suggested power, but his face was so guarded that it ruined the effect. Katie didn't imagine anyone walking past him on the street would dare stop to ask for directions. He was too guarded and edgy. She couldn't decide if it was a good thing or a bad thing that he had found her. She would have died in the City eventually, she was sure of that. But were the odds any greater she would survive with him? Or was it even more likely that he would kill her himself?

After they had finished packing their supplies, she had tried to make up for pulling the gun on him. He had been surprised when she had knelt in front of him, pulled her shirt over her head and then unbuttoned his trousers. And in spite of how hard his cock had been, he had refused her.

"I'll take what I want, not what you give me," he had said, and pushed her away.

She couldn't remember a time in the last three years when her body hadn't been the key to getting what she needed. Katie leaned back against the tree and wished she knew what to do.

Krang walked one hundred paces into the woods and then circled woods around the clearing, checking for any signs that someone might be in the area. When he was satisfied they were alone, after almost a half hour of looking, he headed back toward the clearing. He stopped ten meters away. The girl was still resting against the tree, watchful. He had expected to either find her asleep or gone, and hadn't been sure which would be better.

Katie had cut her hair evenly, no more than half an inch long. She wore the same baggy clothes she had on when he found her. If she didn't talk, she might fool anyone not paying close attention into believing she was a boy. If you looked too closely, her woman's body would give her away. With her short hair, she could almost pass for a camp survivor, except that she was lacking the requisite tattoo, and Krang was not about to show her the truth behind his own tattoo. Katie looked too healthy, though. He remembered Sarah when she came to him, his last night in the camp: her hunger-pinched face, waxen and unhealthy, the deep bags under her eyes, the overwhelming fatigue in every step that she took.

Katie had suffered, but not in the same way. She didn't have the look of death about her, which would be a problem if they ran into other Corabians right away. He had been immersed in the camp for so long that the stench of death hung on him like it hung over the pit. People would look at Krang and see the camp on him. He oozed it. But Katie? She still had her vitality. Somehow she had lived on the streets for three years and not given up. She hadn't let the streets defeat her.

How do you explain her vitality to others? It wouldn't be a problem now, when they were surrounded by Montrovian Citizens who hadn't known defeat until a few weeks ago, but once they went far enough south, where the war had ground on for years, what then? She hadn't been chewed up and spit out by life, even though life on the streets should have done just that. Was it just the resiliency of youth? Maybe his story would be that she had collaborated, but for him. That she had remained on the outside, smuggling him food and medicine. She could have been selling herself to pay for everything. Even selling herself to the guards to protect him.

Then again, that could be a danger. Corabians might resent that he had benefitted from her sacrifice. Maybe that story would serve in a pinch, but he needed something better than that for day-to-day encounters. And the story needed to be simple. Complicated lies always unraveled. A simple story would see them welcomed by their brothers and sisters. If they lived long enough to catch up with the Corabians. He knew the odds were still against them.

He entered the clearing and nodded to her, acknowledging her vigilance. She smiled, hesitantly, and then frowned when she realized what she had done. She didn't say a word until he had settled down a few feet away.

"Where are we going?" Katie asked.

Krang shrugged. "We're following the Corabians. We're going wherever the camp survivors are going."

"To the Homeland? We're going to the Homeland?"

Krang nodded uncertainly. He had no idea what the hell the Homeland was. He had heard the term frequently in the camp, but had never bothered to ask any of the prisoners what the fuck they were chattering on about. Who the fuck cared? None of them were going. Krang shook his head, wishing he had been a little more thoughtful back then. Was it Corabia? Or some spot in Corabia? He didn't think Corabia wanted all the Corabians back. They had made no effort before the war to claim them, that was for sure. The Montrovian government had offered a swap, to bring all the Citizens living in Corabia home for all the Corabians living in Montrovia. It had been done in this region repeatedly, especially after the Ottoman wars that followed World War I. Greece and Turkey had exchanged what seemed like half of their populations.

Katie cleared her throat nervously. "I'll fuck you all you want. Do anything you want, but I won't fuck for you. I'd rather be dead than belong to another Stojespahl. If that's all you want from me, just kill me."

Krang stared at her, not knowing whether to laugh or knock some sense into her. The girl didn't mince words. He still didn't know if he really needed her, but he had a growing suspicion that he did. Her comments about the Homeland were a perfect example. Krang reached out with is right hand, grasping her firmly by the ear. Katie jerked back, bumping her head against the tree.

"Finally you're scared of me," Krang said, smiling

She shook her head, but her tears gave her away.

"It's okay to be scared of me. You should be."

"I've never been scared of anyone."

Krang nodded. "I don't think you have, before now." He let go of her ear, ran his hand down her cheek and neck to her breast. "I'll tell you who and when to fuck until we get to the Homeland. You won't defy me or argue, because you know I will kill you. I've no interest in whoring you for money or fucking you for fun. We can help each other, or we can get each other killed. Do you want to live or die?"

Katie was quiet for a long time. When she spoke, her words were so quiet he barely could hear them. "Live. I want to live."

Krang leaned in and kissed her chastely on the forehead. "Then you'll live." He studied her, trying to figure how much he could risk telling her. He knew that when they joined the refugees fleeing to the south, they would be Citizens. He didn't think he could risk pretending to be Corabian now. He had no idea how cowed the Citizens were, so he needed to be a Citizen, and he needed Katie to believe he was. He didn't know if she could really keep a secret, so he needed her to believe he had a secret to keep, but one that would help if they were captured and she gave it away. And it had to be simple enough not to get him tripped up.

"Katie, where are the camp survivors going?"

The girl looked puzzled. "Everyone knows they're going to the Homeland."

Krang nodded. "Where the fuck is it?"

Katie looked away, signaling her fear. "How can you not know?" she whispered.

"I don't know because no one ever told me."

Katie turned back to him. "How do you grow up knowing nothing about the Homeland?"

Krang laughed nervously. "Look, I haven't been honest with you. I need you with me on this trip because I know absolutely nothing about the faith. Not one single thing. You have to teach me."

"Why didn't your parents didn't teach you?"

"My parents were Citizens. They only taught me to hate Corabians."

Katie stiffened.

Krang shook his head. "I don't share their ideas. I was sent to the camps because I married a Corabian girl. I had hoped it would save her from the camps. I

73

was wrong."

"Why would you risk such a thing? During the war?"

"I don't know," Krang shrugged. "We do things for love. It's probably wrong to even call it love. I was captivated by her. Sarah was a beautiful woman, I used to see her every day, and I knew that she was beyond my reach. She was married, you see, and had a baby. A wonderful little boy. And then one day they were gone. They were stopped by soldiers in the street to be sent to the deportation center. Babies weren't allowed at the camp, so the soldiers took her baby from her and killed it. Her husband was very brave. He attacked the soldier who killed their baby and was shot dead..."

Katie laughed bitterly. "That's not brave, that's stupid."

Krang studied her face. "You're right. No one else will ever tell you this, but what you did was much braver. You survived."

Katie shook her head. "I wasn't brave, or principled. I was only alive, and that was all that mattered to me. And I'm no longer sure that living was worth it. So how did she married you?"

"They left her in the street with the bodies of her husband and son. Just walked away. Her family came and gathered them up and she was gone. I thought she had still gone to the camp. About a month or so later, I saw her in the market. She was still beautiful, but so haunted.

"I convinced her that she could save herself through marriage. I told her that by staying alive, she would keep the memory of her husband and son alive. I loved her, but there was a hole in her soul. She was never really with me, some distance always separated us. When her parents were deported, a few months later, she went down to the depot and boarded the train with them. I went to the authorities and demanded her release. The war was stalemated by then, and I thought they would want to do the right thing. Instead, I was detained, and after several months, I was sent to the camp.

"I arrived only a few days before the Corabian army. I was able to escape after processing and hid in the woods. When the bombing stopped, I went back for Sarah, but the camp was deserted."

"Is she dead?"

Krang shook his head. "No. I saw her just before the camp was liberated. She kissed me and told me she forgave me. I can't forgive myself for letting them take her."

"Do you think she loves you?"

Krang shook his head. "No, I don't think so. I think she is still lost in the memory of her husband."

"Do you love her?"

"I don't know..."

74

"So you risked your life to have sex with her? To have something unattainable?"

Krang shrugged. "Maybe. By the way, Abraham was her dead husband's name. My real name is Walter. Does it sound Corabian enough?"

"There are no Corabian sounding names. Everyone knows that. We come from the same ancestors. The only thing we differ on is the manner in which we practice our faith. We're Christians, just like you. You've lived along side Corabians all your life, didn't you learn anything?"

"I was taught that Corabians came here after the hard work of settling this land was done and took away jobs from the Citizens. You're good craftsmen. You're clannish. You don't have the same morals we have. You claim to be Christian, yet don't believe in the supremacy of the church, or the divinity of Jesus."

"That's the same ignorance that started this war. I thought you people got over those kinds of beliefs by the time you were in grade school." Katie said. She spat on the ground. "We believe Jesus was the son of God, we just believe that we are all children of God."

Krang laughed. "Until the war came, I never gave a single thought about Corabians. I only cared if a girl was pretty, and if she would hook up with me in one of the clubs, not which church she prayed in. It wasn't like she was going to bump into me in any church, unless it was one that sold beer on Sundays. I worked alongside any man, when I was willing to work. I didn't learn anything about Corabians because I didn't care about the differences between us. You drink the same, you dance the same, and you fuck the same. That was all that was important."

Katie smiled, and nodded. "If everyone believed that, there would not have been a war."

"Wrong," Krang said. "Ridding our land of Corabians may have been the excuse for war, but oil was the reason. Money, power, or resources have always been the reasons we went to war."

Katie didn't respond.

"Now, for your story: You hid out during the war in the city, working as a maid for a wealthy old woman who didn't understand what was going on. She just wanted someone to take care of her. The bombardment started while you were out shopping, and you are worried that no one is caring for that old lady. Can you remember that?"

Katie nodded. "Where did we live?"

"In the fifth district, down by the river. You know the old brownstone row houses, across from the park? Maybe a mile from the market?"

Krang saw a look of relief on her face as he made up her story and knew that

75

she was still his.

"This is why I need you. I know none of the customs, traditions or laws of your people. I have no real knowledge of the Homeland. You will be my guide on this journey, and if you do your job well, I will free you. If you fail me, I will abandon you, or kill you. Never forget that if I am revealed, then you will be revealed as well. If nothing else, I have the tattoo. That alone may save my life. You do not."

Katie nodded. "I understand that I need you as much as you need me. I will teach you what I can, but you will have missed a lifetime of learning. The intricacies of our customs will eventually reveal you."

"Let's hope that it doesn't happen until after I release you."

"Wake me when we leave," Katie said. She rolled herself in her blanket and lay down. Within minutes she was asleep.

Krang watched her sleep. He had been honest about why she was valuable to him without revealing himself. Without someone to act as his guide, he could walk across the Homeland and never see it at all. It was more an ideal than a place, that he knew already. He didn't know if it just meant Corabia, or if it was a special place in Corabia, or if it was so mythical that the survivors could stop any where they liked and claimed to have made it.

And he didn't know if she really felt that she needed him enough to not betray him. She was a survivor, and Krang believed that as long as she saw a way to survive she wouldn't challenge him. Krang admired her. False modesty didn't serve anyone. If getting on your knees and sucking a cock meant you would live for another day, then it was the right thing to do. Katie had lived longer than many of those who used her. Krang laughed silently at the thought that she would probably outlive him as well.

Krang looked at her face. Asleep, the girl didn't seem wary, as if all that she experienced just washed away from her. That must be a blessing of the young, Krang thought. He doubted that sleep relaxed him at all. He was always wound up, like a child's top that had been pumped and was ready to be released. Drinking or fucking or even killing had only been a temporary release; as soon as he was done he could feel the tension building inside him again.

Katie was starting to dream, her eyes twitching under their lids. Her breaths, deep and slow moments before, came more quickly together, as if she were panicked.

How anyone could see the girl as a collaborator? How had she betrayed her people? If anyone had been betrayed, it was Katie. Looking at her sleeping, he wondered how her parents could have failed to protect her. Why didn't they run? Why didn't the whole damn bunch of Corabians start running ten years ago, before the war had even started? There were so many signs of the impending blow-up. The legislature took away every right and legal safe hold for the Corabian people and still they stayed. In the steelworks, in the bars, in the market, they all acted as if nothing was going on. And when their friends and neighbors began to turn away from them, to shop in other stores, to not speak with them on the streets, they still did nothing.

They had paid a great price for not acting when they could have.

Katie groaned lightly in her sleep. Krang imagined that she would be beautiful when her hair grew out and the bruises faded. He thought of Emma, whose only survival skill had been to fuck and to get pregnant. Maybe she wasn't so different from this girl. Maybe Emma was stronger than I realized. If she had been sleeping with someone else, if the baby wasn't his, maybe she had simply been trying to survive.

Emma must have realized she had lost me, Krang thought. Just as I knew that I was lost to her. I knew that I could never wash enough of the camp from me to ever really come home. And I didn't want to, he realized. I wanted the war to last forever, so I could remain at the camp forever. What will I do now? Can I truly play the part of a wandering fix-it man? I'm like an addict, he thought. I crave that feeling of power that I had in the camp. The power of life and death. It was like being a God. Nothing can ever replace that. I'll never feel that rush again. Never. I'm lost without it. I should just kill myself now. There is no point to my life without the camp. No point at all.

Why did Sarah ever free me? Krang laughed bitterly. That bitch. She knew being free would be worse for me than being dead...

"Wha...?" Katie jerked awaked.

"Shhh, go back to sleep, Katie." Krang crawled over to her, and laid her head in his lap, gently stroking her brow. Her breathing became deeper as she drifted away. Krang smiled. He still had power over the girl. There would be others along the way. And eventually he would find Sarah. That would be his redemption, his moment of glory, when he stood face to face with her and watched the pride crumble from her face as she realized what she had loosed upon the world.

You almost got me, Sarah. I almost gave in to your tricks, Krang thought. You wanted me to feel the despair that was your life, and to be so reckless in it as to throw away my life. Never. I will never rest until I track you down and teach you the lesson you thought to teach me. I will never forget you, or Abraham, or Capek. If I live to be one hundred, I will hold you in my memory. And when I find you, I will make you pay.

Krang heard the birds begin their morning songs, and watched the sky slowly lighten from black to pink. A new day was dawning.

Chapter Six

A stream of refugees flowed in fitful spurts under the morning's pale sun, walking in ragged columns along the broken highway. Krang, sitting with Katie on a small hill next to the road, watched the bedraggled groups shuffle slowly forward. Their peddler's wagon was pulled up onto the hill next to them.

They had been watching for the better part of an hour, ever since the path they had been following all morning had come out upon the highway. Krang was surprised by how many of the men were wearing suits, and the women nice dresses, as if they were on their way to a church picnic rather than fleeing for their lives. Krang and Katie were dressed down in comparison.

Most of the refugees carried a suitcase or a carpetbag. A few pushed overloaded bicycles. They all looked around nervously. Krang saw a silver candlestick poking from a sack a man was carrying. The man was large, his overcoat open to the morning, his face as red as a robin's breast. What good would a candlestick do him? Who along this road would barter for something heavy to carry? He should have brought food, as much of it as he could carry. Krang wondered if the man would even survived the day's walk. He looked on the verge of having a heart attack.

Krang spat on the ground. Their greed would kill them. How many would die, even tonight, because a fellow traveler coveted their silver or gold? How many would begin to starve to death as early as tomorrow, or the next day, when the loaf of bread and sack of turnips they had brought were gone?

The refugees that passed below them walked in groups that were larger than a single family. They did not speak to each other, but walked with their heads up, looking from side to side, following the footsteps of the person walking before them. It was only when the groups slowed, as they neared Krang, that any of them looked up to see the cart on the hill. The look that flashed across the men's faces when they saw the cart amused Krang. It was as if the men suddenly realized they hadn't brought enough and they couldn't contain their hatred of the fact Krang had, and their lust for it.

What was common to each pack of refugees that marched past? Were they neighbors, Krang wondered, or perhaps several generations of the same family? Or just people who had been living in the same tent in the refugee camp? Had the

Corabian army expelled them from the camp or city, in essence issuing their death warrants?

"I didn't know there were so many," he said softly. He had expected the road to be deserted this early in the morning. Although when he thought about it, it made sense that the exodus would be heavy in the morning, so close to the city. You would want a whole day to walk. Tomorrow would be different, a day's walk from here. Tomorrow some people would have already given up.

They did not move until a natural break occurred in the stream of refugees, a gap of more than a quarter mile between groups. Krang manhandled the wagon down the hillside and onto the road. The wagon was designed to be pushed, not pulled, with two wheels in front and two wooden rear legs near the handles. It was difficult to maneuver among the potholes and debris that dotted the muddy road. In some places the road was destroyed; huge water-filled craters forced them to push the cart through the muddy berm to get around. Trucks and tanks that had been damaged during the assault on the city had been pushed off the road and lay in the ditches on either side. Some still had the decaying bodies of soldiers rotting in the wreckage.

Katie looked at all the destruction in a kind of awe. She had not seen the cost of this war to the Corabian army, only the thousands of dead Citizens in the city. The fighting here had been fierce. She looked into the woods that bordered each side of the road and wondered how many hundreds or thousands of dead, from both sides, lay unburied under the budding trees. Maybe the fighting here explained the ferocity of the attack on the city. Had the Montrovian army killed so many Corabians that obliterating the city seemed justified? Or was it simply that once the blood lust of war came over an army it didn't matter what they killed, as long as they kept on killing? It was too much to contemplate.

Katie walked silently for quite a while before clearing her throat. "You want me to teach you how to become one of our people?'

Krang nodded, grunting his assent.

Katie shook her head. "I don't think that I can do that. You need a teacher, a confirmation..."

"Bullshit."

"I'm serious. This is a lifetime avocation that you are suggesting. There are books to read, classes to be taken, traditions to be understood..."

Krang shook his head. "I'm not trying to fool anyone. I was born a Citizen, I won't lie about that. I converted because of a woman. I don't need to know a lifetime's worth of philosophical arguments, I need to know enough not to be killed immediately when we reach the Homeland."

"You think that we would kill you?"

Krang nodded. "Don't be naive, Katie. My greatest concern right now is that everyone has a reason to kill us. The Citizens may have lost the war, but that doesn't mean that they've forgotten why they went to war. If they discover our truth, we're in danger. And the Corabians? I expect a lot of revenge killing is going on right now. That doesn't even count the armies, which may or may not be done fighting each other, nor your run of the mill asshole thief who kills you for your stuff. This wagon full of food is more valuable than gold right now."

"You're saying that to scare me."

"No, I'm not. I'm preparing you to use that pistol when necessary. I can't afford to have you freeze up, like you did with me. The next man you kill won't beg you for it like your Captain did, and this time you'll need to pull the trigger." He was silent for a moment.

"And I need to know what I would have been taught, if I had married into the faith in normal times."

Katie sighed. "That's the hard part. I'm not sure what you need to know. I was only fourteen the last time I went to a service. I haven't taken most of the classes, or read most of the books. I don't even think that anyone would care what you know, if this war hadn't occurred. I only know what a kid would know."

"That's perfect," Krang said. "I want to know what a kid would know. Someone who hasn't had any doubts about their faith."

"If you think I could live through this war without doubting my faith, you're not the man you seem to be."

Krang sighed. "Do you believe?" he asked.

Katie stared at him for a long time before she looked away and shrugged. "I don't know. I think I do. There were so many moments in the City when I had no Faith, but somehow it keeps coming back. Just a small thought in my head, that I need to open myself to God. I can't always pray. Certainly not prayers of gratitude, although I know I should be grateful for my life. And I don't ask for anything, because I'm afraid I don't have the faith to make it happen. But I still have this kernel of hope. Do you?"

Krang shook his head vigorously. "No. I have no faith in God. If God existed I would not be alive today, and many other people would be. People who were better than me. But I do exist, and they don't, because I was stronger, more powerful. There is no God, but there is me."

Katie searched his face until Krang looked away. She wanted to see past his exterior to discern the truth of his soul, but saw nothing.

"You're so serious," Katie said. "And wrong, by our teachings. God exists through you, according to my father. I was taught God exists as you."

"So I am God?" Krang laughed bitterly. "Isn't that saying exactly the same as what I just said? If all men are gods, and I exist today because I am more powerful than they are, then that is the same as saying there is no real God."

"No." Katie shook her head, excited by the discussion. She had not talked with anyone about the teachings since the morning she ran away from home. Her words sounded like old friends. Krang pushed the cart around a pothole in the road as she continued talking.

"We are taught that you are God, individualized."

Krang shook his head.

"Let me explain it another way. If you take a cup and fill it with water from the ocean, you have captured the essence of the ocean. It's not the whole ocean, yet it is a complete part of the ocean. It is the essence of the ocean." She mimicked handing him a cup full of water.

"There are no sharks in the cup."

"But there is a shark holding the cup."

Krang laughed so hard for a moment he had to stop, setting the cart down and catching his breath. Katie was glad she had been able to make him laugh. He almost seemed normal while he was laughing. After a minute he grasped the cart's handles and began walking again.

"Funny girl, but my point is still valid. There are sharks in the ocean, but not in the cup."

Katie reached out and playfully slapped him. "Don't be facetious. It could be a thimble, a gallon, or a huge aquarium. Each contains the essence of the ocean, the basic components that support life, and yet is not identical with any other. One may have a shark in it, and another no more than plankton, yet each is a bit of the ocean. They are the ocean individualized."

"So I am not the big God, but I am a little God?"

"That was the first way I understood, but that's not really it. You are a child of God, created of the essence of God, inseparable from God. Jesus taught us that the very divinity that filled him is within each and every one of us. We are taught that we can see the divinity in each person on this earth."

"So you can look at me and see my divine essence?"

Katie studied his face intently. He was so guarded and secret.

"Well?"

"I'm still looking."

Krang burst into laughter. "I'll bet you are. You should have been a politician."

"You misunderstand me. I see no light of God burning within you. That is, at least in part, my own deficiency. But you hide your divinity deeply. I can see that it troubles you, so you put it so far down inside of yourself that you won't ever bump into it. Many people do that. But I will continue looking until I see it, and then I will magnify it, and celebrate it, until the whole world sees it."

"You really believe this?"

Katie nodded. "It is what we are taught. God is all good, and as we are of God, then we are also all good."

"What about evil people?"

"I can't really tell you about evil people. I wish that I had been taught more myself, because I struggle with what I have seen and done, during this war. I can't always reconcile the teachings with the world that I see around me, but we are taught that the world, while real in a physical way, is only a spiritual illusion."

"What the hell does that mean?"

"I have no idea," Katie said, wishing she knew more, or was more articulate about what she knew. She loved that he was treating her like she was his equal. "What I am trying to say is that all people have the essence of God within them, no matter how they chose to live. We are taught that nothing a man or woman does is ever terrible enough to remove them from God's grace. That forgiveness is always possible, but never necessary."

"And you believe that?"

"I don't know. Even as a child, I struggled to understand where God's laws and our laws intersected. My father was a great teacher, and renowned for his wisdom. He had students come from all over to learn from him. But he still had a temper and hated it when I defied him. So we all seem to struggle to live what we are taught. My father cursed me as I ran away that last morning. He swore he would never forgive me for defying him."

"But do you believe that God always forgives us?"

Katie stopped. She was crying, an ache in her chest so deep it was like a hole in her heart. What would she give to be forgiven?

"We're taught," she said quietly, trying to ignore her tears, "that God never judges, so there is no need for forgiveness." She paused for a long time, before quietly adding "I just wish I could believe it."

Krang turned away from her as she wiped the tears from her eyes. He was shocked by her sense of guilt, of her obvious desire to be forgiven. Forgiven by whom, he wondered, and for what? She had survived, for God's sake. If that wasn't divine in its own right, then God was a fucking idiot.

"I was taught that God always judges," Krang said. "I was told that nothing I could do was good enough to please that bastard in the sky, but that I had to keep trying. I was taught that the more miserable your life was, the more God loved you, unless you were rich, which was the best proof of all that God loved you. I thought it was bullshit."

Katie nodded, wiping her eyes with the backs of her hands. Krang thought she might have smiled at his comment. Krang grunted as he pushed the cart forward. For the first time that he could remember since he was a little boy, he wasn't angry that a woman was crying, and didn't believe that she was doing it just to manipulate him.

They were caught on the road when night fell. The road had become a levee, perhaps twenty or thirty feet higher than the surrounding country. Heavy forest, filled with brackish marsh water ran to the very bottom of the levee. Krang could see small campfires dotting the levee, where other travelers had stopped for the night. The levee was too steep to try to take the cart off the road. Krang considered just walking through the night, or at least until they found a place they could walk away from the road, but discarded the idea. The road was too torn up to walk at night, and filled with travelers who had no place to go. Continuing on would just attract attention, and the risk of being attacked by someone was just too great. And the girl was exhausted. She had done well today, he thought, never complaining, nor asking for him to stop and rest.

Krang cut them both a small piece of dried sausage from their supply in the bottom of the cart. They chewed slowly and shared a water skin.

"We'll stay here tonight," Krang told her. Katie's face immediately relaxed. "No fire. You can sleep under the cart and I'll stand watch."

"I can stand watch," Katie said defiantly. She covered a yawn with the back of her hand.

Krang laughed. "No you can't," he said. "You'd be asleep in minutes and we could both die. Don't worry, you'll stand plenty of watches before this trip is over. Tonight you can sleep."

Katie wrapped herself in the blanket and scooted under the cart. She was asleep even faster than Krang had predicted. He surveyed the road in either direction. No other refugees had made camp within a few hundred yards of where he had stopped, so that was good. The sky was cloudy, hiding the moon, and Krang was grateful for that as well. Although moonlight might help him see what was happening on the road and down at the bottom of the levee, it would show them off like a spotlight. Krang was being cautious, but he didn't really think they were in any danger tonight.

Katie woke an hour before dawn, as the sky was just beginning to lighten, a habit from her nocturnal wanderings to scavenge in the city. She rubbed the sleep from her eyes after she crawled from under the cart and then nodded to Krang. "Coffee?" she asked hesitantly.

Krang shook his head. He would have killed for a cup of coffee and a cigarette right now, and they had brought a pound of ground coffee with them, stashed in the bottom of the cart, but he didn't want to risk starting a fire. He was rationing his cigarettes, since he had no idea how long it would be before he could lay in another supply.

Katie stepped next to him and leaned in so she could whisper in his ear. Krang could feel her energy, standing next to him in the darkness, coming off her like heat from an engine. Her lips just brushed his ear as she whispered, sending a shiver down his spine. "Why don't you sleep for an hour or two? I'll stand watch."

Krang pulled away and shook his head. He could see the look of bitter disappointment that washed over her face. She started to turn away and he reached out and grabbed her by the arm, pulling her close. He leaned in to whisper, aware of her musky scent. Another shiver ran down his spine and he suddenly remembered when he was fifteen, kissing a girl behind the church, and she had let him cup her breast through her dress. He had thought he was going to die that night, from the sheer joy of that touch.

"It's not what you think," he whispered, watching her pulse beat in her neck. "I trust you. I'm better off with no sleep than just an hour or two." It was a lie, but he wanted her trust. The more she trusted him, the easier she would be to control.

Katie stepped away from him, a little less quickly than she had started, and he thought he had mollified her. She sat with her back against the cart, he legs crossed sideways beneath her and her hands resting, palm up, on her thighs. She began to whisper, so soft Krang couldn't make out her words. He knelt down next to her.

"What are you doing?"

She opened one eye and glared at him, and he knew she had seen through his lie. "You want me to teach you, don't you? This is called praying." She closed her eye and resumed her mumbling. Krang got up, laughing quietly. He stepped away from her, but watched her. As she prayed, her face changed. She lost the look of irritation. Her breathing relaxed and her shoulders loosened. It was the only time, other than when she was asleep, that she didn't look on guard. She was trouble for him, he was sure of it. The desire that had coursed through him moments before could be deadly. He needed a guide, not an easy fuck.

The line of refugees camped along the levee slowly came to life, and by the time Katie was done with her prayers there was movement up and down the road. They had another piece of dried sausage for breakfast. A pale sun broke through the clouds, slowly warming the morning. The refugees moved slowly, first a single man walking past the campers as he got a jump on his day. Then a second, and shortly after a small group of three walking a bicycle. The bicycle seemed to signal to the rest of the refugees, and the groups began to move. Krang was impatient, but wasn't willing to try to navigate through the crowds before him. And what was his hurry? The road was better this morning, the dirt firm and less muddy. Krang tried to maintain some kind of buffer zone from the other refugees around the cart, but it grew more and more difficult to do so as the morning progressed.

If there had been any spirit among the groups yesterday, it was gone today. A night sleeping on the ground had wrinkled the suits and dresses of the Citizens, and several had changed into something more practical. Yesterday people had walked, but today they trudged, heads down, only moving because the crowd around them was moving.

The cart slowed Krang down. It was too bulky to wheel easily around the men and women in front of them, so they had to travel much slower than he wanted. He knew it was probably better for the girl, but he chafed at waiting. Men, walking singly or in small groups, passed them frequently as they made their way up and down the line of refugees. Krang felt uncomfortable every time someone passed them; he could see them eyeing the cart, unable to hide their desire for it. The men were looking for easy targets. By mid-morning Krang was wearing Katie's pistol openly on his hip, giving the men a clear warning to look somewhere else.

He was also concerned about where they would stop for the evening. He couldn't spend another night on his feet. By late morning the road had left the levee and was level with the countryside once more. The forest had receded from the edge of the road for nearly a mile on either side, and grasslands or fallow fields ran alongside. The fighting had been fierce here, and war wreckage littered the fields. A tank battle had taken place at the edge of the trees, and Krang counted seventeen burned out tanks, mostly Montrovian judging from the positions they held.

He looked out over the fields, devoid of life, and wondered why no one was farming. He could see that many of the fields had been planted last fall with winter wheat, which had just broken clear of the ground before the invasion. The wheat was gone, except for random patches of tiny green blades valiantly raising themselves towards the March sun. Everything needed to be replanted. The fields would need extra care this year, would need to be combed over for mines, and have the wreckage and detritus of the armies hauled away, but no one was working in the fields. If it was the same in the south, the entire nation would starve to death before next spring.

By noon, hundreds of refugees were pulling off to the side of the road and just giving up for the day. Krang was sure that some of them were giving up forever. They seemed to be catching up to refugees who had left the City a day or two before them. The road was becoming more and more clogged with travelers and it was almost impossible to keep space around them.

Krang was already wondering if it was time to abandon the line of refugees. Could he fashion an easy way for them to carry their food, so they could strike out cross-country? He shook his head and took in a deep breath to calm himself. Mired in the middle of this flood of lost souls, he was safe. He needed to remember that. All this misery meant he was safe.

Krang glanced at Katie, walking beside him. She had been silent most of the day, other than to answer his questions. She was much stronger than he had expected. She had not asked for a break, or to eat, or for any water.

"Tell me about the Homeland," he asked her.

"I've never been there," she said. "I don't know anything."

"What did you learn about it growing up?"

"It doesn't really exist," she said softly.

"What?"

"This confuses most people," Katie said, "but the true Homeland is a state of being, not a place. The Homeland is that place where you find God..."

"Then where the hell did the camp survivors go? When the other prisoners talked about the Homeland I just assumed they meant Corabia."

Katie nodded. "Yes, I'm sure you did. There are two different Homelands, and only one of them exists as a physical place. In order to understand the physical Homeland you need to understand the spiritual Homeland. It's like your Heaven, except that it's not just Heaven."

Krang shook his head. "You people are nuts."

"No," Katie said. "Just listen. On one level, the Homeland is like Heaven. It is where the soul resides when it is not in your body. It is the Home of our wondrous Father, the God of all Being. Many of our songs and rituals celebrate the moment that our soul passes from this difficult world to the wonder of the Homeland. In truth, however, we don't believe in Heaven the way Citizens do. The Homeland may be referred to as the place we meet God, but we don't truly believe that happens when you die. The Homeland is that state of being that we enter when we meet God every day. It is the place your soul goes to when you pray or meditate. It is the place of your highest consciousness. If you wait until you die to attempt to go to the Homeland, you will never experience it. It is not the reward for living a good life, but a condition of truly living."

Krang nodded. "That's bullshit."

Katie laughed. "Exactly what many people say. In time, you will move beyond that point of view. I think you are complex enough to find the truth in this."

"And the second Homeland?"

"The second Homeland is Corabia."

"The city itself, or someplace within the country, or the whole country?"

"I'm not exactly sure. My father always told me that one day our people

86

would go home. Not in his lifetime, and probably not in mine, but maybe in my children's. I was always confused, because we weren't from Corabia. I've never been there. We had no relatives there that I knew of. My father traveled there, to study and meet with other teachers, but it was never our home. I don't think many Corabians living in Montrovia had real ties to Corabia. I had a friend who had cousins who lived in Corabia, but she had never met them. As far as I'm concerned, my family was no different than the Citizens. I bet my heritage in this country is as long as yours. So I never felt any need for a Homeland."

"Where did the idea of the Homeland come from? We recognize the Holy land in Palestine, like other Christians."

"Jesus was born in Bethlehem, so of course it's sacred. I was always told that Jesus came to the city of Corabia and preached the Word of God there. So Corabia is also Holy city, like Jerusalem and Bethlehem."

Katie grinned at Krang. "I don't feel a need to go visit those places either. I think the desire to return to the Homeland is a desire to be closer to a sacred place. The place our Master Teacher showed us the path upon which we walk."

"You mean Jesus?"

Katie nodded. "Yes. Your people see Jesus as a God, separated from yourselves by his Divinity. So you claim to want to live as he did, but you will always fail, because no man in your world can be a God. Since we believe that all men are endowed with God, we believe Jesus was no more Divine than you or I. Thus, if I strive to live as he did, I may succeed."

"And do you believe the people in Corabia want you all to come back?"

"No," Katie said. "When things started to get bad, before the war, many people inquired about emigrating to Corabia. There was no offer of acceptance. Some of my father's friends even suggested fighting for a piece of the countryside to call our own."

"And would you have fought to create this Homeland?"

"No," Katie said, softly. "If the Homeland exists, it does in my heart, not in the world."

They stopped as the sun was fading from the western skies. A streak of red, like a pillar of righteousness, rose from the far horizon into the sky. Krang stared at it, wondering briefly if it was more likely that God was marking a spot of safety or smiting some poor bastard who muttered the wrong prayer. Smiting for sure, he thought with a laugh. Katie stared at the sunlight with a look of joy on her face, and Krang imagined she saw it as a promise of some kind. She had such a trusting and child-like view of God. It certainly was more appealing that the oppressiveness of his mother's church, but he doubted it was any more valid. God was a selfish bastard who only cared about God. How you prayed or what you believed didn't matter.

Krang wheeled the cart off the road and across a broken field, coming to rest next to a burned out hulk of a half ton truck. No bodies were in the truck cab, or laying near the spot, so he thought this would be a good place to spend the night. They had moved almost a half kilometer from the road, and Krang looked forward to sleeping for a few hours. The field had been the sight of at least one recent battle, and bloated bodies of dead soldiers lay clustered in small groups to the east of the truck. Most of the dead were on the edge of the woods that bordered the field. Krang thought he might find another working gun if he searched the dead soldiers.

A string of campfires dotted the road, and a few burned in the field they were in, but none were close. Katie had picked up small sticks as they walked through the field, but Krang forbid a fire at their camp.

Leaving Katie with the pistol to guard their belongings, Krang grabbed a pair of cloth bags from the cart and began to search the field around the truck, hurrying against the failing light.

Krang worked his way from the truck to the woods, moving from body to body, ignoring the sickly odor of death and decay to pick through the soldier's remains. He dropped every unfired shell that he found in one bag and every empty brass shell casing in the other. By the time he reached the last visible group of bodies he had struck pay dirt twice: he had recovered an old bolt action .30 caliber rifle that would be perfect for hunting, and one of the newer rapid fire carbines. The carbines were smaller caliber, but had a clip that held fifteen shells, and could be fired repeated by just pulling the trigger, with no need to work the bolt. Night had fallen when he finished with the last soldier.

Krang began picking his way across the darkened field to their camp. Now that it was dark, he began to worry about anti-tank mines that might have been scattered across the field. For a moment he froze, unable to take another step, but then he laughed, took a deep breath and moved forward. He wouldn't have noticed a mine in the daylight, so it really didn't matter that he couldn't see where he was stepping now. He was about halfway back to the tank when he realized that Katie had built a fire at their camp.

"Damn it," he whispered, angry that she had disobeyed him. He began to walk faster, trying to hurry without making noise. As he got closer he could see silhouette of a man standing near the fire, and realized that Katie was not alone. Putting the wrecked truck between himself and the fire, he snuck as close as he could without being discovered.

"No," Katie was saying. "My husband went looking for food. He'll be back in a few minutes. You don't need to stay."

"It's not safe out here," the man said. "It wouldn't be right for us to leave you here alone when it's not safe. You just come back to our camp, and everything will be okay."

"No." Katie's voice was beginning to sound desperate. "I can't leave without telling my husband. He would be worried sick about what might have happened to me. I won't go."

Good girl, Katie, Krang thought. You're doing okay.

"We'll leave Karl behind to wait for your husband," the man said. "He'll explain everything."

"No. I can't leave my wagon or my husband."

"What's in that wagon, that made you need to come all this way from the road?"

"We came for privacy. We haven't been married all that long. I told him we couldn't be too close to anyone else."

The men laughed. "Come on now, girl, it's time to go."

Krang began rummaging through the bag of shells, feeling for one that would fit one of the guns. He quickly recognized the pointed end of a .30 caliber shell and grabbed it. Laying the carbine on the ground, Krang slipped the shell into the rifle's chamber. He worked the bolt as quietly as he could, jacking the shell into the firing chamber.

"Let go of me," Katie shouted.

"Your husband is a fool to leave you alone in a place like this," the man said, his voice low. "He doesn't deserve to keep you."

"Let go of me!"

Krang stepped around the side of the truck. There were two men standing near the fire. One of the men held Katie by her upper arm, and was pulling her away from the light. The other man held a bayonet in his hand.

I wish I'd found two shells, Krang thought.

"What's going on?" Krang demanded, stepping far enough into the light for the men to see him. To see the rifle held casually in his hands.

The man holding Katie immediately released her.

"You're back." He took a small sidestep away from Katie. "You shouldn't leave your possessions laying around where they might get harmed."

Krang laughed. "She's capable of taking care of herself. She's already killed one man. I'm sure two more wouldn't have been a problem."

The man with the bayonet spoke up. "You misunderstand, friend. We were not..."

"I'm not your friend. Now leave."

Bayonet scowled. "We all need friends in this world. I shouldn't want to be so alone." He nodded to his friend and they both left.

Krang watched them walking away, wondering, as they disappeared into the blackness of the night, if he should have shot them down as they walked away.

"What the hell happened?" he snapped to the girl.

"They came a few minutes after you left. A group of men came from the road and built a camp. You can see the fire in those trees." she pointed out a stand of trees several hundred meters away. Krang could see a camp fire burning in the woods.

"I just sat here and didn't move, hoping that they wouldn't see me. Since it was getting dark, I thought if I blended into the shadows, I would be okay. Maybe they saw you and decided to look for your camp. I don't know. A couple of them started looking around the field. Once they spotted me and came over, I built the fire to signal you that something was wrong. I thought I was going to die."

She came around the fire and hugged him tightly.

"You still might," Krang said, pushing her away. "They'll be back, all of them this time. How many men were in the larger group?"

"I don't know. Five? Maybe seven?"

Krang retrieved the second gun and the bag of ammunition from behind the tank. Dumping the shells onto a blanket, he told Katie to sort them. Krang stepped behind the truck, away from the fire, where his night vision wouldn't be bothered by the light. He crouched down and let his eyes adjust to the darkness, and studied the tree line where the men were headed. The trees just looked like a darker mass in the darkness, but the light of their fire glittered in the woods. The men occasionally stepped between the fire and Krang, and he was able to track them all the way into the wood.

Katie ended up with two piles of ammunition that would fit their guns, and a third pile of shells that wouldn't. There were maybe fifteen bullets for the .30 caliber and forty to fifty for the carbine. Krang directed her to load the clips on both rifles.

Krang kicked the fire out, and handed the .30 caliber rifle to Katie. He showed her how to work the bolt and jack a shell into the chamber, and how to work it again to eject it once she fired. He made her practice several times, until he was sure she understood how to do it.

"I'm going to go check things out," he said. "If anyone comes back, make them say 'Walter.' If they don't, shoot them. Don't give them time to think about it, just shoot them. You only have six shots, so you may want to save the last one for yourself."

Katie nodded.

"You did good, building the fire," he said. "But if any of them come back, it means they want to hurt you."

"Give me the pistol."

Katie pulled it from her jacket and handed it to Krang. "Be careful," she whispered.

"I'll be careful. I just want to make sure that they don't head back over."

"Do you really think they will?"

"Yeah." Krang shrugged. "We'll know for sure in an hour, when they think we're asleep."

"Why don't we just go back to the road where everyone else is? They won't try anything in front of everyone else."

Krang studied the girl trying to make out her expression in the darkness. "I understand men like them. They've claimed you, and they won't stop until they take you. If it's not tonight, it will be tomorrow, or the next night, or the minute I step off the road to take a piss. And if it's not you, it's some other girl. Do you want them going after someone else?"

Katie shook her head. Krang turned and walked into the darkness.

Krang moved in a direct line towards the other camp, stopping when he neared the tree line. He lay on the ground, watching, feeling terribly exposed. He would like to have come upon the camp from the opposite direction, but was afraid that if he circled around too far from their camp that he would miss them in the darkness as they headed back for Katie. Trees partially blocked his view of the camp, and he was too far away to get an accurate count of how many there were, but he wouldn't miss them from here if they attempted to sneak back to his camp.

Krang was grateful for the cloudy skies as he crawled forward to the edge of the wood, now no more than thirty meters from the camp. Bits and pieces of laughter or shouting would drift by, but he couldn't make out any words. Krang began to slowly move to his right, drifting from tree to tree as he slowly circled in towards the camp. He could see well enough now that he would know if any of them left the camp. Krang kept the men between him and the road filled with other refugees, fearful of being discovered by an overly curious fellow traveler.

Krang stopped when he was on the opposite side of the camp. He crouched outside the light of their fire, and could easily make out the details of the camp. Six men, at least two with guns, sat or stood around the fire, passing a bottle back and forth. Krang could make out the two he had confronted sitting with a third man, arguing earnestly. Krang took up the carbine in his right hand, the revolver in his left, and waited.

Katie sat in the darkness wrapped in a blanket, her back to the burned-out truck, her eyes on the distant flickering fire, and cried. She felt that somehow it was her fault that they had been discovered. Katie was sure that Walter was going to pay for her mistake with his life. Katie didn't understand why she felt this sense of dread. She had made it through the war without being as scared as she was right now.

The first time she'd sold herself, only hours after escaping the deportation that had claimed her family, she had felt no fear. Katie had never done anything with a boy beyond kissing and very innocent touching, yet when the policeman had pushed her to her knees in the alley, she wasn't afraid. She had been angry at him, and disgusted with herself, but she hadn't been afraid of what was happening. She had moved from encounter to encounter with no fear and eventually no regrets, accepting the beatings as easily as the food or cash, and as long as she was alive the next morning, everything had been okay.

Even when she had been claimed by Stojespahl, and had moved off the streets and into his apartment, she never felt an attachment to the room, or feared that she would lose it. She had never cared what would happen. If Stojespahl threw her out, or killed her, what difference would it make? She hadn't run from the deportation because she was afraid to die, she had run because it was the right thing to do. Even when the camp survivors had beaten her, she hadn't felt afraid.

So why was she afraid now? And why was she afraid for this man? She had accepted the deaths of so many people during the war. Was Walter any different from the others? He seemed to feel that he owned her, just as they all had, whether for ten minutes or ten hours or ten months. He had used her, just as the others. He was no different, so why did it matter? Why did she cry for him?

Why didn't something happen?

Krang knelt in the darkness, watching the camp, for more than an hour. Eventually the two men he had confronted reached some kind of consensus with a third, and the three of them rose from their places on the far side of the fire. A fourth man waved them away. He sat on the ground, his back to Krang, studying some papers. The fifth was sharpening a knife on a whetstone; the last had curled up in a ball and gone to sleep.

Krang stood, willing the blood back into his legs. He slowly stepped forward as the men continued to talk, stopping when he was no more than ten meters from the camp. One of his two acquaintances, the one with the bayonet, reached down and picked up a rifle, and turned away from the fire with his companions.

Krang stepped forward into the light, his guns held chest high, firing repeatedly at the three men who were walking away from him. The men were knocked to the ground, the concussions of the shots echoing in the woods. Krang spun, not waiting to see if the first three were dead, to fire on the other three men. In a matter of seconds it was over. The acrid stench of gun powder hung in the air. The man who had been sleeping was still tangled in his blanket, the other two sprawled on the ground near the fire. The three men who had been walking away lay where they had fallen. Krang checked on each man in the party, confirming the kills.

92

Katie saw the bright flashes of the shots before she heard the popping of the guns. She felt the tears begin again, blurring the distant light of the fire. The tightness in her chest faded and she realized she had never believed he would fail. I wasn't crying for him, she thought. Maybe I was crying for them. She clutched her rifle tighter, and watched until the distant fire was extinguished.

"Why did you kill them?"

"I had no choice," Krang replied. "They were going to kill us."

"Don't do it anymore."

"What?"

"You heard me," Katie said, tossing the rifle from her lap. "I don't want the weight of their blood on my soul."

Krang shook his head. "It's not like I shot them when they were sleeping. They were going to come back over here, kill me, and take you. I was only acting in self-defense."

"I'd rather be dead."

Krang laughed. "I don't believe that. You've already proved you were willing to kill to stay alive."

"And I was wrong. I don't need any more blood on my soul, just because I was incapable of forgiving another person."

"This isn't about forgiveness," Krang said harshly. "Your life is just as valuable as any of theirs. More valuable, even, because of your constant struggle to do the right thing. You have to accept the challenge of living this life you were given. I don't care if you do it because you feel it's a sacred gift or because it feels good, but you have to live, or it's all wasted."

"But I don't have the right to choose my life over that of another person. That's God's choice."

"And God chose to make me shoot straight."

"No. God is only good. God does not kill."

"So it would have been good if they had killed us?"

"I don't know," Katie whispered. She was crying again. "I just don't want to be responsible for any more killing."

"You don't know what it means to be responsible for killing," Krang said. He sat beside her, his back to the truck, and wrapped the blanket around them both. "Go to sleep," he said brusquely. "I'll keep watch in case anyone comes to investigate the shooting."

Katie sighed heavily, and rested her head against his chest. It took her several minutes to stop crying. Krang felt her breathing deepen, and knew that she had dropped off into sleep. He was unsure what he had gotten himself into with the girl, and wondered if he should find a way to get rid of her.

I never let Emma fall asleep cuddled against me, he thought. Not even when I thought I loved her. How has this girl gotten to me so deeply, that I care about what she is feeling? It must be guilt, he thought. Somehow, I feel guilty because of what that bitch Sarah is trying to do to me. Since I can't confront her, the conflict is playing out here.

Krang stroked Katie's short hair. Could something as simple as being forgiven have made a difference in the way he was treating her? Krang laughed for a long time, soothing Katie back to sleep when she awoke. I should be so lucky, he thought. I should be so lucky. She is worried about the deaths of six men who wanted to kill her. How many hundreds rest on my soul? And I can't feel a thing.

Chapter Seven

Krang sat against the truck in the darkness, the girl sleeping with her head on his chest, watching as the proliferation of campfires along the road burned out, one by one. He was too alive to sleep, replaying the attack in his head again and again. Sometime after midnight the moon broke through the cloud cover, bathing the field in silver light. Krang suddenly appreciated the earlier blackness, as the silver light created shadows that played havoc with his imagination. Every clump of dirt became a man crawling across the field, intent on taking what Krang owned.

Katie groaned in her sleep, snuggling her head tighter against Krang's chest. Her body fit against him nicely, their shared heat under the blanket keeping them warm. Krang listened to her deep, even breaths as his kept watch across the fields. It felt good to have the girl laying next to him, and that bothered Krang. He had never felt protective of Emma, and couldn't think of a time when he would have let her cuddle against him like Katie was doing. Even after sex, he had never been one to hold Emma. Thankfully, she hadn't wanted any of that from him either, but would roll away for a cigarette as soon as they had finished. Except for sex, they didn't really touch.

They had married after Emma turned up pregnant, but Krang could never say that he had truly loved her. He wasn't even sure that he really liked her. He just liked fucking her. Krang had never resisted when Emma said the baby was his, but he knew she was seeing other men at the time, just as he was seeing other women. He assumed that his willingness to get married must have meant that he loved her. Had he? Or had he simply been too lazy to look for another apartment?

There hadn't been a time when he was with Emma that he hadn't been seeing other women. Not a single day. She had never cared. At least she had never complained, and he had taken that as permission to continue. Krang had never wanted his parent's relationship. His father had been pathologically jealous, once accusing his mother of sleeping with her priest. They had been inseparable, except when he was working or she was at church, but it had seemed to Krang a prison sentence, not a marriage. With Emma, he had been able to pretend there were no needs, beyond sex. It was a different kind of prison, but prison all the same.

Katie stirred in his arms. Krang looked down at her pale, unlined face. When she was awake, she always looked haunted, like she carried with her a great sadness, or some terrible secret. Not the look of overwhelming numbness so many of the prisoners wore, but a deep sadness all the same. Or guilt.

What terrible secrets could she be hiding? She hadn't been alive long enough to have terrible secrets, at least certainly not like the ones Krang had. He understood that she felt some guilt about whoring herself for food, but how else was she supposed to survive? There was no shame in being strong enough to survive. Maybe living through the final onslaught on the city had shaken her so deeply? She must have thought she was going to die every second of the bombardments.

He wondered if his kids felt the same way. Did they store every horrifying thing that they had seen or experienced in some inner compartment, and tormented themselves with it every waking moment? Or were they were more like his prisoners, eventually becoming numb to every experience? Most likely they were dead.

He didn't feel anything about the likelihood his kids were dead. Not sadness, or anger, or even joy. The hell they had gone through didn't mean anything to him. People die. More people die in war.

Krang stroked his hand across the stubble of Katie's hair. She felt guilty about killing Stojespahl, who clearly deserved to die, and who had literally killed himself. She was upset about the six men he had just killed, probably the only justified killing he had ever done. She felt like it was her fault the men were dead. Even if it was her fault, why couldn't she see the righteousness of their deaths? How could she not want them all dead?

And what about me? Krang didn't feel remorse for any of the people he had killed. He had never kept a tally, but he must have killed more than a hundred. Thinking back, he couldn't find one death that bothered him. How could he feel guilty when life was going so well? Good things were happening to him, while others were suffering.

Katie had asked him yesterday if he believed in God. If his choices were to believe in Katie's God who loves everyone, or his mother's God, who was all about punishment and retribution, how could he? God let him skate through the war unpunished while exacting such terrible tributes from others. Was God so capricious as to reward his enemies and punish his faithful? God was either so far removed from our lives as to be powerless, or there was no God. Krang liked Katie's claim that all men were God individualized. He could live with the thought that he was his own God because he exercised the power given him. In which case he would be blessed until the day he met someone even more powerful, and then he would die.

But Katie had power too. Krang still didn't understand why he hadn't killed her immediately. It could have been the sex, but he had never let sex stop him before. And as much as he liked fucking the girl, he didn't think he was going to fuck her again. If he was going to track Sarah down, he had to be able to enter her world. To be Corabian. Katie was his key to that world. To be her brother, or uncle, or family friend, or whatever fucking story he would tell, meant he needed to keep his dick in his pants. Finding Sarah and proving to her that she was wrong about him was more important than having access to an easy fuck.

Katie shifted against his chest. Her mouth was slightly open and the soft rustle of her breath reassured him she wasn't having another nightmare. He yawned and tried to stretch without waking her.

There was something about the girl he liked. Krang shook his head. He was getting weak, he knew it. You survive by only caring about yourself. Once you got caught up in other people's needs, you were easy to manipulate and kill. Still, he liked her. It was partially the set of contradictions she presented, like a puzzle to be solved. She needed him to survive, but she didn't. She had done admirably before he found her. She needed him because she needed to need someone. And she could deny it. And would do so vehemently. And yet she snuggled up against him and slept, like a child.

Krang hated to admit that escaping death had changed him, but he could no longer deny it. He had changed in some fundamental way. He was fighting an overwhelming urge to celebrate the fact that he was still alive. To literally dance down the street shouting and crying. It was as if his cynicism had retreated to a place that it didn't color every thought he had. Krang didn't think of himself as the sentimental type, but was unable to deny the joy that he felt at being alive. Maybe Sarah had changed him in some way.

He felt lost, like a child in the midst of a new city. This environment was new to him. He didn't know how to act in such a place.

Krang shook his head. I'm lying to myself, he thought. I haven't changed, not really. I'm feeling some kind of psychological reaction at having escaped death so narrowly, but I haven't changed. I need the girl as cover, that's why I care about what happens to her. I'm lying to myself to even think I could change if I wanted to. And I don't want to change.

He felt Katie resting against him, felt her breath on his neck. I do want to fuck her, he thought. His cock began to stiffen.

Clouds blowing across the moon began creating strange patterns of darkness and light. Krang looked out across the field, wishing for morning. His cock was so erect it was painful. He was unsure if he trusted himself with the girl. She was his future, his pass to a new world. He couldn't afford to squander her, like a boy with a nickel who sees the candy store. She was the key to finding Sarah. He shook his head trying to clear it, looked across the fields, and cursed under his breath.

The baby lay less than thirty meters from where they were camped. He couldn't believe that he had missed seeing the body before now. Or that Katie had. It was on the path they had followed from the road. Or had the men brought it with them? What if they hadn't been planning on killing them, but had wanted to leave the baby? Krang stared at it, making sure the shadows weren't playing tricks on his eyes. It was a baby.

Krang pushed Katie aside. He climbed unsteadily to his feet, and stumbled across the field to the body. The baby was dead. It lay on its back, lifeless eyes staring up at the night sky. Someone had crushed it's skull against the ground like you would a runt piglet. The baby wore just a long shirt and diaper. The shirt was gathered around the infant's chest. The white cotton was yellowed with age and stained brown from the baby's blood. Bits of skull clung to the shirt. Krang felt nauseous as he stared at the body. He felt the wind pick up around him, carrying a faint, angry murmur with it.

Of course, Krang thought. I did this. This is Sarah's baby, the one that I killed.

The hand that brushed against his face startled him from his reverie. Krang looked up, expecting to see Katie. An old shrunken woman stared at him, her eyes pleading, demanding his attention. Her lips formed silent words, but Krang couldn't interpret them.

Krang shook his head. "I don't know you, Grandmother," he hissed.

He bent down and picked up the body, looking for someplace to hide it. He had to get rid of it before someone else saw it. The baby was no heavier than a loaf of bread, yet Krang struggled to lift it. He felt exposed. He was sure that all the refugees camping along the road could see him. And surely Katie must be sickened of him now. Krang raised his head to look for Katie, but the crone blocked his view.

The murmuring became louder, more forceful. Krang turned away from the old woman. He could see them now, stretching across the field toward the road, silently accusing him as he stood holding the baby's lifeless body. Hundreds of men and women. The field was covered in a blanket of fog, which made his accusers seem insubstantial, as if they were made of the very mist itself. As they came closer, they became more solid, until they were all he could see.

They were all from the camp. His prisoners, the ones he had killed, still dressed in the rags of their uniforms, still sporting their fatal wounds. Each one silently reached out and touched him. The touch was almost a caress; it was much less angry than in the cave, and yet more damning. Krang stood silently, looking each one in the face, silently enduring. He had no choice; they were his children now, his creation, the handiwork of his time at the camp. As they filed past him, one at a time, the caresses became longer. A touch on the cheek became a stroke across his face and neck, or a hug across the shoulder. A man he had once fought with before the war, drunk in a bar, who was now a shuffling skeletal creature swathed in rags, kissed him on the cheek. A boy, just a teenager, stared at him with sunken eyes and held up the pet rat he carried in his hand to show Krang. A woman glanced at him over her shoulder as she walked past, the gesture reminiscent of a former lover.

Finally, only Abraham was left. He stood before Krang, his eyes empty, lifeless. The bullet hole in his face, an angry beauty mark, stared accusingly. Krang shrank away from him, but could not step away. Abraham wrapped his arms around Krang, pulling him into a hug as if he were a long lost friend. The intimacy of the touch, and the pressure of the small dead body trapped between their chests, cut Krang more sharply than any knife could have. He felt his soul leaking away from him in that touch.

Abraham released him and began to walk away.

"Wait!" Krang called. He lifted the boy's body. "Take him."

Abraham looked at the body for a moment, turned, and continued on.

"Stop!" Krang ran across the field to get in front of him.

"Take him," Krang said, holding the body out. "He's your son."

Abraham looked at Krang, smiled sadly, and faded from view. Krang was alone, the field empty, the moon setting on the far horizon.

"Fuck." Krang cradled the body to his chest. "What the hell am I going to do with a baby? And how am I going to tell Katie?"

"Tell me what?"

Krang jerked awake. He was sitting before the stamped out remains of Katie's fire, his back against the burned out truck. Katie was kneeling next to him. Her eyes shined in the bright moonlight, full of worry. He glanced quickly around: there was no infant's body nearby.

"You were having a terrible dream," Katie said. " I tried to wake you, but I couldn't."

There had been no infant. I'm going crazy, Krang thought.

"I'm sorry I was upset with you," Katie whispered. "You saved my life."

Krang felt her hand on his crotch, slowly rubbing his cock. Her caress grew more insistent, stroking and fondling him until he was erect. Krang thought that he should protest, that he couldn't afford to have sex with this girl, but he had no energy to stop her. Her fingers had opened his fly and were pulling his cock through. How ironic, he thought, a few days ago sex would have been a means of my controlling her. Her mouth slipped over his erection. Now she's controlling me.

"Stop," he whispered. "You have to be my ..."

She let his cock slip from her mouth, and placed her hand across his lips, silencing him. She knelt and pushed her pants off and sat astride him, his cock sliding deeply into her pussy.

"Shhh," she whispered. She kissed his mouth and rocked herself against him. She rode him urgently, her hands caressing his face. She leaned forward slightly, keeping his cock inside her, to whisper in his ear. "You saved me."

Krang immediately exploded within her. One spurt, ripped from his heart and bowels and throat. His orgasm was so intense and quick that it caught him by surprise. They rested together for several minutes. Krang felt cleansed from the dream.

"I want you to know that I appreciate what you did," Katie whispered, laying her head back on his chest.

"Next time just say thank you," Krang said, an edge of anger to his voice. "If we are going to make others believe that you are my sister, or my ward, then we can't have sex."

Katie shook her head. "You can't stop me from fucking you. Maybe I love you."

Krang laughed bitterly. "You don't love me and I don't love you. We need each other to survive. That's not love."

Katie ground her pussy against him. "Says who?" she pouted. "And why do I have to be your sister? Why not your wife?"

"You can't be my wife. How am I supposed to search for Sarah if you're my wife?"

"Tell people she's your sister. Then we can fuck all we want."

"If you're my wife, men won't be as willing to help when we need it. If you're my sister, they have hope."

Katie rolled off him. "So you can pimp me."

"I'm not saying that."

"But it's what you mean. If necessary, you need to be able to use me as a whore, to get what you want."

Krang could hear the hurt in her voice. Her feelings weren't his problem. "Look..."

"I know, it's what I do," Katie said, brushing the dirt from her knees.. She tried to wipe away her tears so Krang wouldn't see them.

"You misunderstand," Krang said brusquely. "Although I don't know why I give a damn. If you go around telling people you're my wife, you can never start your own life over. What happens to you when I find Sarah? I can't take you into the Homeland as my wife, and still be looking for my wife. As my sister, you are respectable traveling alone with me. As a woman, you're not."

"So now you fucking care about me?"

"No, I don't give a fuck about what happens to you, but if we're going to do this, we can both benefit. And if you know something good can happen for you, you won't be tempted to fuck things up for me. You don't want the world to think we've been fucking."

"Do you think anyone cares anymore? Our lives have been destroyed by this war. No one cares who I'm fucking." She scrambled to pull her pants up.

"That was true until the day the war ended. We had an excuse then, that we didn't know what the future would bring. People encouraged others to chase their own happiness in the midst of terror. It was a way of fighting back. It was that way in the camp. No one cared who slept with whom, because you were both likely to be dead soon anyhow. But that changed the minute the end of the war was in sight. If anything, people are more socially constrained right now than they were before the war started. They are trying to put meaning back into their lives, to force moral equivalencies to exist again. A man who was blowing up buildings two weeks needs to feel comfortable that a stop sign means stop."

"But if people think I'm your sister, I can never be more than that."

"Why would you want to be more? Have you looked at me? The only thing I've ever been good at was killing people. Just because I found you doesn't mean you want me in your life."

"I decide who I want in my life, and I decide who I fuck. Not you."

Krang shrugged. What was the point? "Fine. But I'm never going to be more to you than I am right now. The day will come when you will want to be free of me, and this is the easiest way to do it. And don't think that us fucking will keep me from killing you, if that's what I need to do."

They manhandled the cart across the field and back onto the road as the sun was breaking above the forest to the east. It took nearly half an hour to reach the road and by that time many of the refugees were breaking their camps. The refugees were more spread out than they had been yesterday morning, and they were moving more in individual groups than as a pack, with many groups making no real effort to get under way.

The road they followed took them further away from the mountains. This was now farming country. If there had been no war, the rolling hills would be under assault from teams of draft horses and plows, but they saw no farmers working the land. Wooded plots broke up the monotony of the empty fields.

The detritus of war lay everywhere: on the road, in the fields and in the woods. From the wreckage and soldiers' bodies, Krang could deduce how the war had been lost. Montrovian soldiers had dug in on the southern edge of each little wood and held on at terrible cost for both armies until sheer numbers of Corabians had overrun the position and the Montrovian survivors had filtered back to the next wood. Krang couldn't imagine how those soldiers must have felt, ceding the

Motherland one acre at a time.

Katie stayed distant from Krang the entire day. It didn't bother him that she was hurt by his earlier comments, because he didn't want her to be attached to him in any way. She was a much better tool for him to use when she was indifferent towards him, than if she thought of him as her lover. He didn't want to be burdened by any feelings for her either; if he needed to sacrifice her at some point in time, it would be much easier if he didn't care about her. Still, she was a great fuck, and he kept remembering how she felt riding him.

The sun grew stronger as the day went by. Today was going to be the warmest day of the spring. Krang threw his coat in the cart, and felt a fine sweat on the back of his neck as he pushed the cart. It felt good to work so hard.

Krang continued to feel a giddiness about having escaped the camp and the sure death that had been waiting for him. Katie was a reward for escaping the camp. It was like Sarah had given him a gift, but hadn't checked the bag and realized it held more than one thing. Not only did he get to live, he got Katie. So why was he still so angry at Sarah?

Sarah had had no right to forgive him for anything. Who was she, to magnanimously bestow a benediction on him, as if her opinion mattered? Did she think that she had done something just by freeing him? Krang had never expected to survive the war. He had loved the camp too much. Even if Montrovia had found a way to win the war, how could he have ever left the camp? He wouldn't have given up his power willingly So he had thought death was the only thing that waited for him after the camp. Forgiveness hadn't been an option.

The camp had confirmed one of Krang's beliefs: the idea of justice was a joke. The only thing that existed was personal power. He tried every day to fuck with God. He had done everything in his power to offend God, to push Him to the limit, and still he had survived. Where was the justice in that? He had killed a baby by crushing its head on the ground before its parents, and then shot the father in front of his wife. Where was the retribution? If God existed, He was powerless.

Krang thought about his mother, about her hard belief. She had watched her husband die of black lung, after twenty years in the mines, and had thought his suffering was buying him his place in heaven. She had gone to church every day, and prayed on her knees for an hour, abjectly begging forgiveness for crimes she couldn't describe or understand. Krang never believed that the fire that killed her was an accident. He was sure that she sat in her bed and watched the flames consume her, in hopes of getting to heaven quicker. For her and her priests, suffering was the key to everything.

But he had not suffered at the camp. He had been the one to make others suffer. To see them cry out for their God and know that no help was coming.

How many nights did I want to see that same look of horror on Emma's face, to stop her damn whining? How many times on leave did I walk past a man who had fired me, and wished I could have him out at the camp to teach him a thing or two?

Krang glanced at Katie, marching stiffly in the line of refugees, her face a hard mask. I admire your ability to survive without taking it out on others. If you stay with me, you will become like me, and the world doesn't need another Walter Krang. You cried last night for the souls of six men who were just like me, men who would kill you for the pure joy of killing. I want you to cry for me some day, but not to become me. When my masquerade ends, if you're still with me, you will be the one to pay for it. If I can do one good thing in my life, it is to save you from that.

Krang laughed under his breath. Look at me God. I have a conscience, you miserable bastard. How the fuck can you do this to me? You let me be *the guard*. Hell, you created me. I was nothing more than an asshole when I went out to that camp looking for a job. I was too fucking lazy to hold down a job, too indifferent to care for my kids, too inconsequential. And you let me become *the guard*. You did nothing to stop me. And now you've freed me? My mother would have quit the church over this. How can you do that to her?

The sun broke through the cloud cover in the early afternoon. Katie was amazed at the change she saw in the other refugees when the sun came out: they smiled and nodded to one another as if out for a picnic. Her own heart soared as well. In spite of everything, she felt a sense of calmness about her that she had not felt since before the war. Somehow, being with Walter made her feel better.

She wasn't naive enough to believe he was traveling with her out of some desire to help her, or even a sense of obligation. He needed her. He wanted her sexually, she was sure. And she liked that. Katie had come to accept that her body was a commodity to be bartered to get what she needed. Walter needed more than her body, however, and that was different from the other men and women who had used her. Walter needed Katie's life. He needed every experience of her faith. He needed her memories.

Katie wiped a trickle of sweat from her brow. She was glad it was spring. Winter in the city had been miserable, this year worse than ever. She glanced at Walter from the corner of her eye. He was outwardly calm, but never peaceful. His eyes were constantly in motion, darting from face to face looking for each new risk. She didn't understand why she felt safe with him. There was no denying his violence. No denying that his threat to kill her was real. Maybe she just didn't care if she ended up in a ditch by the side of the road?

No, she thought, it wasn't that. She hadn't cared before, but now she had some hope. Even though Walter was clearly capable of killing her, she didn't think he would. Stojespahl had constantly berated her, threatened to send her to the camp, or just to kill her himself. How many nights had he taken her with his pistol in one hand? How often had she wished he would just pull the trigger and end her pain? Walter wasn't the same as that.

Katie smiled. There was something else. What secret was he hiding, that he needed her as a diversion? She didn't believe his story about marrying Sarah and being sent to the camps. Not for a minute. He wasn't one to risk his life for love. So how did he know so much about the camps? And who was Sarah?

Was there another reason to get sent to the camps? Had he just managed to piss off someone with enough authority to get thrown in the camp?

Unless... Katie had heard rumors of resistance fighters, living in the caves in the mountains. Most of them would have been Corabians, but a few must have been Citizens. It had been said that some of them infiltrated the death camps. There had been whispered stories of mass escapes. Walter had that ease of killing, which he had demonstrated last night. And he felt no guilt about it, that was sure.

She decided that she would think of him as a resistance fighter. She would be safe with one so easily violent. And unlike Stojespahl, this man was not going to turn her in the minute he grew tired of her. He had more to risk than she did.

Katie giggled again. Forgive me my game, Walter, she thought. I do not know what you are running from, but it can't be as bad as what I have done with my life, simply because I was afraid to die. How much time in hell have I already earned? Maybe my parents were right: this life is only a phase in our existence, an illusion that captures our imagination and weans us away from our true spiritual path. When we try too hard to hang on to it, that's when we end up in hell. I should have gone to the camp with them. I would be happily moldering in a grave somewhere, she thought, but my soul would be free of this place.

A cardinal swooped down from a tree to grab at a crumb of bread lying on the road. The golden sunlight made his feathers glow with an ethereal brilliance that took Katie's breath away. The cardinal alighted on the lower branch of a tree and studied her. As she approached, it dropped the crumb at her feet and flew away.

Katie smiled, her heart soaring. Never mind, God, she thought. I'm okay where I am.

During the afternoon, refugees began asking for food. They offered to barter valuables, or push the cart, anything for food. One woman, with two small children, offered her body. When Krang called a halt for the evening, they moved about thirty meters off the road. Katie couldn't get the woman off her mind.

"Can't we share some of what we have?" she asked.

Krang looked at her, frowning. "You can't be serious."

"I am."

"If we share what we have, then we have nothing."

"We don't have to give it all away."

Krang pointed to line of refugees camped along the road, which stretched out of sight in either direction. "How are you going to pick who to feed? As soon as anyone knows we have extra food, a riot will break out. You think you love them, girl, but you haven't seen them at their worst."

Bullshit, she thought, silently eating her piece of dried sausage. I've fucked them at their worst. "Maybe I should go and suck some of them off," she said brightly, "that would at least brighten their day."

Krang choked on his water and doubled over coughing and sputtering. Katie beamed to see it.

Chapter Eight

Krang lit the cigarette one handed, drawing the acrid smoke deep into his lungs. The tip glowed red every time he inhaled, a spot of warmth in the cool morning air. A single bird, somewhere in the wood to his right, began its morning song, a faint premonition of the cacophony of the morning to come. The road, a hundred meters away, was dark and quiet.

Krang took another draw on his cigarette. He had rationed himself, smoking only two or three a day, but was down to a handful left in his kit bag. He wondered if he should kill someone to steal their tobacco, and then smiled. Katie would hate him, and that would be bad. She slept next to him, wrapped across his chest, her hand resting on his thigh. He wondered if they had time to fuck before the world came to life.

In the month since they had left the city, his resolve to keep her at arm's length had completely disappeared. They fucked almost every night, and Katie was the instigator as often than not. Last night she had not even waited for complete dark, but had sat herself on his stiff cock in the half-light of dusk, unconcerned if anyone could see them. Krang had been surprised that Katie was such an aggressive lover, but he didn't mind her gentle bites or the occasional bruise. It seemed fitting that she expel her demons on him, and it was great sex.

He glanced down at her as she slept, her breath slow and even. Only when she slept was her face peaceful and unguarded, and he thought she was beautiful in those moments. Her hair was almost two inches long now, and her bruises had healed. Although she still wore pants all the time, Katie no longer tried to pass for a boy. Krang sighed. He was growing used to her, and that was a problem. He had only brought her along as camouflage. She was to be the sacrifice, if one were necessary. Krang worried that he might hesitate when the moment came, and lose both their lives, instead of just hers.

On the road, someone nursed a cooking fire into life. Krang drew in another lungful of acrid smoke and flipped his useless butt into the mud. He wasn't looking forward to the day's walk. The journey south towards the Homeland had settled into a numbing routine. The congestion on the road had eased somewhat, as every day more and more of the refugees simply gave up and refused to go on. They would be dead by winter, if not sooner, for there was nothing to sustain them in the empty, lifeless fields. The refugees who continued became more sheep-like every day. If one person stopped, the entire column stopped. If someone made camp for the night, even in early afternoon, almost everyone else made camp for the night. He didn't think they were making ten kilometers a day.

It was bad enough having to manhandle the cart around the columns of bombed trucks, some a half-mile long, that continued to block the road at least once a day, but Krang spent even more time walking around groups that had simply stopped in the middle of the road. Every time they passed someone, Krang recognized the look of resentment of a vanquished people. The refugees could see that Krang and Katie had a destination in mind, someplace to be, when they had none, and hated and feared them for it. The looks he and Katie got from Citizens on the edge of exhaustion were almost the same looks he had gotten from the Corabians in the camps. They saw his power and were cowed by it. It was the most divine irony.

Katie stirred gently against his chest, and he knew she would soon awaken. He would give anything for a hot bath. His cock twitched when he thought about sharing a bath with her, but he pushed the image from his mind. He brushed his hand against the scraggly beard on his face and wondered if he should heat water and try to shave. He had no razor, but maybe he could sharpen one of the knives on the sharpening stone. I'm becoming just like one of them, he thought, irritated with himself. It was so easy to lose himself in the day-to-day crap that seemed important. He needed to keep his focus on one goal: getting to the Homeland and finding Sarah.

The column of refugees slowly came to life as the sun cleared the trees on the eastern horizon. It was another hour before the column stumbled into motion. Traveling was easier here, as the roads were in better condition for more of each day. The fields were still dormant, which meant the nation would starve to death come winter. This area of the country supplied most of the corn and wheat for the entire nation. Krang wondered if the country was already dead, and just didn't know it yet.

Krang was pushing the cart as he walked, Katie walking beside him. She was quiet most of the time, except when he engaged her in conversation, but she wasn't semi-comatose like so many of the refugees stumbling along the road. She seemed content to be within herself, and didn't need to talk all the time. Krang appreciated her more every day.

He watched her as she walked. She was watching a red-tailed hawk that soared in slow circles overhead, a slight smile on her face. If he had to guess, he would say she was happy.

"So explain this to me again," he said, drawing her attention away from the hawk. "You people don't believe in hell?"

Katie shook her head. "I believe in hell. I've visited."

Krang frowned and Katie burst into laughter. Krang loved it when she laughed spontaneously and thought it sounded beautiful. It meant her soul wasn't dead.

"Seriously," Katie said, then dissolved into another bout of laughter that lasted several minutes. "You looked so serious when I said that, like I must be crazy," she said when she regained her composure.

"But you don't believe in hell?"

"We don't believe in Heaven or hell, not like you do. Not as some place your soul goes to after you die."

"So the rest of us are crazy?"

Katie shook her head. "I think they're both very real, but we think about them differently than the Citizens do. What happens when we die? You've been taught your soul goes to Heaven or hell, depending on how you've lived. I was taught our soul goes back to God, regardless of how you've lived. Our soul returns to God without our ego. So I wouldn't exist as Katie in God the way you would exist as Walter in Heaven."

Krang shook his head. "You'll never find me in Heaven."

Katie smiled. "I won't find anyone else, either. Heaven doesn't exist."

"But you said you did believe."

"Sure I do. Remember, our thoughts produce actions. So I can create the world in which I live, to a certain extent. I can live in Heaven right now, if I have enough faith, or I can live in hell. Didn't you feel like you were living in hell in the camp?"

Krang shook his head. "I wasn't. So many others were, but not me." He realized he shouldn't have said anything, the moment the words were out of his mouth.

"You know, my mother was devoted to the church. She went to mass every day, and prayed for everyone. She believed that the more she suffered in life, the more she was assured to go to Heaven when she died. So she was aware she was suffering, but instead of being unhappy about it, she was ecstatic. It was proof to her that she would spend eternity in God's arms. That seemed crazy to me."

"Maybe," Katie said. "I'm always sorry when people miss the chance to live now because they think their life really begins after they die. But look at your Mother. Maybe her belief in Heaven gave her the courage to go on in the face of adversity? So maybe she was creating her own version of Heaven right here."

Krang laughed bitterly. "One that required her to create a catalog of all of her suffering?"

Katie shrugged. "Who am I to say? All I know is that there were moments when I was on the street that I lived in real despair, and my life was hell at those times. At other times, when nothing else had changed, mind you..., I was still blowing and fucking people for food and shelter.., I was able to raise my consciousness and find blessings in my life, and then everything was okay. That's what I meant when I said I had visited hell. My faith isn't strong enough to keep me free of it, but I don't have to live there all the time."

"And what about this war? Isn't the war hell, in and of itself?"

"How the fuck should I know?" Katie said with a grin.

"What would your father have taught?"

"He would have said that what happens in the world doesn't matter. How we respond is what matters."

"Rather simplistic, don't you think?"

"I remember when my nana died, his mother. She lived with us, and had been very active and healthy in spite of her age. And then one afternoon she was tired and lay down for a nap and never woke up. He was clearly sad, but he said that her death didn't matter. Our lives had to go on, whether she was alive or not, so we could chose to be okay, or to suffer a great loss."

Krang looked at her. "And?"

"I was seven, so I chose to suffer a great loss."

"I wish my mother had believed in something more than suffering." Krang shook his head. "No, that's not what I mean. I think her life could have been different. She could have celebrated the good stuff instead of wallowing in the bad stuff. That might have made a difference for me, but she got what she wanted out of life."

"My father said we all get what we want out of life, even if it looks horrible to another person. And he didn't mean to blame people for the conditions in their life. He thought we came here, were born, for spiritual growth, so our lives were created with all the appropriate challenges in place. So it's never a question of whether or not we succeed in life, it's simply a question of whether or not we experienced life."

Traffic on the road grew heavier later that morning. The refugees were bunching up again, the space between groups disappearing. By noon the road was as full as it had been a few days out of the city. News of the roadblock caught them by surprise. It was a few kilometers down the road, and all the refugees were being searched.

Walter wheeled the cart ten meters off the road. "We'll stop here for the day," he told Katie.

"It's barely early afternoon," she said. "Are you crazy?"

"I'm going to take a nap." He lay down, his head cradled on his hands in the shade of the cart, and closed his eyes. In a few minutes he was asleep. Katie sat on the ground next to him, her back against one of the cart's wheels, her arms wrapped around her raised knees, and watched the refugees walking past. She realized that over the course of the past few weeks they had become invisible to her, just another part of the landscape. She hadn't gotten to know anyone on the road, and as others walked past the spot where she sat, Katie couldn't even remember if she had seen them before.

The refugees stumbled past her, exhausted to the point of being near death. Many people didn't do any more but follow in the footsteps of the person in front of them. Did she and Walter look so lost and defeated?

Everyone was dirty, covered in dust from the road, their hands filthy. Katie held her own hands out before her. Her fingernails were short and ragged, and black with dirt. She imagined her face must be filthy as well. She glanced down at Walter. He had a streak of mud across his brow, and his face was dark red from the sun. His beard was full of straggles, and she wondered for a minute how she could even kiss him. That made her laugh, considering what she had done in the city to stay alive. Kissing a dirty face was no big deal. They had quit washing weeks ago. Who could risk water for washing your hands or face, when you never knew if you would find more?   Walter looked for water every morning, disappearing for as long as an hour, but he didn't always find it. Many of the refugees who had died on the road had died from dysentery, from drinking the contaminated water they found close to the road.

Walter's obsession with the cart set him apart from the other refugees. Katie remembered how many refugees had been carrying suitcases and bags when they left the city, or pushing bicycles or wagons. Most of that had been discarded along the way. None of the refugees who trudged past her this afternoon carried anything heavier than a coat, or a cooking pot, or a water skin. And if they had a coat, they wore it, in spite of the heat of the spring afternoon.

Katie looked at Walter again. She had a sudden realization that this was the first time she had ever seen him asleep. He was always the last to fall asleep at night and the first to wake up. Seeing him asleep... not just asleep, but looking relaxed, was a bit of a shock. His bound up energy, the sense of impending explosion, was almost entirely absent. He looked like a normal man.

Who was he? Katie spent most of her days trying to figure it out. She had given up the fantasy that he was a resistance fighter. He seemed indifferent to the war and didn't care who won or lost. All of the death they saw didn't touch him. She still couldn't understand how he seemed to have no feelings about the men he had killed. Six men! Did he hide his feelings so deeply that she could never find them, or did he just not care?

She hadn't met any other camp survivors to know if they were all like him.

But she didn't think so. By his own admission he hadn't been in the camp very long. Katie felt guilty; she had even wondered if the tattoo was a fake. But why would anyone do that? She wondered if he was a deserter. He wasn't a coward, so he wouldn't have run away in fear. Maybe he just grew tired of killing and walked away when he knew all was lost.

Katie sighed. She guessed it didn't really matter who he had been, but who he was now. Not knowing his past didn't take away from the fact that being with Walter made her feel safe. But it was more than just being safe. He treated her like she was an adult. Part of her success in the city was the number of men who had wanted her to be not quite an adult, men who had been turned on by her powerlessness, but that wasn't Walter. He didn't see her as powerless, and didn't want her to be a child. He knew what she had done and he approved that she had done what she needed to survive. He gave her a conduit to release all of her guilt and grief and rage. He respected her.

Well, to a point. He still did whatever he wanted to do. He was clearly in charge.

But he did treat her like an adult. He listened when she tried to teach him about the faith. He argued with her and expected her to hold up her end of the argument. He demanded she be like him and then accepted those places where she refused.

Katie thought she was falling in love with him. She knew that was a problem. He didn't want her, he wanted Sarah. She didn't know what she would do once they found Sarah, but she guessed she could be in love with him until they did. He didn't love her, but that was okay. None of her customers had loved her, except maybe Matilde, who she hadn't been able to love back. What goes around comes around.

She must have drifted off to sleep because suddenly she was aware of Walter standing above her, watching the refugees walking past the wagon, eating from a big piece of summer sausage. Katie sat up, a feeling of panic in her chest.

"What are you doing?"

"Eating. Do you want some?" He squatted on his heels and offered her a piece of the sausage.

"You're eating in front of the others. Won't that make them want what we have?"

"I am prepared to share," Krang said solemnly.

"You, share? When we share with others we have nothing left for ourselves, isn't that right? That's what you've been telling me ever since we started out."

Krang nodded. "Correct, but selfish. Come eat."

"I don't understand you."

"Look," Krang said as he sat down against the wagon, "when we get to the roadblock, they'll confiscate anything they think is excessive, including our food. We might as well give it away as be shot for hoarding."

"Be shot?"

"Haven't you noticed the signs forbidding the hoarding of food?"

"Sure. But they'd shoot us?"

Krang shrugged. "Who knows? This is a different world than the one we lived in a month ago. There were no laws in the City after it fell, but there are here. I'm not willing to chance that hoarding food is one of the many things punishable by death under martial law."

"So we're going to give away our food?'

"Give it away, or sell it. Barter it. Even throw it away. Whatever you want. It just can't be in the cart when we get to the roadblock. I'm putting you in charge of getting rid of it."

Katie took a piece of sausage from him and slowly chewed it. She thought about all the times she had sold herself in the city for nothing more than enough money to buy a piece of sausage and a cup of tea. She was the one with food and resources now, the one who could demand to be serviced for a bite to eat. She didn't understand how things had changed so quickly, that none of these people had any hold on her, no power over her. She had power now, and couldn't imagine using it. Couldn't imagine forcing people to debase themselves for one of her tins of meat. Not even if she came across someone who had used her in the City. Did that mean she was still really powerless?

When the sun was low on the western horizon, casting long shadows from the trees, Katie pulled all of their food from the bottom of the wagon. They had several pounds of cured sausages and the small ham, and perhaps twenty tins of meat. Katie set aside enough food for two days, and cut the rest into smaller portions, dropping it all into a canvas bag. She found herself standing nervously at the edge of the road, uncertain of what to do. She hadn't really talked to anyone other than Walter in the month they had been on the road. She suddenly felt shy, and could feel her heart pounding in her chest.

Katie looked at the refugees camped in scattered groups along the road and realized she didn't trust them. She could feel Walter's world view pressing down upon her. To her left was a larger group huddled around a small fire. Several adults, ranging from her age to her grandparent's. Three young children dozed by the fire. Her heart racing, Katie stepped into the circle of their camp. She squatted down by a young woman she assumed was the children's mother.

The woman looked up, alarmed at the intrusion. One of the men stood, a knife in his hand. Katie shook her head at him and held out the small ham.

The woman looked exhausted, as if each day's walk was slowly eroding her life.

"What's this?" the woman said, looking at the ham.

"We've extra," Katie said. "Please take it."

The woman looked Katie up and down, a look of disgust on her face. "You think we want your food? Now? Who'd you fuck to get it? Or did you kill someone?"

The man with the knife raised his hand, asking Katie not to bolt. "Please leave the ham and go."

The woman turned on her husband. "I don't want the whore's food just because of a road block. I hope she gets shot."

"We want the food. The children need it. We all need it."

"And where do you think a ham comes from, out here?"

"Doesn't matter where it comes from. Please leave it miss, and go."

Katie set the ham down and rose. She could feel her cheeks burning. She wanted to run away and hide. To just throw the food away and forget them all. She turned away from the group.

"Thank you, miss." the man said softly as she walked away.

Katie went quietly down the line of refugees camped along the road, offering just enough food for each person in the group to have something. She was stung by the lack of appreciation, and the accusing looks of those who accepted her gifts. Several refugees refused to take any food from her. By the time she returned to the wagon she was in tears.

"They hate me," she told Walter. "They all knew I had been keeping food from them, and that I was only sharing now because of the roadblock."

"They knew they would have done the same thing," Walter reassured her. "We have been selfish, but being selfish was the right thing to do. You just confronted them with their own greed."

"That doesn't make it right."

"No, it doesn't," Walter said. "And it doesn't make it wrong, either."

The sun seemed to take forever to set. Krang chafed at the idea of just sitting until it was dark. He wanted Katie to believe that everything was going to be okay in the morning; to believe that roadblock wasn't a real problem. He knew this was likely the place his past caught up with him. He had to assume they had a list of war criminals they were searching for, and he had to believe that his name was on the list.

"Aren't we going to go make camp?" Katie asked with a grin.

"We need to sleep here tonight."

Katie pouted. "But I want to be alone with you. Why can't we move into the fields like always?"

"I expect that they will send out patrols tonight. We wouldn't want to be caught out in the fields by a patrol."

"Patrolling for what?"

"Anyone who tries to sneak around the roadblock."

As soon as it was dark, Krang took their oldest blanket and laid it out on the ground, piling their weapons and ammunition on it. He had Katie hold the pistol that she had taken from Stojespahl. The others he wrapped tightly in the blanket and hoisted them to his shoulder.

"Where are you going?" Katie hissed.

"To get rid of these. They are also forbidden."

"And what about this one?" Katie asked, holding up the pistol.

"I'm going to risk them finding that one. I'd rather have one gun than none. I think we can get it through the check point."

Krang walked about one hundred yards from the wagon, and laid the guns on the ground next to a large boulder. He walked back to the wagon and grabbed their small shovel and a roll of twine, and then returned to the spot he had selected to bury the guns. Krang dug a hole, approximately two feet deep and three feet long. In the darkness, it looked amazing like a miniature grave. He bound the guns tightly within the blanket and laid them in the hole, and quickly filled it in. He stood on the small mound and tamped it down with his feet, hoping to make it less noticeable.

Krang was half way back to the wagon when he noticed the soldiers. They were patrolling the field to the left of where he had buried the guns, no more than twenty-five yards beyond the boulder. There were four soldiers and two dogs that he could see. Krang dropped to the ground. He could see their handheld spotlight sweeping the ground, searching for anyone trying to sneak around the roadblock. He was caught in the middle of the empty field with nowhere to hide. A broken hedge ran perpendicular to the road, but Krang didn't think he could make it to the hedge without his movement giving him away. He began to crawl towards the hedge when he saw a small depression in the field and slithered into that. Krang pressed his face to the ground. One of the dogs was whining and getting excited. It barked several times until one of the soldiers cuffed it. Krang realized the soldiers thought the dog was barking at the refugees on the road behind him.

After several minutes the soldiers moved on. Krang silently rose and made his way back to the camp.

Katie was anxiously waiting when he returned. "I could see the searchlight," she whispered. "I was afraid you weren't coming back."

Krang laughed, and reached out and ruffled her short hair. "That would probably be the best thing to happen to you," he said, "to be free of me. I don't want you paying for my crimes."

"Don't say that," Katie said angrily. "I don't want to be alone again. I know I will be, if we ever find your precious Sarah, but until then, I need you. And as for your crimes, they can't be any worse than mine."

Krang shook his head. "You don't really need me," he said softly. "You are a survivor. You can make it on your own." He decided not to broach the topic of personal crimes. They wrapped in their blankets and sat: Krang with his back against the wagon, Katie with her back against him. He watched her sleep for hours until he drifted off.

The sun hung weakly in the east, a pale yellow ball lost among shimmering pink bands of clouds, announcing morning had come. The broken clouds held the promise of later rain. The air was crisp and just cool enough to show Krang's breath, a faint fog when he exhaled. He had made a small fire that morning, and was sipping a cup of coffee and smoking a cigarette. Katie had her hands wrapped around her own cup.

He finished his coffee, and lit a second cigarette. "Ready?"

She nodded. "You're worried about this morning?" she asked, pointing to the cigarette.

Krang realized he hadn't smoked two cigarettes back to back the entire time they'd been on the road. He shrugged, as he stood. She didn't need to know how worried. "Let's get going," he said, grabbing the handles of the wagon.

The road block had a feel of permanence to it. Two tanks sat astride the road, a jeep in between them. The jeep was pulled back just far enough to allow one or two people at a time to pass between it and the tanks. Tangled barbed wire had been run from the road block for several hundred meters in either direction. Soldiers stood every twenty meters or so along the barbed wire, guns at the ready. A larger group of soldiers manned the check point itself, clustered around the jeep and tanks. Behind the roadblock a tent city had been erected. It looked every bit as large as the refugee camp outside the city had been. Krang could see several flags flying from a central point in the camp: the new United Nations flag, the Albanian flag, a Montenegrin flag, and a Red Cross flag. He had heard rumors months ago that Albania and Montenegro had entered the war, hoping to grab more territory for each other. Krang didn't see a Corabian or a Montrovian flag.

Krang had a bad feeling about the roadblock. Rumors were spreading up and down the line like wildfires: the most common ones all had some form of mass shootings in them. Krang had experienced the denial of his prisoners on a daily basis; he knew that the mind simply rejected what it could not handle. He had more reason than anyone else to believe that refugees were being systematically shot, yet his mind was trying to come up with logical reasons why it couldn't be happening. Wouldn't it be rich, he thought, if they stuck me in a camp until I died? He knew that was a distinct possibility. Just because the war was over didn't mean that the countries involved wanted to have hundreds of thousands of refugees wandering the countryside. Especially refugees that last month may have been your enemy, and who had no loyalty to the ruling regime. Was the war even over? Just because Mountain City had fallen didn't mean the fighting had ended.

He looked at Katie out of the corner of his eye to see how she was holding up. She seemed unaffected by all the rumors. She was watching a flock of starlings wheeling about in the sky, a slight grin on her face.

"Why so glum?" Krang whispered.

She blushed at his comment. "I'm just happy," she said.

"You're not worried?"

She shook her head. "In a sick way, I don't care what happens. But I woke up this morning and I realized that I had survived the war. Did you see the sunrise! It's the first time I've noticed a sunrise since before my parents were taken away. I mean really noticed it. When you hold me, I sleep. When you feed me, I eat. I wasn't really doing any of those things in the city. I hadn't tasted anything in years."

Krang was taken aback by her comments. How do I protect her from who I am? How do I make sure that the first time I need someone to take the fall, I don't offer her up? If I keep her with me, I'll hurt her. I know I will, because I've hurt every single person I've known. I've used them for whatever I've needed, and discarded them.

He thought of Sarah, standing before him on the parade ground, telling him what he had done to her family. Atrocities he couldn't remember until she reminded him of them. Killing a baby hadn't even registered on his consciousness. Why had Sarah forgiven him? How could she do that? It wasn't right, to forgive what he had done.

Krang sighed. Sarah was only one, and he had wronged hundreds, maybe thousands. Her forgiveness was meaningless. It's not like God was looking down on him and saying that he was forgiven, and to go out and live a good life. God was probably going to use this roadblock to take His revenge. To exact retribution. To make Krang pay for what he had done by making the girl pay as well, right before Krang's eyes.

"Walter," Katie grabbed him by the arm. "Will you promise to hold me? I mean if this is the end? If they are going to kill us?"

Krang laughed, hoping he sounded sincere. "Don't give in to such nonsense, girl. You can't trust rumors."

They had inched close enough to the road block to see why it was taking so long. Each group of refugees that was traveling together was pulled through the narrow opening by a pair of soldiers and searched. It didn't look perfunctory. As soon as they were pulled aside by the soldiers, another pair of soldiers blocked the road and waited until the group had been processed and escorted away. Then the next group was pulled through.

Krang hoped Katie's pistol was hidden well enough in the cart. He had wired it to the inside roof of the cabinet, behind the sharpening stone.

Ahead of them, a man near the roadblock stepped out of line and began walking quickly back along the line of refugees. A soldier near the roadblock blew sharply on a whistle, and another began to shout at the man to halt. The man began to walk faster, the two soldiers jogging after him. Glancing over his shoulder, the man began to run down the road. The soldier who had blown his whistle stopped jogging and calmly raised his rifle to his shoulder.

Krang knocked Katie to the ground as the refugees before them scattered. Three crisp shots rang out through the crowd's panic, and when Krang raised his head to look the man was on the ground. The soldier who had shot him casually walked up and prodded him with his foot, the rifle still at ready. Convinced the man was dead, the soldier sauntered back to his post, leaving the body lay.

Krang slowly stood, his heart beating wildly. He reached down and helped Katie from the ground.

"I guess it's too late to turn around," she whispered, giving him a radiant smile.

Krang laughed in spite of himself, earning looks of condemnation from those around them.

Katie grabbed him by the arm. "Forget what I said about holding me. You know, if they shoot us? Just run faster than him." She indicated the body with a nod and a wan smile.

"I would never leave you to face that alone," Krang said, shocked when he realized that he meant it. He shook his head. He wouldn't mean it when they were before the rifles. Then he'd be willing to leave her.

The road block operated very simply and effectively. No one got through it. Each refugee or group of refugees was questioned, searched and then marched off to somewhere in the camp. Trucks could be heard coming into and leaving the camp, and occasional shots. Every group seemed to get split apart, the men separated from the women, children from parents. It seemed to operate very much like his camp had. Krang had no desire to be put into a camp, regardless of the irony. And he was determined that Katie would not be made to suffer because she was with him. He would free her, no matter what, even if she didn't want to be free. Soon they were next in line.

The soldiers at the roadblock were Albanian. At least we can understand them, Krang thought, thankful no English or Americans were here. He slowly pushed the peddler's cart between the tank and the jeep and stopped when the soldier ordered. Katie was pressed tightly against his back. They stepped away from the cart. Krang already regretted his decision to try to sneak the pistol through.

An Albanian soldier stepped before them. A corporal, he had not seen the rigors of war. He was corpulent, his round face and heavy jowls and brow beaded in sweat. He was so fat his uniform barely fit him, his undershirt showing in gaps between the buttons of his blouse. He seemed ready to burst like an overstuffed sausage. He smelled of soap and cologne, pungent and cheap. Several other soldiers lounged in the shade of the tank, guns held loosely in their hands, a casual display of power.

"What the hell is this?" the corporal demanded, pointing to the cart.

"My work," Krang replied. "I fix things..."

"The way you people fixed this place? That's a joke."

The corporal nodded to one of the men from the tank, who stepped forward to search the wagon. The second soldier was smaller and lean, not overstuffed, and smiled shyly at Katie as he stepped forward. He looked more like a boy than a man, except his eyes were hard and distant.

Yes, Krang thought, I did bring her for a reason.

"We just want to go to a place where I can find work..."

"Shut up," the fat soldier said.

"My sister and I..."

"I said shut up," the corporal repeated. He leered at Katie, his eyes lingering on her body. "You're the prettiest thing to come through this roadblock in a week."

Katie looked at Krang. Her face was pale and he could see she was fighting to control her anger. Come on girl, he thought, have you already forgotten how to survive?

The smaller soldier stepped forward and gently pushed Krang back a step or two from the cart. He did not move Katie. He knelt down and began rummaging through the bottom of the wagon, pulling out the tools and supplies.

"What are these?" the boy asked, pulling out the bag of empty rifle shells.

"I melt them for the brass," Krang replied. "To repair pots and things."

"No," the boy said, tossing the shells off to the side. "That's forbidden."

On top of the bag of shells the boy threw the garden shears, tin snips, knives, mallet, claw hammer, rope, all the screw drivers, and the sharpening stone. He left the pliers and wrenches and small shovel, but after a moment tossed the heavy wrench into the contraband pile.

He looked at Krang. "I'm sorry," he said. "This is all forbidden in this zone. If you had entered a different military zone, it might not have been."

The fat corporal pushed Krang back another step. "Don't bother explaining," he snapped. "They don't need explanations." He stopped next to Katie, almost touching her.

The smaller soldier sighed. He then went through their meager food supply as well. Katie had given away everything except three salami and some dried fruit. The boy gave Katie one salami and the dried fruit to hold and threw the rest onto the contraband pile.

"That's our food," Krang said, "You can't take that!" He was secretly pleased that the soldier had left them one salami. He hadn't thought any of the food would get through the check point.

"Silence!" The fat soldier stepped up menacingly, then returned to his place as the boy began going through the blankets in the bottom of the wagon. He began pounding on the wooden partitions, looking for secret compartments.

Krang braced himself for the next discovery.

"Corporal..." The soldier pulled back from the cart, a look of anger on his face. "I've got a weapon."

The fat soldier stepped up, his rifle leveled at Krang's head. "Move," he shouted.

Krang eyed him suspiciously. He shook his head dramatically. "It's for protection," he shouted. "The road is a dangerous place to be. I have my sister to protect."

"Move," the corporal shouted.

Krang took a slow step forward and felt the rifle barrel press insistently against the back of his head. He raised his hands over his head and stumbled forward a few steps. Krang cursed silently. He had brought death to the girl. He had fucked up again. Katie was cursing vehemently behind him, berating the fat soldier.

"Corporal!" The younger soldier called out.

The corporal grabbed Krang by the collar of his jacket, stopping him. The younger soldier was pointing to Krang's left forearm, where his shirt cuff had slipped down to reveal his forged tattoo.

"His arm. Look at his arm. He has the tattoo."

"I don't care about a fucking tattoo," the corporal snarled. "He had contraband." He prodded Krang with the rifle.

"The Captain ordered..."

"Fuck the Captain. He had a gun. He could have shot one of us. The rules are very clear."

"I'm gonna report this," the younger soldier said. "Refugee rules don't apply to Corabians, and you know it. If you send him over the hill, I'll make sure you get the firing squad, you bastard."

The fat soldier wheeled about. "You'll be dead first," he threatened.

"Fuck you," the boy replied. "You'll never make up for missing the war by killing them now. You don't even know the fucking difference between them."

"There is no fucking difference," the corporal replied. "They all deserve to die."

Katie grabbed the young soldier's arm. "Please help us," she pleaded. "I'll do anything, if you'll only help us."

He pushed her roughly away. "It's not about you, lady. It's about making sure this fat bastard lives by the rules of war. The thought of killing you gives him a hard on, and I'm not going to let him get his jollies"

The corporal stared hungrily at Katie. "Anything?"

She nodded. Her cheeks were flushed, and she took a deep breath. Krang could see her calculating in her head, comparing the roadblock to what she had done in the city. She took another breath, stood a little taller, making her breasts more prominent. Her face became a mask, the smile a lie.

Krang felt the gun against the back of his head. "Walk, fucker. To the third tent across the yard."

Krang took a step forward. Katie walked with him. The corporal never lowered his rifle, but followed. The smaller soldier was still arguing with him. The group crossed the yard quickly.

"What the fuck do you think you're doing?" the young soldier hissed.

"I'm gonna make sure that they get taken care of personally. She wants to help, so I'm going to let her."

"You're sick." the soldier said. "I'll have no part of this."

"No, don't go," Katie said, grabbing the younger man's hand. "I want you to be there. I want to thank you for helping us, really I do."

Krang stopped outside the door to the tent. It was a standard army issued tent, large enough to sleep a squad. The fat soldier pushed him with the rifle, but Krang didn't move.

"I can't be part of this," the soldier said. "I'm not like him."

Katie reached out and touched him on the arm. "I know you're not."

The fat soldier pushed Krang again, but Krang refused to move. The corporal raised the rifle and slammed the butt of it into the base of Krang's neck, knocking him to the ground.

"Shoot me now," Krang snarled from his knees. "I'm not going in unless he agrees to come in. I'll not have you use her and then kill us anyway."

The corporal giggled. Krang thought it was the most chilling sound he had ever heard.

The boy shoved the corporal. "You fuck. I should cut your throat right now."

The fat soldier swung the rifle around, holding it at ready. "I'm not afraid to shoot you, Liask. You think because you saw combat that you're better than me?

You got busted down to private for what you did, so don't talk to me. You're a butcher. You had no conscience at all, so don't pretend that you've found one now. You'd fuck her if you'd thought of it. Nothing ever stopped you before."

The young soldier seemed to deflate. He pushed past Katie towards the tent.

"I know who I am," he said, stopping by the corporal. "And I know that I am more than capable of killing you, if you hurt either one of them."

The corporal looked at him. "Fair enough," he said with a grin, pushing Katie past them into the tent.

The younger soldier held Krang back for a minute, looked at him and shrugged. "I'm sorry."

Krang nodded, and stepped into the tent. Katie was already on her knees, unbuttoning the corporal's trousers.

"Why the fuck did you tell them I was your sister?"

Krang was taken aback by Katie's anger.

"I was trying to protect you..."

"By pimping for me? I don't want that from you. Don't you want me anymore?"

Krang looked at her intently, in the tent's half light. Slowly he shook his head. "No."

"Bullshit," Katie hissed. She stepped forward and began hitting him in the chest and face, again and again.

Krang just stood there, letting her blows rain down upon him, until she stopped. He wrapped her in his arms and held her while she cried.

"Why don't you want me? Is it really about your fucking Sarah??"

Krang shook his head. "No. I don't want you in my life because I don't want you to get hurt. I don't want you to be guilty by association. I don't want any more of what happened today. And everywhere I go this kind of shit follows me."

"Isn't that my decision? To be willing to risk it?"

"I don't have to let you walk into this. I don't want you to get hurt."

Katie stepped back and looked up at him, her eyes wet with tears. "You've saved me from more of this than either of us will ever know, but I understand that you can't stop it all..."

Krang shook his head. "I don't want to be your savior fuck, if you know what I mean. I don't want to be a replacement for these bastards..."

"That's not what I was saying," Katie interrupted. "I'm not the girl who lived on the streets anymore. I'm not here because you forced me to come with you. I could just walk away from you in the middle of the night. Or shoot you. I'm here with you because I like being here with you. I like you."

Krang nodded. "I don't want you to like me. I'm not a person you can afford to like..."

Katie smiled. "You're sweet. It's about Sarah, I know. You're committed to finding her. I'll help you do that, and then I'll disappear. It's still better for me than being alone now."

"You don't need me."

"And you don't need me. It's perfect." She stepped away from him and began rummaging through a duffle bag at the foot of a cot.

"What are you doing?" Krang asked.

Katie looked up at him and smiled radiantly. "The bastards took all of our stuff. I'm taking it back."

Chapter Nine

The dim light of the tent, and the warm, closed air reminded Katie of summer afternoons in her father's church, when she had just wanted him to shut up and let everyone go. She was suddenly tired and wished it was safe to lay on one of the cots and take a short nap. She grabbed a duffel bag from under one of the cots and dumped it out on the floor and rummaged through the contents, pulling out several pairs of socks and cotton undershorts. The undershorts would be too big for her, but at least they would be clean.

Katie saw a tin flask lying in the gear that had come out of the duffel bag. She opened it and sniffed. Some kind of alcohol, stronger than wine. She took a gulp, coughing as the liquid burned down her throat. Katie sputtered and choked, but the booze cut through the cloying taste of the fat soldier's cum. She had tried to blow the second soldier as well, but he wouldn't let her, even though she had seen his cock pressing against his trousers.

Katie took a second drink from the flask, swishing the liquid around in her mouth and then spat it out on the floor of the tent. She offered the flask to Walter. As he drank it, she wondered what would be different between them. Would he refuse her, now that he had seen her with another man? Or was he like some of the men who had bought her, who got more excited by watching her fuck someone else first? Or was he truly indifferent to what she did?

Katie rummaged through every duffel bag in the tent, while Walter kept watch at the door. She took two canteens, matches, foot powder, two t-shirts for her and underclothes for him. She also took a jacket that was lying on one of the cots, and two mess kits. Then she took as many tins of rations as she could find. Everything was shoved into the duffel bag she had emptied.

Even with the rations, the bag wasn't very heavy. Katie slipped the straps over her shoulders and nodded to Walter. He opened the door a few inches and peered out, then grabbed Katie by the hand and pulled her out of the tent. The bright sunlight blinded Katie after the dimness of the tent. She blinked rapidly, squinting against the sun, until her eyes adjusted to the light.

The second soldier had told them to follow the main road through the camp and then south towards Corabia. He had given them a yellow pass that guaranteed free passage; Katie held it in her free hand, so everyone could see it, but no one paid any attention to them.

The camp was huge and chaotic. Makeshift canvas barracks, mostly behind barbed wire fences, ran for as far as she could see. Trucks rumbled past them on the road, and soldiers were everywhere. Thousands of people seemed to be crammed into the camp; all of them must be rushing about or being marched from one place to another.

The sense of desperation was overwhelming. So many people were talking or arguing at once, everywhere it seemed, creating a deafening buzz that was only interrupted by the horns on the trucks as they tried to clear the road. The looks of misery on her fellow travelers faces had been replaced by terror. Katie wanted to run away and she had been told she was free. Refugees stared accusingly at Katie and Walter as they walked freely through the camp while the refugees were huddled together under guard. Cutting through the cacophony was the crisp report of gunshots, coming in sudden bursts, as if by firing squad.

Katie didn't think she could last a day in this place. On the streets of the City, she had always had an out. Even dead end alleys had doors and windows in them. Someone was always willing to help you for a fuck or a blow job. Even if it had only been an illusion, there had always been a sense of freedom, but this place offered nothing.

After ten minutes of walking, the barracks ended. The camp became more depot than camp, with caravans of supply trucks lined up and ready to go. Pallets of supplies and stacks of mortar shells filled the empty fields. Trucks, moving in long lines like giant green ants, kept bringing more supplies into the depot, or left, their beds filled with unhappy refugees. The chaos of the camp just faded away, without a fence, or guard post, or any defined end, the pallets of supplies becoming more haphazard until there were no more. They walked on the berm to avoid the speeding trucks. After a kilometer or so the road switch-backed up a hill, rising a few hundred feet above the plain on which the camp was situated.

Katie was suddenly exhausted, as tired as she could remember being since they left the city. The climb up the hill was just too much. She felt the duffel bag weighing her down and wanted to dump it by the side of the road. She could feel tears running down her cheeks, but didn't understand why she was crying. The afternoon sun was too warm. She stumbled, falling to her hands and knees. Walter pulled her up, and took the duffel bag from her back. He took her by the hand and pulled her off the road, making her sit in the shade of two pine trees. Walter made her drink from one of the canteens. The water was sweet and still cool, and she closed her eyes wishing she were floating in a pool of cool water. Floating forever, never having to take another step.

"We'll stay here tonight," Walter said. He pulled one of the tins of rations from the duffel bag and made her eat it. Katie was still tired when she finished, but she felt better. She had quit crying, and that overwhelming sense of despair was disappearing.

"What is that place?" she asked. "It's not a refugee camp."

"No, it's not," Walter agreed. "It's more like the camp I was at, but not exactly the same either. I guess they're hunting down soldiers who are trying to get away, or maybe even all the men who could be soldiers. Men of a certain age."

"And they're killing them?"

Walter shrugged. "All of them? I don't know. They're killing some of them, but how many, I don't know."

"We were almost killed, weren't we?"

"The pistol was a mistake," Walter said. "I'm sorry."

"Why are they doing this?" Katie couldn't get her head around what she was seeing. Suddenly she was very aware that her family was gone, having disappeared into something just like this. Was there any hope they were still alive?

"Why not? Revenge? Fear? Who the hell can say? Those were Albanian soldiers. Maybe they want this hell hole for themselves."

"Don't tell me that you can ignore this, after being in one of those camps? We have to do something about it."

"I don't know what I think, to tell you the truth. All of those people don't deserve to be treated this way, but I can tell you that some of them do."

"How can you say that? No one ever deserves to be treated like that." Walter wasn't listening to her. He had a puzzled look on his face like he was miles away.

"Walter?"

"Sorry." He shrugged again. "I don't know what you want to do about this, except throw your own life away. They won't hesitate to kill you if you interfere."

"Are our lives worth anything in the face of this?"

Walter grabbed her by the arms, pulling her towards him. She could see the flash of anger in his eyes and for some reason it comforted her. He was back to normal.

"Your life is always worth something. You are the future, for someone. I'm not. You survived the war, and I didn't, or I shouldn't have. I don't feel anything about that camp. I don't feel bad for those people. You can throw your life away, but it won't make any difference. If you want to sacrifice yourself, do it when someone will benefit. No one benefits now."

Katie stared at him, blinking back tears, not saying anything.

"I'm amazed that you can feel anything for these people who did so much to you."

Katie began to cry. "They didn't do anything to me. I sold myself. I betrayed myself because I was afraid to die. It wasn't anything they did. It was the war."

Walter pulled her to him, hugging her tightly, letting her cry herself out. The afternoon sun was warm, and Katie felt a comfortable sense of drowsiness. She let him hold her until she fell asleep.

Krang wished he had a cigarette, but they hadn't found any among the soldier's gear. The whole encounter at the roadblock had been one big fuck-up. He knew he should simply be happy they were still alive, but he wasn't happy at all. He was acting out of character and it bothered him.

He didn't understand this girl and why so much mattered to her. Why she felt so much. As he stroked her short hair, he wondered what had happened to change him. Was it Sarah? Or Katie herself? Something had ruined him. God set me up, he thought. God made me change just to hurt me, the bastard. I would have preferred a bullet to this.

If Emma had been crying, I would have left. I sure as hell wouldn't have comforted her. I won't be able to protect myself, or Katie, because I'm losing my edge. I should just send her on her way and walk down into the camp and give myself up. Climb into one of the pens and let them discover me and shoot me. Krang shook his head. Katie is getting to me, making me forget who I am. I am the bastard son of a bastard God, and I survived. I have a task to complete before I die: to prove to Sarah that she should have minded her own damn business and left me to my fate.

Krang dozed fitfully. He wanted to be on the road, putting miles between them and the camp. He half believed the fat corporal would change his mind and send a patrol out to hunt them down. But Katie had reached a breaking point, and was on the edge of being catatonic. How many times had Krang see prisoners endure the most horrific punishments and then go to sleep? Sleep had been the best defense some of them had against him.

Krang knew he could step right back into that camp and become *the guard* again. He had felt the call of it at the roadblock, his heart quickening. There was something so seductive about being in control of all those people. He didn't even want to think about it. He sighed, and closed his eyes, and made it through a miserable night. He drifted in and out of sleep. For the first time since his escape he felt overwhelmed. How do you survive what I have lived? Life cannot ever be as vivid as it was. Why bother?

Katie slept soundly through the night, not waking once. Krang gave up trying to sleep an hour or more before morning. He watched the girl sleeping. She looked peaceful but he was in a foul mood. She was weighing him down. He wanted to be through with her. When she woke, she smiled at him eagerly, her hand brushing the front of his pants, but Krang pushed it away. He was in no mood for her today. No mood for anything.

126

Breakfast was eaten in silence. By the time they had finished eating the road south was busy with trucks coming and going. They packed up the duffel bag and headed back towards the road.

I don't want to drive a fucking truck for the rest of my life, Krang thought, watching the convoys racing away. What I want is what I had in the camp and that's gone forever. When they reached the road he pulled the pass they had gotten from the fat corporal from his pocket and pressed it into Katie's hand.

"Take this," he said brusquely. "This may be good with the soldiers, but what about the locals? They'll know why we got through the roadblock and may not like it. I want to go back into the camp this morning, and steal a gun."

Katie nodded. "Okay, let's go."

"No, you can't come with me. I can pass as a soldier, and I have the tattoo, so if I get caught, I'll be okay. If you get caught, we can't believe we'll get another chance like yesterday." Krang paused for a moment. "You go ahead and start south, and I'll catch up to you."

He pointed south along the road. "See where the road branches? The trucks are all going on the left branch, so you take the right. I don't want someone to try to pick you up, even with the pass. In fact, walk through the field until you get there. That'll be safest. Figure you'll have a two hour head start on me, so make camp somewhere you can see me coming down the road. Go far enough that I won't find you until dark. I don't want anyone to see us meet up." He could hear the lie in his voice.

"I don't like that idea," Katie said. "Why don't I just wait here?"

"What happens if I leave in a hurry, or if a patrol decides to sweep this hill? You need to be out of here, because once we split up you have no protection."

"I have the pass."

"I'm unwilling to risk your life to find out if it's any good. I'll watch you 'til you're on the road, and then I'll go. I'll only be an hour or two behind you, I promise." He hated himself for not being able to tell her the truth. He was saving her life, whether she wanted him to or not.

Krang kissed her on the forehead, turned her around and gave her a little push. He watched her cross the field, her shoulders shaking as she cried. Krang watched her until she had reached the split in the road and taken the right branch. He turned and walked north along the road until he was at the top of the hill overlooking the giant camp below. Sarah, he thought, I am going to undo what you have done.

As Krang made his way down the hill to the camp, he contemplated his decision to surrender. Surrendering was the same as swallowing a bullet. But Krang had known from his first day at the camp that death was the only way out. Death had seemed a reasonable trade off for being *the guard*. He had never objected. The life he led now was never part of the equation. Sarah had changed him. He had accepted her gift without ever considering the cost: once he decided he might actually survive, the world had power over him, just as he had had power over the men and women in his camp. Now that he wanted Katie to survive, he was compromised even more.

There was truly only one solution to his dilemma. Krang had to choose when he died. Death wasn't so bad when it was your choice. It was just that simple.

And Katie was safer without him. Krang thought about that for a long time. She was safe from being punished for his crimes, that was true, but was she really safe? How could any seventeen year old be safe in this madness? But she wasn't really safe with him, either. That was the real problem. Krang knew he couldn't protect her. Sooner or later, he would fail. And then he would have to watch her suffer, like he had watched her blow that fat bastard in the tent. Krang knew he couldn't take it. He was unable to stand with Katie and just be with her if something bad was happening. He was a coward.

Krang spat, a bitter taste in his mouth. He was so fucked up now, doubting himself. He wasn't *the guard* anymore, but he didn't know who the fuck he was. He wasn't any different from anyone else now. And it sucked.

Once in the camp, Krang made his way directly to the processing area. He marched as quickly as he could past the flat bed trucks filled with crying refugees that lumbered through the mud towards an unknown destination. No soldier tried to stop him. The closer he got to the processing area, the more alive he felt. Adrenaline began rushing through his body, making him feel stronger and quicker.

I haven't changed, he thought with a smile. Sarah, you were wrong about me, wrong about yourself. You should have accepted your anger, rather than being ashamed of it. You should have wanted to pull the trigger, rather than spare me from it.

The muddy track Krang followed opened up onto a scene of total bedlam. The cries of the refugees, some in anger, some in fear, filled the air. The fear was such a palpable thing. No one wanting to step over the line that guaranteed death, but the refugees seethed at the idea that their meekness might deliver it all the same. Krang smiled to himself: he was home.

A group of soldiers huddled together, warming themselves against the morning cold in front of fire burning in a metal barrel. The barrel glowed red-white at the bottom, gradually changing to a dull brown near the top. Krang walked directly towards the soldiers, his heart lifting. He owed God a life and would pay it now, and be done with it all. He would never have to watch, impotently, as Katie suffered. That was freedom enough.

Krang slapped one of the soldiers on the back. "I'm lost," he said with a grin.

The soldier whirled round, his hand scrabbling for his pistol. A look of fear quickly turned to anger.

"You dumb fuck! I should shoot you."

Krang stared into the face of the fat corporal.

The corporal broke into a grin. "Where's your little sister? She wants another piece of me?"

Krang was shocked into silence.

The corporal reached out and grabbed him by the arm, pulling him along. "I wouldn't say where she was either, if I were you," he said with a conspiratorial grin. "Come on, I don't want this to get any further than between me and you. Let's get you the hell out of here."

Krang was pulled along numbly. What the fuck is going on, he thought. This can't be happening to me. How can I screw up killing myself?

The corporal was pulling him towards the line of men sitting on the ground under the eyes of a couple of bored guards. "I've half a mind to just stick you in with these sons-of-bitches and have you shot, but then I'd never get another chance with your sweet sister, and I am not done with her, let me tell you. No sir."

He pushed Krang to a stop before the line of condemned men. "Look at them bastards. They're all going to die today. I bet you want to pull the trigger, don't you?" He laughed. "Sorry, we don't let none of you do that, even if it would be the right thing to do."

Krang looked at the line of men: mostly young, some old, two or three no older than teenagers. One man sat quietly on the ground, ruffling the hair of his son. The boy couldn't have been any older than a year and a half.

"Don't be feeling sorry for any of 'em, except maybe that baby. They all deserve to die, that's for sure. And we got no place for the little kid. It's just the way it is. Come on, I've got to get you out of here," the corporal pulled on his arm

Krang had a sudden thought of Katie, and suddenly had a purpose for the chance encounter with the corporal. He pulled his arm free and stepped over to the man sitting on the ground with the boy. Krang crouched before them, gently lifting the boy from the man's lap.

"What's the boy's name?"

"Mirek." The man smiled at Krang, a look of peace and gratitude flooding his face. "Who are you?" he asked.

"Krang. Walter Krang."

The man smiled again. "Bless you, Walter Krang. The world will remember you forever."

Krang stood quickly, the boy light in his arms, and jogged after the receding form of the fat corporal. The boy cried quietly as he lost sight of his father.

The corporal glared at Krang as he caught up. "I'm in a good mood today. I won't be the next time I see you. You're a dumb fuck, so stay away from me."

Krang held the boy gently in his arms as he walked away from the camp. What are you doing to me, God? Why did you put that fat prick in my way this morning? I wanted to make things right, he thought.

Oh, fuck. There is no God, never has been. Krang shook his head. If God had ever existed, he would have struck me dead the minute Sarah kissed me on the cheek and said she forgave me. Me, of all people. Damn it, I liked who I was. I never asked to be changed.

The boy slowly quit squirming in Krang's arms. His head drooped onto Krang's shoulder and he fell into a deep sleep. Krang could feel a drop of spit from the boy's mouth roll slowly down his neck. He laughed softly. I hated being a parent, he thought. I hated having those kids around me, demanding my time and attention, wearing Emma out so she didn't want to fuck, just getting in the damn way. What the hell am I doing, taking this boy? Like I'm going to rescue him? I couldn't protect my own kids, now I'm supposed to give a damn for someone else's? And so what if the kid had died? What is one more death on top of what's already happened in this place?

The boy snuggled deeper into Krang's shoulder. Another dribble of spit ran down Krang's neck. Krang found it impossible to wipe the tears from his eyes with both arms wrapped around the sleeping boy. I don't know who I am anymore, he thought. It took me thirty years to become *the guard* and just a few weeks to lose him.

Katie walked numbly, the duffel bag heavy at her back, her eyes blurred from crying. She had been walking for an hour. She hated that she had been dismissed. She didn't think it was because she had sucked the soldier's cock. She'd had to do that, and Walter had seemed okay with it, so what had set him off? He was always impatient, had she just slowed him down too much?

She didn't believe his story that he was going back into the camp to steal a gun. She had noticed his agitation in the camp. He had been distracted, somehow distant. It was the same after they got away. His mind had been somewhere else. Maybe being back in a camp had made him a little crazy?

In spite of Walter's directions, Katie refused to go any further. She found a maple tree near the road that was just leafing and sat, staring down the road she had followed, hoping against hope to see Walter. Katie leaned against the maple tree. She tried to clear her mind with deep breathing exercises. The slow, deep breaths helped calm her.

The sky was a brilliant blue, although a band of clouds to the west hinted at rain later in the day. The field to her right was awash in dandelions, the bright yellow flowers glowing like thousands of little suns come down to earth. Some kind of hawk or eagle circled overhead, lazily hunting on the warm updrafts, never once flapping its wings. Katie took another deep breath, and knew she had a choice to make. Life would go on, if she chose, or she could wallow in her fear of losing Walter.

I never really had him, she thought. He made me feel safe, but that was an illusion. Everything comes from God, and only God. God protects me, not Walter. So if he does not come, I will go to the Homeland on my own. I will find my family by myself. She would give Walter until the following morning and then she would leave without him.

Feeling like she had a plan, Katie looked around the fields to take stock of her situation. To her right, across the field of dandelions, she saw a winding row of trees and wondered if they might be growing along a creek. Katie took a stick and wrote WALTER in the dirt of the road by the maple tree, and then picked up her duffel bag and went exploring. The trees didn't hide a creek, but a small pond. Katie stuck her hand in the water and winced. It was cold, but she wasn't going to pass up this opportunity. She hadn't bathed in weeks. She pulled clean clothes from the duffle bag and then stripped, enjoying the feel of the sun on her skin. She hadn't been naked since before the city fell.

Katie took a deep breath and plunged into the pond. The icy water shocked her, and she came up spluttering. She had no soap, so she scrubbed herself as best she could. She dunked herself three times, trying to get her hair clean. The she climbed out, her teeth chattering, and dried herself with her dirty clothes.

As the sun warmed her, she was tempted to stay naked and enjoy the feel of the sun on her body, but she didn't feel safe without Walter, so she reluctantly dressed in clean clothes. She washed her dirty clothes in the pond, and then laid them on the ground to dry. She sat at the edge of the trees and watched the road.

In the early afternoon she noticed a figure in the distance, on the road. It moved slowly, and looked misshapen. She couldn't tell who it was, but it moved without the grace she associated with Walter. As the figure neared, she decided it was tall enough to be a man, but as he got closer, he began to look too tall. The she realized it was a man, with a child riding on his shoulders. Her heart sank in disappointment. She kept an indifferent eye on the figure, until he was just a few hundred meters away. Now she could make out his features. Walter. It was Walter, with a child. Katie jumped to her feet and ran towards the road. She shouted his name, afraid he would walk past her, and he stopped and watched her running across the field, a look of amusement on his face.

When she reached them, Katie hugged Walter so hard she nearly knocked them to the ground. She began to giggle, tears coursing down her face. She kissed him, her heart flaring with desire, then pulled the child from Walter's shoulders, hugging him to her breast, kissing him and laughing. The boy rolled in her arms, looking to Walter for safety.

"Who is this?" she finally asked breathlessly.

"This is Mirek," Walter said, overwhelmed by Katie's welcome. "I couldn't find a gun, or any more food, so I stole a kid instead." He grinned.

Katie held Mirek on her hip, and leaned in and kissed Walter passionately on the lips. "I thought I lost you," she said. "I had the strangest sense that you were giving up on me, and that I would be alone. Instead, you went out and did what I didn't have the courage to do, for all my talk. You stopped them from destroying a life. You won, Walter. I think I love you."

Walter reached out and gently stroked her cheek. "I told you not to love me. I'm not the man you seem to think I am. And I won't be here for you when you need me the most. You need to start planning your life without me."

Katie stiffened, and then smiled weakly. "We're walking in the same direction, okay? And I'll love whoever the fuck I want to love, you included. I know that you think everything will fall apart, and maybe you're right. I refuse to live another day afraid of the future. All I have is right now. The future doesn't exist. So don't be an asshole."

Walter nodded, smiling at her frankness. "Right. Don't be an asshole."

Dusk was gathering around them as they walked along the road. Krang was too aware of Katie walking beside him, the boy in her arms. She was so clean and he wanted her, but he felt dirty next to her. He needed to find a place to wash. They needed to make camp soon, but some part of him didn't want to interrupt the moment. She had been trying to explain her view of Jesus for the last hour and although Krang thought he understood what she was saying he kept asking questions because he liked the way her voice sounded

"So you don't believe that Jesus is the Son of God?" he asked, for the third or fourth time.

"It's complicated," Katie said with a laugh. "We believe Jesus is a son of God, as we are all the sons and daughters of God. He is no more divine than you or I."

Krang laughed. "Everybody is more divine than I am."

Katie shifted Mirek in her arms. He nestled against her silently, content with watching them talk. "No. Everyone is a child of God, and therefore divine. How you choose to live your life may be another problem, but you are a divine being."

"I still don't get it then. Why all the animosity between our people? You haven't said anything that is so incompatible with what I heard in church to account for the war."

"Nothing accounts for the war," Katie said angrily.

Krang nodded. "And anyone who truly believes this war is about religion is a fool. But what is so different to even allow the pretense?"

"The difference is simple. You worship Jesus. We don't worship Jesus. Jesus is simply teaching us the truth about ourselves. He is not even showing us the only path to follow to reach God, for that is different for each person. He is just teaching us about our abilities. That's why we call him the Master Teacher rather than the Savior."

"More word games."

Katie sighed. "This is an example my father used to say: It's like if we went to a movie about God, and we were able to see the projector from our seats. The projector is what lets us see the movie, right?"

Krang nodded.

"Well, you've been taught to worship the projector for showing you God, rather than worshiping God. We understand that without Jesus we wouldn't know God, but choose to become our own projectors..."

"Your own Jesus? I'm still not sure I get it."

Katie groaned. "It's not your fault. There are books, okay? They'll explain it better than I can. I never read the books, I was just a kid."

"But you don't worship the books..."

"Of course not."

"But you're saying we do..."

"I didn't say that..."

"Not literally, Katie. If I read the Bible, it shows me a path to God. I can consider the Bible to be a sacred book for what it shows me, I can venerate it, and make it central to my understanding of God, but I wouldn't want to worship the Bible itself. I wouldn't want to pray to the Bible, or believe that it will intercede with God on my behalf."

"Right, it's just a book."

"And that's what you're saying about Jesus."

"Exactly."

Krang took the baby from her arms, and walked on in silence, contemplating their discussion. His mother had dragged him to church for years and he had despised her for her faith. Katie's faith seemed much more alive and less transactional. He didn't believe in her version of God anymore than his mother's, but he like the way Katie's faith lay on her.

133

Krang looked at Mirek, quiet in his arms, and then the fallow land they were walking past. He was struggling to maintain some sense of identity. He felt like an idiot: blissfully happy. Not even happy; happiness was transitory. He was filled with joy. Joy that wasn't going to go away, even if things got worse. And that scared him. He knew things could get worse in a hurry. In fact, feeling so good, so light within the world, was an invitation to God or fate or whatever power was out there to bring Krang to his knees, but he couldn't let the feeling go. He felt like he was glowing from within with the word "Idiot" hanging in the air above his head. The whole world would be able to look at him and see what a farce he was living.

Was cheating death such a sublime thing as to turn him inside out? Krang shook his head, and felt Mirek nestle against him. Was saving a baby so heroic? Could this one act of lunacy - how were they going to care for this kid? - in any way atone for all that he had done before? Was he even at a place that he felt a need to atone? Was such a thing even possible? Could anything make a difference after being *the guard*?

Krang knew that he was in trouble. It would all fall apart at some time or another. Katie would find out who he was, and then suffer for it. This child would probably pay the ultimate price for Krang's sins. Wouldn't it have been better just to let the boy die with his father? Krang wished he had the courage to walk into the woods and hang himself, and save Katie and the child from his crimes. And in spite of all the doubt, still the lightness in his heart. *His soul?*

Katie stopped beneath an evergreen tree and sat down to rest by the side of the road. She held out her arms for the baby, so Krang gave him up and sat next to her.

"Why did you take him?" she asked.

Krang shook his head. "I wish I knew. I'm not sure that I did anything but postpone the inevitable."

Katie kissed the Mirek's cheek. "You gave him a chance."

"I may have done nothing more than guarantee him a life of fear and pain. I don't know that I did good."

"But your heart was in the right place."

Krang shook his head again. "I don't think so. I think I was trying to buy my salvation."

"You can't buy salvation, or earn it. Here's a secret: your life is your salvation. Live it. You can be in heaven every day."

"At what cost?"

"If it's costing you, then you're not in heaven."

"And if it cost's other people?"

"Then it's also costing you, and you're in hell, even if you don't recognize it."

134

"So your heaven is as mythical as mine."

Katie burst into laughter. Mirek struggled in her arms, so she set him on the ground. He crouched alongside the road, watching a line of ants moving in the dirt. "That may be," she finally said.

Krang reached out and stroked Mirek's fine hair. "I didn't do it for the boy," he said. "I did it for his father. I've never seen a man so unafraid to die for himself, and so afraid for someone else...."

Krang paused, an image of Abraham on the train platform flooding his memory. "No, that's wrong. I have seen it before... once...." he trailed off into silence, his eyes closed. He could feel the weight of the baby in his hands. Of her baby, Sarah's baby. Could feel the force with which he struck the ground. Could hear the wet slap of Capek's skull on the concrete station platform, could hear the "pop" of his pistol, feel it's light recoil, as he shot Abraham. The only time he ever killed a man left-handed. What a fucking legacy, to be able to kill with either hand.

Krang could feel them hovering around him. The souls of all the dead. They were with him, of that he was sure, Abraham in the front, a smile on his face. Krang nodded to himself. They were his family now, more than Katie and Mirek, or Emma, or his kids. He had to lead them home, to the Homeland, and then join them, pay his price to them, make Sarah proud of him. He would find her and give her the baby, and show her the souls that he had brought with him from the camp. He would make her promise to take care of Katie. And then he would be done with this life.

Krang felt Katie's hand brush his face.

"Sorry," he said brusquely. "I did it for the boy's father. I did it to take away his fear. Not of dying, he was okay with that. To take away the fear that his son was going to die because of his actions. To lift him out of that hell."

He looked up at Katie, into her worried eyes. "And it did. It really did."

Chapter Ten

The land rolled so gently that the small rises were like waves capping miles apart. The flat troughs between the waves were free of evidence of war as far as they could see: no tanks, no burned out half tracks, no dead soldiers lying in the fields. Only farms spread out a few miles apart and small villages that they avoided. The farms were slowly being reconstituted as men returned from war. They passed a small number of farms that had fields of winter wheat coming up, and several that had at least made an effort to get the fallow fields plowed. Many families had at least had time to put in gardens, even if they hadn't had time to put in their crops.

They had been on the road for six days since escaping the detention camp, feeling more hopeful every day as the fallow weed-choked fields slowly transformed back into viable farms. Montrovia wasn't completely dead after all.

Krang felt as if Katie and Mirek had always been with him. It was as if they were his reward for escaping the fall of the camp. It was a dangerous thought, but Krang hadn't been able to shake it. Katie had become even more passionate, offering herself every night and even during the day when the boy was napping. Mirek was still learning the mechanics of walking, and whenever they stopped he explored everything in sight on his wobbly legs. If he fell, he would look up to Katie in surprise, but never cried. He babbled pleasantly most of the day, but didn't say any real words yet. Katie had fashioned two t-shirts into haphazard diapers for the child, and spent most of her free time trying to find ways to clean them. Krang was amazed at how quickly they had bonded.

The rations they had stolen had run out this morning. Krang had spent the morning worrying about finding food for Mirek. The boy was hungry and upset. Krang had decided at dawn that they would have to stop at the next farm they came to and try to beg food. Even the pangs of hunger hadn't ruined the fantasy of his new family.

Until now. The farm spread out below them like an oasis. Acres of winter wheat, dark green, sprang from the ground in stark contrast to the overwhelming grayness of the overcast sky. The fields shimmered in a fertile symmetry, the barns and outbuildings looked freshly whitewashed, and the large house showed no signs of damage from the war. It was almost as if the war had never happened.

Except for the bodies hanging from the oak tree in front of the house.

Krang looked at Katie. "Let's go on," he said. "There will be other farms."

She shook her head. "Mirek needs food. Unless you're planning on stealing a cow, we need to barter with them."

"Barter? They're all dead."

"Don't let your city upbringing show so easily. A farm this size needs more than eight men. In fact, since the farmer just lost eight men to the hangman, we probably could find work and stay for a few days."

"I don't like it. It doesn't feel right."

Katie laughed sadly. "Does it feel any different than any of the other killings we've stumbled across? Whoever hung those men left the farm intact and we need food. I'm not afraid of dead bodies and I don't see anything else out of order. I think it's a risk we take."

Krang nodded, not pleased to hear Katie reflect his ideas so clearly. "Okay. You two stay here, and I'll go see what I can arrange."

"We'll be less threatening if we go as a family."

Krang shook his head. "No. I don't trust this situation. I want you to wait here."

"It's not any safer here than it is a quarter mile down the road in the front yard of that house."

"No."

Katie shook her head, shifted Mirek onto her hip, and started towards the farm.

Krang grabbed her by the shoulder. "I told you to stay here."

"I am not going to stay here. I almost lost you last week and I'm not going to risk that again. We go together, or we don't go."

"I will not have you making these decisions. You need to do what I tell you..."

Katie pulled free from Krang's grip and took a step back. "I will do what I think is necessary, Walter. You don't own me. You don't even want me. You don't want this child. I know I'm playing at being your wife, that I have this fantasy of making a family. And I know that you don't. That as soon as you find Sarah, I'm out of the picture. I know I'm here because I'm easy sex, and I can live with all that. What I can't live with is being left behind. I don't care if this is dangerous or not, I can't live with being left behind..."

"I'm not leaving you behind! I'm just making sure that everything is safe. I need to be sure that we don't end up hanging from that tree, too."

"And you can stop that? I won't have you abandon me. I will be dead before I am abandoned. That's going to happen soon enough as it is."

Krang shook his head. "You underestimate yourself. You've proven you can

137

survive without me..."

"I don't want to go back to that life, don't you understand? I don't care if it's only an illusion that you can make me safe, I don't want to let it go. I don't want to live each day thinking about who I have to fuck to stay alive. I'm ashamed of who I was. Look at all the people who died for something they believe in while I survived. I don't deserve to be alive..."

"You deserve life more than anyone I've met," Krang snapped. "You did the right thing, not throwing you're life away to make a point."

"I didn't have any faith!" Katie said in a rush. "I'm only alive because I was a coward and willing to do anything to stay alive, no matter the cost..."

Krang grabbed her by the shoulders. "You didn't live because you were a coward. You lived because for you living was more sacred even than dying. You're alive because you had the courage to keep on living, in the face of horror. You never gave up. I'm overwhelmed by your strength..."

"Then why don't you love me? Why do you want to walk away from me?"

Krang took a step back, looking into her face. What could he tell her? "I can't reconcile my past with today. I can't make sense of my life. I can't accept that I have come from that place of death to a place that demands that I live, and that I somehow celebrate life. Death was my guardian angel in the camp. My constant, intimate companion. Death was my God, my lover, me. I was less than human..."

"And you, like me, did what you needed to survive."

"No," Krang shook his head vigorously. "I did so much more than survive. I fed off the misery of others. I grew as they diminished. And every day I became less human, less worthy of life, or love, or peace. And I haven't changed. I could feel it all coming back when we were in the detention camp. I haven't changed at all. And yet I'm here.

"Sarah gave me a gift that I don't deserve, and I don't know whether to thank her or curse her. I don't know if I am seeking her out to claim her, or just to know that she survived. I don't know who I am, I just know that I'm not who you think I am."

"And I'm not who you think I am. You don't even know if I told you the truth about my life. You don't even know if my Daddy was the commandant of the camp."

Krang began to laugh. That's one thing I do know, he thought. He realized that he couldn't control her. He didn't even really want to. And it was pointless to keep having the same arguments over and over, like he used to do with Emma. "Fine. We go together."

Katie was wrong about the bodies. They weren't hired workers. The bodies were only hours dead, dressed in their Sunday best. An old man and woman who should have been worried about nothing more than their vegetable garden and grandchildren; a younger man, late thirties, broadly built, clearly the old man's son; two girls, one Katie's age and one not more than five or six; and three boys, all teenagers. Their hands had been bound behind them, bailing wire looped around their necks, and their bodies dragged up the tree.

Katie sank to the ground, hugging Mirek to her chest, sobbing.

Krang stepped past her, looking towards the house, searching for any sign of who might have done this. He saw another body laying face up in a drainage ditch that ran alongside the road. Krang stepped down into the ditch to examine the body. The man wore faded overalls, and had been shot once in the face. A machete lay in the ditch near his head. Krang pulled the body from the ditch, and laid it as gently as possible on the road.

"Come," he whispered gently to Katie. "We have to go before they come back." He pulled her to her feet, and with his arm around her waist began walking her away from the farm.

"No," Katie shook her head, pulling away from him. "We have to bury them. And we have to make sure there is no one else here who might need our help." She looked up at Krang, her face streaked with tears. "What happened here? Did he do it?" She pointed to the body in the road.

Krang shook his head. "I don't think so. I think he was a hired man, and that he came out here with the machete to either cut them down, or to try to save them, and that whoever did it killed him, too."

"Who would do this?"

Krang shrugged. "Could be soldiers. Maybe they were collaborators? Could be Corabians or other refugees. Maybe they refused to offer food? Could be a neighbor down the road who always hated the old man, and saw this as the perfect opportunity to do something about it. Nobody is going to investigate. Nobody is going to prosecute."

Katie looked at the ground. "Kill me and Mirek before you let someone do this to us," she whispered. "Promise me that."

"I can't," Krang said. "I can't promise to protect you in this world. I don't have power, any longer, and I'm terrified. That's why I tried to leave you back at the camp. You have power around men, or at least some of them. You have a better chance on your own than you have with me or the boy."

"I don't want to fuck my way to freedom any longer. Not for me. I would do it in a heartbeat for Mirek, or for you, but I won't do it for myself. I just can't do it any longer."

Krang stared at her, knowing she meant what she said. "Damn it, Katie. It's a sin to throw away your life on a principle..."

Katie flashed her most brilliant smile at him. "You forget, Corabians don't believe in sin." She nodded towards the house. "Let's get this over with."

Krang picked up the machete from the ditch and followed the girl.

The woman was crouched in the corner of a darkened bedroom, cradling an infant in her arms, rocking back and forth and mumbling incoherently. Katie gave Mirek to Krang, and motioned for him to open the drapes to let in some light. She crawled across the floor slowly, approaching the woman cautiously, her hand held out as if she were befriending a dog.

"She's hurt, Walter," Katie said softly. "She's covered in blood."

Krang backed towards the window, never taking his eyes from the pair on the floor. Katie had reached the woman, her hand resting on the woman's shoulder, but the woman hadn't acknowledged her presence.

Krang pulled the drapes open, flooding the room with light.

Katie shrieked and scuttled away from the woman. "Oh my God, the baby's dead," she cried.

The woman looked up incoherently, then slowly focused on Krang standing by the window.

"No," she wailed, trying to scramble further away from him.

Katie slid forward and enveloped the woman in her arms, rocking her against her chest. The woman stiffened momentarily and then collapsed against her. "They're all dead," the woman whispered hoarsely, "my babies are all dead..."

"Shhh..." Katie hushed her, holding her tight. "I know. I saw them. Don't worry, we'll take care of them. Let me have the baby."

The woman looked up at Katie blankly. Her faced was streaked with the blood, where she had cradled the infant against her. Her expression was that of a lost child, trying to understand how her world had suddenly collapsed.

"Let me take care of the baby, and of you." Katie reached down and pulled the infant gently from the woman's arms. She didn't want to hold it, but didn't know what else to do. "Walter, help me."

Krang stepped forward and put Mirek into the woman's arms. "His name is Mirek and his parent's are dead," he said gently, before reaching down and taking the dead infant from Katie. He carried the body to a cradle on the far side of the room and laid the baby down.

The baby had been shot while in the cradle, the bedding was blood-soaked. The bullet had nearly torn the child's head apart. Krang looked at the body coldly. He felt nothing. No anger, no outrage. How could I feel anything, he thought as he wrapped the body in the loose bedding. I've done the same thing. I've killed a baby in front of its mother. I can understand why this child had to die. Krang picked the baby up, and carried it from the room.

Where are you, spirits? I demand that you confront me, he thought, and make me feel this. Where are you Abraham? When will you make me pay for what I did to your son? And you God? When will you punish me? Not this bullshit. I don't count this as punishment. Making me angry at someone else for doing what I've done? What kind of justice is that?

Krang shifted the body to one arm, and grabbed the machete with his free hand. And I don't need any of that cocksucker justice where you hurt Katie and the boy to make me pay for what I did. If you want me, come and take me. Put me back in the pit and let the vermin eat me alive. I can deal with that. But don't you fucking hurt my people. I've done enough of that myself. He continued the dialogue with himself while he finished checking the other rooms on the second floor, and then checked the first floor again. The house was empty.

Krang stepped out onto the side stoop. He gasped for breath, and sighed as a gentle breeze moved over him. Krang laughed softly. The aroma of manure was the best thing he had smelled in years: it wasn't tainted. He needed a shovel, or a pick, to bury the baby, and then the others. There were several barns clustered together on the other side of the yard, plus a small whitewashed brick building near the garage. That's either a smokehouse or a tool shed, Krang thought, marching briskly towards it. Either way I'll be happy. The brick building had small windows just under the roof line, and a pair of wooden sliding doors with an unlatched lock. Krang held the dead baby in his left arm, cradled against his body, the machete ready in his right hand. He nosed the door open with his foot.

The door slid back on a well-oiled metal track, letting light flood into the shed. Krang was surprised to see people staring at him in shock and fear. The men and women were packed into the shed, standing quietly, eyeing each other nervously. They wore overalls, dungarees and other work clothes, appeared well fed and healthy. There were maybe fifteen men and five women. Most of the men were young, in their teens or early twenties. Krang guessed the women belonged to the older men. No one said a word. Krang silently handed the baby's body to the first man inside the door, and motioned for him to step out. The man accepted the body, cradled it gently to his chest and walked past Krang, who then nodded to the second man to come forward. Krang reached out and grabbed the man by the hair and slammed him against the door frame. He brought the machete up until the point was digging into the man's throat.

"What the fuck happened here?" Krang whispered to the man, who tried to shrink into the door frame. He turned to the others. "Did you people do this? Tell me or I cut his fucking head off!"

The men were silent, looking at the floor, not at Krang.

"Well?" Krang shouted, putting enough pressure on the machete to break the skin. "I've cut him now."

The man gasped, a trickle of blood running down the machete blade. He tried to shake his head but couldn't.

"No," one of the women called out. "It wasn't us. We wouldn't have done this. This is our home."

"Why the hell didn't you stop them?" Krang snarled, shoving his victim to the floor. "Why did you let them butcher this family? They shot a baby in the head, for the love of God, and what did you cowards do?" He grabbed another man by the throat.

"Stop," pleaded the man who was holding the baby. "We could do nothing. You saw Karl, you have his blade. They were too many, they had guns, we would have died."

Krang whirled on the man, pointing the machete at his chest. "They hung children from a telephone pole in front of their mother. Isn't your life worth that?" Krang's eyes blurred over, he could feel tears running down his cheeks, but he didn't feel weakened by them. "Why didn't any of you have the courage to stand up and act? Why couldn't you have been with your friend, and risked your life to save another? If you all had acted together, you would have saved them..."

"Or we would have died." A man to Krang's left said quietly.

Krang spun on him and swung the machete violently, catching the man across his temple with the broad side of the blade. The man grunted and crumpled to the ground.

"You can all still die," Krang snarled.

He spun on his heel, took the baby from the man outside and marched away. The workers trailed after him, silent. Krang stopped near the house, and gently laid the body on the ground.

"Get the rest of them," he said. "Bring them here so we can bury them."

The man who had held the baby shook his head. "We can't cut them down. They are to remain as a warning to the rest of the farmers of what will happen..."

Krang glared at him until he fell silent.

"Cut them down, and bring them here."

"They'll be back to make sure the bodies are still hanging,' the man began again. "They will kill us all."

"I'll kill you now," Krang hissed, "if I don't have each body here in the yard in fifteen minutes."

"They'll be back..."

"Let them come back," Krang said with grin. "That's what I want. Let them come in here and meet me. I am the avenging angel of God and I will strike them down in their shoes. I have lived with death for the last three years. I am death. Your's. Their's. Anyone's who crosses my path. So don't fuck with me, or I'll take your head off. Cut them down."

The men left silently. The five women stood uneasily, waiting. Krang waved them away. "Cook some dinner, something." The slipped away before he noticed. Krang stared at the dead infant lying at his feet. The trauma to its head left it unrecognizable.

Krang jumped as he felt a hand slide around his waist. Katie smiled at him, reached up and brushed the tears from his face.

"I'm not afraid anymore," she said. "I don't think anything can hurt me when I'm with you."

Krang pulled loose from her grasp. "Don't say that. Don't tempt God. He has enough perversity already, don't give him a reason to do more." Krang sighed. "It probably doesn't matter. Your fate was decided the minute I met you. I'm sorry for that."

"Don't be afraid for me. I think you're blessed, and I am by association."

"Where's Mirek?" Krang asked.

"She's feeding him. He took to her breast like she was his Mother, and she took to him as quickly. When she heard him cry, she came out of that trance and became a mother again." Katie's eyes glistened, but no tears fell. "I think I've lost my baby already."

Krang felt a moment's panic at the thought. Wasn't the baby Sarah's? Wasn't that why he had found him, to be able to give back what he had taken? Krang wasn't sure that he could leave the child here, he had a debt to repay, and the boy was part of that payment. He took a deep breath and let the thought go.

"We need sheets to wrap the bodies in, so that we can bury them. Can you find some for me?" he asked Katie. He left Katie standing on the porch, and went looking for a spot for the burial. He found it in the back yard, between two oak trees, near a stone bench, in sight of the kitchen window. Krang sat on the bench and looked out over the yard. He could hear the cries of the men as they worked to cut the bodies down from the telephone poles. The sun was an orange globe hanging pregnant above the horizon. The afternoon heat held the promise of a hot summer.

In his mind's eye, Krang could see exactly where the grave would be. They would reseed immediately, and by the end of the summer, someone looking for the grave would need a marker to find it.

Krang closed his eyes tightly. He could see the pit from which he had been reborn. Nothing sacred, the pit had been an open wound upon the face of the earth. The pit had been as much a promise of coming death to the camp inmates as it had been a place to dispose of bodies. Using trucks and bulldozers to move the dead had reduced them to so much rubbish, of no more consequence than yesterday's garbage. The guards would shoot the wild dogs and other scavengers that came down to the pit to search for food, but never out of any sense of outrage or morbidity. It was simply a way to pass the time, a game on which to bet. They were as likely to set a man running for the trees and shoot at him as they were to shoot the dogs.

Krang could remember his Corabians in the pit stirring and eventually climbing out, coming to find him. How ironic was it that the pit had been filled, finally, with the bodies of his friends? Now the prisoners they had killed would never be free of that horrible place. The weight of his comrades would hold them down forever. If Gerri and the others were in hell, as they deserved to be, then they were holding all the others down there with them. Tormenting them still.

It was no wonder that Sarah had wanted him free. Not to forgive him, as she had said, but simply to spare herself the pain of seeing her husband's grave defiled by Krang's presence. To live with the memory that we would be forever together would have killed her. Why hadn't the others seen that? Why hadn't they forced us to dig another pit, one just for us? Then they could have pissed on our bodies from the side of the pit as we had done to them. Then they could have had revenge. What kind of revenge was simply killing us? We were all dead anyhow.

Krang lit a cigarette. He inhaled deeply, feeling like he hadn't smoked in days. He heard a small cough behind him, and turned to see Katie standing there, sheets in her arms. Her hair was so short, her face smudged with blood from the dead baby. She wore her womanhood uneasily. He had never noticed before how the child peered out from behind the facade of whore. What force brought you into my life? Am I to save one life, for everyone I took? Is my trail of spirits reduced by one every day that I see you through to the next? Or are you my torment, my penance, my future pain? Are you destined to die to punish me?

Krang patted the bench beside him, nodding for Katie to sit with him. The gentle pressure of her body next to his brought a smile to his face. He grabbed her hand in his, and sat, silently, while he finished his cigarette. Katie coughed softly. Krang glanced at her from the corner of his eye, feeling strangely like he had as a boy so long ago, when he was trying to work up his nerve to kiss a girl for the first time.

"I was always told that something good comes out of every action," Katie said quietly. "That God is everywhere, and that even in the face of terrible devastation, something good will eventually take hold.

"I don't think that I can believe that, anymore. I don't think that anything good can come from what happened here."

Krang shrugged. "It appears that Mirek found a mother. That could be good."

"But at what cost? Did all her family deserve to die so that Mirek could stay here? Wasn't I good enough to take care of him? Am I so terrible a person that I am not even allowed to raise an orphan? You risked your life to save him and all I could do was give him away."

Krang wrapped his arm around her shoulder. "You fail to see yourself as the

144

world sees you. It is an act of love to give the boy up." Krang could feel her shaking as she cried silently beside him. "The boy will be fine here."

Katie nodded and wiped her face with her hands. "I know. It's just that I'm so alone, Walter. I don't deserve to be loved, and yet I think maybe you do love me, in some small way. But I also know that you will leave me when you find your wife, and I think that will kill me..."

Krang stiffened, the vision of Sarah kissing him on the cheek flooding his mind.

"Katie," he said quietly, "she's not really my wife.... She torments me. She freed me from the camp. She took justice from God to make me remember her. I don't know why I'm looking for her. Part of me wants to hurt her, to take back the power that she stripped from me. When she freed me, she destroyed me. And another part of me wants to throw myself at her feet and beg her to let me repay her in some way. Of course, there is no way to ever pay my debt to her. My sin is too great even for God to remove..."

"No sin is too great for God to remove." Katie looked at him, her eyes shiny with tears.

"You can say that for one reason," Krang said with a sad smile. "You have not sinned before God. You celebrate life. I cannot promise you that I will be with you forever, for I have a great debt to pay, and I cannot know when it comes due. But I promise you that I will never abandon you, or leave you for Sarah, or any other woman. You must promise me, however, that you will live on when I am gone."

Katie shook her head. "I can't do that, Walter. I've lost too much already. And I won't hold you to your promise about Sarah, for I see the hold she has on you. Just promise me that you will not leave me before you find her. I will die if you leave me before then."

Krang sat silently for several minutes before replying. "Katie, I have to tell you that I'm afraid that you will die if you stay with me. I am cursed, or perhaps I am the curse. I bring death," he waved his hand vaguely to indicate the farm, "where ever I go."

"You can't believe that you are responsible for what happened here, Walter. You have given yourself much too grand a role in the workings of this world if you think you had something to do with this."

Krang shrugged. "Maybe, maybe not. All I know is that at some point you must leave me or die."

Katie squeezed his hand tightly. "Do not fear death, Walter. Death is simply a transition to the next phase of our life, a re-birth to something new. I no longer fear dying. I ran from death three years ago and learned that other things can be worse. I fear the moments of pain of knowing that I am alone and unloved. I fear

145

the moments when I am forced to pay for the choices I have made in this life. I'm not sure I have the strength for that."

Krang leaned in and kissed Katie gently on the cheek. "You don't have enough distance from the events of your life to judge yourself. The price that you have to pay for surviving the war is living. You are paying that price now. The worst thing that you have done in your life is taking up with me: I am likely to bring pain to you. I am cursed."

Katie laughed. "Now who is too close to judge? You sound like you think you are death itself, or some kind of monster."

"Maybe I am."

"Many men killed in the war, Walter. It may not be good, but it was a war. Just like the men you killed that night at their camp. As much as that bothered me, you did it to protect someone..."

Krang laughed bitterly. "I have no room on my conscience for those men. They may be the only justified killing I've ever done. I didn't kill because of the war. Rather, I saw the war as a license to kill. It gave me the excuse to act. I must have always had the desire to destroy in my heart.

"I am the closest thing to a monster that you will ever find. Do not hold me in your heart; I don't want you hurt when God claims His retribution. I will deserve whatever happens, but I don't want you hurt when it does."

Katie stood up. She leaned down and laid her face against his. "I see the goodness in your heart, even if you don't." She kissed him lightly on the cheek, and went back into the house.

Krang dug the grave alone, while the others watched. He refused to let them help. His eyes stung from the sweat dripping from his brow. His back and shoulders ached, yet he felt energized. How many more graves do I need to dig? It was as if each shovel full of dirt released the weight of one spirit from his soul. If I cannot take back what I have done, I can at least pay it off by helping others. Krang stopped for a moment to catch his breath. No, he thought, shaking his head. That's not right. I can never pay for what I have done. I can stop thinking about it, momentarily, when I do something truly outside of myself. I can let it go for a minute or two. And that is all that I should ever hope for. I have no right to ever be free of what I have done. Krang began shoveling again.

The woman stood between Krang and Katie, holding the sleeping boy against her chest. She stiffened each time the workers laid one of the sheet-wrapped bodies gently in the grave, but never cried. When the last body was lowered into the grave, the woman stepped forward and scattered a handful of tulip petals over the bodies. She stood silently for a moment and then turned and walked away.

146

Krang nodded to the men, who began to shovel dirt into the open grave. He wondered if someone should have said something, anything, in memory of these people. Maybe silence was enough. He thought of the reverence with which these bodies had been handled. The bodies had been lifted to men standing in the grave, and gently placed on the ground. The father had been cradling the infant. They were still dead, as dead as any inmate from the camp, but Krang knew these souls would never wander. It was the love that made a difference, he thought. In the camp, I dehumanized every person I saw. It was more than killing them: I terrorized them, mutilated them, tortured them and killed them. I destroyed with an absolute randomness that meant there were no rules to follow to safety and life. But humans can somehow handle that. They persevere.

But I wouldn't let them bury their dead. I wouldn't let them grieve, or love. I used a bulldozer and a dump truck and made them refuse. Garbage. Trash. Less than human. That's why their spirits follow me now.

Krang could feel the weight of their souls huddling around him in the evening's half-light. He knew they were all there, save the one or two who had been released today. They haunted him, and their silent observation was worse than the most violent attack would be. They didn't even judge him, Krang knew. They were only here to witness his life, to lay testament to the foolishness of Sarah. They would condemn her, not Krang.

The tears slid silently down his face, but he did not wipe them away. If the woman could not afford to cry for her family, for fear of falling back into madness, Krang would cry for her.

147

Chapter Eleven

Krang sat in the middle of the road next to the hanging tree, balancing the chair on its back two legs. No moon shone in the overcast night sky. He fingered the shotgun in his lap, checking the magazine again in the darkness. Krang had stationed six of the farm workers in the underbrush on the right side of the road to create the ambush. The men were absolutely silent, and Krang wondered from time to time if they had fled in fear. It was late; they had been waiting for several hours for the killers to return. Lev, the foreman, had been convinced that they would come back that night.

"Good." Krang had whispered when Lev told him he was sure they would come back for Marie that night.

Lev had looked shocked. His brother had been the man killed in the ditch with the machete.

"Where are your guns?" Krang asked.

Lev shook his head. "The guns were all confiscated years ago, when the war began. The war was not popular here. We couldn't afford to lose our young men to a war that didn't mean anything."

Krang laughed. "Do you take me for an idiot? This is a farm. You have guns for hunting, for shooting varmints, for fun. Where the hell did the old man keep them?"

Lev raised his hands and shrugged. "The old man supported the war. He..."

"So it was the son who defied authorities? It was the son who kept his workers free of the draft? The son brought this upon the family?"

"Bily was a generous and loving man. He kept the farm alive throughout the war."

"And Bily hid the guns. Where the hell are they?"

After much whispering amongst themselves, Lev sent one of the men out into the barn. The man came back with a bundle wrapped in oilcloth. It contained seven guns, and several boxes of ammunition. Krang had claimed a 12 gauge shotgun and a box of buckshot shells. He would be close and wanted to inflict maximum damage. The best shot among the group, a boy in his late teens, was given the deer gun, a .30 caliber bolt action rifle. The other men who were going had small bore shotguns, used for hunting rabbit and quail. They were still powerful enough to kill a man.

"If you're good, take them out with head shots," Krang told the teen. "If you think you might miss, just knock them down with body shots and we'll finish them off later."

"I won't miss," the boy said. "I can take out a running deer at fifty yards..."

"These aren't deer," Krang said coldly. "It's not the same thing to kill a man..."

The boy reached out and silenced Krang by grabbing his wrist. "They were my friends. As much my family as any man here. I will not miss." Krang could see anger on the boys face, but his voice was calm.

Krang nodded. "Just make sure they're not still shooting. If it takes three or four shots to knock one of them out of action, take them. But the minute one of them is down, go on to the next man."

The boy nodded, flashing Krang a nervous smile.

They went down to the road before dark to set up the ambush. The road ran in between a ditch and a small hill. The hanging tree grew just beyond the ditch, the only cover on that side of the road. Scrub trees and bushes grew on the hill, providing plenty of cover for the men, and allowing them to be positioned above who ever would come down the road. Lev was sure the killers would come back along this road.

Bily had been unwilling to pay tribute to the men, who were trying to take control of the countryside. They had shown up one afternoon in the village a few miles from the farm, demanding tribute. The first killing had been the village magistrate. Bily had wanted to hunt them down then, but his father had talked him out of it. The villagers had agreed with the old man. They were all afraid that resistance would just get more men killed. That had been a week ago, and now Bily and his family were dead.

Krang had distributed the men in the brush above the road. Krang was troubled that other than the boy, not one of these men seemed to want revenge. Lev didn't seem to relish avenging his brother's death. Instead of anger, the men only showed fear. The men were so afraid, Krang had gone back to the house and returned with the chair, sitting in it in the middle of the road just to show some bravado. And then they waited.

To Krang's surprise, Katie hadn't argued with him about the ambush. "For whatever reason Walter, you are good at killing. So be good at it, and come back to me." She said it so casually, he thought. But she is right, I am good at killing. It seems to be the only thing I am good at. Killing the body. Killing the soul. Killing hope.

149

Did God make me this way? Am I nothing more than a divine killing machine? Krang shook his head. That would mean that everyone I'd killed had deserved it. Even I don't believe that. Some of the guards at the camp believed the Corabians deserved to die, but they were nothing. Petty bureaucrats killing with a glee that was all about efficiency and helping Montrovia. Krang sighed. I wasn't like that. I never believed in all the bullshit that was put out. I had lived among the Corabians all my life: they were no different than us. And I never believed in the war. I was relieved when it became apparent that I would be hired as a camp guard and spared from the army. I had no desire to expend my life in that fight.

I killed in the camp because I liked it.

Krang thought about his first days at the camp, before he became *the guard*. He had felt nervous, as you do on any new job. In Krang's experience, you had to figure out what it took to keep your boss off your back within your first week or you might as well quit. He had known that quitting the camp hadn't really been an option. He would end up in the thick of the fighting, unless he were already working in a war related job. The camp was it.

Emma had been thrilled when he got the job, and he had despised her for it. He wanted her to be disgusted, but she seemed somehow titillated when he told her of how the Corabians were forced to strip in public and walk naked through the camp to pick up their uniforms. She liked to hear about the littlest indignities that were inflicted upon the prisoners. Krang had become more brutal in his telling of the camp, just to shut Emma up. After a few weeks, she no longer asked him how his day had been. He hadn't even killed anyone yet.

Krang couldn't remember any pivotal moment when he changed. The first man he killed had been trying to escape. The prisoner had gotten over the fence and was running for the trees and Krang had shot him through the back. He had felt no glee in the killing, only a satisfaction that the man hadn't escaped. Krang had noticed a look of respect on the faces of his comrades, and fear on the prisoners.

That was what he had liked: respect and fear. Not the killing itself, but the fear it caused. And the more random his killing became, the more fear he generated. He created power for himself. By the end, he was more powerful than the commandant. That was why the prisoners had hung Bitmeyer, but not Krang. They still feared *the guard*. A machine gun at 25 meters might do the trick, but to stand before him and put a noose around his neck.... It would never happen.

Krang looked into the darkness and saw them: all of his souls, waiting patiently to be freed. They stood in a loose semi-circle behind him, their eyes intent upon him, still dressed in the rags they had on when they crawled from the pit. He knew they were always there, whether or not he could see them. He didn't

150

know what they wanted from him, but he didn't fear them. They could not cause him harm, it seemed. He was sure that if they could have, he would have been punished long ago. They were his witnesses. Krang knew he had an obligation to them. He had to complete their journey in this world, free them from their purgatory. Following him around must be hell. He had to free them from hell.

And what of God? Krang couldn't pinpoint the moment in his life that God disappeared. It was long before the camp, before he was even an adult. The world had never seemed fair enough to him for there to be a God, or for anyone to claim that they were his chosen people. My mother prayed for hours every day, and for what? I am the best example that there cannot be a God, he thought. I have defied all decency and not been punished. And what of Katie's thought, that sin is its own punishment? What has my sin cost me? What have the deaths cost me?

I have lost a family that I didn't know, a family I didn't love. Will there be some point in my life when I grieve my children? I grieved more seeing Katie give Mirek away this afternoon than I did when I lost my children. Maybe I'm the dead one, he thought. Maybe these souls that follow me are living and I am the ghost. Life holds no beauty for me, no mystery, no joy.

"I would pay you back," he whispered soundlessly, somehow knowing the souls could hear him, "if there were a way to do that. I would release you if I could. I will dig a thousand graves across this countryside if that will make a difference. I will give my life willingly to protect Katie, not for love of her, because I am incapable of loving anyone, but because she is of your people, and I hold a debt. I will gladly give my life tonight, avenging the deaths of this family to release their souls from this place. Does it count for you, if they are not Corabian?"

Krang chuckled. He would die this evening: either himself or another like him. It was fitting.

Krang heard the low whine of the truck's engine long before it crested the hill. The driver was struggling to find a lower gear to make it up the hill and Krang thought the driver might strip the gears before the truck finally labored over the top of the hill like a pregnant sow waddling towards her pen. The truck's hooded headlights left Krang hidden in the darkness.

Krang whistled to alert the others, made sure a shell was in the chamber and flipped the safety off. He took a deep breath and smiled.

The truck came down the hill too fast, bouncing over the rough gravel road. Krang wondered if his attempt to do the right thing was going to end up with him run over by an inattentive driver before he saw the truck's nose drop as the brakes were applied. The truck slowed to a rumbling stop in front of him. With the hooded lights, Krang could see very well. The truck was a two-ton work truck, with a flat bed and side rails good for hauling supplies or livestock. Three men rode in the cab of the truck and Krang could see several more standing on the flat bed, hanging on to the side rails. Krang could see the men had guns.

"Get the fuck out of the road," one of the men in the back of the truck shouted. He leaned slightly forward across the roof of the cab, a rifle held in his right hand.

"I can't," Krang replied. "I'm waiting to meet someone."

The man laughed. "This is our road, and no one is coming."

Krang shook his head. "I'm waiting to meet you."

All the men in the truck bed had turned forward to watch Krang.

"What the fuck for?" the man demanded.

"I was told that you would be back tonight to check on Bily and his family, that you would kill anyone who cut them down. I wanted to meet the man who said those words."

The man in the back of the truck laughed. "Why do you want to meet me?" he asked, tension climbing into his voice. He rose up slightly, his gun angling downward in Krang's general direction.

"Because I cut them down." Krang knew he had only an instant to act, and put his trust in the men who were hiding in ambush. His job was to disable the truck.

In one fluid motion, he brought the shotgun to his shoulder and fired into the cab at the driver. The buckshot shattered the windshield, sending a maelstrom of glass and lead into the cab. The truck stalled, jerking as the engine died. The man in the back of the truck brought his rifle to his shoulder and his head exploded in a shower of gore. Krang pumped a new shell into the chamber and fired at the second man, and pumped and fired at the third man, who was scrambling to get out the right side door.

The hillside next to the truck erupted in fire, massacring the men in the back of the truck. The shots went on for what seemed like minutes, even as Krang pumped and fired again on the third man, catching him with a second shot as the door to the cab pushed open. The man fell from the cab to the road and lay still. Krang was surprised at how bright and loud the flashes of powder from the guns seemed in the darkness. The men in the truck bed were slaughtered. Only one man got a shot off, spinning away from Krang and towards the ambush, but his shot passed harmlessly over everyone's head.

Once the men quit firing, the stillness was absolute. The entire attack had taken less than a minute. Krang hadn't even fired the last two shells in his shotgun. None of the men on the hill said anything. The acrid tang of gunpowder mingled with the sickeningly sweet smell of blood, reminding Krang of other men he had killed. There was no sweetness here, either. Krang motioned for the others to join him on the road. He walked up to the right side of the cab and pulled the bodies out into the road. The man who had been trying to get out the door had been caught in the back of the head by the buckshot. Not much was left of his head. The driver's face was missing. Krang's shot had caught him head on. The man in the middle was young, not more than sixteen.

One of the men began to retch.

"That's the magistrate's nephew," another man said.

Krang glared at him. "Save your sorrow for someone who deserves it," he hissed. "Throw the bodies in the back of the truck."

He pulled a knife and handed it to Lev, nodding towards the rear of the truck. "Make sure they're all dead."

Lev nodded, and flashed Krang a tight grin. "You did it," he said. "You killed them."

"You killed them," Krang said, to all of the men. "You did this." Krang watched Lev climb into the bed of the truck and methodically check each man. He killed two by cutting their throats. He could hear them beginning to talk, to recount their actions, tell who they had shot. Only the boy, the one who had fired first and most accurately, cutting the leader down before he could shoot Krang, was silent. Krang could see the hurt in his eyes as he looked at the magistrate's nephew. They must have been friends at some point, Krang realized.

Krang drove the bloody truck, with the dead in the back, to the village about five miles from the farm, and was followed by Lev in Bily's truck. The bodies were dumped unceremoniously onto the public square of the village. There had been nine men on the bed of the truck, plus the three in the cab. Lev was confident that all of the men who had come to the farm were dead, but several of the other farm hands insisted that other men had been involved with the gang. The man who had challenged Krang from the back of the truck was unfamiliar to anyone. The others were all men who had grown up in the area and had known Bily. Krang left the wire nooses that had been used to hang the family with the bodies.

"If anyone else is involved," he told Lev, "they will understand what it costs to mess with you."

Katie was sitting on the porch when they returned. She watched the truck drive past the house without moving. She was standing on the top step when he reached the porch. Krang had expected her to run to him, like she did the day he found Mirek, but she didn't move, just watched him with dark eyes. She hugged him when he stepped on the porch. Krang squeezed her tightly, breathing in the scent of her. He stepped back, searching for words to explain what had happened.

Katie raised her hand up to his mouth. "Don't tell me," she said, shaking her head. "I don't want to know. You did what you thought you had to do, and I forgive you for it."

Krang stiffened, her words like a knife in his heart, and walked away from her. He slipped a cigarette between his lips, cupped his hands around it against the light breeze, and lit it. Then he went and sat on the bench in the back of the house that over looked the family's grave. Krang could sense that Katie had followed him, although for the longest time she stood silently behind him. Finally, she reached out and touched his shoulder.

"Why are you angry with me?" Her voice was quiet but he could hear the pain in it.

He shook his head slowly. "How dare you forgive me? I risked my life to protect you and this woman, and you offer to forgive me?"

Katie took in a deep breath. "I am done with killing, Walter. I told you that. I have no strength for it, even if it means my own death."

"I could not let those men return and kill again. Now others are safe. They would have killed her."

"Maybe that's what she wants, Walter. Maybe she doesn't have the courage to kill herself, so she wanted them to come back and do it for her."

"And Mirek? He should be killed too?"

Katie didn't say anything.

"Is that what you want? Someone to help you kill yourself?"

"No," Katie said quietly. "I just don't want you killing for me. I don't want you acting on my fears and angers. You take on a terrible burden when you kill. You separate yourself from God. I don't want you to destroy yourself for me."

Krang grabbed her and pulled her around in front of him. "I am condemned beyond any hope, do you understand? I have the blood of hundreds of people on my soul. Their spirits follow me to act as witness against the day I meet my judgment. I am already damned and you can do nothing about it. Nothing."

Katie jerked her hands free of his. The look of fear on her face reminded Krang of the first moment he looked into her face, in the grocer's shop. He smiled. Finally she understood who he was. She reached up and held his face gently in her hands.

"I forgive you your desperate need to punish yourself, Walter. I forgive you your fear of love. I forgive you for when the demons you are struggling with slip out and hurt me or others. I forgive you for those moments when you see no other answer but to kill. I forgive you for trying to drive me away.

"I know you think you're some kind of monster. I am too. I sold my body to survive, to anyone who would pay me. I sold my self respect, my traditions, and

154

my family. I watch my family go to their deaths and did nothing. I denied God, in order to stay alive. If only I had had the strength to kill, Walter."

"No," Krang said. "You're romanticizing what I did. Killing didn't require any strength or valor on my part. I would be a much better person if I had sold myself to stay alive than to have done what I did. I applaud your courage."

Katie climbed into his lap. "So you forgive me too," she whispered. "And I forgive you."

Krang held her tightly, not speaking. How would you feel, he thought, if you knew who I really was?

No one from the village came to investigate the dead marauders. After a day or two, everyone settled into a new routine. Krang helped oversee the field work, getting the men back in the routine of running the farm, although they didn't need him. He spent most of the day with Lev, watching as the older man ran the farm, and the rest of his time wandering the fields alone. Katie helped Marie. She brought Lev's wife, Lily, into the house to help with the cooking and cleaning so Marie could bond with Mirek. Marie never lost a certain faraway look, and Katie was sure that she spent much of her time mired in grief, but she was animated and joyful when she was with the boy, and that gradually spilled over to everything else. Once Marie walked the fields with Lev and took control of the farm they were no longer needed, but still they stayed.

Krang spent many hours sitting in the backyard overlooking the grave. He could think there. When he was working, or walking in the fields, the activity kept his mind quiet, but when he wasn't working his mind ran. He found a certain sense of peace by the grave. He would sit there every morning, and again every night, and think about his life. Even the evening he knew it was time for he and Katie to leave the farm for good, he still sat by the grave for an hour, trying to understand.

 Krang thought they probably could have left after the third week, and definitely after the fourth, but he was lost. They stayed at the farm for ten weeks. What had motivated him since being freed from the camp was finding Sarah. He had wanted so badly to find himself alone with her, to force her to acknowledge his power over her. He had needed to make her take back her forgiveness. To kill her. That hatred, even more than the will to live, had kept him alive.

Krang had never understood why Sarah had forgiven him. He just couldn't fathom it. And now, he understood even less, but realized that what he had thought of as weakness had been a great strength. Sarah had promised him that he would think of her and Abraham, and the boy Capek, everyday for the rest of his life. She had been right. But she hadn't forgiven him to punish him, to make him contemplate his sins. She hadn't freed him in hopes that he would be haunted by

155

the souls of those he had killed. She had forgiven him so that she could be free of him, so that she could find peace. Krang was amazed at Sarah's strength. He could not forgive. His strength was in his capacity for violence. The men respected him because they had seen what he could do with a gun. They viewed his willingness to risk his life as a sign of courage. Katie was right when she said she wanted no part of killing, even if it cost her life. But Krang wasn't that strong.

Sarah, what do I do now? Krang shook his head. I don't want to hunt you down and kill you anymore. But what do I want? I feel nothing. I am not truly alive, and maybe never have been. I am living a lie, one that has served me well. I imagine there is a price to pay for this life sometime, but I don't know when it will come due. Krang laughed. I am like a vampire, he thought. I feed off the deaths of others. I am a physical incarnation of evil, yet in some way I am to be pitied, because I only act out of my nature. Someone needs to drive a stake through my heart and kill me. Is that why I found Katie? Is she the one, so tainted physically yet pure spiritually, who will take me down? Will I pick at her resistance, day after day, until one day she can't take it anymore and she kills me? Krang thought about that and shook his head. I'll kill myself first, he thought. If she kills me, it would kill part of her soul, and I won't do that.

Or is she here for me to kill? Is that God's plan, that I fall in love with her, and then kill her myself? How fitting would that be, to destroy the one thing I truly love.

Sarah, I came out here to find you and kill you. To make you pay for what you did to me. I hated your arrogance, that you thought you had the power to forgive me. Power I had stripped even from God. Now I have to find you and apologize. I cannot ask your forgiveness, for you have already given it. But I can stand before you and apologize, and pray that you will break down and act on the pain and rage that you must feel towards me. I can stand before you with my head bowed, and let your rage wash away my sins. I can give you the gun.

No, he thought. I can let you take me before the tribunal, and be judged for my crimes. By a jury of my peers? A jury of your people. I can let the collective rage of your people wash away my sins. You must promise me, Sarah, that you will protect Katie. She is the one deserving of forgiveness from you and your people. You must take her under your wing, make her your younger sister. You can tell them that I kidnapped her, that I forced her to submit to me. You tell them that I am a monster, and she is my victim. And then you can help Katie understand what must happen.

Krang lit another cigarette. He inhaled slowly, watching the smoke curl lazily from the end of the cigarette. God has blessed me, he thought in wonderment. God has given me these months with Katie that are outside my previous experiences. I have never known a person, not even my children, for whom I would gladly lay down my life, but now I know Katie. It is bittersweet to know my life could have been different, but it is worth knowing.

Krang sighed. He didn't quite understand how it had come to be the end of summer, but it was. And two and a half months of sitting, watching the sun sink across the valley, seeing the last rays of light setting on the newly dug grave, had changed him. He couldn't deny who he had been, but he couldn't deny who he was becoming, either.

Chapter Twelve

A gentle fog was forming, hovering a foot or so above the ground, as they stood outside the house. The moon had set, but dawn was still two hours away. The summer air was warm and humid, but Katie was still shivering. Lev's wife, Lily, hugged the girl.

"Marie can't say goodbye," Lily said. "She doesn't want you to go."

Katie nodded, but couldn't stop a sob from escaping. She wiped her eyes with the back of her hands.

Lily hugged the girl again. "I'll make sure Mirek always knows that you were his mother for a few days."

Lev came around the side of the house, pushing a produce cart. Krang had seen it before in the barn: Bily had used it to sell food in the village. It was slightly bigger than the cart they had lost at the road block and had a tarp on four poles covering the bed and creating shade. An oilcloth sling hung underneath the cart, holding the shotgun Krang had used in the raid.

Lev broke into a broad grin as he drew near. "I've stocked it with food and water, enough to last a week or more. This is our gift to you for all that you have done for us." His grin faded when he saw Katie struggling not to cry.

"I know you feel like a thief, sneaking away in the middle of the night," he said, as gently as he could. "I've a couple of men I don't trust to have your best interests in their hearts. Men who may have been happy to see Bily and his family killed, thinking something would somehow come to them. This is safest, for you to go when no one knows that you are leaving."

Katie nodded. "Won't they try something tomorrow?"

"These are lazy men, without gumption. They won't know which way you've gone, or where you are headed, and it would be too much work to try to find out. You'll be safe."

Lev turned back to Krang. "Let's put this in the truck. I'll take you down past the village about ten or twelve miles. There's a commerce route there, running north and south. If you stay headed south, you'll eventually find Corabia."

Krang nodded. "How far do you think it is? To Corabia?"

Lev shrugged. "Six hundred kilometers. There is still fighting south of here, closer to the border. I don't know how bad it is. When we invaded Corabia, we never got more than sixty or so kilometers over the border before the fighting bogged down. They eventually threw us back, but then couldn't get too deep into Montrovia either. It was a stroke of genius to jump the lines and attack the north, and it spared us, but the south is still embroiled in war."

"I thought the government had collapsed?" Krang asked.

"It's the army that's still fighting. There are rumors that the army isn't unified any longer, that two or three generals have become warlords and are fighting amongst themselves, the Corabians, and the United Nations for control of the region."

"Don't forget the Albanians," Katie said, spitting on the ground.

Lev nodded. "Don't forget the fucking Albanians," he said, spitting as well.

The sun hadn't broken the far horizon when Lev dropped them at the side of the highway. He and Krang lifted the vendor cart from the back of the truck and set it on the road. The highway was a simple two lane road, made of crushed gravel and tar, but it was wide, smooth and undamaged, with a large berm on either side. There was no sign of other refugees.

They walked in silence for a long while.

The half-light of dawn and the patchy fog steaming from the ground gave everything a mystical look. Krang was certain that if he looked back, he would see his spirit companions trailing behind him, made more real by the dawn's insubstantiality. Once again he had the feeling that his dead were somehow more real than he was. That his entourage was more alive than he was. He shook his head to clear the thought.

"Why do they hate us where ever we go, Walter? Will we ever find a place where no one hates us?"

Krang shrugged, pushing the cart ahead of him.

"Is this what it means to be Corabian?"

Krang laughed. "Lev's men don't hate you for being Corabian," he said. "They hate you for giving Marie a reason to live. If you hadn't shown up with Mirek, she would have died in that room, and they know it."

"I thought Bily and Marie were good to the men who worked their farm."

"They were. But jealousy and desire aren't stopped by someone being good to you. I'd bet that Bily's treating those men as his equals actually inflamed their desires, rather than diluting them. And they saw his death as an opportunity to take what they wanted."

Katie was quiet for a minute. "I don't understand people. At least when I was on the street the rules were simple."

"Were they? Didn't men beat you and steal from you?"

"Yeah, but that was the rule. I was on my own."

159

"Then you understand the world now. You're on your own. Don't think you can count on anyone, especially me."

"What about the Homeland?" Katie asked. "It's a safe place for us."

"Your people were never much loved in Corabia, Katie. Corabia saw all of you as Citizens, not Corabians. They didn't fight to free your people, they fought because Montrovia invaded. What are they going to do with all of us? Where will we live? And what of the people who live there now? Are they going to agree to give up their land, for us? It could be war all over again."

"I am sure the authorities will have cleared the land out for us," Katie said.

"So they're sending us to one giant concentration camp?"

"It's not like there isn't plenty of unclaimed land all over right now. With so many dead in the war, there is bound to be land..."

"Then why do we march south? Why don't we grab a plot of land here, and become farmers and raise a family?"

Katie stopped. "I'd like nothing better, Walter, if I thought you meant it. But you aren't ready to settle down yet. I can see it in your eyes. You still have something you need to accomplish. So we go to join the others in a sacred place. And if we don't go there, you never find your Sarah!"

"I told you..."

"I know what you told me, Walter, but I'm not blind. I can see the hold she has on you. Nothing will stop you from finding her."

They walked on in silence, watching the morning sun rise around them. Krang studied the girl from the corner of his eye. They hadn't talked about the future since the night of the ambush. In the ten weeks they had stayed at the farm they had been able to live in the moment and not worry about what the future would bring. They had shared a bedroom in the main house and grown easy with each other. Their lovemaking had lost a sense of urgency, but, if anything, had increased in quantity. He had liked the ease between them.

Katie had turned away from him and was pretending to watch the sun coming up. Her body was stiff with her anger. In spite of her anger, Krang thought she looked beautiful. She just seemed to glow with life and vitality. Even her anger was worth experiencing, because of the sense of life behind it. He was sure her sense of hope would soon wash away the anger.

What of me, he thought, turning away from the girl. Do I hope? He shook his head. Hope was never good for him.

A bead of sweat ran down his back. It would be hot today. That was the most he could hope for. He thought of Sarah in the camp. Did you have hope when you freed me, or just despair that nothing could bring them back? He pictured her, standing before him on the parade ground, in her rags, a blanket around her shoulders to ward of the chill March air. He could see the bandanna covering her thin hair. He realized with a start she had been losing her hair, a sign of malnutrition. When she had smiled at him, her teeth were going bad. She had come out to the parade ground, her hand in her pocket, where she held the shiv, searching for him, and then she had turned away.

Krang had thought she had turned away because she needed to build her courage up to confront him, but suddenly he knew that wasn't true. She had been coming to kill him then, just as she had said. She had been planning on stabbing him with her shiv and watching him die. What had happened as she looked at him? What had she seen that had made her turn away? She would have been a hero to the entire camp if she had stabbed him, even if it hadn't killed him. And if she had stabbed him, the illusion of his power would have been broken and they would have torn him apart.

What had happened to make her forgive me? He shook his head. Had her mind buckled under the pressure of killing him? He saw now that it wasn't his strength that had saved him, but was it her weakness? It must have been. No sane person would ever think his actions could be forgiven. So if she was crazy, what did that mean for him?

"If God exists, then why did he allow this war?"

"You have to get over the idea that God either exists as some supreme being that controls everything or doesn't exist at all. It's not true." It was late afternoon of their second day on the road and Katie was lecturing him. "God didn't allow it."

"Then why did it happen?" Krang loved pushing her, testing her faith.

Katie shook her head in irritation. "War comes from people, not God. This war may have been fought in part by zealots who used the name of God to justify their actions, but God had nothing to do with it. God is only love. There is no room for war in God."

"But we had a war..."

"Yes, we did. But it wasn't God's war."

"So how does God punish those who go to war in his name?"

"God doesn't punish. God is only love."

Krang could hear the exasperation in her voice. In a perverse way, he felt like he was growing her faith by challenging her on it all the time. "I was taught as a small child not to judge others, for God would judge them."

"And you left everything to God?"

"No," Krang admitted with a bitter laugh. "I never left anything to God. I'm just saying I was taught that God is the final judge of all of our actions."

"No," Katie was firm. "God does not judge. God does not punish. God is love, so God loves."

Krang shook his head. "But what about those who go to war in God's name. Surely there must be some punishment for that."

Katie glanced at Krang as he pushed the cart along the road. "You've been to war. Isn't that punishment enough?"

"And you're saying God has nothing to do with that?"

"God doesn't punish us, we punish ourselves."

Krang shook his head. "I disagree. The camps were like hell for the prisoners, but how were they responsible? They didn't choose to be there. I won't blame them for what happened."

"But you think God sent them there?"

Krang shrugged.

"You're in hell now," Katie said quietly.

"What?"

Katie nodded. "You're in hell now. You've agonized over everything that you've done since you left the camp. You question why you're alive and others are dead. You didn't even travel with the others when they left the camp." She looked at him deeply. "Were you one of the ones who stayed behind and killed the guards and their families?"

Krang blanched. "No," he said shaking his head violently. "I did not kill the guards or their families, or the villagers who sold supplies to the camps, or any of the others who were killed at the end. I did not do that."

They walked in silence for several minutes.

"I escaped a day before the end," Krang said softly. "I knew what was going to happen, but I wasn't there. I got out through the pit, and ran off into the mountains. I hid for several weeks before I came down into the city and found you."

Katie smiled at him. "Maybe that's why you're in hell. You feel like you deserted those who needed you. You kill so easily, but for some reason you don't understand, you didn't want to kill when the others expected you to. You're questioning every action, over and over. You already feel like an outsider among the Corabians, and then you add the sin of escaping and leaving the others behind. It is no wonder that you're in hell. You punish yourself because you want God or the others to punish you. To take your guilt away. I know this, because I do it myself. You are very rarely here, in the present, Walter. But when you are, I truly like you."

Krang shook his head. "I've warned you not to like me. You can't afford to, Katie, or I will be your death. You may travel with me.... No, not even that. The world must know that I 'm forcing you to take me to the Homeland. I 'm forcing you to teach me more about your people, so that I might hide among them. I'm forcing you to have sex with me. No one must ever think that you choose to be with me. I don't want you to end up paying for my sins."

Katie was quiet for a minute. "You are so mysterious, Walter. I told you, God does not judge you, and will not punish you."

Krang laughed bitterly. "I'm not worried about God, Katie, just men. I'm worried about the Corabians. I'm worried about the soldiers occupying Montrovia. I'm worried about Montrovian soldiers, returning home in defeat, seeing me walking with you. I'm worried about the man who sees us cross his land and fears us."

Krang stopped and let the cart rest. He took Katie's hand in his and squeezed it, liking the warmth of it.

"God doesn't concern me, Katie. If there is one thing that my life proves, it is that God doesn't exist. Or if he does, then God is powerless. Or else so bitter and dried up that he simply doesn't care what happens and does nothing to intercede. God is not my worry."

"I used to feel exactly like you."

"And?"

"And then I met you."

Krang laughed bitterly again. "You didn't meet me. I hid in wait for you. I attacked you and raped you. I was going to kill you."

Katie shook her head. "No. You never consider what I was doing at that moment. I could tell that someone had entered the store. I was trying to protect a goldmine that you wanted to take from me. You didn't rape me, I seduced you. You were rough, but I could have resisted. I had my gun."

"You couldn't shoot me. You tried."

"I chose not to shoot you. I could have if I'd wanted to. I could have shot you, or I could have shot myself. I decided to have sex with you instead. Sex was how I protected myself."

Krang laughed. "You are too much."

"You don't believe me? I killed Stojespahl..."

"Under extreme duress. He was practically begging you."

"No," Katie said softly. "That's not true. I lied when I told you that story. I wanted you to feel safe around me."

She walked on slowly, waiting for him to catch up before continuing.

"Stojespahl deserted his post as the city was about to fall. He showed up at the apartment, drunk, wanting to fuck. I knew I couldn't let him get away. I fucked him until he passed out. I took his pistol and then I sat on his chest and woke him up. I made him watch me. I put the pistol under his chin and told him how I despised him and how he was going to have to pay for what he had done to me. He begged me to run away with him. He kept telling me how much he loved me, and when that didn't work, he told me that the Corabians would kill me. I laughed when he said that. That was what I was hoping for. I was still sitting on him when they broke down my door and found us. I shot him while they were in the room. That is why they didn't hang me as a collaborator. That and the sex."

"I'm no different than he was," Krang said. "You need to be able to put a bullet in my head when the time comes. It may be the only thing that will save your life."

Katie snorted and shook her head, but didn't say anything.

Krang looked at her. In the weeks they had spent on the farm, she had changed. She had always had a kind of hollowness, a fragility underneath her hard shell, which was gone now. If you knew her, you could still discern the sorrow behind her smile, but in many ways she seemed restored. When she smiled, she looked like she was a normal teenager. Even with her short hair. Her hair was about four inches now, and looked like the style he used to see in the clubs.

How do I give her any kind of normal life? She deserves a normal life now. A husband, kids. Friends to celebrate holidays with. How do I make sure she gets that and not a hangman's noose?

The road they followed wasn't busy, but had a regular stream of traffic. A truck would lumber past them, maybe one or two an hour, and occasionally a horse-drawn wagon. This was farming country, and the farms were as fertile as Bily's had been. Krang estimated they walked less than ten kilometers the first day and about the same the second, as they got their legs under them again. Krang didn't stop at any of the farms they passed, nor the village they saw in the distance near the end of their second day; he was content to live on the food Lev had given them and still distrustful of others. Katie always waved when vehicles went by, and spoke with the farmers in their wagons, but other than that they made contact with no one.

Late in the afternoon of their third day they saw a squatter's town, in a field next to the road. There were maybe fifteen shanties lining the road. The shanties were constructed of whatever materials had been available: cardboard, wood, tar paper, even canvas hung over a tree branch to make a tent. Several small gardens had been laid out in the field behind the shanties. This was the first sign of refugees they had seen.

Four men sat on boxes by the side of the road, staring at the pair as they walked by.

"There's no room for you here," one of the men said, as they drew abreast.

"Not planning on stopping," Krang replied. "Where are you from?"

"We came up from the south late last year. The fighting was so heavy we had to flee. I think they're still fighting down there, so be careful."

"How far?"

"A week or two pushing that cart."

"Where you from?" a second man asked. He was wearing pants that had been cut off at the knees.

"The eastern mountains," Krang lied quickly, not giving Katie a chance to answer. "We thought one of the port cities might be safer."

The man shrugged. "Haven't seen any folks from the west. Maybe it is safe there."

Krang nodded his thanks and walked on.

They began to see more of the shanty towns every day, the further south they walked. None as big as the first, they were often only two or three shacks stuck in a field. Several shacks had already been abandoned. Krang couldn't tell if the occupants had died, or simply left in search of something better. At least once, they came upon shacks that were inhabited by men who had deserted the army, and they still carried their guns as a warning to anyone who might challenge them.

While Krang was always cautious around the shanties, Katie wasn't. She would laugh delightedly whenever they saw a group of huts on the horizon, and no matter what Krang said, he couldn't keep her from walking ahead to talk with whoever lived there. She suddenly seemed fearless, with no concern about who the person she was talking with was, or what they might have done in the past. It was as if the past and future didn't exist for her.

All the shanties wee occupied by refugees who had fled from the south of Montrovia. They heard stories of fierce fighting, but none of the refugees had arrived in the last several weeks, so no one knew if the war was still underway. No one seemed to know who was winning, either. Each refugee had a different story about who had been involved: Corabians, Albanians, the U.N., even break-away Montrovian units fighting the army for their own territory.

Katie walked alongside Walter, enjoying the sun on her face. She had worried that after living in a house and sleeping in a real bed for so long that the road would be difficult, but after five days on the road everything seemed easier than before. She wasn't afraid anymore. She wasn't afraid of Walter, wasn't afraid of being discovered or called a collaborator. Seeing the farm return to normal after such a tragedy made her think she might find a normal life as well. Walter seemed more relaxed, too. He wasn't any less vigilant, she didn't think, just a little less expectant of something bad.

"So how do I tell him?" she asked herself for the hundredth time. She thought it was funny that he hadn't noticed. He seemed so different from other men, but this was one place he wasn't different at all. She hadn't had her monthlies since just before the farm. She'd had some nausea, but nothing she couldn't control. The times she'd thrown up, Walter hadn't been in the house. Marie had known, Katie could see it on her face. She had come into Katie's room one morning, when Katie was vomiting into the porcelain wash bowl and gently rubbed her back. The unexpected tenderness had made Katie look up and she'd seen the look on Marie's face. A combination of joy and terrible sorrow. She had smiled at Katie, but hadn't been able to stop the tears from falling.

Katie guessed that she was two or three months pregnant. They had some time to make it to the Homeland, but they couldn't afford to dawdle. She wanted the baby born in Corabia. She didn't want to have to risk carrying it through a war zone. When she thought of what it would have been like to have an infant with her when the city fell, she understood Walter's outbursts. How would she be able to protect her baby in a war?

Katie pushed that thought from her mind. The further south they walked, the more normal life seemed. The Corabian army had leapfrogged through some parts of Montrovia, not inflicting terrible damage, in hopes of reaching the capitol and ending the war once and for all. What fighting was left was sporadic and they would just need to walk around it. They hadn't seen signs of any soldiers since the roadblock giving Katie hope they would avoid them forever.

Katie couldn't deny the hope she felt. She didn't know if her family was alive, but if they were, they would be in Corabia and she would find them. She would have a family of her own. She was in love, something that she had never thought would happen when she was working the streets of the City. She had thought, with the clarity of a sixteen year old, that her life would be the same until she died. She hadn't even been aware how numbing the thought had been. How it had limited her choices.

The only worry she had was Walter. Every time she looked at him she saw the shadow of Sarah hanging over him. She wished she knew more about their history. Walter was at his most unguarded when he spoke about Sarah. The weird mix of rage and... It wasn't lust, or even love. Adoration? It was impossible for Katie to understand. All she knew was that Sarah was a threat. Not to Katie, but to Walter. She thought Walter believed the promise he had made to her at the farm. Katie didn't believe it. She was resigned that Walter would leave her at some point. She thought he loved her, but he had so much conflict in his soul. So much pain. She worried every time he left her alone that he was going to go somewhere and kill himself, to atone for whatever he believed he had done. Katie had long ago decided it didn't matter. If he could accept her past, she could accept his. She wasn't even curious about it now, except for understanding the hold Sarah held on him.

Katie also worried that if they found Sarah, Katie would like her and give Walter up. Sarah had the original claim. She secretly hoped she hated Sarah, so that she could fight for Walter with all her might. She might not win, but she would be able to explain to her child that she had tried. Katie unconsciously ran her hand over her belly, and then laughed when she realized what she was doing. There was nothing to feel, yet. So how do I tell him?

Krang struggled to live in the moment. They had been on the road for a week now. So much walking, so much silence. The weather had turned hot and very humid, so even though the mountains were behind them, each step required effort. Katie seemed caught up in the land around them, to take strength from the very physicality of it. She shined with sweat, and smiled when her legs ached. For hours at a time, the only sounds Krang would hear were the wheels of the cart squealing softly on the hard, dried road and Katie's breathing. She was so alive.

The road seemed to bring back the edge to their love making. There were moments when Katie seemed as wild as Emma had been. Yesterday afternoon she had made him stop the wagon by the side of the road and had pulled him behind a stand of trees and demanded he fuck her. A farmer had come down the road on horseback and Katie had refused to quit. She had begged him to not stop, to not worry about the cart, to just keep making love to her. Krang had been the one who was red-faced when they stepped from behind the trees to assure the farmer that the cart was nothing he needed to worry about. Katie had been nonchalant, even as she buttoned her long skirt.

The road left too much time for contemplation. Arguing with Katie about her faith provided a pleasant diversion, but much of their time was spent in silence. Krang struggled to understand what was going on in his life. Was he *the guard,* or wasn't he? How had Katie come to be in his life? Did he love her? What about Emma and his children? And the biggest question of all: why had Sarah forgiven him? He felt a rage whenever he thought of Sarah but could no longer determine if he was angry at her or at himself. How could she be so much more human than he was? How could any person forgive him for what he had done?

Krang didn't know what he was supposed to feel about his time at the camp. The things he had done had broken every law, every moral code that existed. He had been feared and respected, even admired for his very willingness to break those barriers. He had never felt a moment's guilt for anything he had done at the camp. He didn't know how to feel bad about it, even if he felt that he should feel bad. It was as if someone else had done those things, but Krang wasn't going to let himself off the hook. He knew it was wrong, wrong beyond all reason or excuse or understanding. How could he have been so wrong? And where was God in all this? Shouldn't God come to punish him?

Krang feared giving himself over to Katie's optimism. He felt that the minute he did, he would be damned. As long as he remained *the guard* he would be safe.

167

Krang feared that the minute he changed, God would come to punish him. By changing, he would be admitting that what he had done was wrong, and then he would have to pay for it. Krang didn't mind being punished for what he had done. He welcomed the idea. But he refused to be punished for changing. He refused to be punished for loving Katie. And he refused to let Katie be punished for loving him.

Watching Katie walking before him, Krang almost sobbed. It hurt, physically hurt, to know that she was as good as dead as long as she stayed with him. Because he was dead. What she had already suffered, her naive faith, none of that would matter. She was his sacrifice to the legacy of the camps. He had to find a way to save her. To save one person from *the guard.*

Krang no longer needed to find Sarah. At least not to hurt her. He wanted to let her go, to know only that she was living her life. He wanted to know that she had remarried, had another son, maybe two or three, and that she had found some level of happiness. He wanted to stand before her and give her the opportunity to repudiate what she had done: to unforgive him. He wanted to stand before her and feel the wrath of God emanating from her being. She should be his executioner, it was only just. Would she understand the truth about Katie?

Krang glanced over his shoulder to see if his spirits were still traveling with him. They were nearly impossible to see in the daylight, but he knew they were there. He could *feel* them walking behind him. He could feel the weight of their souls with every step that he took.

"You must protect her," he said to them. They didn't answer; they never did.

Krang smiled to himself. That would be the best thing, if she were to be protected by Sarah. Katie would feel the sting of his death, but she could become a sister to Sarah. They could heal each other. That would be good.

The moon had risen early, blood-red, and hung forebodingly in the evening sky. It wasn't dusk yet, but night was ripening on the countryside. They had been looking for a good place to stop for the evening, but had found nothing that Krang liked. As they crested a small rise in the road, a fire flared in the distance. It was too big to be a campfire, yet seemed too small to be a house burning down. A bonfire? The flames looked inviting against the deepening purple of the evening.

"Let's stop here," Krang said, eyeing the fire.

"No, Walter," Katie said, a hint of excitement in her voice. "Let's go on. I want to see who is up ahead. It must be a lot of people."

"It could be another checkpoint," Krang said.

"Maybe," Katie acknowledged, "but there are no floodlights, and I don't see any trucks or tanks, so I don't think so."

"It could be a local militia or a gang of marauders..."

Katie laughed. "Or it could be travelers who stopped together by the side of the road to talk and eat..."

"I'm not comfortable with it."

"You're not comfortable with anything," Katie pouted. "Let's just see who they are. If you are still uncomfortable, we can keep right on moving."

"It might mean walking another two or three kilometers tonight. Or even all night long."

"I know," Katie said. "I'm not trying to throw my life away here. Look how the trees come down almost to the road there. If we need to escape in a hurry, there should be plenty of cover to help us."

Krang nodded, still unhappy. It had been months since they had spent a night on the road camped near any other refugees, and he didn't want to start now. "Let's compromise," he said. "We'll find a place to hide the wagon and we can walk down. If it seems safe, we can stay for a while and talk, but we don't stay the evening."

Katie nodded, her eyes shining with excitement.

Krang looked towards the fire. He didn't think anyone from the camp could see them in the darkening gloom. He pushed the wagon off the road towards a stand of trees one hundred meters away. The trees surrounded a small clearing that would make a perfect camp. Once it was dark, they headed back to the road. Krang debated taking the shotgun with them, but decided that appearing in the camp up ahead armed might be more dangerous than showing up empty handed.

Shouts and laughter from the group carried on the wind as they approached. The fire was so big that it lit up the area around it and Krang could see refugees while they were still quite a ways down the road. He was shocked at how brazen the group was. He had counted fifteen people before they were within fifty meters of the camp.

Krang put his hand out and stopped Katie when they were still outside the circle of light created by the bonfire. There were twenty adults in the group, and one infant being held to a woman's breast. And they were Corabians.

They had lost some of the skeletal look that marked the camp survivors but were still recovering from being undernourished. All of them were thin, and their eyes seemed much too big in their faces. Their skin had lost that waxen paper look, as if it had been so thin to be translucent, but they didn't yet look healthy. Krang didn't recognize them, they weren't from his camp, but he thought they should turn around and leave well enough alone.

Katie broke free of his hand and stepped forward into the light.

"Halloo!" Katie called out, as Krang reached to stop her.

"Stay where you are." One of the men in the camp called out urgently. Now everyone had turned and seen them.

Krang raised his hands where everyone could see them. He didn't want anyone to shoot them accidentally.

Several men from the group came forward, with either pistols or knives in their hands.

"What the hell do you want?" one man demanded. He carried a heavy machete in his hand. He was short and thin, his skin still tight on his frame. Krang thought he must have been close to death when his camp was liberated, for he looked more scarecrow-like than the others, but he was clearly one of the leaders of this group. His pants were cut off below the knees and he wore no shoes.

"We saw your fire," Katie began, "and we thought it would be nice to have some company..."

"We don't want any fucking company," the man snarled.

"Shut up, Hans." A woman stepped forward from the group near the fire. She looked healthier than Hans. All she wore was a man's undershirt and boxer shorts. She was also without shoes. "Of course we welcome your company. I am Marenka."

Marenka stepped forward and shook hands with Katie and then Krang. Her eyes widened in surprise when she saw Krang's forearm.

"They are from the camps, Hans. We must take them in." She pulled Katie towards the fire.

Hans shook his head and spat on the ground near Krang's feet.

Krang shrugged his shoulders, nodding at the two women, and said "What can you do?"

"You were in the camps?" Hans asked, incredulously. "For how fucking long?"

Krang shrugged again. "A few months. Less than a year..."

"Fuck! There's only one way to look like you do."

Krang nodded slowly. "Yeah. I escaped."

Hans' eyes narrowed. "Escaped?" He shook his head. "No one escaped."

"Maybe not from your camp. I did."

"How?"

"It was dusk, the guards were being changed. There was a deep open pit grave on the west side of the camp. I simply walked over to the pit and tossed myself in, then burrowed under the bodies. I lay there most of the night, and then snuck away. I spent the rest of the war hiding out in a cave I had known about since I was a boy, stealing food from farmers."

Hans nodded slowly, considering the possibilities. "And the girl? She escaped with you?"

"No." Krang shook his head quickly. "She hid out in the city, and fucked her way out of trouble every time she got caught. She killed an officer when the city fell. Sat on his chest and put a bullet in his head."

Hans glanced at Katie sitting near the fire. "Cute girl."

Krang laughed. "Yes, she is."

"Come, sit by the fire. We can talk there." His features relaxed as they took a seat. "We have to be vigilant here," he said, waving broadly to indicate the land around them. "They don't exactly like us. Sometimes they challenge us."

Katie was already deeply in discussion with the woman who had greeted them, but looked up when they approached. Twenty men and women sat in a loose circle around the fire. They all bore the signs of the camps: stick-like figures with huge, wounded eyes. Fragile and tough at the same time. It was like looking at a collection of scarecrows posed around a fire for Halloween. It was odd to see them looking free.

"This is Walter," Katie said proudly. "He saved my life."

Krang nodded sheepishly to the group. He felt oddly displaced. Six months ago, if he had met any of these people, Katie included, he would have had the power of life or death over them. He would have used that power to degrade them and kill them. And he wouldn't have had a moment of hesitation or regret. He had never believed that what he was doing was right, it was simply allowed. And by taking what was allowed further than anyone else, Krang had created an identity. He became.

And now? He hadn't given his power away, but it wasn't there anymore. These people could do anything to him. Of course, if they decided to kill him, or torture him, that would be nothing less than just. Simple karma. Krang could live with that. It would probably be better if someone would just recognize him and kill him. It was such a struggle to live without *the guard*. He couldn't go back to being who he had been before the war, because he hadn't been. He had never really existed. He couldn't just drift through life hoping that tomorrow would be better, or at least no worse, than today. Krang could no longer marry Emma just because marrying her was easier than thinking about whether or not he wanted to marry her. Krang realized now that Emma wouldn't have been upset if he had refused to marry her. She would have simply expected him to pay for an abortion.

"Where are you headed?" Hans asked.

"Huh?" Krang was startled by the question. "I'm sorry; it's been a long day."

"Where are you headed?"

"Ah." Krang nodded. "To the Homeland. Do you know where to find it?"

Hans laughed. "In my heart," he said with a smile. "Where are you from?"

"Mountain City," Katie broke in eagerly. "There was a camp there. I think it may have been one of the first..."

Hans nodded. "We were to the southwest, closer to the sea. We were lucky. They had decided to empty the camp before it was liberated, so they packed us into a train and sent us off. We got parked at a siding for six days while transports rumbled by night and day. Our people were dying, hundreds every day. A bomber mistook us for a troop train and bombed the siding, and that freed us, those that survived." He nodded to the group. "Almost three thousand left the camp..."

Krang flinched. He felt the souls of those others searching him out, waiting to join his entourage. "This is all that survived?"

"No," Hans shook his head. "Perhaps three hundred, maybe four. We were all whisked away by different groups, and we have not seen the others since. The Citizens helped us. Gave us food and clothing. Out of guilt, I am sure. We didn't trust them and refused to get into the busses they provided. We are heading south, to the Homeland."

Krang nodded.

"Will you join up?"

Krang looked at the earnest face, skin stretched so tightly. Hans grinned, looking more like a death's head than ever.

"Join what?"

"The liberation army. I hear they are taking anyone who wants to fight."

Krang scratched his head in puzzlement. "We've heard there is still fighting south of here. Even the Albanians are involved. Why would you want to join up?"

"The war for the Homeland," Hans said impatiently. "I've studied the maps. Much of southern Montrovia was clearly Corabian at one time. We will take that back for the Homeland."

"Haven't you had enough war?" Katie asked.

Hans shook his head. "I didn't get to fight in this one at all. When our citizenship was revoked, I was discharged from the army. I am ready to liberate the Homeland."

"Liberate it from whom?"

"Whoever occupies it. They must leave. Leave or die. After what was done to us, we must have the Homeland."

"But some of these people didn't do anything to you."

"No," Hans said. "But they might have."

"So you will kill them and steal their land?"

"No," Hans said. "I am not a barbarian. I will only fight those who refuse to go. If they agree to go, we will put them on trains and send them away."

"And where will they go?"

"Who cares?" Hans asked. "It is not my worry."

Krang smiled at the seductiveness of Hans' argument. He could soon be right back where he had been, relocating those who stood in the way of the dream for a

Homeland. Krang wished that he could say that he would have none of it, but his racing heart gave him away. He could become a hero to his new people. A father of the Homeland. There was a sweet irony in the idea. He glanced out into the darkness, looking for his ghostly entourage. Would you rest, he wondered, if I killed others to take your places? Like at the ambush? Would that satisfy you?

"There will be no new war," Marenka said. She had a very intense, determined look on her face. "We do not go to drive others off the land that they live on. We have heard that the war has made the Homeland unlivable. The fields are unsafe, littered with armaments. We will reclaim it, make it whole again."

Hans shook his head. "I don't agree."

"If there is a war, old man, you will not fight it. I will not have you survive the camps to die now. And I did not survive the camps to commit atrocities on others."

"We must claim what the world owes us. No one has the moral strength to give it to us."

The woman shook her head. "I will not let you become a monster out of some sense of having been wronged." She looked at the entire group. "Or any of you. I will cut your throat in your sleep before I let you harm an innocent human being out of a sense of greed, complacency, or entitlement. Do you want to become one of them?"

Another young woman spoke up. "But Marenka, sometimes you must act. Like with the collaborators in the camps. We had to do something."

Marenka spat into the fire. "Bullshit. No one had to throw anyone into a pit toilet to see them drown in shit and piss. Not even the guards would have deserved that. Not even the one we called *the executioner*." She got up and stepped away from the fire, shaking her head in frustration.

Krang got up and followed her, stopping several feet outside the circle.

"Excuse me, Marenka?"

"Yes?" Her face was pinched, her brow furrowed.

"I don't mean to intrude. Are you okay?"

Marenka laughed gently. "I should be by now. I am usually alone in my sentiments. It requires so much energy to keep them on the right track. There is so much anger, especially Hans. Many of us lost family in the camps. My husband disappeared on a work detail, but Hans..."

"His wife was killed in front of him?" Krang asked.

"In front of all of us. Hans had snuck into the women's section of the camp to see her. He did it every few days. He had been caught once before, and threatened with death. This time, *the executioner* dragged his wife out onto the parade ground, and her sister and mother and killed them. He lined them up in a row, one behind the other, and shot Maria, Hans' wife in the head. He said he did it to save bullets, because he could kill the three of them with one bullet. Hans has never been the same."

"Tell me more about *the executioner*. Who was he?"

"Tomas Sobek. I'm sure you had a guard just like him. A perfect terror machine. We called him *the executioner* because he loved to kill."

"And you don't think that he should be tossed down into the toilets?"

Marenka shook her head violently. "No one should. Who are we to be so cruel? Do we gain anything by becoming them?"

Krang stared into her eyes, searching for something he might have seen in Sarah's eyes the afternoon that she freed him. His throat felt tight as he asked the question. "So you forgave him?"

Marenka laughed sarcastically. "Hell no. I want to testify against him at an inquiry. I want to see him hang. He and every other guard that ever worked at a camp. Even if they only worked there for a single day. Anyone who can allow such inhumanity has no place in this world."

Krang was shocked by the fury in her voice. He stiffened involuntarily, and stepped back. I should not be surprised, he told himself, Sarah was an aberration. Yet he felt a sense of hurt hearing the venom in her voice.

"Even if they only worked for a day?" Krang asked.

"Even if." Marenka shook her head as if to clear an image from her mind.

"There was a kid who worked at our camp. His name was Willi. Willi never hurt anyone. He called all the men Sir and all the women Ma'am. He threw up every morning, before roll call started. Everyone saw him. He would give his breakfast to the prisoners..."

"Even Willi," Marenka said vehemently. "He should have done something."

"What could he do? He was only a boy. If he had spoken up he would have ended up dead."

"He could have run away."

"But don't we bear some responsibility for what happened?"

"How could you blame us?"

Krang shook his head. "I'm not, really. But if you think the boy Willi should have risked his life, shouldn't all of us have done the same thing? In our camp, if the prisoners had rushed the guards, the prisoners would have won. Many would have died, but they could have overcome the guards."

Marenka studied Krang intently, and then laughed deeply. "You are like Hans, unable to accept that you didn't fight your way to freedom. That you didn't throw your own life away to save someone else. You ran away, he stayed and suffered. If he had done something, he would be dead, but they would all still be dead, too. Who could fight back in that situation? We were powerless. The hope of surviving was such a weight on our souls. No one could risk anything."

174

Krang nodded.

"What happened to this Willi that you liked so much?"

"He was shot with the other guards and their families when the camp was liberated."

"Good." Marenka smiled.

Krang shrugged. "I thought from your comments at the fire that you were different than the others."

"I am," Marenka said. "There is a difference between justice and terror. No one, however terrible their crime, needs to be tortured, or treated cruelly. But I can't forget what happened. I can't say let them go. Try them, and if they are guilty, hang them. Just don't be cruel about it."

"And what about God? Why not leave them for God to judge?"

Marenka laughed again, low and throaty. "I am not a teacher. I don't know what God will choose to do to *the executioner*. But my need for justice isn't divine, it's personal. God requires men to do his good works. This is just another example."

"Did you meet anyone from our camp, along the road?"

"A few."

"Did you meet a woman, her name is Sarah Jezek..."

"She is Walter's wife," Katie said from the shadows behind Krang. She stepped forward and wrapped her arm around his waist.

"No," Marenka said, "I don't remember Sarah Jezek."

"How long have you been there?" Krang asked Katie.

"Long enough," Katie said with a nervous giggle. "I didn't want you to have sex with her."

Marenka laughed. "I am with Hans, now."

Katie linked her arm through Krang's. "And I am with Walter, until we find Sarah."

Marenka raised an eyebrow. "I do not know whether to wish you good luck, or not."

"That's okay. I'm never sure myself."

Krang felt strange on the short walk back to the wagon. Was Sarah crazy? Was that why she had forgiven him? Marenka was clearly a compassionate woman, and yet she had no compassion for her oppressors, only a sense of justice that said there were moral limits to how you punished them. Why was Sarah so different? Could she teach me, Krang wondered, to see the world as differently as she saw it? Could I survive from her point of view? He glanced behind him at his spirit companions, and knew that they were of Marenka's, or probably even Han's opinion. Throw Krang face first into the pit toilet. Let him struggle to hold his breath until his lungs were going to burst, and in the final humiliation, let him suck a mouth full of shit and piss into his lungs and die. That would be fitting. And Krang knew he couldn't disagree with them.

Chapter Thirteen

Katie hung back like a child trying to avoid a chore as they walked to their camp, scuffing her feet in the dirt and kicking at rocks in the road. Krang couldn't figure out what was bothering her.

"Did you want to stay longer with the others?" he asked her for the third time.

"No," Katie, shaking her head. "Not that."

"Then what the hell is going on?" Krang demanded. "Are you pissed at me?"

Katie shrugged her shoulders. "I'm trying to decide if I should tell you something."

"Tell me."

Katie shook her head. "You won't like it. I don't really want to tell you, but I have to, sooner or later."

They reached the trees where they had hidden their wagon. The small pines formed a semi-circle that hid the clearing from the road, but the camp was open to the woods beyond. Krang could see the dark silhouette of a range of steep hills in the distance. The stars were brilliant tonight. The blood moon was silvering as it rose higher in the sky.

Krang surveyed the camp; it was undisturbed. He walked over to the wagon and pulled out a pair of old blankets for sleeping.

"Come on," he said gently, holding out a blanket. "Let's lay down."

Katie wrapped herself in her blanket and lay on the ground, Krang lying behind her, his arm resting over her hip. Krang knew he could count on one hand the number of times he had held Emma like this. He would have preferred separate beds back then, once they had finished fucking.

"Let's see," Krang said softly. "You already told me that you sat a man's chest and blew his head off with a pistol, but you're worried that this will change the way I feel about you."

"Don't make fun of me."

"Let me guess: You slept with women as well as men while you were hiding out in the city."

Katie elbowed Krang in the side. "You're still making fun of me. Of course I slept with women too. I slept with anyone who would pay me or who was a threat to me. This is serious."

Krang felt his cock stiffen at her confession, but ignored it.

"What's bothering you?" He massaged her shoulders gently. The tension in them let him know she was really frightened.

"I'm afraid if I tell you it will change our life."

"I understand. But why put off the inevitable? You'll just be unhappy until you have to tell me."

Katie nodded. She took a deep breath. "I'm late," she blurted.

Krang shrugged. "Okay," he whispered into her hair.

"You are such a man sometimes," Katie said. "Late for my monthlies. I'm pregnant."

Krang was shocked. How could she be pregnant? Don't be an ass, he thought. You've been fucking every day. But how could she be pregnant? How do you have a baby out here?

His heart soared. A baby? Could it be? "When?"

"At least a couple months ago..."

"No. When will you have it."

"February, I think, or March."

Krang relaxed. He kissed the back of her neck. "That's plenty of time."

"But how? There are no midwives out here. It could be months before we run into one, and that would be too late."

Krang was confused by what she was saying. "Why do you need a midwife now? I mean, if you're sure you're pregnant, what could a midwife do for you now?"

"They have ways to take care of it."

Krang didn't want to understand. "You want an abortion?"

Katie nodded. "That would be best, wouldn't it?"

Krang shrugged. His disappointment left him ashamed. "I guess this is a difficult world for a baby. And there are plenty of orphans that need families. I just thought..."

"You want me to have this baby?"

Krang was quiet for a minute, thinking over what she was asking him. "Yes." He felt her grow stiff in his arms, pulling herself away from his body just enough his chest wasn't touching her back. What was wrong?

"I can't give this baby up." Her voice was as sad as he could imagine hearing.

"Give it up. Why?"

"When you find Sarah. It will be hard enough to give you up. I don't want you to want to take my baby as well."

"I'm not going to take your baby away from you. Our baby. I'm not even going to leave..."

"I know the hold she has on you, Walter. I can see you lost in her every day. You just disappear while we're walking. You can tell me you don't love her, you might even believe it, but I can see the truth on your face. I'm not going to have this baby just to give it to her the way I gave Mirek away."

Fuck.

I have to tell her now, Krang thought. If I don't tell her, she wants to abort the baby. If I do tell her, it will ruin everything. He wondered if there was anything he could say to her to make her understand that he loved her, but what would he say? He owed her the truth. If I don't tell her, then she and our child will be dragged down with me. If we become a family, then I'm conferring my sins upon them. She has to be willing to accept whatever might come about later. And something will, eventually.

Suddenly he felt the presence of his entourage. He lifted his eyes from Katie and saw them standing in a tight circle around where he and the girl lay. The spirits were nodding solemnly. They were more solid than ever before.

"Tell her," they whispered, again and again. The soft chant filled the silence of the night comfortably. Krang was surprised that Katie couldn't hear them. Was this why they followed him, to see his undoing?

He always knew this day would come. It was the end of their time together. Unless..., unless she could forgive him, as Sarah had.

He felt a tear spill from his eye and run down his cheek, but did not wipe it away. I am sorry God, that I do not deserve this woman. I am sorry that I must pay sooner or later for what I have done, now that I see a different path. I wish I could say that I am sorry for having done it, but I must be honest. To say I am sorry now would be the worst hypocrisy, since I wasn't sorry when I was doing it. If I could take it back Father, I would. But I am not a dreamer, so I will simply accept the consequences of what I have done. Protect Katie, and this baby.

"Katie," Krang said softly. "I would love nothing more than to raise this baby with you..."

Katie squealed with delight, rolling to face Krang. "Really?"

Krang nodded, saddened by the look of joy on her face. "Before we can do that, I must tell you who I am. Then you will have to decide what you want to do."

He looked into her eyes, sparkling with joy. I will tell you, he thought, and then you will send me away. You have to. You will tell me how much you love me, but that you must protect our child from my crimes. You will cry, sweet tears of sacrifice and love. And we will both be joyous and sad.

"Your name isn't Walter?" Katie asked with a grin.

"Now who is joking? Let me speak." He stopped for a moment, coughing to clear his throat.

179

"My name is Walter Krang. I told you once before that Sarah was not really my wife. She is not. I was married, am married, to a woman named Emma, and we had four children. I believe that they died when the city was bombed, but I have no proof of that. I do not love Emma, and I don't think that I loved my children. I know that I have not mourned them. They were events, distant places that I traveled to, from time to time. I'm not even sure I would recognize them if I saw them on the street.

"Sarah was a woman from the camp. She saved my life by helping me escape...."

Katie nodded eagerly. "I can accept that you were married, Walter. I know that people grow apart. I am sure that in time you would have divorced your wife. If it turns out that she is still alive, then that is what you will have to do." She leaned forward and brushed her lips against his.

Krang stiffened and pulled back from her.

"What?"

"I am not done. Emma is not the problem. Sarah isn't the problem."

"Don't tell me that I'm the problem!"

Krang laughed in spite of himself. It wasn't a happy laugh. He felt the weight of the night sky crushing him against the earth. It was hard to breath. His spirits were growing impatient; their chant had grown ragged and spiteful.

"You don't know what I've done. You don't understand who and what I am..."

Katie reached out and touched her fingers to Krang's mouth and silenced him. "I know that you have killed men and are very good at it. I understand."

Just let it be, Krang thought. She doesn't want to know.   He shook his head. I can't let her pay for my sins. I won't do it.

"I wasn't a soldier. And I am a killer. I killed hundreds of people. In the camp."

Katie looked puzzled.

Krang took a deep breath and went on in a rush. "I was a guard. I was *the guard*. In the camp. I lived to torment and kill. And I never felt more alive anytime in my life than when I was working the camp. The camp was more important than anything else. It was more important than Emma and our kids. I was like God: I had the power of life and death."

Katie drew in a ragged breath. "And Sarah? What about Sarah?" she asked in a soft, child's voice.

"Sarah is a special person."

"Did you fall in love with her?" Katie asked hopefully.

"No." Krang said. "I killed her son and her husband. When she stepped off the train, I pulled her boy, his name was Capek, he was nine or ten months old,

180

maybe a year, I pulled him from her arms. When her husband Abraham reached for the child, I shot him in the face, as he stood next to Sarah." Krang's voice began to crack. "Then I raised the boy, I raised Capek, that was his name, I raised him over my head and swung him down and crushed his skull on the platform, and then I tossed him aside like a dead piglet. And later that night, I found Sarah in a cabin and I raped her in front of all the other women. I took everything that I could from her. And then I forgot her. What I did wasn't even important enough to me to remember it two years later."

"How can you tell me this now?" Katie asked flatly. Her voice had no timbre, no depth to it, as if she wasn't there.

"Sarah came to me when the camp was liberated. All the guards were rounded up and held on the parade ground. We were all to be machine gunned and tossed into the pit on top of the others. But Sarah, she came to me the night before and she forgave me. She kissed me on the cheek and showed me how to escape."

"Why?"

"I don't know," Krang said, his voice breaking. Tears ran freely down his face. "Why would she do that to me? I'm not worthy of forgiveness. My place was to die in that camp with the others. But she set me free, and told me to remember her husband and son until I die. I hated her for that, you know. She took away my power more completely than any bullet could. I don't understand why I'm still alive." Katie stared at him, her eyes somber and unblinking. He couldn't tell what she was thinking.

"And then I met you. I think God has brought you into my life to take you away from me. To make me happy and then destroy me, by making you pay for my crimes. That is why you cannot stay with me. If I love you, I will be the death of you. That is my karma."

"My family was in that camp," she whispered, shocked, just loud enough for Krang to sense it. She shook her head as if to clear it.

"Why are you looking for Sarah?" Katie asked. Her hands were clenched over her stomach as if she were going to be sick.

"At first, I wanted to find her so I could kill her. I wanted to prove to her that she was wrong, that she had no right to forgive me. I lay in the dark in that cave and fantasized about what her life would be like and how I would come along and destroy it. At that point in time I still wanted nothing more than to be *the guard*. I wanted to have power over her, not to have given my power over to her. I no longer feel that way. I can't go to her and thank her for letting me go, that wouldn't be right. I want to do right by her. I think that what I want to do is tell her I'm sorry."

Katie shook her head. "You want to make her to forgive you again?"

"No." Krang was adamant. "I want to give her the opportunity to

181

acknowledge her hurt. I want to let her scream at me, hit me, turn me in. Give her the opportunity to put the noose around my neck. I want to make up for what I did..."

"Bullshit." Katie snapped. "You just want to make her take back what she has done. You're so crushed by her strength that you are trying to find a way to tear her down. To make her unforgive you. She destroyed you with that kiss..."

Krang shook his head. "No. I just want to give her the chance to let her pain go."

"To let your pain go. She stands in such opposition to everything you have ever done. You can't just walk away from your life. You can't undo who you have been. And you can't undo what Sarah has done and who she has been. I won't let you."

"Okay," Krang said. "I won't."

Katie stared at him, her eyes dark with anger. "What about my family? Did you kill them? My sister? Did you force her to suck your cock for a meal? Did you shoot her? She was only eleven? What did you do to her?"

Krang shrugged. "I don't know."

"I can't be around you. Not right now. Get out. I can't watch you destroy another life. I won't be part of that. Get out."

"Katie..."

"Get out!"

"Listen to me..."

"Listen to you? I can't stand the sound of your voice. You speak so calmly, so dispassionately, about your actions, which are abominations before God. You think the world should have sympathy for you. You made me love you by hiding who you really are." Katie rolled away from him. "I cannot stand to look at you. All I can see is all those people, stuffed into trains, coming to you. My family. So you could kill them..."

Krang reached out and touched her on the shoulder. He hadn't imagined her responding this way. He had expected that she would be upset, and that she would see the need to send him away, but he hadn't thought that she would hate him. She should be sending him away to protect the baby, but tearfully, and full of love. That was how it had been in his head.

"What about the baby?" Krang asked, hating the desperation in his voice.

"Fuck the baby." Katie pulled away from his touch and crawled a few feet away. She glared at him, her face filled with revulsion.

"Don't ever touch me again." She scrambled across the campsite to the wagon and reached underneath, pulling the shotgun from its sheath.

"I abhor killing," she said emotionlessly, "but I did it before, and I can do it now. Get out of this camp before I kill you."

Krang nodded sharply. "I'll leave. I only wanted you to know the truth..."

"There are truths that we cannot bear to know, Walter, and this is one of them. I knew you did something bad during the war. That, I could rationalize. I can't rationalize this away. And I am not Sarah, I cannot forgive you. The magnitude of it overwhelms me. I am sickened by it."

Katie touched her lower belly with her free hand. "I will find a way to rip your child from my womb, even if it kills me. I cannot bear the thought of a part of you inside of me. Do not come back until morning. After it is light, then you may collect your things. I will be gone by then."

Krang turned his back to her and stepped away from the camp.

"Walter...."

He stopped and turned to look at her in the moonlight. Tears ran down her face.

"Take this fucking gun, I don't want it. I'm not you. I refuse to kill anyone else, ever." She held the shotgun out to him. He walked back to her, took the gun from her hand and left.

Krang turned to look back when he was about twenty five meters from the camp. Katie had collapsed into a fetal position near the wagon, and was rocking herself gently back and forth. Krang sighed, and headed off across the fields. He was headed for the hills that he had seen earlier, hoping to find a vantage point to see the lay of the land. He walked without thought.

The full moon hung away to the west, its light recasting the night with a silver tint. A river roared faintly through the gorge below, twinkling in the moonlight like far-off stars. Krang sat on the edge of a limestone cliff, two hundred feet about the river, his feet dangling over the edge. He thought that he had never seen such a place of beauty. He looked at the moon, mysterious and aloof, and counted the hours until dawn. It wouldn't set tonight, he realized. If he stayed here until the sun rose he would be able to see both the sun and the moon hanging in the sky together, light and reflection.

He felt that way about himself. That he was light and reflection. He was *Krang the guard,* and just Krang. They were different, and yet the same. One could never be free of the other. Which Krang would be the sun and which the powerless reflection? Could he ever overcome who he had been and what he had done?

Krang shook his head. Look at my life, he thought. What am I? What is my essence? Is it the sum of my actions or my thoughts?

"What does it matter?" he asked himself softly. "My actions and my thoughts have always been the same. There is no space between them that I could point to and claim was a separation."

I need to be more honest than most men, and not forgive myself because of a moment of doubt somewhere along the way. And I, of course, never had that moment of doubt anyway. Not even once.

Krang thought of his parents, whom he had despised so greatly. His father had struggled to provide for his family in the depression that had gripped the city for decades before the war. His father, so tall and gangly and hesitant. So unsure of himself around others, and such a tyrant when only Krang or his mother were with him. He would work two or even three jobs, when there was work, and then languish for months when there wasn't. Krang had laughed at him behind his back, to see him so beholden to others for an afternoon's work. He had gone with his father many a summer day, from mine to mine, steel mill to steel mill, seeking work.

His father would stand, cap in hand, and beg other men for the right to feed his children. Krang's father had been a soldier too, in a war that had sent him away for two years when Krang was a baby. He had come back from that war without any pride or respect for himself. And yet, every year, on Remembrance Day, his father had pulled out that uniform and worn it to church, to pray for his fallen comrades, and had walked in the pitiful excuse for a parade that the city offered. He would end up his day in a brew house, drinking free drinks paid for by the very men who would not give him a job, men whose money and connections had spared them from the war.

Krang laughed. They were not spared in this war. More than one of them now trailed him in his spirit entourage.

His mother had been no better than his father. Years of hard life had robbed her of beauty. Krang was the youngest of six children. Three had died before reaching school age. His mother had miscarried two or three times after he was born, the last time while he was in the first years of high school. He had looked at her, old and worn out, and wondered how his father could even touch her. She was a very pious woman, and had dragged Krang to church services every Sunday. She was content in her view that life was hard, and that her reward would come in death.

Did you get your reward, mother? Did you, father? Did all the hardship and pain of your lives earn you something after all? All of those years of denial - did they amount to anything? Does it even count if you do it with a view of the afterlife? Did it count? And if it did, why am I surrounded by the spirits of those that I have killed? Shouldn't they be with you, in some kind of heaven, enjoying the results of their suffering? Or do you haunt those who tormented you?

Krang glanced around, looking for his spirit entourage. They stared back at him silently.

"Does each of you have ghosts as well?" he asked, his voice shattering the

184

silence. "Am I carting my parents through hell because one of you is? Am I?"

They stared back at him, unblinking, fading in and out of his view. How many of them were as guilty as he? Krang wondered.

"Did any of you die a fitting death? Did any of you think 'This is my reward?'"

No sound broke the silence.

Krang nodded. It was more likely that they had led lives like his mother and father, eking out a living of some kind in the face of an indifferent society, only to find themselves thrown into hell rather than heaven. But was their hell any worse than his father's? Suffering from black lung from years in the mines, from emphysema, dying horribly from lung cancer? Krang remembered his mother, sitting so stoically beside the bed of his dying father, never once confronting the God that had deserted her. Never once seeming to have expected anything else from life but this moment of suffering. Never saying anything to her husband, except goodbye.

She had died in a fire in her sleep, six months after his father had gone. Krang had never believed that her coal stove had exploded. He had always thought that she had finally given up, and in a moment of pain, set her home on fire. He just hoped that she had one moment in which she told God the truth: that the promise had been broken, that no amount of afterlife, however sweet, was enough payment for the torture of this life.

The camp had been filled with his mother and father, a hundred times over. And he had despised those surrogates as deeply as he had despised his parents. None of them had ever demanded anything better than what life had delivered to them. Even at the end, they had not demanded more. What satisfaction did they gain from gunning down the guards and their families after the war was lost?

Krang couldn't count the number of suicides in the camp, sometimes three or four in a single day. And not once had one of those throwing their life away ever attempted to take out a guard, or the commandant, or anyone. They would hang themselves with a rope that could have become a garrote. Cut their throats with a blade that could have been planted deep into a guard's chest. They could have struck a blow for something. A sacrifice against oppression. Anything. It never happened.

"I tried to goad you into action," he said to the spirits. "In three years, only Abraham acted. He stepped forward without regard for himself. And Sarah was more courageous still. She may have been wrong, but at least she acted. By God, she did something to make a difference in her world."

Krang thought of Emma. I never acted either, before the camp. I did whatever was expected of me, even in rebellion. What was I rebelling against? My parent's empty life? And so I filled mine with too much drink, and too much fucking and a pregnant girl that I was only with because she would fuck me, and I said sure, I'll marry you. I wasn't even honest enough to tell her I didn't love her. Not even at the end, when I spent my leave with a whore. Hell, I wasn't honest enough to tell myself that I didn't love her. I couldn't tell myself that I was incapable of loving anyone except myself.

And then you bring me Katie, and take her away. You're fucked, God. Nothing more than a pissant bully. You create us to torment us. That is the meaning of life. To be kicked in the ass by you, again and again. Just when I think nothing can get any worse than this, you kick me in the ass again. So what's next?

"What the fuck do you want from me?" Krang shouted into the night, the echo reverberating through the valley until it died away to nothing. "Do you want me to jump or blow my head off? Which will give you greater pleasure? Which is a more fitting death for one such as I? What the fuck is it to be?"

Krang sighed. He couldn't even be angry. He had no right to complain. At the very least, he deserved torment.

Krang drummed his heels on the face of the limestone cliff. He sighed, looking up at the moon, wondering if today would be the last day he would ever see it. Was there any reason to go on? Without Katie, without the hope of their baby, what was he? Nothing more than a haunted man. Haunted and hunted. A man that was worth much more to the world dead than alive. If only he could change what had happened. He could have lived a different life, if he had simply had the courage to try. As it was now, his life stretched out beyond him, marking him. As visible as his spirit entourage. He could never escape who he had been and what he had done. It was funny for him to even think that he would want to. To feel ashamed for his life. Ashamed because a seventeen year old girl was offended by him. The whole world had been offended by him and that hadn't mattered. But Katie....

The look of revulsion on her face haunted him. It was the same look he had so enjoyed in the camps. Fear. Loathing. A desire to kill him. Krang thought for a minute about returning to camp. Katie had the courage to act. She could kill him. I could give her the shotgun, he thought, and ask her to do it. She could sit on my chest and look me in the face and put that damn gun under my chin and blow me into oblivion.

He shook his head. Katie could do it, but that would make her break her vow not to kill again. I don't want to do that to her.

The moon hung, motionless, silent. Its face was cold and filled with hatred, the light marking Krang as different. He basked in that alien glow, back to wondering which of his beings was the light, and which the reflection.

Katie lay in a fetal ball, wrapped in her blankets, struggling to catch her breath. The nausea came in waves, spasms wracking her body. She must be having a miscarriage, she thought. Her hatred must be expelling the baby. She looked up at the moon but could find no solace in it; it seemed cold and dim, and reminded her of Walter. Katie slowly regained control of her breathing, and the cramps began to subside as well. She had been hyperventilating, that was all. The baby was safe, although she didn't know if that was a good thing or not.

"How could I have slept with him?" she asked herself. How could I not sense that he was evil? Was I so blinded by my own fears of being alone that I chose not to see the truth? Or was he so skilled at hiding himself that no one would have been able to discover him?

She spit several times, trying to rid her mouth of his taste, of the feel of his tongue, of the texture of his come. She had made a habit of waking him every morning by sucking his cock. She had loved it. Katie gagged, rolled free of her blankets and rose to her knees, and retched, dry heaves making her shudder.

God, why did you do this to me? How could you bring me to this place? And what of the baby? It was no more than a parasite, swimming in her womb, living off of her labor. She would refuse to eat, to drink. She would starve it to death and expel it from her body, even if doing so killed her. She could not bring another being like him into the world. She could not do that.

Katie thought of her parents, of how she had dishonored them. The war had changed them, especially her father. She would be dead to them, her life in the city and this pregnancy enough to drive them away. If they were even alive. Krang had probably killed them. He probably took great pleasure in killing them. And she had thought she loved him.

She threw up again.

Her mind raced, dragging her in its wake. How did he come into being, that he could do such things? Was it his destiny? Simply the way he was raised? Was the thing in her womb tainted with his evil? Would it innately possess his ability to inflict terror and death on others? And even if it wasn't evil, even if she could teach it otherwise, how could she, at seventeen, bring this child into the world alone? Where was God in all of this?

Katie shook her head, trying to clear her senses. She took a sip of water and rinsed her mouth, then sat with her back against the wagon wheel, and rearranged her blankets. She would pray and meditate. That was what she had been taught to do. Turn inward, connect with God, and the path will be revealed. She closed her eyes and tried to slow her breathing, to still her racing heart. She took in a deep breath, held it a moment before letting it gently out. She did this again and again. After several minutes her mind began to quiet and she felt calm enough to pray.

"Father-Mother-God, I thank you for your presence in my life. You are good in this world that has been lacking in good, and you are good in my life. I give myself into your hands, and know that you will guide me and protect me on this journey." She settled more heavily against the wagon.

"Peace," she whispered, drawing in a breath. "Is mine," she said as she exhaled. She repeated this mantra again and again, trying to free herself from the confines of this place. She was searching in her mind's eye for the eye of God. She let the images float in her consciousness, following them with her will. Bright circles that seemed to draw her down, deeper into herself. Coolness and darkness, the solitude of being at the bottom of the lake, being drawn upward towards the light. The speed with which she propelled herself towards that light, that connection. The moment of breaking through, like breaking from underneath the water into sunlight, her body bursting into the air and heat and joy of being.

She found a moment of peace. All was well with her soul, despite what was happening around her. She was a child of God, nothing could change that. She drew in a deep breath and opened her eyes, feeling still and free.

I must go on, God, she thought, and find the path that you have laid out for me. I walk in faith that you will show me what I must do. I don't understand why you brought him into my life, but there must be a reason. Even the child is part of your plan. I will trust that you will let me know if I must destroy it, and if you do not, then I must love it. I must teach it only love that it may never be as he is, but only as You are.

Katie took another deep breath, letting it our slowly. Why did Krang exist?

She tried to imagine herself in his place. Could I have done any of the things that he did? I killed easily enough, she thought. I took a pistol and blew a man's brains out, staring into his eyes when I did it, trying to make him feel my rage and my pain. It didn't matter that he pulled the trigger, because I would have, soon enough. And as soon as it happened, I knew it was wrong. I didn't fight back against the Corabians, didn't try to protect myself. I really wanted them to kill me. But they just damned me, and left me alone. Left me to stew in my own juices, to go crazy with guilt and grief and loneliness and pain.

Until Krang came along. He didn't leave me alone. He needed me, and I wanted to be needed. But he had done worse things than I, even if I didn't know it. How could he kill a baby like that? And the father? I don't understand. Or maybe I do. Maybe what he did is no different than what I did. Maybe it doesn't matter what the circumstances are. Once you kill someone, maybe you can kill anyone. Maybe she was just like him.

Katie shivered violently. She hadn't enjoyed killing Stojespahl, she knew she hadn't. She may have lied to herself at the time, convincing herself that she had a moral right to kill, but she hadn't enjoyed it. She had viewed it simply as a necessary thing, to escape him. She had killed to save her life. And Krang, weeks later, had also killed to save her life. And again to save the life of Marie and the workers on her farm. What was the difference?

Krang seemed unable to feel the impact of what he did. To feel sorry, or guilty. Katie had broken down several days after she had killed Stojespahl, crying for a night, mourning for his wife and daughter, the one she reminded him of, somewhere in Montrovia. Mourning that her actions would deprive them of a man that they saw as good....

Had anyone seen Krang as a good man? His wife and kids?

"Why did you tell me this, you bastard?" Katie shrieked, her voice ripping apart the silence. "Why couldn't you leave me in ignorance?"

She had loved him before he told her. She hadn't been able to tell that he was evil. She was too damaged herself to sense his evil. She knew he was hiding his past, but she was caught up with his present, and she hadn't been able to tell. She had found him blustery, but malleable. Almost gentle, in a way. And his interest in learning about *the way*. He had truly wanted to know. And he hadn't cared that she was Corabian. Stojespahl had refused to ever kiss her mouth. Ever. He didn't want her germs, he had said. Krang had kissed her. Everywhere.

Why did he tell me, God? Why did he think he had to? He knew I wouldn't love him anymore. Did he just want to get rid of me? Of the baby?

Katie drew in a deep breath, trying to regain her calm. She didn't think so. He had told her, again and again, that he didn't want her to pay for his sins. He told her to scare her away. So that when he was arrested and executed, she wouldn't be. As if he were honorable.

Katie laughed bitterly. He was a monster, the worst kind of man, but he wanted to be honorable to her. To protect her. Because he loved her. A man who had proven himself incapable of loving anything other than himself had fallen in love with her.

What would the people he had terrorized think, she wondered. What would they think to see him in love now? And what would this Sarah think? He had killed all that she loved. Would she hate him now that he had found love?

How could Sarah have forgiven him? Katie thought of the shock she would have felt, seeing her son and husband killed so brutally. The rage. I hate him just from knowing that my parents and sister were in his camp. I don't know for sure that he ever saw them. The camps were big; he couldn't have known all the prisoners. But Sarah had seen him kill her family. From just a foot or two away. She must have been consumed with hatred. How could she forgive him? Did she really think that forgiving him would change his life? Why would she care? And how did she have the strength to free him in front of a camp full of his victims? No matter what her reasons were, that must have cost her plenty. She must be hated now by many of them. So why would she do it? What about this man would make her act?

189

Katie couldn't think of a single attribute that Krang possessed that would have prodded Sarah into an act of forgiveness.

It must have been something in Sarah. A fault? Or was she just sick of death and any life saved was to be celebrated, even his? Katie thought Sarah must have been so strong. So free. She couldn't have cared what anyone else would think. But how had she overcome the hatred she must have felt?

Unless.... Katie nodded. It must have been. She forgave Krang as a means of healing herself. She couldn't exact any revenge on him that would bring her peace. She could think of nothing that would bring her peace. So she went to the teachings. And the teachings tell us to forgive our enemies. To forgive those who have harmed us the most. To give them gifts. That is the pathway to heaven. And it is one of the teachings that is most overlooked, because it is so hard to understand. But Sarah figured it out. She forgave Krang, and found peace. She forgave Krang and freed her soul from the camp. Sarah walked out of the camp truly free, leaving no part of herself trapped behind with the memory of her husband and her son.

Katie felt tears rolling down her cheeks. I am forever tied to that room, to that bed, to the look of fear and terror on Stojespahl's face as I killed him, but Sarah is free. She roams this world with no part of her tied to the past. And knowing that, I still don't know what to do. I don't believe that I have her courage. I can't forgive him.

Krang sighed, the shotgun held tightly in his hands. There wasn't any point in putting it off. Yet something was bothering him. It wasn't that he wasn't afraid to die. He hadn't been afraid at the camp, he hadn't been afraid in the fields, he hadn't been afraid at the farm, so that wasn't it. He opened the breach of the gun, checking that the shells were in place. He had thought about killing himself frequently before the camp, even after he and Emma were married. Life had seemed... empty. But he had never thought of killing himself once he started working at the camp. He had not felt that ennui for even a moment after walking through the front gate. The very air was different in the camp. Electrified. Full of tension and passion. All the death of that place had suddenly made life so very worth living. It wasn't the killing, not his killing, that had made life important. It was the insurmountability of death.

Krang had never accepted death as the natural conclusion of life. As a child he had been fascinated with the stories of remote villages where the inhabitants seemed to live almost forever. There was always the possibility that someone's reported death, especially if they lived so far away that traveling to a funeral was out of the question, was simply a hoax. That was why he had never been able to kill himself as a young man, because he didn't believe that he would really truly die. He thought if he tried to kill himself that he would awaken in some new land, a hole blown in the side of his head, forced to live with the shame of the world seeing him forever as one who tried to kill himself. As weak.

But at the camp.... Death was real, overwhelming, a constant companion. It couldn't be negotiated with, yet it was so capricious that it might never strike you or yours. Krang had struck up a friendship with Death at the camp. They would walk through the place together, reveling in the others' fear of them. They smoked cigarettes together, fucked women together, became inseparable. And Death had changed because of Walter Krang. He laid aside the black robes, got rid of the damned scythe and put on a uniform. He stood taller, proud. He no longer snuck in among his victims, trying not to be seen until the last moment, but walked openly among them every day. Death spoke with them, comforted them, amused them, and blessed them by claiming their neighbors, friends and family. For everyone who died that wasn't you was a blessing.

Where are you now? Why have you abandoned me? All of our old friends are here with me, they have followed me from the camp to bear witness to my life, and you are not here. Have I disappointed you?

Krang shook his head. I must be seriously crazy. A girl who I kept around just for a good fuck now owns my life. I see spirits following me day and night. I think Death is a real person, and my friend. How fucking bad off am I? No one can make friends with Death. The son-of-a-bitch always turns on you in the end. Always. Talk about a cocksucker. I wouldn't do that to anyone. I never pretended in the camps. I didn't befriend anyone, like so many others did. I took what I wanted, and everyone knew I would, but I didn't lie and offer protection that I couldn't provide in exchange for sex, or money, or conversation. And I didn't punish anyone for rejecting me, like so many of the others did. I just did what I did. Everyone knew where they stood with me, which was nowhere. How many of the other guards stood before a family that they had promised to protect, having fucked the mothers and daughters, and often even the fathers and sons, and still put them on the edge of the pit and shot them? I never did that. At least I was honest with them.

Krang felt the tears flowing down his face. What the fuck kind of person am I? My great moral victory was that I was honest about the fact that I would rape you and kill you? I offered no hope to anyone, no reason to live another day. I fed on their misery and fear and pain and anger and hopelessness. God, how could you have let me do that?

Krang opened his mouth and jammed the barrels of the shotgun in as far as it would go. The acrid metallic taste gagged him. His right hand slid down the barrels and found the trigger guard, slipped inside and pulled the triggers.

191

Katie sat bolt upright. What was that noise? She laughed nervously to herself. I am so on edge. She imagined that Sarah must be calm and peaceful. Only the calm have such moral strength. I wish I could understand how she found the courage to offer forgiveness. What had her family thought?

Katie had argued with her parents, in the hours before they climbed into that bus. Katie remembered her mother's look of disapproval when she had bolted from the group, her father waving her away in annoyance, cursing at her. They saw her as disobedient. Did they ever forgive me? Did they ever reach a point in which they wished they had come with me? Katie had cried when she ran away, full of anger that her parents were being so complacent, hating them for taking Bela to her death with them. Did Bela ever forgive me for leaving her behind?

And I never forgave them for being so stupid and small-minded. For trusting those with power over our lives not to destroy us. I never forgave them for climbing into that bus and rumbling off to their deaths. I never forgave them for leaving me to a world of blowjobs and back alley fucks, of beatings and rapes and hunger. Of leaving me for Stojespahl, and for his gun. I never forgave them for having to scrub his blood and brains from my face.

And they are gone, and I cannot forgive them. It doesn't matter if I might say that I do, I cannot look them in the eye and give away my pain. I cannot be free of them; they are not here to hear me say it. To recoil from it, to protest it, to take offense at it. To let it work for me. Maybe I can forgive them their absence now. Maybe I can do that.

Katie took a deep breath. And what of Krang? Has he changed? Is he capable of changing? Does it even matter? She couldn't think that it did. And yet he had told her what he had done. He told because in some way he thought he was doing right by her. That he was protecting her. That he was forcing her to take her leave of him, to take her freedom. Could he have changed? It doesn't matter, she thought. I don't care if he has changed or not, I cannot love him. But maybe I can forgive him, she thought. Or at least I can try. When he returns, I will say to him that I forgive him, but that I must continue this journey without him. I will join the group we met this evening.

Can I really forgive him? Katie shuddered. I can certainly say those words, but can I mean them?

"Sarah, you must be so strong," Katie whispered. "I must find you and learn from you. I must raise my child to be strong like you. I must try to act like you." God, you have always taught us that forgiveness is your most precious gift. Why did you make it so difficult?

A brilliant white light shattered the darkness, blinding Katie.

"Don't fucking move, bitch," a disembodied voice screamed out from behind the light. The voice spoke Albanian, like at the roadblock.

Katie froze, her arguments lost in the swirl of activity around her. She could make out figures running past her camp, melting in and out of the darkness. In the background she heard the noise again, the noise that had startled her a few minutes earlier. It was the deep rumble of a diesel engine, the sound of a heavy truck.

Soldiers surrounded her, pulling her to her feet.

"Put her in the truck with the others," a man hissed to one of the soldiers holding her. Moments later she was being pulled up onto the open bed of a two-ton truck, pushed into a mass of people that huddled against the back of the cab. Hands reached out pulling her in, stroking her.

Marenka was whispering in her ear. "Where is your man?"

Katie shook her head. "We argued. He went for a walk. I don't know..."

"Good," she whispered, her head nodding vigorously. "He will be free, and perhaps can free us. We are being relocated. Apparently the war is not over here. We are to be sent to the south, closer to the Homeland. It is a good thing."

"Unless they just plan to shoot us," Hans said bitterly. "They are not so different than the others, and they have no love for us."

The truck lurched forward, throwing Katie into the group. It trundled across the field and onto the road, picking up speed as it headed south.

Chapter Fourteen

The shotgun, spinning end over end, arced away from the cliff and fell slowly towards the bottom of the gorge. The silvery light of the moon flashed off the spinning gun in pulses, as if signaling the stars. The gun arced far enough away from the cliff to be swallowed up into the black canopy of the forest and disappeared soundlessly.

"Fuck! Fuck! Fuck!" Krang's voice echoed throughout the gorge. He thought about throwing himself from the cliff after the gun, but knew it wouldn't matter. The shotgun had worked during the ambush. He was using shells from the same box. He should have been able to blow his head off. It should all be over, except they were conspiring with God to keep him alive. Krang closed his eyes to avoid seeing his spirits, but he could sense them all around him. They were celebrating. They didn't want him dead yet. He could tell they wanted to see him suffer more.

Krang opened his eyes, looking into the gorge where the gun had fallen. He hadn't meant to throw it away. In fact, he was sure that it would still work, if he were to find some way down there to retrieve it. Fuck it all. Krang looked over his shoulder. The spirits were crowded around him, faintly glowing in the moonlight. They looked so very solemn, standing in insubstantial silence, faces blank of expression, yet Krang could sense their mirth.

"Laugh, motherfuckers," he muttered.

Krang scooted back away from the edge of the cliff. He climbed to his feet, working his jaw to reduce the soreness of swallowing the shotgun barrel. He spit weakly, trying to work up enough moisture to swallow. Without thinking, he began to retrace his steps towards Katie and the baby. A sense of dread enveloped him as he understood why he hadn't died.

"Did you kill them yet?" Krang asked the first apparition he passed as he walked away from the gorge. "Did you? How mutilated will her body be? Am I supposed to crave revenge? To want to hunt down the bastards that killed her, but never find them?"

The spirits slowly dissolved as he walked through them, reforming behind him. He glanced over his shoulder, looking for Abraham, but couldn't see him.

"I'm going to deny you all," he said, anger rising in his voice as he stared at his ghostly entourage.

"And I'm going to deny you, motherfucker," he said, looking up to the night sky searching for some sign of God. "What the fuck purpose do you serve? Is it only to tear us apart? You did nothing to stop me from destroying all these people, just so tonight you can have the pleasure of punishing me by taking away the only person I've ever loved. You're supposed to be a God, not some petty bureaucrat who gets off on screwing people. I was willing to do anything to protect her, including kill myself."

Krang stopped, looking up through the canopy of trees to locate the moon. The faint light was a beacon for his hatred. God was no more on the moon than here, Krang knew, but it felt better to have a place to direct his wrath.

"I refuse to give in to you. I won't seek revenge. I'll be fucking bigger than you are. I'll give my life away, to every person I see. I'll give whatever I have, whatever I can do. My money, my health, my body, my soul. I'll give until I'm used up, or someone kills me. I'm going to fuck you God, by refusing to be the person that you have decided that I am.

"And if you want to continue to punish me by hurting others, go the fuck ahead. Kill those who are truly innocent, who believe in you and have lived their lives in order to celebrate you. Take them from me every time I meet them. You are no better than I am, you fucking monster."

Krang sank to his knees, and then sat back, still looking upward. His eyes were no longer focusing on anything. Tears were flowing down his face, but he ignored them.

"You are a monster. Nothing more. You gave life to me, and protected me in all that I did." He paused for a moment, gathering his breath, and then went on. " I reject you. I reject myself. I will have no part of this any longer. I will follow Sarah, who had the courage to forgive, and Katie, who had the courage to love. I will show you, bastard, that I can be better than you. I will show you."

Krang dropped slowly forward, curling into a fetal ball, mumbling and crying. Soon, he slept.

Katie, sitting in the back of the truck surrounded by Marenka and the others from her group, let her thoughts drift. She easily ignored their fearful chatter, not caring at the moment what might happen. None of it was important. What was important was understanding what Krang meant to her. Was he only in her life to impregnate her? Or was he to come back?

She watched the moon shining intermittently through the treetops as the truck sped down the road. Could she forgive him? Could she have the same strength as his Sarah, and forgive him? Not to have him back in her life, she couldn't imagine that, but to let him go. She had to admit that she had never seen that part of him that was *the guard*. She didn't even know if he was telling her the truth. But he must have been, because no one would make up such a horrible story about themselves.

Why did he tell her? He must have known that she would leave him, but she didn't believe that he wanted to be rid of her. He had seemed happy when she told him she was pregnant. He had changed so much in the last few months. She had watched him open up, unfolding like a rare bloom. Had it only been an act, something to put her at ease? She couldn't believe that. He would have slipped up sometime, and she would have seen through his act. But how could someone who had done those things he claimed to have done be capable of loving anyone? There must have been a reason that he told her. He must have felt like he was doing the right thing, even though he had known it would make her leave him. But why tell me now?

He has been waiting for someone to catch him, she realized. And he didn't want me and the baby caught and punished with him. He was sacrificing himself to protect us. And yet he killed all those people. Katie shook her head, her vision blurred with tears. No one ever changed. No, she thought, that's not right. Her father had changed, as the war got underway. He had been consumed by his fear, and he had changed for the worse. But no one ever got better. None of the men in the city ever changed just because they spent time with her. If they were mean, they stayed mean. If they were shy, they stayed shy. How could Walter change? It doesn't make sense.

The truck was out of the trees, crossing an open plain. The moon hung in the sky, shining like a faint promise. The others were arguing softly, some believing they had been rescued, others fearing they were headed to their deaths. Katie didn't really see a difference.

Sunlight filtering through the trees woke Krang. He was stiff and cold, having slept uncovered on the ground, and rose shakily to his knees. Krang struggled to stand up, feeling hung over. He laughed softly to himself, it had been months since he had had a drink; he really didn't like this feeling of nausea and vertigo. How could I have gotten so drunk all the time?

Krang looked around the small clearing he had slept in, trying to gather his bearings. He slowly remembered the evening before. He hadn't been drunk. What a stupid fuck I was, he thought with a grin. Trying to kill myself? For what? And throwing the gun off the cliff, that was stupid. I'm sure a quick cleaning and some new shells would have made everything work.

He laughed again, remembering his heroic words of the night before.

"I guess it's easy to challenge a God that I don't believe in," he said quietly to the forest, knowing that even if he couldn't see them, his spirit entourage was still there. "I hate to disappoint you all, but I'm not that man that I claimed to be last night. I'm not dedicating my life to anything but self-preservation. I survived the damn war, and I am going to make the most of my life now, whatever it takes. And I'm going to go back down there to Katie and tell her she has no choice in the matter. The child is mine, and she is mine, and I shall have them."

I don't care if she hates me, he thought as he began walking slowly down the steep hillside. I'm used to being surrounded by those who hate me. I'll be more comfortable with that than with her love. Being hated doesn't make me feel guilty. It's what I deserve.

The camp was deserted when he got there. She must have walked out shortly after he did and gone straight back to Marenka and Hans and the others. Their blankets were still lying on the ground where they had talked, and the wagon was undisturbed.

He was irritated that she was gone, but not really surprised. That's why I told her, he thought, to drive her away. I don't want her to hang next to me whenever they get around to hanging me, so it's all for the best. Krang felt confused and unsure of himself. His mood swings were unnerving. One minute he was desperately afraid for her, the next just pissed off. It was like he was some little voodoo doll for her to play with. And he was worried about her.

He was angry, however, that she had walked out without anything. She hadn't taken her blanket or even her water skin. She is being stupid with her life, he thought, just to spite me.

Krang gathered the blankets and folded them, laying them in the bottom of the wagon. I tried to start out as a peddler, he thought, and now, after several months and not one repair done, I have a better wagon. God has blessed me again. Krang laughed, and began pushing the wagon towards the camp they had visited last night.

The sun was shining harshly over the mountains when they boarded the train. Katie felt like a zombie, unable to do anything but what was asked of her. She hadn't slept at all last night. She looked at the fear on the faces of the women around her and had to laugh. Look at me, she thought. Look at how I hated my parents for not resisting, and here I am climbing on a train anyway. I know these are not cattle cars, but it could just be so much window dressing. How will I ever know who to trust? Maybe it would be better if it were all over. Maybe the uncertainty is too much to live with. But what else is there?

Katie followed the group from the truck onto the train; like her they carried no luggage or supplies. Everything had been left behind when they were ordered onto the truck. She hung back a bit, letting the others go ahead of her. She was tired of their questions about Walter. They had expected him to somehow rescue them, and she could see on their faces that it was somehow her fault that he hadn't. A soldier offered her his hand when she reached the steps. Katie thought about ignoring him, but changed her mind and took his hand. He grinned broadly and helped her up. She nodded her thanks before entering the first car.

The train was filled with camp survivors. They looked like they had come from a camp that had only recently been liberated. Many of them still wore remnants of uniforms. They looked more like the group that had beaten her in Stojespahl's apartment than Marenka's group. For a moment, Katie was afraid that she wouldn't be accepted here, but she quickly noticed that no one was looking at any of the newcomers. They all seemed lost in their own thoughts and unaware of what was happening around them.

As Katie made her way down the aisle behind the others, she saw a single open seat in the second car and slipped into it. She wanted to be away from Marenka and the women from the truck. She was sick of their whining pessimism. If this train was taking her to her death she didn't want to worry about it every second of the trip.

The open seat she took was next to the window in a grouping of four seats: two on each side facing each other. Across the aisle were another four. The whole thing reminded Katie of the living room in her parent's house, set up to encourage conversation. Katie didn't feel like talking. She was seated with two women and a man. The woman sitting across from her, also next to the window, holding on to the arm of the man, was very pregnant. Her short ragged hair and gaunt features made her belly seem even bigger than it was. The woman was clearly tired, yet seemed to possess that power and a peace that Katie had only seen in pregnant woman. Do I have that look, she wondered? She shook her head. She hadn't earned it yet, at just a few weeks pregnant.

The husband was a small man, made smaller by the pregnancy. He was more skeletal than many of the survivors. It made him seem almost like a child next to his pregnant wife. Katie glanced into his eyes briefly, and then looked away. She saw a fatigue there that frightened her. He was close to death, she was certain of it. He was only alive on the will of his wife, of her need for him to be there when her child was born. Katie didn't know if he had the strength to hang on after the child was born. He wanted to be free of this place.

How great must his wife's love be, Katie thought, to sustain him when he has lost the will to live? Maybe the child will do the same for him, and together they can pull him back from the brink. Katie felt fat and over-fed looking at the two of them.

Next to her, in the aisle seat, a woman was sleeping. She was just a few years older than Katie, in her early twenties. She had not been in the camps, of that Katie was certain. Katie was shocked by her beauty. The woman's skin was clear and pale, and dark brown hair curled lazily below her shoulders. Although she wore no make-up, her lips glistened slightly, and her cheeks glowed with vitality. She slept with her arms crossed over her chest. Katie thought that her face had a look of great sadness to it, a look Katie expected all beautiful women to possess. That sense of aloofness that made men, and other women, stay away. Somehow the thought made Katie comfortable. She smiled quickly to the pregnant woman and her husband, closed her eyes, and leaned her head against the window. She didn't want to talk to anyone.

The train shuddered to life, jolting Katie awake. She shook her head trying to gather her bearings. She remembered the raid, and the train. It rolled slowly from the station, past the line of trucks that had been used to gather everyone up. Katie felt a knot of fear in her stomach as the train, in starts and spurts, chugged back in the direction they had come. Towards Mountain City. Towards the camp. She wondered how quickly the train could make up the four and a half months it had taken for them to walk here. Would it be a day? Or only half-a-day? What would the city look like now? Was the camp still standing?

The train was gaining speed, gaining a smoothness and rhythm that betrayed Katie's fears. It seemed so comfortable, in the seat, and she was so tired. The pregnant couple was already sleeping. Katie looked sleepily at the beautiful woman and wished she could lay her head on the woman's shoulder. Katie leaned back in her gently rocking seat and sighed contentedly when the train peeled away from the road, arching out over a river and curving to the south. She thought, through her sleepiness, they are taking us home. To our new home. Our Homeland.

Sweat ran from Krang's brow into his eyes, burning them. The sun seemed fixed overhead, turning this open stretch of road into a burning hell. The wagon seemed heavier than ever. Krang had considered abandoning it several times, but who he was supposed to be without it?

It wasn't the heat that was really bothering him. He was still trying to understand what had really happened. Marenka and Hans and the others were gone, their camp emptied just the same as Katie's. Everything left behind: clothing, pots and pans, water skins. There was no blood, no dead bodies. He had found tire tracks in the dirt. Krang didn't think whoever took them meant them harm. Why take them at all, if you just wanted to kill them? No one was around for miles. But who had taken them? And had they got Katie as well?

199

He had spent the morning telling himself that Katie's defection didn't matter, but was finally ready to acknowledge that it did. She had hurt him. Her inability to forgive him crimes that she had not been victim of, nor seen him commit, just staggered him. How could she, who had known that he loved her, fail to love him back? And how could Sarah, who had only seen his depravity, find it in her heart to forgive him?

Krang realized that he had never expected her to leave. He thought that somehow she would compartmentalize his life, as he was doing, into camp and post-camp. Hadn't he been a wonderful person, post-camp? Okay, he had killed several people, but they all deserved it. Shouldn't she be able to see that he had changed?

A single oak tree grew beside the road, perhaps a half kilometer ahead. Krang decided that he would stop when he reached it and rest in its shade. He would walk at night, pushing the damn wagon then, and protect himself from the sun. He almost collapsed when he reached the tree. He set his wagon so the tree was between it and the road. The road bisected a broad prairie; several kilometers to the north were the hills where he had tried to kill himself. To the east, perhaps a kilometer away was the forest. It was nearer to his west, only a half kilometer. Above the tree tops he could see the spire of a church. If he hadn't been so exhausted he would have burned the damn thing down, just to prove a point. He sat heavily against the tree.

Krang leaned back into the tree, feeling the roughness of the bark digging into his back. Heat shimmered across the valley floor around him, making the world seem unsubstantial. He felt drained of vitality, as if his very life forces were slowly melting away. He couldn't see the spirit entourage in the light, and worried that they might be lost to him. The heat might make them fly up to heaven and be gone forever. And then what? What if he had to rely on only himself for guidance? Could he live his life differently than he had, without a constant reminder?

So many days in the camp had been like this one: the hellish heat that sucked a person's energy away. No one moving, not even the prisoners, because none of the guards had the energy to force them to work. There were always more suicides on a day like today than any other type of day. The despair would rise from the cabins as thick as the heat. You could feel it, and see it, and know that it was at work. Many of the guards would find an excuse to sit in the office before a fan, but never Krang. He would be in a tower, or better yet, walking the compound, reveling in their despair.

Sarah's face came to him briefly, as she leaned forward to kiss him on the cheek, full of peace. A look of calm unlike anything he had ever seen. Then her husband, the look of rage on his face, and sudden surprise as the nine millimeter tore a hole over his right eyebrow and he flew backward. Krang could feel the weight of the baby in his hand, remembered the quick pleasure of the left handed shot, as the baby arced over his head and down to the loading platform. Even now, his arm and hand and shoulder carried the memory of that moment, the feel of the baby being crushed against the loading dock. Krang realized that he would never be free of that memory, not for one moment, not until he was dead. It was in his flesh, his body trained by that action to do it again and again.

Krang rolled to his hands and knees, retching in the brown grass, his body revolting against itself. He vomited again and again, dry heaves, as if his body wanted to tear itself apart. Finally he collapsed in the dust, tears streaking his face, his arm and shoulder tingling. I crushed a baby's skull in front of his mother and laughed, he thought. I shot her husband in the face and it was just an ordinary day. It wasn't even special. I wasn't high, I wasn't drunk, just hung over. I hadn't been provoked. I was just being myself. And she forgave me.

How do I redeem myself?

Krang shook his head. There was no way to redeem himself. He had been right the night before, sitting on the edge of the gorge, when he stuck the shotgun in his mouth and pulled the trigger. It wasn't his fault that nothing had happened, that neither barrel had fired. He had tried to do the right thing. And he had been stopped.

Krang smiled weakly. God is beginning to reassert himself in my life, that was all. He has found a way to break me down. I put up walls that could not be breached by anyone or anything, not even by crushing a baby's skull. I was beyond feeling, beyond needing to breathe or eat. I was almost a God myself. No, Krang shook his head. I was a God, deciding every day who would live and who would die, who would love and who would cry. Krang giggled at the rhyme.

And then that bastard put Katie in my life. Why her? Have you seen her hair? I've fucked many women who are much more beautiful than she and never felt a thing. But this girl, she gets to me. And then she gets with my child. And then he takes them away. And keeps me from killing myself.

Krang rolled on his back, looking up at the deep blue sky that stretched endlessly above him. "Do what you must. I have no doubt that I deserve it. Just don't hurt anyone else to punish me. Don't run little kids over with trucks, just so I can see them die. You can't show me worse than I have already seen done by my own hands.

"I just don't understand why you didn't stop me. The first man I killed, the one who was escaping. Why didn't you blow the rifle's breach and kill me then? Or one of those nights I drove myself back to the camp, drunk. There were many of them, and the road from the city to the camp so full of places to make a mistake. Why didn't you let me drive over the edge of the fucking mountain and be done with it? I was so drunk on some of the trips it was as if you were looking out for me. Protecting me. Why the fuck would you do that?"

Krang shook his head in disgust. The problem, he decided, is that God is no better than me. Both of us seem to take our power from the misfortune of others. Not even from their misfortunes, because neither of us gives a fuck about that, everyone has misfortunes. We derive our power by destroying the power of others. Break them down to feed ourselves, Krang thought. Like a fucking vampire. That's what I am, a vampire. Too bad the sunlight doesn't kill me.

Krang rolled over on his hands and knees, scrabbling together a small mound of twigs and dry grass. He lit a small fire, one that burned very hot because everything was so dry. Krang picked up all the loose and broken branches from under the tree, adding them to his fire until he had a small pyre going. He pulled his knife from his belt and set it at the edge of the fire, so the blade was immersed in the tiny conflagration.

Krang watched the fire burn itself down all afternoon. The blade on the knife glowed red, then white. Krang took his shirt off, wrapped it around the palm of his right hand several times, and picked the knife up from the fire. He could feel the heat of the blade through the wooden haft of the knife and the layers of cloth.

Krang looked at the partially obliterated tattoo that he had forged on his left forearm in the cavern after his escape from the camp. He saw it as a sign of his sin, an acknowledgment that he would do anything to stay alive. It was a symbol of his inability to feel empathy with another human being. And he never felt the pain of getting it. He needed another symbol. A symbol of his desire to overthrow his past, to acknowledge the pain of others. A symbol that no one will ever be able to take from him.

Krang pressed the white hot blade of his knife against the fake tattoo. The pain, burning like an electric current right into his soul, made him double over. The knife jumped, and Krang pressed it harder against his arm. The smell of his burning flesh, at once familiar and haunting, was nauseating. This was his flesh burning, not some corpse fished from the camp latrines. The heat of the fire, of the late afternoon sun, of the knife on his arm, and the smell of his flesh brought him to his knees, vomiting yet again. The knife fell away, sweat dripped into Krang's eyes, and he bit his tongue to fight the pain. Even the taste of blood in his mouth, however, did not comfort him; Krang knew that he could not find absolution in this simple act of self-mutilation.

Krang kicked the fire out and lay on his side, curled in a fetal position. He called out for Abraham. He needed to show him the scar, to show him that the change had begun. Krang held his arm up to be seen.

"Fuck! Fuck! Fuck!" he screamed. The knife had slipped. Instead of obliterating the tattoo, the angry red burn seemed like a beacon on his arm, underlining it.

Chapter Fifteen

Krang slept in the shade of the big oak tree as the sun slowly lowered itself into the western sky. He slept as a battalion of soldiers filtered through the forest a half kilometer to his west, taking up defensive positions around the church and the edge of the tree line. He slept as another two battalions, complete with tanks, crashed through the trees to his east and began crossing the open prairie. He slept as fighter planes streaked across the sky less than two hundred feet above his head, west to east, trying to stop the waves of approaching enemy. He slept as though he were dead, arguing with the dead, his dead, that God had failed him and the world by letting him live.

Abraham would hear none of it, shaking his head and shouting back. "You must see us to our holy place. You must take us home and free us from the horror that was our lives. This is your obligation to us."

Krang was equally emphatic. "I can do nothing for you now. Release me and let me die."

"You must take us home."

Thunder rumbled in the distance, making Krang look away from Abraham. "A storm approaches. I must seek shelter."

"There is no shelter from the storms of man," Abraham replied. "You taught me that. All I wanted was to be anonymous at the camp. To just survive. And to see my family survive. But you stormed into my life and all was lost."

Krang looked Abraham in the eyes. The bullet hole was a beauty mark above Abraham's brow. "You were a brave man," he said quietly. "You acted to save your boy. If you had all acted, I would be dead, and the boy, maybe he would be alive. You did what you could."

"But it wasn't enough."

Krang could see the tears glistening on Abraham's cheeks. "No, it wasn't enough."

The thunder rumbled again, deeper. It was close enough to shake the ground. Krang turned his head, searching the sky for signs of the storm. He had never felt thunder shake the ground like this, yet the sky was crystal clear, the sun shining brightly.

The next shell took the top off Krang's tree, showering him in dirt and debris. He awoke from the dream to find that he was still dreaming. Night had fallen, yet the world glowed with the brightness of hell. Fire turned night into a parody of day. The tree under which Krang lay was engulfed in flames, dropping burning branches to the ground. The ground around the tree was also ablaze, coated with oil or gasoline, trapping Krang in a circle of fire.

Krang struggled to his feet, disoriented and worried about Abraham. Had the world ended? He spun around looking for a break in the ring of fire that encircled him. Finding nothing, Krang held his breath and stumbled forward into the flames, hoping to break free. The heat forced him to close his eyes and cover his face with his hands. He ran as fast as he could, wondering how his campfire had gone so wrong. He wasn't sure he was going to live. The heat was so intense, he could feel his skin being scorched and smell his hair burning. Suddenly he was free of the fire; the air was cooler and he could draw a breath again. He opened his eyes, but could see nothing. The heavy smoke made them sting. Krang stumbled on, trying to get as far away from that hell as he could, until he stepped into nothingness and found himself tumbling through the air. Falling, his first thought was of pitching forward from the camp into the pit, but he couldn't be back at the camp, could he?

Krang hit the ground hard, rolling to a stop in fresh dirt. He was lying on his back, the soil feeling cool on his skin. All that remained of the fire was an orange glow in the direction of his feet. He was drawing ragged breaths, winded more by fear and heat than exertion. Krang reached up to inspect his face and head. His eyebrows and hair were mostly gone, and his face felt burned, but there were no blisters or open sores. He could see. He smiled.

Lines of shooting stars crisscrossed the sky, first red, then green. Lightning exploded to his left. A single star flared into supernova, spinning crazily back and forth over his head. There was no rain, only the terrible roar of the lightning. Krang settled back to watch the storm dreamily, his mind struggling to make sense of it. No wind. No rain. Just terrible thunder. The fighter planes that streaked over Krang were so low he thought he could have reached up and touched them. One of them was on fire and Krang swore to himself that he could see the young pilot, panicked, fighting to free himself from the plane. He laughed at his imagination.

An explosion rocked the world, feeling every bit like a bomb detonating. Krang shook his head. This couldn't be. The war was over. He and Katie had come so far south from Mountain City that they were in the prairie that made up the borderlands between the two countries. The war here had been over for a year or more. Who was left to fight? Krang rolled onto his hands and knees. He was crouching in a shell hole, about four feet below the lip of the hole. He crawled to the top and peered over. The tree he had been sleeping under was gone, but his wagon was intact, lying on its side. The remains of a fighter plane burned in a swath across the field, illuminating a tank rolling slowly towards him. Krang could make out soldiers running behind the tank, crouched over, using the tank as cover.

Glancing behind him, Krang saw the defensive positions in the tree line, tracer fire arching lazily past him towards the approaching troops. Several flares spun lazily on parachutes, robbing the night of its dark safety. The whitewashed steeple of a church, illuminated by the flares, rose behind the tree line like a beacon for the approaching soldiers.

Krang had no idea who was who. He looked from one line to the other, but couldn't distinguish if they were Corabians, or Montrovians, or Albanians, or U.N. soldiers. The tank, now less than fifty meters away, didn't have any identifying marks that he could see.

A rocket roared into life from the tree line, racing just a few feet above the ground, over Krang's head, and into the advancing tank. The rocket exploded against the front of the right tread, stopping the tank's forward progress. The tank shuddered and then spun crazily to the left, away from the lost tread, crushing several of the soldiers running beside it. The hatch cover flew open and a soldier started to scramble out, but another rocket struck the turret and the tank was gone in a flash so brilliant Krang was blinded for several seconds.

A soldier struggled into the shell hole, falling over the lip of the hole and rolling to the bottom. He was burned severely, and struggled for breath. He grinned at Krang, his teeth unnaturally white against his blackened skin.

"I'm fucked if I look as bad with no hair as you do," he hissed with a desperate grin. "She'll never sleep with me now."

Krang looked at him. He was a boy, no older than Willi had been. His accent was flatlander. Krang couldn't tell if he was Montrovian or Corabian. They all spoke the same damn language and wore the same clothes, and in this region had the same fucking accent. That was the problem with a civil war. All this over some fuck-up argument about God.

"Who's over there?" Krang asked, nodding towards the trees.

"I'm dying," the boy whispered.

Krang slid down beside him. "Fuck that," he said harshly. "You're just a little burned."

The boy labored to catch his breath. "I've got shrapnel all in my chest. I was inside the tank and the next thing I know I'm sitting out here, twenty meters away and I feel like I've eaten a box of razors." He pulled his hand away from his neck and blood spurted weakly.

"Where's your first-aid kit?"

206

The boy shrugged his shoulders and grinned, blood dribbling from his mouth. "I think the back of my head's gone."

Krang shook his head. "No," he began, but stopped as the boy pitched forward into his lap. The back of his head was a mass of blood and pulp. He felt for the boy's pulse, but found nothing. Krang fought the urge to roll the boy's body away. No one had ever held a body gently in the camp, not for even a few seconds. He could give the boy that much.

A group of soldiers ran past the crater, stumbling forward in a half crouch. What he could see of their uniforms and insignia didn't tell him who they were. Another group ran past and this time someone looked down into the crater. He stopped.

"Leave him," the man shouted.

Krang just stared at him.

"Come on, it has to be now. We'll come back for him. He won't lay in the mud forever."

Krang set the boy down and climbed shakily out of the crater. The soldiers were streaming across the battlefield, running in loosely massed groups, shadowing the tanks. Everywhere he looked, he saw them running towards the far side of the field. The tree line was a brilliance of twinkling eruptions: tracers arching gently across the fields, rockets pounding towards them, flares soaring upward. A fantastical party. The roar of the battle was so overwhelming it was like standing in profound silence.

The man pushed Krang forward, towards the erupting trees. "Go," he shouted. "We must finish this now."

Krang stumbled forward, almost falling several times, and then began to run in earnest. The ground was torn up from shell fire and covered with corpses, so it was a very choppy, madcap dash Krang made towards the tree line. He felt free, running towards his death, no gun in his hand. Krang began to laugh. He aimed himself for the busiest pocket of fire. The church steeple, glowing peacefully behind the line, became his target. The soldiers ahead of him began a crazy dance, marionettes jerking on their strings, as they twisted and crumbled and dropped to the ground. Three tanks, side by side, exploded as one, showering the men around them with shrapnel and burning fuel. But the wave of soldiers just kept coming.

Krang glanced over his shoulder and saw his entourage, spread out behind him, chasing after him, cheering him on. He ran past the burning tanks. Krang soon outpaced the soldiers that had been ahead of him. Most had tried to find cover in the field and were returning fire towards the tree line. Krang ran on. He was alone, ahead of everyone, caught in the stark glare of the flares swinging gently on their parachutes. A machine gun position was directly in front of him.

207

The fire they were putting out was non-stop. One hundred meters, seventy-five. He ran directly at the tracers, a grin on his face. Fifty meters. Twenty-five.

A shell whistled over his head from behind and the church steeple disappeared in a ball of fire.

Krang burst into the tree line in full speed, running past the fox holes and gun emplacements that had been firing at him. The soldiers didn't even glance at him, or his army of spirits, as they poured withering fire on the advancing enemy. Officers were directing the fire, shouting out orders in the same flatlander accent as the advancing soldiers. He still couldn't tell which side was which.

Krang dropped to his knees to catch his breath. I must be dead he thought, his chest heaving. They no more saw me than they saw the others from the camp. I must be dead.

The sound of the battle changed abruptly as the charging soldiers reached the tree line. Krang leaned back against a tree and watched as the battle line was overrun. The soldiers were fighting hand to hand now, beating each other to death with the butts of their guns, and ripping each other apart with bayonets. Reinforcements charged up from the direction of the burning church, entering the melee shouting like banshees. The soldiers swirled around each other, fighting as relentlessly as wild animals. In a matter of minutes, Krang could no longer tell which soldiers had come from which position. He wasn't sure they could tell any longer either, but were just killing each other indiscriminately.

Maybe the battle will go on until they are all dead, Krang thought.

Krang got up and began to slip away. At least I don't have to kill anymore, he thought. I will never take the life of another person; never add another soul to my army of dead.

A soldier ran past, hitting Krang in the jaw with his elbow as he fled, knocking Krang to his hands and knees. Another soldier followed, stepping on Krang's hand as he tried to rise. The second soldier raised his rifle and shot the fleeing man in the back of the head, showering the ground with the man's blood. He stepped off Krang's hand and reached down and helped him to his feet.

"Sorry about the hand, old man," he shouted. "I had to take my shot." He disappeared back into the melee.

Krang shook his head to clear it, cradling his hand. "Fuck," he said savagely. I'm not dead. How does this keep happening to me? Now I'm living some kind of charmed life, like some fucking Greek hero who can survive anything. How depraved is God to keep me alive? What value am I to the world? To anyone?

The fighting seemed to stretch on in all directions without end. Krang began to walk, still hoping for a bullet to cut him down, but it never came. Watching the carnage unfold around him, Krang vowed that he would no longer participate.

"No more killing," he said quietly. "If I'm charmed, I don't need to kill to stay alive." I don't think it will make any difference, he thought, but I won't kill. He walked on, the fighting thinning around him. Krang wondered if the shell that hit the tree and woken him had damaged his hearing, because the action seemed so removed, as if he were seeing and hearing it through a thick sheet of glass. As he wandered on, the trees thinned and the battle faded away. Krang broke free of the trees. He took a deep breath, feeling like he could breathe again. He was standing on the edge of a field of soybeans, a farmhouse and small barn visible on the far side. Krang took another breath, and walked across the half kilometer of beans. It was quiet enough here to forget the battle raging behind him.

As he approached the house, Krang could see that he hadn't yet escaped the war.

A group of soldiers stood idly around the farmhouse. The rear door of the house was thrown open, and a young soldier pushed a woman and her young daughter out of the house. The others immediately began to jeer and yell out sexual comments at them. The soldier pushed them away from the house towards the edge of the field. Krang left the beans and walked more quickly across the yard towards the house. He passed a rusting tractor parked in an island of weeds and picked up a long crowbar lying on the tractor seat.

The soldier raised his rifle to the back of the woman's head. Krang was no more than twenty feet from them. The woman looked into his eyes, imploring him to save her.

"Stop!" Krang shouted.

The soldier fired his rifle and the woman collapsed. The girl spun towards her mother. The soldier pointed his carbine at her head and fired again. His shot caught her in the temple and she went down as well. Krang stood directly in front of him, the bodies at his feet.

The soldier turned to look at Krang. "What did you say?" he asked.

Krang swung the crowbar, catching the soldier across the upper arm, knocking him to the ground. He felt the soldier's arm break under the blow. The soldier bellowed in pain. Krang stood over him, staring. The soldier was no more than a boy. Another boy.

"I was just doing what I was told," the boy whispered through tears. "This is a secure area. I had no choice. They should have left this morning with the others."

Krang looked at the boy and nodded. He could see the fear on the boy's face, the resentment. He could hear the justification in the boy's voice. Krang raised the crowbar over his head and brought it down, again and again. The savagery of his attack delighted him. He could feel the boy's blood speckling his skin, could feel the boy's skull turning to pulp with each blow.

The boy's short scream had brought the other soldier's running. One of them knocked Krang to the ground.

"Son of a bitch," he shouted. "Why the fuck did you do that?"

Krang looked up at him dumbly.

"Why did you kill him? What did he do to you? I have half a mind to blow your fucking brains out right now."

Krang nodded numbly. "Yes. Do."

The soldier shook his head. "You disgust me. He was a good boy. He'd do anything we told him to do. Get away from me." He kicked Krang viciously and stalked away.

Krang got to his feet and looked at the boy. His features were no longer recognizable. Krang didn't feel the rage that had gripped him, only despair.

"Why did I do it?" he wondered.

He looked at the mother and daughter. Killing the boy hadn't done anything for them. They were still dead. He looked around quickly, fearing that one or more of their souls might have joined his entourage, but he didn't see them. There were so many souls following him, however, he could not see them all.

Krang found a shovel and pickaxe in the tool shed behind the house. He went into the house and stripped the sheets from the main bed. Krang spread the sheets on the ground near the garden, and then carried the bodies of the mother and daughter and lay them side-by-side. He worked quickly in the cool night air, stripping to the waist as the work warmed him. The ache in his muscles and back reminded him of Marie and her family. He began to breathe deeper, to feel the sweat running from his face. The grave began to take shape. Krang smiled to himself. Perhaps I have found my avocation, he thought. I have killed so many, now it's time to bury them.

A machine gun on the far side of the yard opened fire, spraying tracers across the bean field. Krang glanced at the machine gun emplacement, and at the woods he had come through, and saw the battle that he had escaped breaking into the open field. The soldiers surrounding the house were firing indiscriminately, cutting down their retreating comrades as well as the advancing enemy. The action near the trees fell silent for a moment, the only sounds the firing of the soldiers around the house and the bite of Krang's shovel into the soft earth of the garden.

Suddenly all the guns on the tree line were turned on the house, and what had been a battle between two groups became a brutal assault pouring withering fire on the machine gun nest. Tanks boomed shells against the house, reducing it to burning rubble in minutes. The soldiers dug in around the house began cursing and shouting, knowing their comrades in the field were firing upon them. Krang laughed. The bastards deserved every shot, he thought. Too fucking stupid to risk leaving them alive. He still didn't know who were the Montrovians and who the Corabians. How could you tell them apart? At least they weren't the fucking Albanians.

Krang kept digging, and in the course of the next hour the battle raged past him, past the rubble of the farmhouse, past the fields of wheat on the other side of the house, and was swallowed up by the far trees more than a kilometer away. When the grave was as deep as his shoulders, Krang wiped the sweat from his face, tossed the shovel out, and climbed from the grave.

The mother and her daughter were wrapped gently in the sheet and lifted into the grave. Krang winced as he threw the first shovelfuls of dirt on them, and struggled to breathe as he covered them completely. After a few minutes he stopped, and walked over to the body of the young soldier he had beaten to death with the crowbar.

"I wasn't going to bury you," he said softly. "I didn't want to offend them by shoving you in there with them, and forcing them to stare at you forever. But I've changed my mind. I don't think you hold your sin any longer. I hold it for you now. I pried your sin from you with that crowbar, took it stroke by stroke. I absolve you, and ask that you lay with them and comfort them until the end of time."

The boy was light and Krang managed his body easily. He slipped the boy into the grave and then stood and stared at the mutilated corpse. The boy's blood had dried on Krang's face and hands. Krang felt a moment of anger, of that deep rage that had filled him earlier, but couldn't tell if it was directed at the boy or himself. He shook his head sadly, and began shoveling in the rest of the loose dirt.

I'm such a fuck-up, he thought. I can't do anything right. I hadn't even finished saying I wouldn't kill again before I was beating the boy to death with a crowbar. And the soldiers didn't stop me. Do you want me to kill, God? Am I just here to kill for you? Even if I claim justice in this death, in all the deaths since the camp, what about the camp? Do I have to take a life now for every one I took then?

Krang sat on the grave, feeling his pockets aimlessly for a cigarette, but coming up empty-handed. I am not one to take your vengeance on the world, he thought.

"Katie said you are not seeking vengeance," Krang whispered. "She said you are only about love."

I can't see that, he thought, shaking his head again. Except maybe I haven't been looking. Maybe I'm still blind to the truth, and can only see with the eyes that I made for myself. Eyes that only see violence. Could that be it?

Krang patted the cool earth of the grave, and lay back looking up into the night sky. The smoke from the battle was clearing away, stars slowly coming into focus. Morning was beginning to hint in the east, an hour or so away. Krang drew in a deep breath, and felt his body relax into the earth. He willed himself to dissolve, to join the three at peace below him, but it wouldn't happen.

"I'll dig your graves, God. I'll take care of your dead, as I take care of my own. But I won't keep beating people to death for you. I won't do it." He closed his eyes and smiled, and drifted off to sleep.

The early morning sun, shining through the train window, woke Katie from a deep sleep. The sun was just high enough above the horizon to shine in the train's window. She stretched lazily, feeling the rhythm of the train rocking beneath her. Rubbing the sleep from her eyes, she watched the world speed by outside her window. The train was making its way through rolling hills browned by the sun. She had no idea where they were, but thought they must have come far south already. Katie stretched again, glancing at the pregnant couple. They were both still asleep, almost dead in sleep.

She rolled to her left to see her other companion, the beautiful woman, but the seat was empty. Katie immediately felt panicked, wondering where the woman could have gone. Katie could feel tears spilling down her cheeks, and bit her lip in annoyance. Why am I acting like a silly schoolgirl? I don't even know her. Yet she felt an affinity to this woman. How had she lived through the war, her beauty intact? What strength of spirit had that required?

Katie stood slowly, her hand on the wall until her legs understood the motion of the train. She slipped into the aisle and made her way to the rear of the car, to the toilet, but it was empty. Katie thought the woman might have wanted to be alone, but where would she find a place to be alone on this train? Katie was afraid that the woman had thrown herself from the train, because she had looked so sad. She started to walk through the cars towards the rear of the train, but stopped. Katie remembered seeing a flatbed behind the coal tender, half-filled with wood that could be used to keep the steam up if they ran out of coal. That car was to the front, before the first passenger car.

Katie quickly made her way up the aisle, past her pregnant couple, crossing between cars, and through the first car. She could see the woman through the tiny window in the door at the end of the car. The woman was crouched on the flatbed, huddled on her knees against the chopped wood. She was kneeling at the edge of the car, staring at the ground racing past, rocking slowly back and forth, as if trying to get up the nerve to launch herself from the train.

Katie pulled the door open and stepped onto the small platform at the front of the car. The sound of the door slamming broke the woman's reverie and she turned her head towards Katie. The rushing wind and roar of the steam engine made talking with the woman impossible. Katie mimicked jumping to the flatbed with her hands, hoping to get to the woman before she jumped from the train. She looked blankly at Katie for a moment, then began to shake her head and motion her back with her hands. Katie looked at the ground racing beneath the train. They were moving so fast the ground was a blur. Just looking down made her feel dizzy. She held on to the rail with one hand and inched her way to the very edge of the platform. To reach the flatbed she would have to take a step, a large step, over that open space between the cars. The flatbed had no platform on it to match up to the one on which she stood, no place for her to grab as she made her step. It was quite a bit taller as well.

Katie stepped all the way to the edge, until her toes were at the end of the platform. She still held the railing with one hand, her arm awkwardly trailing behind her. The woman had risen to her knees, a look of horror and fear on her face. She was waving her arms wildly, trying to get Katie to stay where she was. Katie smiled at her, let go of the railing, and jumped forward. She landed on the violently rocking flatbed, staggering, trying to remain on her feet. The woman reached up and grabbed Katie's hand, pulling her down to her knees.

"What the hell did you do that for?" The woman shouted.

"I woke up and you were gone," Katie said softly, suddenly unsure of herself. She had to lean in and speak in the woman's ear to be heard.

"Why is that any concern of yours?"

"I just found you," Katie said. "I'm not ready to lose you." Katie was surprised by the words that slipped from her mouth.

"Lose me? What am I, your mother?"

Katie shook her head, feeling a blush burning in her cheeks. "I was worried for you. You looked so sad, earlier. I didn't want anything bad to happen to you."

The woman laughed viciously. "Nothing bad can ever happen to me again," she whispered bitterly.

"Don't say it like that," Katie said. "You'll make it happen."

"What are you, superstitious?"

"No," Katie said quickly. She felt unsophisticated beside this woman. "I just believe in the teachings, in the fact that we manifest, for good or bad, what we think about and talk about."

The woman nodded softly, and reached out to ruffle Katie's cropped hair. "You wouldn't think I could keep forgetting, but I do. I wasn't in the camps like the others. I'm not Corabian. I don't know any of your teachings."

Katie nodded, touching her hair absently. "I wasn't in the camps either, but I am Corabian."

The woman laughed again, joyfully. This time it was a beautiful sound.

"I'm Katerina or Katie for short. What's your name?" Katie asked.

"Lisle."

"That's beautiful! Why are you on this train?" Katie asked.

Lisle shook her head softly. "I 'm not really sure. I suppose because I am not safe among my own people." Lisle had a faraway look, and then shook her head. "When I was younger I fell in love with a Corabian boy. Apparently, I have been contaminated by his caresses..."

"Oh." Katie looked down at the flatbed on which she was riding, tears stinging her eyes. She felt the woman touch her cheek, and looked up.

"I didn't say that well. I don't believe I was contaminated, but my people do. My family does. It is not safe for me, in my village. You would think that after four years of war we would have killed enough. There is at least enough hatred left in the world that if I stay in my village, they will kill me. My own family will kill me...." She began to shake as tears spilled from her eyes.

Katie slid next to her, taking Lisle in her arms. Katie didn't say a word, just sat and held her as the train wound its way through the countryside towards an unknown destination.

Krang walked slowly through the forest, the early morning fog isolating him from his surroundings. He had slept deeply, but only for a few minutes, and awoken refreshed. The sun was still low enough on the eastern horizon that morning had not yet broken under the trees. He was looking for a place to wash up, a place to scrub the boy's blood from his face and hands. He carried the pickaxe and shovel on his back, secured to a rucksack he had found at the farmhouse.

The bodies, materializing suddenly out of the mists, lay in a haphazard pile on the edge of the clearing, surrounded by soldiers. More soldiers, stripped to the waist, were digging a mass grave. Krang nodded to the soldiers standing in the clearing and slipped his rucksack from his shoulder. He pulled his shovel free and joined the men at their digging.

Krang worked silently for several minutes, enjoying the feel of the shovel digging into the earth. The exertion seemed to calm him, to cleanse him. He became aware of the man next to him, who was struggling to dig. The man would half-heartedly lift a spadeful of dirt from the grave and toss it towards the side, more often than not scattering it back into the grave. He was agitated, and not focused on the digging.

Krang reached out and touched him on the arm. "Are you okay?" he whispered.

"Fuck you," the man hissed. "You're going to kill us as soon as we're done."

Krang looked at the man, seeing the fear on his face. "I'm not with them," he said, pointing to the other soldiers. "I didn't realize you were fighting each other. I'm sorry."

"Then they'll kill you too."

Krang shook his head. "They won't kill me. I can't die. It's my punishment, to not die. I have to live with the world as I made it, and I can't die. So I travel with my friends." He pointed off to the woods, to his entourage.

The soldier gasped. "They're all dead," he whispered.

Krang looked at him, alarmed. "You can see them?"

The soldier nodded.

Krang shook his head sadly. "I'm sorry, then. You're already dead, in truth if not yet in body."

The soldier moaned softly.

Krang shook his head. "Don't let it worry you," he whispered. "You'll be okay with it."

The man shook his head.

"Did you enjoy this fight?" Krang asked.

"Fuck no," the man whispered. "I hate this shit. It tears you apart, the waiting. Waiting to die, every time we go into battle. I hate it."

Krang nodded. "Now you'll be at peace. You won't hate it anymore. No more dreading each day wondering what it will bring. Wondering if you will survive. Your worst fear will be realized, and as always it won't be as bad as you imagined. Living the way you've been living, in fear for yourself or for your friends, right? That's pure hell. You'll be released from all that. It's time. And if you need to, you can always come with me." Krang nodded towards the silent spirits. "We have room for you."

"Do you mean it?"

"Yeah."

"Thank you," the soldier said. He lifted another shovelful of dirt from the grave

"Do you believe in hell?" he asked after several minutes.

Krang laughed. "Absolutely."

"I think I'm going to go to hell. This war..." the man paused awkwardly, "it's just that I've done things that are wrong. Things that I know are wrong, yet when I was doing them, it didn't seem that way."

"You were at war..."

"But that's not an excuse. Take this. None of these men will dare open their mouth to say this isn't right. I know they won't, because I never did. And it's not just the killing that's wrong. I mean, we are at war, so I couldn't just stop killing..."

He laughed. "Imagine how quickly this war would have ended if we had all just refused to kill anyone? No, it's not the killing. It's the casualness of it. I could kill a man and then sit down next to his corpse and eat lunch without even washing my hands. I never felt a thing. So I think I deserve to go to hell."

Krang nodded. "You're right. We all deserve it, when you think of it that way."

The man nodded. "I'll miss my wife when I go to hell. She is a good person..."

"You miss her now?"

"More than anything. If I had had any courage at all, I would have gone AWOL months ago and spent my time with her. If I'm going to die, at least that would have been for something worthwhile."

"Let me tell you a secret," Krang said softly, resting on his shovel. "You're in hell now. This is hell. There is no other. When you are released from this place, you will be free forever. I know hell. I've done such terrible things, and I have a witness for each one of them. And I must live and witness myself. I must experience this world as I have made it: full of hatred, and ugly beyond belief. And I must experience it alone, as I chose to live it. I will stand up with you, even in your place, but they will not kill me..."

One of the soldiers standing above the grave blew shrilly on a whistle and ordered the men out of the grave. Krang stood on the edge, catching his breath. The grave was a deep gash in the earth, longer than it was wide, fresh dirt mounded around its lip. The diggers began to toss the bodies of the dead into the hole.

Krang jumped back down into the grave. He picked up the two bodies that had already been tossed in and carried them to the far end and lay them neatly side-by-side. Krang walked back to the other end, and gently took each body as it was brought to him and placed it in the grave. Forty times he carried a man home, stepping gently around the bodies already on the ground. He was exhausted when he climbed from the grave.

The soldiers made the men stand on the long lip of the grave, facing in. Krang stood with the man he had talked with to his left and the other five men to his right. He reached out and grabbed the man's hand, squeezing it.

"What's your name?" Krang asked gently.

A soldier stepped up behind the man farthest to the right and shot him in the back of the head.

"Damek," the man said tightly, jerking Krang's hand.

The soldier stepped to his left and shot the next man, and stepped to his left and shot the next man.

"Who are you?" Damek asked.

"I'm the grave digger," Krang said as the man to his right fell into the grave.

"Tell my wife I love her," Damek said, as the soldier raised his pistol. The shot rang out and Damek tumbled forward, his hand slipping free of Krang's.

"Get them covered up," the soldier said, holstering his pistol. "And clean up. You look like shit, and you smell."

Krang nodded. He began to gently shovel dirt back into the mass grave covering the bodies. He looked around for any sign of Damek, other than the lifeless body that lay in the grave, but he had not joined Krang's entourage.

The soldiers slipped away through the forest without a word.

Krang continued to shovel, working as hard as he could. He was breathing heavily, sweat dripping from his body. He knew that he was crying because his eyes kept blurring up, but he didn't wipe them. He just shoveled until the grave was mounded over, and then he sat on the mound and rested. He wished he had a cigarette. The acrid smoke would clear the ugliness from his mouth and lungs, would free his mind for a moment from the rigors of thinking.

How had he become different from all these others? He couldn't understand why he was suddenly invulnerable. What cruelty: to watch the world die around you and know that you will not. At least in the camp he had the illusion that someone might rebel, that someone might rise up and take him down. What if his pistol had jammed when Abraham had stepped forward? On that crowded platform, with no way to separate them, if Abraham had actually reached Krang, the guards in the tower would have opened fire with their machine guns and cut everyone down. They would all be dead: Abraham, Sarah, and Krang.

Krang rose wearily from the grave and walked across the clearing. A small creek ran through the woods just beyond the far edge of the clearing. Krang stripped, leaving his clothes in a pile at the creek's edge, and walked into the cool water. Using handfuls of sand and fine gravel from the creek's bottom, he began to scrub himself. He rubbed hard enough to wash the blood away, to leave his skin pink and bright and clean. Then he grabbed his clothes and scrubbed them as well, sitting in the water until his body was numb from the cold. He was having trouble thinking, holding onto his thoughts.

"Maybe I can die," he mumbled. Maybe I can sit here and let the water wash my life away, minute by minute. If God won't take me all at once, maybe he will take me piecemeal. He shook his head. I am dead, he thought. I must be. It's the only explanation, that I am part of my entourage of dead, rather than they a part of me.

He looked at his reflection in the water, seeing himself for the first time in several weeks: his hair and eyebrows burned away and his skin scrubbed pink. Looking at the rippling image, all he could think of was that he looked like a newborn baby.

Walter stumbled from the creek, laying his clothes out in the morning's strong sunlight to dry. He crawled into the shade of a tree and fell asleep.

Chapter Sixteen

Walter woke late in the day, stiff, cold and more than a little disoriented. He lay on the ground and stretched, working the stiffness from his arms and legs, trying to remember how he ended up in the forest when he had fallen asleep on the great plain. He was naked and felt cool, even in the August heat. He could see his clothes hanging from the lower branches of a tree. Krang struggled to his feet and staggered to the tree, having difficulty finding his legs. The clothes were dry and relatively clean. He pulled them from the tree. His balance was off, so he sat on the ground and dressed slowly, staring at the mound of the mass grave. Why wasn't he buried there?

He brushed his hand across his head and felt the stubble of his hair. The touch of his hand against his scalp brought the last day flooding back to him. He looked down at his arm and saw the burn, red and blistering, underlining the fake tattoo. Rather than obliterating the fake tattoo, the scar seemed to call it out, demanding that it be seen. He stared at it in wonder, almost as if he were looking at a scar on someone else's arm. He could barely feel the pain of it.

Beyond the grave, he could see the cast-off packs of the men who had been buried. Walter crawled across the clearing, feeling too weak to stand, and searched the belongings, finding several tins of rations. His stomach was growling like he hadn't eaten in weeks, but Walter realized that couldn't be true. Unless he had slept for more than a day, he had eaten dinner with Katie and the others just two evenings ago.

The tins had simple metal keys that wound a strip of metal from around the top of the tins to open them. It took him five minutes to get the first tin open. His fingers were too clumsy to pull the key free of the tin, then too big to slip the metal tab into the slot on the key. He felt like he was learning how to open the tins for the first time. As the top slowly peeled back, juice and fat dribbled over his fingers. Walter licked at the juices, his mouth flooded with the oily taste of processed meat. He pulled a chunk of the meat from the tin and stuffed it into his mouth, closing his eyes and grinning as he chewed. This was eating. The tin was empty after another handful. The meat overflowed his mouth, making it hard for him to chew. He began to laugh, feeling the oil running down his chin.

Walter ate two more tins of food in rapid succession, and was holding his fourth when he realized he should save the others. He dropped the tin of food back onto his small pile, sat back against a tree and looked over the clearing as he licked fat and grease from his fingers.

The early evening sun cast a golden hue on everything. The clearing was dominated by the shallow mound of the grave to his left. The creek in which he had washed was to his right. Small blue and white flowers grew by the edge of the creek, their colors made even more brilliant by the sun's warming light. The clearing looked more like a painting of an ideal woodland scene than reality. The shadows under the trees gave the golden highlights of the sun an intensity that Walter found especially moving. The grave mound, bathed in golden light, glowed on one side, fairly alive, and yet rested in dark shadows on the other, an appropriate indicator of what lay beneath.

Walter motioned for Abraham to come out from the trees and join him in the warmth of the evening sun. The shade approached hesitantly, as if afraid the golden hues might cast him away.

"Don't be afraid, my friend," Walter called softly, waving his arm to urge him on. "You are as alive for me in the daylight as you are in the night." He waited until the other man approached and sat across from him, the angry wound on his face clearly visible.

"I thought you and the others were just a figment of my imagination, a way for me to torment myself, but Damek saw you. So I will tell you what I am doing, and you can decide what you and your companions need to do. If you are with me in the hopes that I will beg your forgiveness, you will be disappointed. I cannot ask you to forgive what is unforgivable, and nothing I can do now or in the future will ever serve as absolution for what I have done. I am an abomination."

Abraham smiled, the lift of his lips echoing the sadness in his eyes. He nodded at the truth of Walter's claim.

"But you must understand that Sarah forgave me. And she freed me that I might remember you, and your son Capek, for my entire life. I need to let her know that I will do this, not because she made me say it, but because I understand that I must.

"So I go to find your Sarah. At one time I wanted to kill her, at another to give myself over as her slave. Now I simply wish to acknowledge her courage, and tell her that you will live forever in my memory."

Abraham shook his head solemnly, as if trying to deter Krang from his task.

"I don't ask your permission," Krang said. "I do what I must. I will not harm her."

Abraham slowly rose, saying nothing, and made his way back towards the

220

forest.

"Wait," Walter called to him, silent until Abraham turned to look at him. "I want you to know that I have found my life's work." He pointed to the grave mound. "I will bury the dead, wherever I find them. I have never been good with the living, so I will honor the lives of people by caring for them in death. Never again will I allow someone to throw a body in a pit, or bulldoze the dead like so much trash. It isn't much, I realize that. But it is what I can do."

Abraham nodded and moved soundlessly into the forest.

Walter found a small dispatch bag and two canteens among the soldiers' discards. He also found a pair of boots that fit him reasonably well. The bag, filled with twelve tins of rations, he slung over one shoulder; the canteens he wore on his belt. He slipped his shovel and pickaxe into the rucksack harness he had made at the farmhouse and was ready to go. His heart ached at leaving the clearing, fearing the darkness of the forest around him.

The light followed him into the woods. The canopy of leaves overhead was thin enough that each step he took was bathed in light. The path, meandering through the wood as if created by a wood sprite, glowed in the golden hues of the setting sun. The path was lined with wild flowers, a hundred hues glistening and beckoning him onward. Walter walked, unconcerned about where the path headed.

The forest gave way in less than fifteen minutes, breaking out into a field of wheat that shimmered in the late sun. The golden stalks were ready for harvest, and the fields, untouched by any sign of last night's battle, stretched on for miles. Walter could just make out a thin, dark tree line against the horizon. The wheat swallowed him up as he walked across the field, swaying gently around his legs, leaving no signature of his passage. He wondered if somehow the tanks and soldiers had also passed magically through this field, leaving no sign of their being, or if they had been so awestruck by the placidness of the field that they had simply turned aside at the last minute, and fought their way back through the forest?

Walter walked in silence, the sun warming his back. He was alone in the field, no birds following him, no rabbits darting fearfully from his path. It was a moment of solitude, the first he could ever recall. He had been alone before, many times in his life, but never at peace. Even as a boy the future had pulled at him, the past had taunted him, and the present confounded him. Right now, Walter felt like he needed nothing more than what he had at this moment. And his newfound purpose - to bury the dead - was an extra blessing.

Night caught up with him swiftly, but Walter just kept going. He wasn't sure how long he had slept at the grave, one day or two, but he wasn't tired. He reveled in the stars thrown against the silky black of night. The moon which lighted his path seemed, for the first time in his life, warm rather than cold and distant. He was saddened to see it set, in the early morning hours, but content with the knowledge that it would always be there, would always light his way.

When the first faint light of morning broke before him, it carried with it the sounds of the morning birds, and Krang knew he had returned to the land of the living. Suddenly weary, Krang turned to the south. He would walk until dark, he thought, and then he would sleep. Hopefully, he would find this place of peace again, at least in his dreams.

Chapter Seventeen

The two girls huddled against the wood on the flatbed for the better part of a day, until the train shuttled into a rail siding in a small town. They had chatted a little, about nothing important, because the rush of the wind and roar of the engine meant they needed to shout to be heard. As the train pulled into the siding to take on coal and water, Katie was shocked to see thirty or forty soldiers disembark and form a cordon around the train. She hadn't noticed any soldiers on the train.

One of the soldiers saw them sitting on the flat bed and rushed over, gun at the ready. He was about thirty, tanned and thin. His uniform was clean, but worn. He looked tired or bored.

"What are you doing out here?" he shouted. Katie was relieved he wasn't Albanian, although she couldn't tell from his accent if he was Corabian or Citizen. He pointed his rifle at them in a menacing way.

Lisle raised her hands and nodded for Katie to do the same. "We just came out for some air," she said.

"Do you see any others who've come out for air since we stopped? What makes you think you can?"

"We didn't come out since we stopped," Lisle said. "We came out earlier."

The soldier looked back at the first car, realization dawning on his face. "Why the fuck would you do something so stupid?" he asked.

"We're not exactly like the rest of your prisoners," Lisle said.

"You're not prisoners," he snapped, looking at the girls more intently.

"Then why all the guns?" Katie asked, pointing to the cordon of soldiers.

"To keep everyone on the train, including the two of you. We've had a few instances, and don't want no more."

"Instances?"

"With the villagers. They're not always happy to see the refugees. So now we keep everyone apart, for safety. Maybe we need to keep you two apart as well, for your own safety. Are you girls running away from home?"

Lisle laughed, that light and airy joy that Katie had heard earlier.

223

"We weren't in the camps like them," Katie said, "but we both belong on this train." She didn't offer any further explanation.

The soldier ended up walking them through the train to a baggage car at the very end. The door to the car was locked with a big padlock. The soldier fished a key from his pocket and ushered them inside. It was half-full with boxes of military rations, and a pile of duffel bags belonging to the soldiers who were guarding the train.

"You can stay here until we cross the border. At the border you have to be inside the main cars. If they find you in here at the border, you'll be thrown off the train, or even arrested. If I see that you've been in the food, I'll throw you off the train myself." They heard the door being locked when he left.

Lisle sprawled out on the duffel bags and patted the spot next to her, calling Katie to come sit.

The train shuddered into motion, pulling slowly away from the rail siding. They had been stopped for almost an entire day as the train took on water and coal. None of the refugees had been allowed to leave the train. They could see out a small hole in the wall of the baggage car. Katie watched the countryside slide by as the train picked up speed. Lisle tugged on her arm, pulling her away from the little window.

"You asked me earlier how I ended up on this train," Lisle said, "and I wasn't..."

"I shouldn't have asked," Katie interrupted. "It's not important."

"It's very important," Lisle said. "I've only told one other person the whole story, because he saved my life. And you told me so much."

Katie grinned. "I always say too much. I shouldn't have said anything."

"How long could you keep the baby a secret? In a few months the whole world will know."

"But my baby isn't your concern."

"It is now," Lisle said, reaching out to grab Katie's hand. "I want to help you. It gives me something to be focused on other than my own troubles." Lisle gave Katie's hand a hard squeeze.

"When you told me that you didn't want to lose me, after being so stupid as to jump on that car while the train was moving, I thought you were a silly little girl. But now, knowing your story, I know you. I haven't had a friend for such a long time. I won't walk away from you. And I need to be as honest with you as you have been with me, even though it hurts to talk about."

Katie could see Lisle's eyes glistening with tears, but they didn't fall. She nodded, silently urging her new friend to continue.

"I'm twenty-two now, so I was your age when the war began. I was madly in

224

love. People don't think a seventeen year old can really be in love, but that's bullshit. I know that your love for Walter was real, and how much his loss hurts you. I suffered a loss, too. Krejci was a beautiful boy. He was my age, and had dark curls, dark eyes, and a look that just melted me. I had known him since he was a child; his father managed our gardens and orchard. Krejci was my first kiss, out behind the drying shed. He was my lover the summer before the war broke out. We taught each about our bodies: how to caress them, how to kiss them..."

Lisle blushed, a far off look in her eyes.

"Such sweet, forbidden kisses. I loved the taste of him. He helped me become a woman. We knew it couldn't last. Our parents would never allow marriage, so it was just an innocent exploration, but that summer Krejci was my life. And Krejci was Corabian.

"I always thought that we were careful," Lisle said. "I never told my girlfriends or my sisters. I always looked to make sure no one was watching when I snuck off to our spot in the orchard. I still don't know who saw us."

"One night, a few weeks after the war started, Krejci never came home. We had been out late; much later than we should have. I had to sneak into my house or I would have gotten a beating from my father. I pretended I had been in my room, studying for exams. Krejci's father came by the next morning, asking for permission to take the day off. He wanted to look for his son."

Lisle's voice had become flat, emotionless. Katie thought it was more heartbreaking than if she were sobbing.

"They found him in the orchard, at our secret meeting spot. Right at the place where we made love. He had been hung. They beat him first, and castrated him. His cock had been stuffed in his mouth. A note was pinned to his naked body with a nail. It said he had been punished for taking what didn't belong to him. Everyone else thought it meant he had stolen something, but I knew the truth. He had taken my virginity."

Lisle stopped for a minute, her breath coming raggedly as if she had been running hard.

"I was so alone. I couldn't share my grief with anyone. I think I went out of my head for months. Were they going to do the same thing to me? I didn't go to his funeral. I couldn't."

Lisle shook her head slowly, tears spilling down her cheeks.

"I was too scared to go to the funeral of the man I loved. I thought if I went, it would confirm what everyone must suspect. Krejci's father hated me. He knew somehow. Krejci had never told him, he swore to me he wouldn't, but his father stared me after that with such hatred in his eyes. I was afraid to be home alone if he was working in the garden. I thought he might kill me, too."

Katie wrapped her arms around Lisle to comfort her. She could think of nothing to say, so she just held her friend and listened.

"Our town wasn't big, only ten thousand Citizens, and just a couple thousand Corabians, but when the deportations started, our rail station became a regular stopping point on the way to one of the camps. And my parents, who I had always thought of as good people, showed me the truth. I never knew their souls were so ugly.

"My father was almost gleeful when Krejci's family was deported. The poor families, laborers like Krejci's family, were the first to go in our town. My father went on for days after they were gone about how glad he was to be rid of him. This man had made my father wealthy, doing more of the work required to keep the orchards and gardens productive every year, and my father was treating him like a beggar on the street. It made no sense to me."

Lisle stopped for a minute, wiping the tears from her face. When Katie tried to comfort her, Lisle shook her head and pushed her away.

"If I don't tell it now, I'll never be able to tell it at all," she whispered. She wrapped her arms around her body as if she were chilled.

"Crowds of Citizens began going down to the rail station every day. They would shout and taunt the Corabians who were being deported from our town, or if no one was being taken that day, they would just harass the Corabians on the trains taking on water and coal. My parents went several times. I saw them. My mother, so beautiful and regal to me, shouting filth at her neighbors. I saw someone throw a stone that hit an old woman in the cheek and my mother laughed. You have to understand that I had always adored my mother. Everyone seemed to love my mother, to want to talk with her. Men would meet us on the street together and flirt with my mother by asking if we were twins. I had so wanted to look like and be like her when I was younger, but suddenly it made my skin crawl to know I looked like her.

"My father became rich beyond his dreams buying up the property of his old business acquaintances. He would regal us at the dinner table with tales of how badly he had cheated his former friends. I didn't recognize him anymore."

Lisle stared at the floor of the baggage car.

"My father changed too," Katie said. "He went from preaching that God is all good and loves you no matter what you do to trying to follow every law he found in the bible. He was suddenly sure God would punish us for the slightest transgression. And he applied that to the law of men as well. My Father still wanted to prove that he was a good Citizen. He refused to leave for Corabia when the first edicts were issued, those against Corabians owning property, because he was a Citizen, and he convinced most of our people not to leave either. To prove his loyalty, he was among the first to sign up for transportation. We had heard the rumors by this time. The camps in the south were death camps. Everyone talked about it. But he went, and he took my Mother and my sister Bela with him. To their graves.

"This man I loved with all my heart cursed me when I ran away. He made me choose between sucking cock in an alley or getting on a train to go to my death. He couldn't protect me."

After several minutes of silence, with both women lost in their own thoughts, Lisle continued her story.

"Eventually, I quit being afraid. It had been several years since Krejci was murdered, and no one had said anything to me. I began to think that maybe they didn't know who he had been with that night. I relaxed. When the war went bad, and the army began retreating, I relaxed more. The war swept through our town in just a few days. We all hid in our cellars and no one was hurt. Within a few weeks we had a battalion of Greek soldiers garrisoned in the town. For the first time since the war began, it felt safe. Do you know what I mean? To feel safe again after years of terror? I think I actually smiled and laughed a few times. I never forgave my parents, but I didn't worry they would find out about Krejci any longer.

"One night in February, Mother sent me to the church, with a note for the Priest. I never made it. A group of men, maybe four or five, were waiting near the church. The only thing I can remember is being grabbed and pulled backward against someone, a knife against my throat. 'You didn't think you were going to get away with it, did you?' he whispered in my ear. All that fear and panic and shame came flooding back to me and I couldn't even scream for help.

"When I woke up later, I was in the hospital. I had been unconscious for weeks. I had been beaten so severely that even after I regained consciousness the doctors still thought I would die."

Katie pulled away from Lisle and stared at her new friend. Lisle's face looked flawless, no scaring or broken bones. She reached her hand up to trace the line of Lisle's face.

"How?"

Lisle broke into laugher, a bitter edge to it. "They didn't touch my face. They broke my ribs, both arms, one of my legs, six of my fingers..." She shrugged.

"How long were you in the hospital?"

"Six months. I was only released a few days ago."

"Are you safe to travel?"

Lisle laughed again, a joyful peal that cascaded through the baggage car. "I'm safer here than back there," she said with a grin. "They did a good job in the hospital, caring for me. I had to learn how to walk again, and they were very patient. I had a guardian angel.

"When I woke up, really woke up, enough to be aware of my surroundings,

227

someone was standing in my room, reading my chart. He smiled at me, but never said a word. I thought he was a doctor, until he was leaving the room and I saw his uniform. He was a soldier. He came every day and checked on me.

"I learned that he was a Captain, stationed with the Greek battalion left in our town. He was a translator, and worked with the doctors at the hospital to be sure that the Greek soldiers who came into the hospital got good care. His battalion didn't have a medical unit with it, so they just used our hospital. Apparently he had been in the hospital when I was brought in, and didn't like the manner in which I was treated. I think I would have been left to die if he hadn't been there. He told the doctors that he would shoot them if I didn't recover. The doctors worked very hard to save me after that, but I don't think he really would have killed them over me."

Katie shook her head, thinking of Walter. Of course he would have, she thought. It's what certain men do.

"His name was Captain Aesop, like the fables, and he told stories. Once I was strong enough to talk, he would sit with me for a bit every day and tell me stories. We never talked about the war, or what had happened to me. He would tell me about life in the islands. He was a fisherman before he was drafted into the army. He told me about the different places he had been in the world. He never stayed long, just enough to see how I was progressing. When I was struggling to walk again, he stayed longer, shouting encouragement at me from across the room."

"What did your parents make of this Greek Captain?"

Lisle shrugged. "My parents never met him. They never came to see me when I was in the hospital. When I was ready to be discharged, Captain Aesop had a package for me. It was a new dress, what I'm wearing now. He said my other things were ruined and needed to be destroyed. He didn't realize the nurses had already brought my things into the room. The Captain was right, my clothes were ruined. Everything was covered in blood stains. The note that had been pinned to me when I was dumped at the hospital was still pinned to my ruined blouse. It said I didn't deserve to live, that I was an animal who fucked Corabians.

"I stuffed it all in the trash and put on my new dress and then modeled it for the Captain. He smiled when he saw me, and nodded, and then left to check on his soldiers. My mother was waiting for me outside the hospital. She had a bag in her hand. She told me I wasn't welcome in her home. She told me that my father would kill me if he saw me, so I had better leave town now. She told me I had dishonored them both and was no longer their daughter."

Lisle stopped for a moment, biting her lips to regain her composure. She shook her head as she continued.

"She never even asked me if it was true. The fact that it had been said publicly was enough for her to cast me out."

Katie gathered Lisle in her arms and held her while the older girl cried. She thought of Marie and her family and what Walter had told her and all the hurt and loss from the war. She cried with Lisle, and held her, until Lisle stopped. When Lisle spoke again, she spoke very softly.

"I walked out of town. I didn't know where I was going. Captain Aesop eventually found me. He was driving a Jeep and he made me get in. I thought he was going to take me back to his garrison, give me a place to live, but he didn't. He spent the entire drive complaining about how barbaric we were. That we deserved the pain of this war because we weren't quite human, as far as he was concerned. He showed none of the compassion he had showed me in the hospital. He drove me about thirty kilometers out into the country, to an Albanian check point and handed me over to them.

"The Albanians put me on the train that night. We have spent the last week shuttling around the country, picking up Corabian refugees. Camp survivors, except for you. I have no home and no salvation on this train. They will turn me away when we get to Corabia, and that's the same as killing me."

Katie held Lisle tighter. "I won't let them. I won't leave you. You're my sister now. We'll make up a story about how we survived the war together. Someone hid us. Something."

It was almost morning when the door to the baggage car slid open. The soldier who had allowed them into the car stepped inside. He frowned when he saw them sitting on the duffel bags. The girls scrambled to their feet, holding onto the wall of the train for support.

"We're going to be stopping soon for more water and coal," he said. "A group of government officials are going to board the train at the station. They will explain what's going to happen once we arrive in Corabia."

"Are we getting close?"

The soldier nodded. "I don't know how much time we'll spend stuck in sidings, letting other traffic use the track, but we're only a day's ride away. Our train is low priority, so we have to pull aside for all of the other trains."

Katie nodded, excited about seeing the Homeland. She glanced at Lisle, but couldn't read her face.

"You have to go back inside now. If the officials found you in here, it would bad for you, and for me."

"Will we be safe?" Lisle asked.

"Most everyone is sleeping now, so I don't think you'll have any problems."

"What about when everyone wakes up?"

"You don't have any choice. I can't leave you back here."

"Could we go back up front, to the flatbed car behind the coal tender?"

The soldier shook his head. "You'd be arrested and sent to prison, or worse, if they think you're collaborators. Let's go."

The girls followed him from the car, stepping into the darkened passenger car. As they walked through the train cars, past sleeping refugees, Katie was afraid they weren't going to find seats together. She felt a wave of panic wash over her at the idea of being separated from her new friend. She had only known Lisle for two days and yet she felt calm and safe in her presence.

Katie grinned broadly when they saw a pair of seats together about halfway through the train. Katie turned and pointed them out. Lisle laughed gently at Katie's smile. Katie bit her lip to keep from crying in embarrassment. She didn't want to be thought of as a child by this beautiful woman. Lisle nodded for Katie to take the window seat and she slipped into the seat by the aisle.

Lisle yawned. "It's so late," she whispered. "We should really sleep. Do you mind if I lean against you?"

Katie shook her head no. She settled back in her seat. Lisle leaned in next to her, resting her head on Katie's shoulder. Lisle was asleep within minutes, her breathing deep and slow. Katie watched her sleep, her face peaceful, until the rocking of the train lulled her into sleep as well.

Katie woke to the sound of another train thundering past them. They were stopped in a siding. A freight train roared past them, right outside her window, seemingly close enough to touch, shaking the train, and leaving a barren vista in its wake. They were crossing a semi-arid plain, full of scrub juniper trees. Katie was unsure if they were in Corabia or Montrovia. There was no natural boundary between the two countries, only a political one engineered a hundred or so years ago. Like the people who lived there, who were indistinguishable at a glance, the two countries were also too similar to tell apart. Katie had heard stories, as a child, of entire villages in these border flat lands that considered themselves Montrovian or Corabian, only to find out during an official census that they belonged to the other country. She didn't understand why anyone would go to war for this.

The train stopped every few hours to allow other trains to pass. Sometimes they idled in the sidings for two or three hours in a stretch. At one stop trains were passing them every little while. At the next they sat for hours and nothing came by. At each stop, a group of soldiers would dismount the train from the baggage cart and cordon off the area to ensure that none of the refugees slipped away from the train. Katie didn't understand why they were being treated like prisoners, if this was Corabia. None of the soldiers ever spoke. They just stood silently, guns at the ready, as if there was something precious in the wasteland behind them.

It took three more days before they reached the city. The train would move in spurts, shuttling from one siding to the next. Katie spent the time in conversation with Lisle or dozing. None of the Corabians near them seemed to care that the girls were obviously not from the camps. It was clear to Katie that they noticed, for she caught them staring, but no one ever said a word to her, or even shot her a dirty look. Everyone seemed somewhat dazed that their own ordeal was about to end.

Katie thought something different was happening when the train stopped on the tracks. It hadn't pulled into a siding to allow another train to pass; it had just shuffled to a shuddering stop in the middle of the arid plain. She could see nothing from her window except two army trucks parked near the track and a group of men walking towards the train. The men climbed aboard the train near the front car, and immediately the train jerked into life again, slowly building speed.

Two men, dressed in drab suits, entered the car where they were sitting and called for quiet. One of the men was older, his hair receding, his white shirt tucked over a large stomach. The other was young and lean, deeply tanned, and clearly the more comfortable of the two. He had loosened his tie from his collar, and undone the top button of his shirt.

"Welcome to Corabia," the younger man said.

The car erupted in a ragged cheer. Katie found herself joining in, feeling overwhelmed by the knowledge that she was home. She glanced at Lisle out of the corner of her eye and saw the older girl was white as a sheet. She squeezed Lisle's hand to reassure her.

"We're from the Relocation Services Office," he continued in a loud voice, trying to be heard above the noise. "We're here to tell you what is going to happen when you detrain, in about an hour or so. We have some rules to share with you to make the relocation process as smooth as possible, so please pay attention."

The older man stepped forward. "None of you are Corabians," he said. "You don't automatically belong here. The people of Corabia have been gracious to take you in, so you must obey the rules..."

An angry buzz surged through the train car.

"What he means," the younger man shouted, cutting off the beginning protest, "is that you're coming into a city where people already have lives, jobs, families and friends. It's not an easy process to assimilate everyone who has nowhere else to go, so please be patient with us.

"You will be provided housing, and food, and medical care at the relocation center. We will work with you to try to determine if you have other family in Corabia. Ultimately, you will be relocated from the city to another location within the country. Wherever possible, we will send you where others from your town or village have been relocated, to help with your transition, but we can promise nothing."

"We can't lose our country just to take you in," the older man said.

231

"Go to hell," someone in the rear of the car shouted. "We're the same as you."

The younger man stepped forward, his hands raised. "You must understand that we share many things, most notably our faith, but we are very different as well. Most of you come from families that moved north from Corabia generations ago. You are welcome here, but you are different from those of us who never left."

More groans and complaints rose from the men and women in the train car.

The younger man grinned at the complaints. "Please be patient. We have a process for this, but it will all work out. You are all welcome, unless you are found to have committed crimes before or during the war…

"What crimes?" a man near the front called out.

"Murder. Rape. Collaboration. Anything really…"

"We've all been in the camps for years," the man said. "What crimes could we have committed?"

"You'd be surprised at what's been reported by one refugee against another," the older man said.

"Let's move on," the younger said. "When we pull into the station, you will board buses to go directly to the Center to be checked in. It's just short drive from the station. Once there, get in any line. It doesn't matter which line you stand in, everything is the same from line to line. We've had refugees worried that something bad will happen if they stand in the wrong line. All the lines are the same!

"We will ask for a complete history, so you can be matched to any relatives or neighbors who might already be here. If you managed to hide your papers during your time in the camp, please present them. We are trying to create a census of who survived and an accounting of who didn't. We will ask about your family. We will ask about everything you knew about the camps: who was in charge, who were the guards, who killed whom. I know this is painful, but it is necessary. We want to bring those responsible for the camps to account, so your help will be required."

A noise ran through the car, light and urgent. "Hang the bastards," someone shouted.

The young man nodded. "We will catch them and hang them. Just like what's been happening at Nuremburg."

"Hanging's not good enough!" someone shouted and everyone laughed. Katie thought it was a horrible sound.

Lisle looked more and more frightened as the men spoke. "They will send me back," she whispered to Katie. "If they don't even want all of you, they won't accept me. They will send me home to be killed."

"No," Katie whispered. "We will protect each other. I'll say that you are my sister. Who will know? If we ever meet someone from Mountain City we will tell them something else. But for now, you are my older sister. And you must help me. If they think I am a collaborator, they will turn me away. We survived because father hid us before he was transported. We hid and we stole to live."

"No," Lisle said, shaking her head. "We are too well fed, you and I, compared to them. Especially to the ones who were just freed. They won't believe us. Even if they believe we are sisters they will think we collaborated. The war was so long, how could two girls survive? We need a better story, or they will hang us."

Lisle thought for a few minutes.

"Let's tell the truth, or a version of it. We will tell them that father hid us with a neighbor. He paid him all his money, and trusted thirty years of friendship. But the man reneged as soon as father was transported. He sold you on the streets to pay for our food. As for me..."

"He kept you for himself," said Katie, "and when the war was lost, he beat you until you almost died. You were in the hospital for a long time before we could flee to the south. And here we are."

"They might believe it. What if they have questions about our family and friends?"

Katie nodded. "Let me answer. I know Mountain City. My father knew so many people, and he traveled here, so they may know of him, too."

"They will know he didn't have a third daughter."

"Eventually we may be found out, but at least this should get us in. If someone here does know him well enough to know he has two daughters, not three, they certainly won't remember that Bela was three years younger than me rather than older. By the time anyone knows, we can figure out what we need to do to be safe." Now that they had a plan, they settled back in their seats and watched anxiously for the city to appear.

The train ran down a long dike, neatly tended fields on one side and the rocky coast of the Adriatic sea on the other. The Montrovian invasion had stalled before it reached this point. This land had never seen war. Katie was excited to see the Adriatic. She had never been close to it before. Her father had always promised that they would vacation at the sea when they were older, but they had never gone. Katie put the window down and let the breeze from the sea wash over her. It smelled funny, salty and musty, and she wrinkled her nose. The grey waves receded until they merged with the sky. It was a bit overwhelming, and she felt her heart beating hard in her chest. But she was excited for more than a glimpse of the sea. She was in the Homeland, the place her ancestors had lived. The place where the faith had been born and nurtured through countless generations. She had never visited Corabia, and yet she felt so excited to be there. It was like coming home, in some strange way. Like Corabia was all that was left of her family.

The train pulled away from the sea, giving Katie her first glimpse of the city. She gasped when she saw the skyline suddenly appear before her. Katie had thought that Mountain City had been a large, complex place, but it was nothing next to this. Someone had told her that more than a million people lived in the city of Corabia, but she hadn't believed it. She hadn't even been able to imagine it. Katie grabbed Lisle's hand and squeezed, overwhelmed by the immensity of the city before her.

Corabia was a sprawling metropolis that went on as far as Katie could see. The skyline was dominated by granite and brick buildings that soared fifteen to twenty stories into the air. The tallest buildings in Mountain City had been the apartment complex where she had lived with Stojespahl. The four buildings of the complex had been five stories tall and they had overlooked the city like lords on a throne. They wouldn't even have been visible to her now. The soaring towers, their facades glistening with windows, made an incomplete semi-circle around the city. Katie guessed there must be a hundred of them at least. They didn't match, like the four apartments had, but that added to the majesty of the scene. Red brick, yellow brick, dull gray limestone, and shiny black granite all thrown together in a way that seemed to scream that the city was so rich it didn't know what to do with itself. And they just went on and on and on.

Nestled against the sea, the older walled city, built in traditional stone, looked out of place next to the modern towers. The incongruity of the low stone buildings with the modern towers made the city seem even more modern. It was simply growing away from its medieval heart. Beyond the walled city, against the sea, the docks were packed with ships. Men, made tiny by the distance, swarmed the ships. Cranes lifted covered pallets from the vessels onto rows of waiting trucks. It was unlike anything Katie had ever seen.

The train slowed as they approached the city, inching through a sprawling cemetery as it neared the station. The cemetery seemed to mimic the larger city, with a smaller walled off section at its core, full of older rough hewn stone markers, surrounded by taller, modern granite spires and statues. The cemetery seemed as large to Katie as Mountain City itself. She wondered if it was the only cemetery in the city. How many graves do you need each year in a city of a million people?

The train pulled to a stop in a large covered station with several concrete platforms. Other trains were in the station, but were several tracks away from Katie's train. She could see passengers jostling each other as they moved along the platforms, either rushing to catch a train or more slowly heading into the station. Katie felt a stab of disappointment. Everyone looked so normal. It was as if the war had never happened here. No one stood on their platform to meet their train, just more soldiers in a loose cordon. At least these soldiers weren't carrying guns like the refugees were criminals.

No one in their carriage moved. Katie could see that some of the Corabian survivors were stepping down from the cars at the front of the train and being herded along the platform. She was unable to move. Her heart was hammering in her chest, and suddenly she felt afraid. She looked at Lisle and could see the fear on her friend's face. Katie leaned over to whisper in Lisle's ear.

"It will be okay," she said. "We're sisters."

A soldier came to the door of their car and nodded for everyone to leave. Katie and Lisle waited in the short line to disembark. Once they reached the platform, they were swept along in the crowd to a row of waiting buses. They were almost put on separate buses, so Lisle grabbed Katie by the hand and didn't let go. They stepped against the tide of refugees to move to the next bus in the line to be sure they remained together. The driver of their bus was a young man with a dark tan and greasy hair. He gave Lisle a broad smile when she climbed on the bus. The girls sat together near the front of the bus.

The bus trundled into the crush of traffic outside the train station. Katie had never seen so many cars and trucks in one place. The noise of the city was overwhelming. The sidewalks were packed, filled with people who seemed intent on getting somewhere. The crush around her bore no resemblance to Mountain City. The market in the city had been as much about people gathering together as it had been a place of commerce. It was where everyone came to gossip, and flirt and just catch up. The people on the streets here shared none of that, all intent on their own activity. Even thought there were many more people, they all seemed more alone than Katie could believe.

Lisle grabbed Katie's hand and hung on, squeezing hard. Katie realized this must be even more overwhelming for her friend, who had come from a much smaller town than she. The trip on the bus lasted twenty minutes, although they only went a few blocks. The bus waited for a break in traffic and turned into a walled compound, driving past an ornate gate with a decorative metal arch. Inside the gate, the streets were almost empty. The people Katie did see were strolling, not racing from place to place. The bus pulled up before a large gymnasium that looked big enough to hold several thousand spectators. When they disembarked, Katie could see the arched roof of the train station in the distance. It would have been quicker to walk, she thought.

A man stood outside the bus, directing them through an open set of double doors. He reminded them that any line would do. The refugees moved slowly, as if they were sleep walking, studying their surroundings suspiciously. Katie kept Lisle's hand in hers as they followed the group into a cavernous auditorium. Lines of refugees snaked across the room, and a small group of men and one woman sat on the floor of the auditorium under the gaze of a bored policeman. Katie watched as another woman was sent from the front of her line to the group in the center of the room. The woman screamed and shouted, and had to be pulled by two men and forced to her knees with the others. She quit shouting, but cried loudly for several minutes.

Lisle's grip on Katie's hand grew tighter. Katie glanced at her friend, suddenly afraid for her. Lisle's face had drained of color. A line of sweat had broken out on her brow. She was breathing fast, shallow breaths, almost gasping for air. The line they were standing in hadn't moved in the twenty minutes they had been inside the building.

"I can't do it," Lisle mumbled, more to herself than Katie. "You go on. I'll just go back." She tried to step out of line.

Katie tugged hard on Lisle's arm, refusing to let her out of line. "What are you doing?" she whispered.

"I can't end up there," Lisle said, pointing to the group sitting on the floor. "I won't let them do that to me again. I'll just leave."

"You're with me," Katie said. "Everything will be fine." She wished she could believe it.

Lisle leaned forward so she could whisper in Katie's ear. She pointed out a policeman with a dog, standing against the far wall of the auditorium. "He'll smell me," she said, "and know I'm different. They'll see it on my face. If they find out, they'll take me in the back…" She shook her head, a look of terror on her face.

Katie didn't know what to do. Lisle was about to bolt from the room and that would ruin everything. She had never seen anyone in such a state. She reached up and cupped Lisle's face in her hand. Lisle jerked away at the touch, but couldn't move because Katie still had her hand. Katie reached up again, gentling her, feeling Lisle relax to her touch. She leaned forward.

"If the dog can smell anything, it will be Walter's seed in my belly. You can't leave me to them. You have to protect me, because you're my older sister. I'm lost without you."

Lisle nodded. She seemed to be able to focus on the idea that Katie needed her to be safe. Her breathing slowed. When a young man came by with a pail of water and a ladle, Lisle drank deeply. She seemed herself by the time they reached the front of the line.

A man beckoned them forward. He sat behind a small folding table on a folding chair. The man was older, in his fifties, maybe, with thinning gray hair and a round, sallow face. He peered at them, bird-like, from a pair of dirty glasses. His dark suit had stains on the lapels and his tie was loosened around his neck. He looked disheveled and completely overwhelmed. He had a stack of big ledgers piled up around his feet. An open blue ledger was on the table.

He motioned them forward impatiently. The table held the ledger, a bottle of ink, and an assortment of pens.

"Where?" he asked, smiling benignly.

Katie looked around the gymnasium, wondering how they had gotten to the only table with a character straight out of a Dickens novel, like her father used to read to her before bed.

"Where?" she repeated.

The man grimaced and shook his head. "Another stupid one," he mumbled, shocking Katie. "Where are you from?"

"Mountain City."

The man stared at her blankly.

"In Donat's Coal Basin," she said. "Up North in the mountains."

"Oh," he said, nodding. He put the blue ledger on the floor at his feet and picked up a green one.

Katie was disappointed. The blue ledger had several pages of names in it. The green ledger didn't have an entire page completed. She could tell none of the names were her family's. Her heart sank at the realization none of them had made it. She looked away, biting her lip, trying to keep from crying, when she realized that all the tables in the gymnasium had a green ledger.

The man recorded their names and ages, but stumped them when he asked for their occupations. Katie was about to say something about her life on the streets when Lisle interrupted her.

"Children," Lisle said. "We were just children when all this started. I hadn't yet taken my examinations for university and Katie had just started the upper school."

"Where are your parents?" the man asked.

"Sent to the camps," Katie said. "Along with our little sister, Bela. She was eleven."

"Are you asking me to believe your parents just turned you loose…"

"Oh, no," Katie said. "We had a huge row about it. We had heard the rumors and begged father to run away, but he wouldn't. He thought it was his duty, as the leader of our village church, to go where his flock was going. Our neighbor heard the argument and promised father to look after us."

"So you lived with your neighbor through the war?"

"No," Lisle said. "Not the whole war. He turned out to be a wicked man. He took her…, our father's money, but then he turned against us. He wanted me for himself and locked me in the basement, except for when he used me. He finally grew tired of me and beat me nearly to death. I was in the hospital for several months. I'd be dead if the soldiers hadn't arrived."

The man turned to Katie, a distasteful look on his face. "And you? He kept you locked up as well?"

Katie shook her head, suddenly feeling ashamed. "He sold me to a soldier, Captain Stojespahl, who put me on the streets to earn a living."

"You have a special talent?"

Katie gave the man her most brilliant smile. "I fuck really well."

The man frowned, and then shook his head disdainfully. "What happened to this Captain? How did you get away?"

"I killed him," Katie said. "The day the city fell. He told me Lisle was in the hospital and was going to die. He was drunk, and fell asleep, so I took his pistol and put it under his chin…"

"And you shot him?" the man asked, his face agog.

"No," Katie said, giving him another smile. "I woke him up so he would know what was happening and then I shot him."

Katie was suddenly afraid that her admission to murder might get her sent to the center of the gymnasium, but the official seemed pleased with the story. He neatly wrote both girls names in the ledger and gave them identity cards.

"Go to that table over there," he said, pointing across the gym, "and they will assign you to the women's dormitory and get you a ration card for the dining hall."

Katie started to turn away, but Lisle hadn't moved.

"We need something more private than a dormitory," Lisle said. "We can't be in a great big room with everyone else. It won't work."

"It's what we have," the man said. "We don't have space to give everyone a private room. You've all been living in barracks anyway…"

"It won't work," Lisle said again. "We haven't been in barracks." The color had drained from her face and she was sweating again. Katie didn't know what was bothering her, but Lisle looked like she was going to be sick.

"We don't have special rooms, except for the sick," the man said. "You're the healthiest person to come through here in months. Maybe you don't need to be here…"

"Maybe I don't," Lisle said. "The barracks won't…"

"I'm pregnant," Katie blurted out.

"What?" the man said.

"I'm going to have a baby."

The man shrugged. "We don't give private rooms just because you couldn't keep your legs together."

Lisle leaned forward, putting her hands on the man's folding table so her face was just inches from his. "The woman from the train have threatened the baby. They've said they'll cut it out of her."

238

"Why?"

"Didn't you listen to what we told you?" Lisle hissed. "She was forced to work the streets. The father is Montrovian. The women want to kill the baby."

"Maybe they should," he said. "Wasn't this whole war caused by this kind of thing? Mingling of the blood?"

"I'm going to pretend you didn't say that," Lisle replied. "I'm not going to report you to your supervisor. I am going to promise you that if anything happens to Katie or the baby, I will come back to this gymnasium and kill you. Do you understand me?"

In the end the man relented, and sent them to talk to a woman about an apartment.

Krang sat atop a small rise, the forest at his back, and surveyed the village before him. It was no more than a half mile away, across a sloping barren field, an odd mix of old brick and mud cottages, surrounded by a vast array of hastily built shanties that stretched off in all directions. The village had probably been home to a few hundred people before the shanties had sprung up, but now might house as many as a thousand people. Refugees? Soldiers who came home with families and needed a new home? Krang couldn't tell. And from this distance, the village appeared to be recently deserted. No one walked the streets, or tended the gardens. Except for the field directly in front of him, surrounded by pickets with red ribbons, which Krang assumed to be a mine field, the outlying fields had all been planted. A single burned out two ton truck sat astride the road that entered the village. If anything, the scene was eerily reminiscent of when he and Katie had first seen Marie's farm house. The only thing missing were the bodies hanging from a telephone pole.

Krang laughed. Villages like this one didn't have electricity or telephones, so there would be no telephone poles. He still expected to find a massacre. He stood and stretched, slung his satchel over one shoulder and the shovel and pickaxe over the other and began to make his way down a narrow path that skirted the mine field towards the village. It had been several days since Krang had seen anyone, and he felt excited about the prospect of talking with someone, if anyone was alive.

The path Krang followed eventually merged with the main road running into the village. He studied the village as he walked, and his heart sank. In ten minutes, nothing had moved, and he heard no sounds beyond the song birds from the woods and the gentle wind rustling the leaves of the trees. It was a dead village. Krang stepped from the path onto a dirt road, one hundred meters from the shanties. He passed the dead truck. It was not a recent kill. Hundreds of bullet holes peppered the cab of the truck and the fuel tank had ruptured. Who ever had died here had been buried long ago.

The road into the village was blocked with a makeshift gate covered with two red ribbons. The gate was leaning against two fifty-five gallon steel drums, but open on the sides. Krang paused for a moment, wondering why the gate was there and if someone had planted land mines at the sides of it, then started around it.

"Stop!"

Krang froze, and looked up in alarm. A man was crouched in the scant shade of small tree, no more than twenty feet beyond the gate. The man was drab and small and blended into the dirt of the road. If he had not spoken, Krang would have walked directly past him, he seemed so insignificant. The man struggled to stand, using makeshift wooden crutches. His right leg was missing above the knee. He hobbled over to Krang, stopping ten feet away from the gate.

"Go away. We have the cholera here. Or maybe plague. Something. People are dying. Go away." His voice was weak from disuse, and Krang had to listen intently to understand him.

Krang studied the man, trying to determine if he was sick, or simply exhausted. He stepped around the gate and approached the man.

"Maybe I can help," he said.

The man looked at him hopefully. "Are you a doctor?"

Krang shook his head. "No. But I can bury your dead, so that those of you who are able can spend your time on the living."

The man nodded slowly, disappointed. "We need a doctor, but God sends a gravedigger. I suppose after the horror we have been through it makes sense. If nothing else, it's typical."

Krang looked past the man, down the simple road that bisected the village. "Is anyone else alive?"

The man nodded. "The village council has ordered everyone to stay in their homes until we stop dying. We don't know what is killing us. Five died last week, and even more this week. They only come out to take their dead to the church, and to pull water from the well in the evening. I think it's the water that's killing us, but what can you do? Without the well we're all dead anyway."

Krang thought the man looked no more alive than any in his entourage, but he didn't say anything.

The man nodded over his shoulder. "Go on down the street, past the shacks to the village proper. On the left you'll see the church. It's got no steeple or any bell or the like, but it has a stone front, and you'll recognize it. That's where the dead are. We haven't been keeping up with putting them in the ground."

He turned around and hobbled back to his spot beneath the tree, folding himself up in a way that was just a razor's edge from simply collapsing. He waved Krang on towards the village.

240

Krang nodded, and walked on. The shanties he walked past were made from scraps of lumber, broken crates, animal hides and cardboard, packed so tightly together that it appeared you would have to walk through some of the ones bordering the road to reach the ones behind. He could sense people staring at him from the dark interiors of their shacks, but saw no one. Krang felt more alone than he had in the last week of solitude.

The church was small, but still the largest building in the village. It was a wood-frame story-and-a-half with a stone front. The remnants of a sign stood next to the street in front of the church. Someone had burned the sign to the ground, so only two posts remained, blackened at the top from the fire. Krang smiled. He imagined the sign had been erected by the army, whether Montrovian or Corabian he couldn't say, and the people of the village had burned it to the ground as a way of rebellion. The sign certainly wasn't to name the church, although there had been a church in Mountain City with a sign out front. A village this small didn't require signs for anything, and any way, this church didn't need a sign to tell the world what it was. It was clearly and immediately a church, even without the sign, the steeple, or the bell. It just was a church. Krang was struck by the power that the building had, to so declare its nature and intent without the benefit of recognized symbols. If I believed in God, I would believe that God was in this place, he thought. As fully and completely in this church as He was absent from the camp.

Krang dropped his satchel bag on the ground near the door, leaning his pick and shovel against the front of the building, and entered. A single large room filled the entire first floor, except for a small room at the rear of the building that he guessed was the minister's office. A brass cross dominated one wall, and three small stained glass windows cast colorful shadows. The church had no pews, just wooden benches stacked neatly against the wall.

The seven bodies, covered with sheets, lay on a tarp on the cleared area of the floor, three of them children to judge by their size. The shrouded bodies seemed out of place in the peaceful room, but where else would you put your dead? Krang turned and left through the front door looking for the cemetery. He circled around the side of the church, and saw a stone wall running from the rear of the church. A narrow steel gate was pulled shut, the only break in the stone wall. Krang went back for his tools and satchel.

The cemetery was centuries old, commanding the steep hill which lay back of the church. A low stone wall encircled the original portion of the cemetery, a small relatively level plot of ground directly behind the church, but that ground had been used up decades ago. Someone had torn two openings in the stone wall and the cemetery had expanded down the hill. Several attempts had been made to encompass the new cemetery with a similar stone wall, but eventually that project had been abandoned. It appeared that recently, people had been stealing stones from the wall to cover the tops of shallow graves and protect the dead from scavenging animals.

Krang walked down the hill, looking for a suitable spot. It was early afternoon. He hoped to be able to get two or even three graves finished before the light gave out. Krang saw a mound of fresh soil off to his left. Someone had started to dig a trench. With a little work, Krang thought he could expand it to fit the seven bodies resting in the church. Krang dropped his tools, and stared at the open wound in the ground. He wished he had a cigarette. It seemed like it had been months since he had smoked. Krang shook his head. This reminded him of the soldiers' grave in the forest. It wasn't right, he thought, to dump them namelessly into a hole in the ground, so much rubbish to be got rid of. Their families had a right to have a place to come and grieve, to tell them of the exploits of their children and grandchildren. To somehow keep them in the family.

He would turn the trench into three graves, one for each child. It was already deep enough, wide enough. He could bury them distinctly, and still take advantage of what had been already done. Krang looked at the ground around him. The soil here was rich and deep, with no rock outcroppings to make the digging difficult. A tree shaded the area from the worst of the afternoon sun. It would be tight, but Krang could fit the others in, he knew he could.

Taking a bit of string from his pack, Krang laid out the four adult graves. Then he moved a little further down the hill and laid out three more. They will need them, he thought, whether I am here or not. Using the pick to break up the soil, Krang fell into a steady rhythm. He liked the feeling of the sweat running from his pores, as if the very work cleansed him. He had never worked before, not really. In all the years before the camp, when he had held jobs in the mines and the metal works, all of his energy had been spent avoiding work. There had been times, he knew, when the anger of co-workers, or the attention of supervisors, had forced him to exert enough energy to work up a sweat, but even then it had been aimless, with no care for how it all came out, and always less than everyone else. How many jobs had he quit, when he had run out of ways to not work? And how many times had he not been allowed to quit, but been fired?

Krang smiled to think of it. What a leech I was. And Emma really no better, moving from office to office looking for the perfect job. She would have been happy finding a boss who required no more than a blowjob a day. And I would have been happy for her to find it. My father must have hated me and he must have certainly been embarrassed by me.

And what of the camp? It was unreasonable to call that work. The inmates had been the ones to do the work. He just stood over them and forced them to do whatever he wanted. And because he knew the work was meaningless, just

242

another way among hundreds to kill the Corabians off, it hadn't mattered what had happened then either. So he had never worked, not really worked, in his entire life.

Pushing the shovel blade deep into the dirt and feeling the resistance as he lifted it out delighted Krang. Each shovel full of soil that he deposited beside the grave had a rich aroma, a tanginess that spoke to him of life, not death. It was as if he were building houses, not digging graves. And Krang loved it. Even the fatigue, the pain in his lower back and shoulders, the blisters on his hand. Within an hour, Krang was straightening the walls of the first grave.

The people of the village came to watch him, silently, in ones or twos. When Krang stopped, while digging the second grave, he found that someone had left him a meal, wrapped in a kerchief, and several cigarettes. Krang smiled, lit up one of the cigarettes, and smoked it in solitude. He had been in the village for several hours, and except for the man at the gate, not one person had said a single word to him.

Krang sat on the edge of the grave, his feet dangling inside it, and bit deeply into an onion, reveling in the sweetness of it. How can I see things today that would have escaped my notice a year ago? How can I eat an onion and smoke a cigarette, my shoulders aching, and feel content? How can I hold Katie safe in my mind, and trust that she and the baby are alright? And in missing them, know that she is free and safe without me, and be okay with that? And even want her to find love again?

Krang took a deep drag on the cigarette, and exhaled languidly. The laugh welled up inside him slowly, a deep resonant sound that filled him with joy. He looked away from the graveyard, up into the deepening blue sky of the evening.

"Sarah," he whispered, "wherever you may be, know this: you have changed me. I think you would approve of who I have become." He shrugged. "Or maybe not. We'll never know. I have no idea where you found the courage and strength to forgive me. I would not be able to do that, I am sure. I promise you that I will not let the world forget your husband and son, or any of the others whom I killed. I will build a memorial to them, so the world never forgets the horror that we caused at that place."

Krang looked up and saw his entourage filtering into the graveyard from the forest. Even they filled him with a sense of peace. They were his eternal witnesses, proof that he had not just dreamed his previous existence. They would keep him honest, stopping him from revising his history, stopping him from editing the camp out of existence. And I would otherwise, he thought. I would pretend to myself that it had never happened until I believed it. They are my saviors.

Night fell and Krang kept working on the graves. A three quarters moon rose in the east, hanging low in the sky, lighting his work. He finally climbed from the third grave, then sat with his feet hanging into it, and smoked another cigarette. Would it have made a difference if I had dug the graves of each man I killed? Krang wondered. If instead of forcing them to dig their own, or using the backhoe to dig great big pits, if we had done it ourselves? I think I would have had to see them more as individuals if I had to bury each of them.

He shook his head. I could look a man in the face and kill him easily enough, so maybe burying them wouldn't have meant a thing. Except that I hated to work, so I wouldn't have killed anyone if I knew I was going to have to dig their grave. Krang lay on his back in the cemetery, his head resting on his satchel, and watched the stars until he fell asleep.

Krang buried the children first. He had finished the fourth grave in the morning, just before the day's heat rose from the ground in waves so thick you could see them, and then returned to the church. Someone had left wooden markers, with names painted on them, and burial linens, next to each body. Krang had carefully undressed each child, piling the garments together to be burned. He washed each of them in water he brought from the well and wrapped them in the clean linen. Krang was amazed that in the midst of such horror, after years of war and death, someone still had fine linen for burying the dead; and yet he was saddened that the living deprived themselves of such finery, in order that the dead might have it.

The children were laid to rest in the trench grave, separated by walls of stone. He placed a small branch of evergreen with each of them, and quickly covered them up. When each grave was filled he hammered in the markers. Krang cried silently, tears streaming down his face, from the moment he began washing their bodies until he had finished burying them. He never wiped away the tears. They were, to him, a sign of his guilt.

The adults were buried without tears, but with as much care as the children.

Krang dug a small pit behind the church and placed all of the clothing and other possessions that had been left with the dead in it. He soaked everything in oil from a lantern he found in the church and burned them, smoking a cigarette. The tears began again, still silent. He couldn't understand why, after surviving years of war, these people had to die now. Of all the atrocities they had seen, why had it been influenza, or the measles, or cholera that had the strength to kill them? And why them, rather than him?

He dug three more graves that afternoon, and ate the simple meal that was left for him, then curled up next to the children's grave to sleep. He left the next morning, without having spoken to anyone beyond the man at the gate.

The washed out moonlight flooded the room through the bare window, bathing the empty twin bed in its harsh glare. Lisle lay in darkness, curled on the second twin bed, her body wrapped gently around the girl. Katie had finally drifted off, after crying for hours. She was afraid that Lisle was going to leave, and she was right. Once morning came, Lisle would leave this place that didn't want her. Lisle gently disentangled herself from the girl, being careful not to wake her, and went and lay on the other bed. She breathed in deeply. She needed space to sleep, not that she expected to sleep tonight, but it would have been impossible to sleep touching the girl.

The room was a simple box, with the one curtainless window, two beds without linens, and a closet without a closet rod or door. The beds were so close together that Lisle could reach out and touch the sleeping girl without moving. It was hot, but Lisle wouldn't disrobe. Katie was sleeping in her shift, and still had beads of sweat on her neck. The girl's breathing had calmed and she seemed to be untroubled, now that she was asleep.

Lisle was exhausted and wished that she could sleep, but she knew the nightmares would start if she did, and tonight she didn't have the energy to deal with them. Even though she could never remember the dreams, the fear they created left her feeling paralyzed. It was her one clear memory from the attack: being too afraid to run away or fight back, even though she knew what was going to happen. When she fell asleep it was as if the attack was happening again, right now. She never knew what made the dreams come. Some nights she had them, some she didn't, but she suspected that the fear she had felt all day, since arriving in the city, was likely to bring them on.

Lisle watched the rise and fall of Katie's chest, timing her breathing to that of the girl. After only four days, she had already grown closer to Katie than anyone since Krejci died. Could she trust her life in Katie's hands? Did it matter? Lisle had this feeling she wasn't supposed to be here. Not just in Corabia, but *here* at all. The attack should have killed her, and but for the intervention of one Greek captain, it would have. She should be dead.

Lisle had woken up on the train when they pulled into a siding to take on water. She had looked at the girl sleeping in the seat next to her, surprised to see the empty seat taken. Surprised that the girl looked more like her than the other refugees on the train. She had wondered, for a fleeting instant, if the girl were another Citizen being thrown out of Montrovia. But she had known it wasn't so.

Maybe because it was the middle of the night, the soldiers hadn't put up their regular cordon around the train. Lisle had stood and stretched, and wandered forward on the stopped train. She was thinking about running away when she saw the flatbed car between the coal tender and the passenger cars. She had instantly thought it would be easier to kill herself than wait for someone else to finish the job.

Unlike the other cars, where you could easily step from one car to the next, the deck of the flatbed wasn't aligned and was at least two feet from the end of the passenger car. It was hard enough to climb onto it when the train had been stopped. Lisle had decided to throw herself down between the cars of the train, to be crushed on the track under those beautiful steel wheels. She hadn't thought it would hurt, it would all be over so quickly if the train was going fast enough. Once the train had begun moving, it had simply been a matter of getting up her nerve. She had almost been ready when she saw Katie standing at the edge of the platform, like an idiot, trying to jump onto the flatbed. Lisle had been sure Katie was going to fall and die under the wheels of the train, and it would have been her fault.

Lisle had been so angry at Katie that night. Angry at Katie for butting into her life. Angry that Katie would risk her life over a schoolgirl crush. Angry that anyone could feel that way about her, without knowing the truth. Katie still didn't know the truth, not all of it. Lisle would never share all of it, but she had felt compelled to share something.

She looked over at the sleeping girl. Katie looked so innocent, like she was without a care in the world. She was innocent, in spite of all that she had done. And somehow that meant that Lisle needed to protect her, but what could she do? How could she risk staying here?

Lisle sighed, feeling the single tear trickling down the bridge of her nose. She could feel her body beginning to itch, along the scars, and bit the inside of her cheek to distract herself. She wrapped her arms around herself, allowing the warmth of her body to ease the tension she was feeling. Lisle watched Katie sleeping until she drifted off herself.

Chapter Eighteen

Katie stared out the window of the apartment watching for any sign of Lisle on the street below. Lisle had been gone all day and Katie was anxious for her return. Katie smiled to herself. She was always worried that Lisle wasn't coming home. She shook her head trying to dispel her fear. They had been in the refugee village for a month and their lives were falling into a normal pattern. It seemed surprising, considering the first night's tears. Katie could still feel the shadow of that horrible night haunting her, when she had been lying on the unmade bed in the little room, listening to Lisle explain why she had to leave.

In the morning, Rena had saved them. Rena was a few years older than Lisle, had lived in Corabia all her life and had gone to work in the refugee center straight from University. She had laughed when she entered their room, unannounced, and found them still sleeping on the twin beds. Rena had come to see them because she was curious about the two sisters who were expecting a baby. Since no one knew if they would be relocated before the baby came, she moved them into family housing. The new apartment had a kitchenette that opened onto a small sitting room, a bedroom, and a small attached bath. She had arranged for the big bed to be replaced with two single beds. Rena had shown them how to draw linens from the laundry, where to shop with their ration cards, and where they could find second hand clothes for sale. Lisle had been so grateful that she had broken down and cried.

Rena had also told them where to go to see about jobs. Katie now worked part time in a nursery at the hospital, watching kids whose parents were either too sick to take care of them or who needed to be watched for a few hours so their parents could see a doctor. Lisle ended up with a position as a clerk at the library, spending her days re-shelving books. She had told Katie she found a sense of freedom spending so much time alone, in the stacks, with no one watching her. She could never be betrayed by the books.

Rena still stopped by at least once a day to check on them, and was their only real friend.

They lived in a corner apartment, and Katie could see two different faces of the city from where she stood, just by turning her head and looking out a second window. To the south of the village, between it and the harbor, was the modern downtown of Corabia. Katie could stare at those buildings for hours. They seemed so tall, reaching twelve to fifteen stories each. One building, all marble and glass, soared to twenty-five stories. She had been told that these buildings had three or even four elevators to take workers to the right floor. Mountain City didn't have a single building with an elevator in it. Katie wanted to go into the downtown just to ride up and down in one of the elevators, but Lisle wouldn't go with her. She went to the edge of the downtown every day to go to the big library where she worked, but she had no desire to explore the downtown.

Looking out the second window, facing east, Katie could see the old city of Corabia. Right outside her window was the public garden, cared for by all the refugees, that grew vegetables for the cafeteria. Beyond the garden was the old cemetery, and beyond the cemetery the walled city. The cemetery reminded Katie of home as much as anything she had seen. Enclosed by a low stone wall, it was full of mausoleums, family crypts, small stone markers and excessive statuary. Her grandparents had been buried in a similar cemetery in Mountain City. She smiled every time she saw it. The walls of the old city rose next to the cemetery, blocking her view of the sea. From her window she could see over the wall and into its narrow, twisting streets of the old city. Katie loved to walk in the old city. She understood now that the Corabian quarter in Mountain City had been an inarticulate copy of the wonder of what lay before her. She could feel the history of her people every time she wandered through the streets of the old city.

A breeze lifted the curtains gently, bathing Katie in cool air. The windows were her favorite thing about the apartment because of the breeze. It made the late summer heat bearable. Katie liked to strip and sit in the darkened room playing with her belly, even though she wasn't really showing yet, and talk with her child. She had been embarrassed at first, with Lisle watching and listening, until the day Lisle had sat next to her and whispered to the baby herself.

Katie left the windows and went in sat in the rocking chair that dominated the room. Other than a small table and two chairs in the kitchenette, the rocking chair was the only piece of furniture in this room. Lisle had bought it with her first pay, proudly telling Katie that no pregnant woman was going to live in her house without a rocking chair.

In the last month, Lisle had become her sister, and her best friend. Katie had never realized how much the silence of her years on the streets had cost her. None of her customers had wanted to hear her say anything except how big their pricks were or how good they made her feel. Walter had let her talk, but he had seemed amused and distant from everything she had said, and he never said anything about himself. Lisle listened, held her when Katie shared some terrible memory and then told her own stories. They spent most nights sitting in the dark, side by side on one of the two twin beds in the bedroom, talking. They often fell asleep that way, Lisle huddled under a thin blanket, resting against each other, although Lisle always slipped away to her own bed before morning.

Katie was worried about her friend. Lisle didn't seem to feel comfortable, even after a month. She might have a moment of fun, laughing with Katie about some silly thing Katie had said or done, but she spent most of her time on edge. Lisle was sure that she would be discovered and sent away, or worse. She had terrible nightmares from which Katie had trouble waking her. Katie would listen to Lisle's incoherent rambling and moaning, and watch as her arms and legs began to twitch and thrash. Katie would climb into bed and hold Lisle, whispering to her that everything would be alright. Sometimes that calmed Lisle, but often it didn't. One night she had actually slapped Katie across the face hard enough to leave a bruise.

When Lisle finally woke from the dream, she could never tell Katie any details, but it was easy for Katie to see the fear still on Lisle's face. Katie would comfort her, and wish she had a clue about what to do to help. She was willing to do anything to make life better for Lisle, but was at a loss for answers. She loved to hold Lisle, to sleep next to her, to touch her and stroke her hair, but that didn't really help. Lisle shrank from every unexpected contact, and allowed herself to be held only lightly. She would snap at Katie and tell her to get away.

Katie had found a church for Lisle, a real Montrovian church, with two tall towers in front and lots of stained glass windows. She had hoped that would help Lisle feel at home, but Lisle refused to go. She said it would just convince everyone of what they already suspected, and she couldn't risk it. Katie had offered to go with her, but Lisle wouldn't even talk about going after the first conversation.

Katie had also found a church for herself. She had gone to one service, in a modest stone church on the edge of the walled city. She had picked it because it was small, like her father's church had been, but that had been a mistake. Seeing someone else sitting in the teacher's chair, where her father would have sat in his church, had simply been too much. She had cried through the service, and hadn't gone back. She was aware that perhaps half of the refugees in the village didn't go to service. Many of the refugees were angry at God and refused to go to church, others had a similar experience of loss when they tried. There was, however, a very strong core group of refugees who celebrated service several times a week, and always tried to convince Katie and Lisle to come with them.

Katie did find that she could pray again, and she made time in her day every morning and night to offer words of gratitude. She believed she was blessed to be in Corabia, to be pregnant, and to have Lisle as her family. She didn't understand what had happened during the war, but was willing to let it go. It was, that was all. It didn't define her anymore than her months with Walter defined her.

A bell tolled in the distance, and Katie smiled. Lisle would be home from the library soon. She would have stories today, as always, of young men who stopped by the circulation desk to flirt with her. Lisle would be vicious in her parody, and very funny. It was what passed for entertainment in their home.

Krang sat on a log by the side of the road, the remnants of his entourage gathered silently about him. It was nearing dawn, and he had walked most of the night. He had found that his sleep patterns had changed. He rarely slept more than a few hours, usually in the first part of the evening. Most nights he walked, or if he had a grave to dig, dug, or simply sat and watched the night unfold around him. He had come to know the stars intimately, to sense the coming of the dawn, to expect the first sounds of the birds.

Krang studied the ghosts that were still with him. They were slowly evaporating; their hold on this world dissolving as they lost touch with the pain and anger that had compelled them to follow him. The ones who remained with him were the most angry, the most hurt, the most incapable of forgiveness. Krang sat silently in the darkness, watching them as they watched him. They had begun their haunting as his witnesses, but in truth, Krang was now witness to their lives. In the horror and carnage of this war and the last, the world war, when tens of thousands had died in single nights as cities were firebombed, and tens of millions had died altogether, they could be easily overlooked. Krang knew that should not happen.

They stood guard silently, their accusing eyes never leaving him. The hundreds had been reduced to handfuls. Krang welcomed their hatred, trying to understand who they had been in life, so he could know what he had destroyed. Some he had known: Emerik, the butcher his mother had used from the time Krang was a small boy; an old woman, Mama Dubravka, who took in laundry; the boy who had delivered their paper. What was his name? Jakov? But Krang hadn't really known them. He didn't know what they gave up when they came to the camp. Not things, so much, but those parts of themselves that were lost forever in their deaths. Had Jakov ever kissed a girl? Had he known the exquisite joy of making love? That fleeting, hurried, fumbling attempt in the old band shell one spring evening with his first love?

And what of the old woman, Mama Dubravka? Her husband was long dead, and she never remarried. Was he so good she could never replace him? Or was she simply so tired of his bullshit that widowhood was a pleasure? And Emerik the butcher, who would look at him in the camp, not with accusation, but with hurt.

Had he really believed Krang was human enough to value their relationship? Who were these people he had ignored, both before and at the camp?

Their lives were no different than those of his parents, or his friends. Nor were they different than the life he was living now, where meaning came from what he actually did, not who he fucked or how much he drank. Of course, his ghosts didn't see any similarity. They only saw *the guard*, and that pleased Krang. He needed their hatred and their incomprehensible pain to remind him of his truth. Their eyes were what drove him to his knees, sick with himself, trying to somehow vomit out what he had been. What he was. Krang could never pretend it was all in the past. He didn't believe people changed. Once a shit, always a shit. As if that trite phrase could ever capture the horror of what he had done. But what could?

Morning would be here soon, and his apparitions would fade in the light. They never left him, and if he tried he could feel their anger even on the brightest of days. With the return of morning, he would see once again the unending plains across which he trudged. How many weeks had passed since Katie had left him? Krang couldn't say any more. The hills had given way to rolling plains that seemed unending. He walked south, keeping the morning sun to his left and the afternoon sun to his right. He would reach the Homeland sometime, and make up for what he had done.

Lisle sat on her bed, studying Katie. Katie wore a thin sweater to compensate for the cool November evening. Her pregnancy looked good on her. She looked so vibrant and flush with life. In the last few weeks her belly had bloomed like a rose unfurling. There was something Lisle saw in her expression, in the way she carried herself, that made her believe Katie was going to love being a mother. She would be complete in some way she hadn't been before. And that was why they were arguing.

Lisle wiped her eyes with the back of her hand. She didn't need to be crying. She took a deep breath. "I really don't belong here. I should leave before someone finds out that I'm a fraud."

"No one is ever going to find out..."

"Katie, I don't feel safe. There are undercurrents of threat all around me. You read the papers and hear what is being said, even in the legislature. It's like Montrovia all over again, except I'm the Corabian."

Katie shook her head. "It's not the same. The laws don't pass here. Sure, we have our share of bigots, but most Corabians want our society to be open to all, as it has always been. No one has burned any churches, or destroyed a business just because it's run by a Montrovian."

"No, but there was an attack..." She shivered to think about it: a Montrovian couple walking home at night had been attacked and beaten by a gang of men. None of the witnesses had stopped the attack or called authorities until after it was over.

"And the police are working on those. They'll catch the men responsible."

"But it's already too late for the victims, isn't it?" Lisle shook her head angrily. "This isn't easy for me, but I think I should go. I've been reading the papers. There are refugee centers in most of the larger cities in Montrovia. As long as I don't go back to any of the western cities, I should be okay. You're safe here."

Katie shook her head wildly, her voice rising. "You can't leave me! I don't have anyone else. I lost my family, I lost Walter, so what am I supposed to do? You're the only one I have."

"You have everyone in this fucking country! They all love you: the nursery where you work, the doctor you see about the baby, the others in this building. You're everyone's favorite." Lisle cringed once the words were out. She was jealous of the ease with which Katie had adapted to this place while she hated it. She hadn't wanted that to be the truth.

"Only because they don't know me. Because they don't know I fucked every living thing to survive the war. Because they don't know the father of my baby is a monster who delighted in killing Corabians and I loved him. If they find out anything about me Lisle, I'm in as much danger as you are. We have to stay together."

"But I hate it here!"

"You hide yourself away, Lisle. We've been here for over two months and you've made no friends. You hide in that damn library and hurry home, and then what? Do you go out with any of the men who ask you out? Do you? Do you even talk to them? You make me turn them away."

"If you want them so much, why don't you suck their pricks in the hallway? It's all you claim to be good at, anyway."

Lisle closed her eyes. She hadn't meant that. She was in danger of destroying this friendship, but what could she do? Katie didn't understand how difficult it was to just get out of bed in the morning, let alone walk through the streets of this place. *I should tell her the truth*, Lisle thought, *but I won't. I'll never do that.*

"No one wants me, Lisle. I'm pregnant with someone else's baby. Who would want me? You're the beautiful one. You're the one they want."

Lisle crawled from her bed and sat on the floor before Katie. "Don't hide behind the baby, Katie. You don't want any of those men, either. You still love Walter, and you're waiting for him to come get you, just like you're waiting for your family to come get you."

"They're all dead. No one is coming for me..."

"You don't know that. And when they show up, you'll leave me here, alone. I can't risk that."

"You're my family, Lisle. No one else. I will never leave you, no matter what else happens. I know we've only known each other for a few months, but I'm closer to you than anyone I've ever known. If you leave Corabia, I have to leave too."

"But you have a life to build here, Katie. You can't leave now. You need to be here in case your parents or your sister turn up."

"They're all dead. You're my family."

"You don't know that they're dead."

Katie stared at Lisle, with haunted eyes that glistened with tears. "We saw no survivors from that camp on the road, Lisle. Walter said he thought about a thousand people survived, but we never saw a sign of them. And don't you think he would tell me if my family were alive? That last night, when he told me the truth? He didn't even try to lie and tell me they might be alive. Walter wanted to be honest with me, so I know I won't find them."

Lisle nodded, seeing the need on Katie's face. "All right. I'll stay. But not forever. I have to leave sometime."

Katie flashed an incandescent smile. "We can leave after the baby is born. We can go to America."

"America?"

"Why not? None of this hatred exists there."

The village sat astride a small crossroads, enveloped in the heat, dust from the browned fields coating everything. Krang wished it would rain, but the clouds in the sky were tight and small, offering no hope. It had not rained in weeks and he felt as parched as the fields around him.

The streets of the village appeared empty for an early afternoon. It was so hot that people took refuge from the heat wherever they could. It took less than a minute to reach the village square. The square had a stone cistern, with a bucket and a winch. Krang slowly pulled a bucket of water up from the deep well. He took a sip, letting the tepid, metallic-tasting liquid wash the dust from his mouth and then spat it on the ground. He lifted the bucket so he could drink from it, letting the water spill over his face and chest. It felt cooler running over him than it did in his mouth, but he knew he would be dry again quickly.

Krang took his bearing of the village. It was typical of what he had seen for the last several weeks. Theses villages seemed to spring from the dirt themselves, and be composed of more dust than anything else. Why was it here, other than the odd coincidence of two roads, going nowhere, happening to cross? For what reason could it exist? He doubted more than a few hundred adults lived here, hanging on against an indifferent world.

If he was lucky, and the villagers were not, he might find someone who needed to be buried. He looked around for a general store. He could always find the most recent news at a general store, but saw nothing around the square that would serve that purpose. A village without a general store was an accursed place, indeed, he thought with a brief smile.

An old woman sat on a chair in the shade of a small house at the edge of the square. She was dressed in black for mourning, but Krang knew that the likelihood was her husband had died sometime in the last five years, not that she was mourning a recent death. He approached her anyway.

"Excuse me, mother," he asked. "I am a gravedigger. Do you know of any who might need my services?"

The old woman stared at him, then raised her chin and nodded to the west. "Darcia lost her daughter in the night. The child lay down to sleep, but never woke. It is for the best, but she will never believe that. Darcia is at wit's end, for the priest won't allow the child to be buried in sacred ground. He thinks Darcia's a whore."

Krang nodded, wondering what was gained by holding a child ransom to her mother's behavior. Power, of course. "Where will I find her?"

"They have a cottage at the end of the street, to the west. A dwarf cherry tree sits in the yard. It's next to the church."

Krang thanked the old woman and took the west crossroads, looking for the house of grief. The village was well off compared to many Krang had passed through. There were no visible signs of the war. The cottages were neat and tidy, many with small fenced yards and personal gardens. The church was brick, with a steeple, looming over the houses that surrounded it. He was able to find the cottage easily, nestled beside the wrought iron fence that surrounded the church yard. The cottage was unremarkable compared to any of the others he had passed. Krang stepped on the low porch and knocked on the door. An older woman opened the door, looked out at him and nodded, as if she had been expecting him. She was as unremarkable as the cottage, and as stoic, the look on her face one of resignation and acceptance, not grief. She reminded Krang of his mother. He set his bundles down and followed her into the house.

The mother, Darcia, was young, perhaps just a few years older than Katie. She was thin and very pale, with great dark circles under her eyes. The older woman was clearly her mother. Unlike her mother, the younger woman wasn't stoic. Her grief shone on her face like a multi-cut diamond, beautiful in its intricacies. This was clearly the hardest day of her life. She exuded hurt.

A young man sat at the kitchen table. He wore the worn and stained uniform jacket of a Montrovian veteran, the right sleeve pinned above the elbow.

254

"She's not to be buried in the church," the young woman said. "I want her here, outside my window."

Krang raised an eyebrow.

The woman broke down. She cried silently for several minutes before regaining her composure. She looked into Krang's eyes, opening herself to him.

"The priest has denied me. She was born while he was away," she said, nodding to her husband, "too long after he left. We have made our peace, but the priest won't allow us any comfort. He refused to offer last rites, even when I begged. It is my sin, not hers, but the bastard wouldn't relent."

"Darcia," the older woman said, her voice rich with anger. "We do not speak of the priest this way. He is right and you are wrong."

The young woman nodded at her husband. "And with his arm, he cannot dig the grave."

Krang studied the young mother, who was beside herself with guilt. He could see on her face that she was sure that she had caused her daughter's death. That it was punishment for her indiscretion. He knew it wasn't so, but had no words that would comfort her.

"I will bury your daughter," he said, "for the price of a dinner. It doesn't matter what, just whatever you would make for yourselves. A few cigarettes would be nice, if you have any to spare."

The young woman looked at her husband, who nodded, then at her mother, who also gave her assent. She nodded to Krang.

"I don't have any cigarettes," the soldier said. "I quit smoking after I lost my arm. I always needed two hands to light a cigarette. Some of the boys in my battalion could do it with one, striking the match on their thumbnail, but I never could. I hope that will not inconvenience you."

Krang nodded and went into the yard to situate the grave. He picked a spot behind the house, in view of the kitchen window, that was shaded by a towering oak that grew in the church yard, its branches flowing over the woman's yard like ivy grows on brick. Krang imagined that the blessings used to consecrate the church grounds flowed into the oak and would drop upon the grave when the leaves fell in the autumn. He knew that a wrought iron fence couldn't keep God's grace from the child.

It took just moments to dig the grave. The soil was rich and black, in spite of the dried conditions, and Krang couldn't shake the image that he was planting a seed of some kind, although he couldn't say whether it was of hope or hopelessness. He fashioned a small casket from a trunk he found in their barn, which he lined with the baby quilt that had been in her bassinet.

Krang took the child into the kitchen and washed her body in the sink, using water he pumped himself from the well. He dried her, and then dressed her in the

255

gown her mother had made for the christening that had been denied her. As he prepared the child for burial, holding her small body in his hands, feeling the soft texture of her hair, he could only wonder at what he had become.

What kind of man can kill a child? Cradling her to his chest, Krang tried to will her back to life.

"God," he whispered silently, his eyes closed, "you owe me. Bring this child back. In the face of so much death, how can her death be necessary? Take me, and give her back to these people who love her." He opened his eyes. She remained lifeless and inert.

He gently laid her in the trunk and left the house, wishing he had a cigarette. His heart was racing. He stumbled out to the grave he had dug, standing over the place where he had violently rent the earth. The hole was an obscene parody of a grave, barely one foot by two. Krang shook, unable to control his breathing.

Images of Sarah's boy, his skull crushed and flapping violently on his shoulders, assaulted Krang. He could feel the weight of the boy in his hand, could feel the impact of his body on the loading dock, could hear his own laughter, and the retort of the pistol. His left hand snapped at the sound, the recoil feeling real.

Krang fell to his knees before the grave, vomit spewing from his mouth. He wretched again and again, long after his stomach was empty. He shivered as if feverish.

"God, what have I done?" he asked, sinking back on his heels. "How can I live, knowing what I've done? You won't let me die. I tried to kill myself, but you won't let me die. If you have some special hell for me, just do it. The waiting is much worse than anything you can do to me.

"Stop treating me like I'm special. I never believed. Not before I met Katie, and not even after. I don't deserve your Grace. You can't give it to me. This child and her parents deserve it. The dead cat I saw by the road this morning deserves it, but not me. I only deserve to die in horror."

He waited, but nothing happened. Krang leaned over, touching his forehead to the ground. "You won't give me what I deserve," he whispered. "You are indeed a cruel God." He brushed some loose dirt into the grave, covering his vomit, then rose unsteadily to his feet.

The baby's mother was waiting for Krang back in the kitchen, standing beside the trunk, her hand resting gently against her daughter. Her face, so pinched with grief when Krang first entered the house, had softened, and she smiled at Krang as he returned. Her eyes were deep and dark.

"I saw you praying for my daughter," she said, her smile growing radiant. "I cannot pray now. I was so afraid for her soul," she nodded towards her daughter. "I made her the christening dress, but she was never allowed into the church. They denied her for my sins."

Krang reached out and touched the woman gently on the cheek. "Her soul is in heaven, mother. Do not fear."

"Do you really think so?" Her look of hope cut Krang like a knife.

He nodded, swallowing down his grief before he could speak. "I see the souls of the dead when they linger in our world. I take them with me. Your daughter is not here, she is home again."

The woman began to weep, silent convulsions racking her body. She grabbed Krang by the hand. "Thank you, thank you, thank you... You are beloved of God, to come to my home, and see my daughter safely home." She turned back to her daughter, leaning down to kiss the still form of the dead child.

The older woman, a tear on her cheek, stood on tiptoe and kissed Krang on the cheek. "God has blessed you, and through you, my family. I am grateful."

Krang buried the child in silence, feeling the eyes of the family on him as he worked. He took his leave without saying anything, not stopping to collect the promised meal. He walked to the south in the humid heat of the late afternoon, hoping to sweat all memory from his body, knowing that he never could.

His mind was in a frenzy as he walked. He wanted the peace he had found after burying the soldiers; peace he had found in moments of solitude since, but it wasn't to be. He couldn't free himself of the knowledge of the child, so small and helpless, denied grace, or of the child he had killed. The memories flowed again and again. What he really couldn't get his head around was God. Where was God in all of this? What was the point of God if Krang could be Krang? How could he be so cruel and then bring comfort to a grieving mother?

"I surrender," he said to no one in particular. "I give up. If you exist, God, why do you refuse to punish me? Do you want me to say I'm sorry?

"I'm sorry! I hate what I've done. Does that make it better? That I know that no one on this earth right now is less of a fucking human being than I am? Is that what you want? That I'm like a cockroach living on filth and misery?"

He laughed bitterly when God didn't answer. We're so alike, he thought. That's what proves You're real: that You're a bastard just like me.

He finally gave up for the day when the sun touched the western horizon.

Katie was walking through the refugee village, enjoying the late afternoon sun. The street she was on was almost deserted, even though it was late and people should be coming home from work. The village was emptying at a quickening rate: it seemed like every day they placed more of the refugees out into communities across Corabia, and the trains bringing the refugees in had slowed considerably. Katie doubted they were bringing a trainload of refugees a week. She didn't mind that the village was being drained of refugees. The more the village emptied out, the more light hearted Lisle became.

257

Katie turned the corner onto her street. Two young men were working on the front of the apartment building, repairing something on the facade. Katie stopped and grinned. They weren't repairing anything. They were hanging a wreath. A Christmas wreath. It was the beginning of December, she realized. She hadn't celebrated Christmas since her family had gone to the camp. Katie felt a moment's panic. What will I do? Then she shook her head and grinned again. It was going to be Christmas, and she would celebrate with Lisle. And with this baby in her belly.

The midwife had come to see her that afternoon. She had done a thorough exam, and Katie had wished Lisle had taken off from the library to be with her. Katie bit her lip. That wasn't true. For the first time in a very long time she had wanted her mother. As the midwife examined her, Katie had cried for her mother. The midwife had told her she was about five months pregnant, perhaps a month less along than she had thought. She had this fantasy that she had gotten pregnant the very first time she and Walter had sex, but of course that wasn't true. She would be ready to have the baby now if that had been true. It had to be at Marie's. She may have missed a period due to stress, or just lost count of her period because of the time on the road. She supposed it didn't matter. She had told Walter the baby would come in March and now the midwife told her April.

Katie suddenly had to pee. The baby had a habit of rolling on her bladder in a way that created great urgency. She had almost wet herself several times. She gave the wreath one more look and then entered her building. Katie climbed the stairs as quickly as she could, and then fumbled with her key in front of the door. She shook her head, knowing her anxiousness was only making things worse. Taking a deep breath, she calmed herself and let herself inside the apartment.

The bathroom door was shut, meaning Lisle was inside. Lisle liked to take a bath every evening when she got home from work. Katie sat on the hard wooden chair at the kitchen table, waiting on Lisle to leave the bathroom. The baby pressed heavily on her bladder. Her need to pee was growing urgent, but she was trying not to disturb Lisle. The urge to go swelled suddenly. Katie bit her lip gently for distraction.

In the months they had lived together, Katie had come to realize that Lisle was the most private person she had ever met. Lisle never shared the bathroom. She dressed in the dark, or behind closed doors. Although men came calling almost every day, Lisle refused to even have a cup of coffee with anyone. They argued every time Katie tried to encourage her to go on a date.

The men had not come calling to ask Katie out. The war had changed many things, but it hadn't made men comfortable with the idea of dating a woman pregnant with someone else's child. Katie wasn't bothered though. She wasn't really ready to date someone. She wasn't even sure that she could. She had used sex as a tool for survival for so long that she didn't know if she could ever have a normal relationship with someone. And, as much as it bothered her to acknowledge it, she missed Walter.

Katie shook her head. She couldn't get the idea that he may have killed her family out of her head. She knew she could let go the camp, except for that. Katie hated herself for being so weak. How could she still want to love him? She should hate him, period. She had always known that her time in the City had proven that she had no moral compass, and would do anything to stay alive. Her fear and weakness was an insult against her family, her people, and her God. But loving Walter, and being unable to let him go from her thoughts after knowing the truth of him, that was unforgivable. God must hate her. And the world, when it realized how bad she was, would certainly punish her.

Katie had argued this out in her mind so many times. The Walter she knew wasn't the man he had claimed to be the night she sent him away. He could be violent, Katie knew that. But torturing people? She didn't know that man. She wasn't in love with that Walter. Katie bit her lip in frustration. She wasn't even good at being bad. She couldn't just love him in spite of everything, because she couldn't get her family out of her mind. What if she had had sex with the man who killed her sister? How could she ever forgive herself?

Katie couldn't hold her pee any longer. If she didn't go now, she was going to have an accident. She went down the hall to the bathroom and stood before the door, her hand raised to knock. She knew knocking on the door would freak Lisle out. Lisle wouldn't let her in. She would have to get out of the tub and dry off and get dressed and by then Katie would have peed all over the floor.

She quietly opened the door to the bathroom. Lisle was soaking in the tub, her head thrown back, her eyes shut. Lisle is so beautiful, Katie thought, watching her. She stepped into the bathroom, pulling up her dress and pushing down her underpants. Katie sat heavily on the toilet as her pee sprayed out. She groaned involuntarily.

Lisle's eyes snapped open. "What are you doing?" she shouted. "Get out!"

"I couldn't wait any longer," Katie said. "I'm sorry."

Lisle grabbed a towel and pulled it into the tub, covering herself. "Just finish up and get out" she hissed.

Katie wiped. "What's the big deal?"

"I don't want you to see me," Lisle said, an edge of panic in her voice.

Katie bit her lip again, fighting back tears. "I won't look. Why don't you trust me?" she whispered.

Lisle giggled nervously, a small desperate laugh. "It's not you, Katie. No one can ever see me..."

"What are you afraid of?" Katie opened her eyes and saw the tears streaming down Lisle's face. Lisle's left thigh broke the water as she tried to sink further

259

into the tub. Katie couldn't make sense of the marking on Lisle's thigh: a jagged, twisted line ran to her knee. It took a second for Katie's brain to register the mark was a mass of scar tissue. A raised twisted scar was visible on Lisle's left thigh where it broke free of the water in the tub. Katie leaned over the tub and pulled the towel away from Lisle's grasp.

Lisle raised her hands to cover her face, involuntary sobs shaking her body. Angry pink scar tissue ran across her breasts and stomach down to her pubic hair. Her upper thighs and arms were also scarred. There were hundreds of scars, an inch or two long, criss-crossing her body. Only her face, her arms below the elbow and her legs below her knees were unmarked.

Lisle sighed, a sad, anguished sound. She looked at Katie from behind her hands, shaking her head.

"They ruined me, Katie. The men who attacked me, they cut me up with a knife so that no one could ever find me beautiful again. They ruined me."

Lisle rolled slowly onto her stomach. The scars continued across her back and buttocks, the cuts even more densely packed together. The scars formed triangles and rectangles and parallel lines. Barely an inch at a time was untouched. The idea clearly had been to mutilate, not to kill.

Katie felt her gorge rising. She choked the bile back and fell to her knees beside the tub. How could anyone do this, she wondered, as she stared at Lisle's back. The scars were deep pink welts that left no part of Lisle body untouched. Her sides were as damaged as her front and back. No matter how Lisle rolled in the tub, she couldn't hide the scars.

"Oh, Lisle, why didn't you tell me?"

Lisle rolled back to look at Katie. "How can I tell anyone about this? They might as well have cut my womb out. They destroyed me as a woman."

Katie shook her head wildly, and reached out and gently ran her finger along one of the scars on Lisle's stomach. "Your beauty has nothing to do with how you look," she whispered.

"Yes it does," Lisle said. "In my mind, it always does. The funny thing is I prayed to not look like my mother any more. I was so superior, thinking I would do anything to be different from her. And this is how my prayers were answered. No one can love me like this."

"I love you Lisle," Katie said quietly.

"That's not what I mean," Lisle sobbed. "No man will ever want me as a lover like this."

"Any man that doesn't want you is a fool," Katie said quietly. She ran her hands lightly over Lisle's body, tracing the raised scars with her fingers. Katie leaned across the tub and gently kissed the ugliest scar she saw, an X mark on Lisle's right side just below her ribs. Lisle stiffened, her body panicked, but Katie calmed her, running her hand along Lisle's cheek. She looked into Lisle's eyes, then leaned forward and kissed her softly on the lips. She returned her kisses to Lisle's torso, kissing each scar as she saw it. Each kiss, in Katie's mind, was a healing kiss, healing Lisle's fear and pain. At some point, the kisses became more energized and passionate. Lisle sighed. Katie brought her left hand up to Lisle's breast, squeezing gently, brushing the nipple. She kissed her way up to Lisle's mouth, slipped her tongue between Lisle's lips, feeling her friend tremble and pull gently away. Katie slipped over the edge of the tub, kissing harder, her right hand sliding down to Lisle's pussy.

Katie had sold herself to many women, as well as men, so she knew how to touch Lisle in a way that would please her. But Katie wanted Lisle to take more than just an orgasm from her; she wanted her to take her love, to know that she was loved, so much so that Katie would give all of herself to make Lisle happy.

By the time they were done, Katie had pulled Lisle from the tub and into her bed, and now they cuddled under a thin sheet, Katie's head nestled against Lisle's breast. Lisle was flushed; she sighed contentedly and gently caressed Katie's belly.

Katie was suddenly afraid that she had done the wrong thing, and that Lisle would leave her. "I'm sorry," she said, her voice breaking. Her vision blurred as tears filled her eyes. "Please don't hate me..."

Lisle laughed. "How can I hate you?"

Katie shrugged, unable to stop the tears.

Lisle leaned forward and brushed the tears away. "It's okay," she said softly. "It was the right thing to do. I love you for thinking that I'm beautiful. I'm not sure I can do that again, but I love you for risking it."

Katie smiled. "Really?"

"I'll always love you, Katie. You really are my family now, and I promise to never leave you."

"You'll leave when you meet the right man."

Lisle shook her head. "I don't think so."

"The scars don't mean anything."

"Not to you. But to most men? I'm not sure I can ever risk giving myself away and finding that out."

Katie beamed. "But you already did. You'll find the courage to again, for the right man."

Lisle shook her head. "We'll see. I'm more worried about losing you than about you losing me. You love Walter."

"I can't love him. Not knowing what he did."

"If you knew that he didn't hurt your family?"

Katie snuggled closer. "It's not even that, anymore. I can't love him because I

261

know I would forgive him anything right now. Even killing my family. And I hate myself for that. I was so independent. I didn't need anyone. I didn't love anyone. Sex was a tool to get men to give me what I needed. Even with him at first. I had sex with him to own him. But somewhere along the way I realized that he respected me, while the rest of the world despised me. He respected me. And then he owned me.

"So I can't risk loving him anymore. I can't give myself away."

They lay in silence as the room darkened around them, until they fell asleep.

Chapter Nineteen

Krang sat on the stone wall of the small cemetery, in the shade of an oak tree, waiting for them to bring out the bodies. He didn't even know the name of the village he was passing through. He had dug three graves this morning. Two were side by side, for a husband and wife, although if Krang had decided where to bury them, they wouldn't be together. The third grave was the one before him, under the shade of the oak tree. Two of the bodies, the wife and her alleged lover, lay in the church, washed and wrapped for burial. The body of the husband wasn't ready yet. They were going to hang him in the village square at noon. He had killed his wife and the farmer while they were talking during the weekly market. Shot them each: the farmer five times, while his wife stood there in horror, and then his wife, once in the head. He would have killed himself on the spot, but in his rage had used all the bullets in his revolver. He had suspected an affair and was unable to forgive them.

Forgiveness. What did it mean to forgive? Did it mean to forget? Krang shook his head, that couldn't be it. Sarah had not forgotten what he had done to her family and he couldn't imagine that she ever would, yet she had forgiven him. And with more than just words: she had done something she could never take back. She had freed him from certain death.

Krang didn't think that he had ever truly forgiven anyone. When he felt he had been wronged he fought back, with words and fists. Even when he said he forgave something, it was always with conditions. Always believing in his heart that he had been wronged.

So what strength had Sarah called upon to forgive him? Did it mean that she let go her hurt and anger, that she simply chose not to take offense at his actions? It couldn't be that simple, Krang thought, even if that seemed to be the manner in which her forgiveness manifested itself within his life. What gave someone the strength to forgive?

When he reached the Homeland, if Sarah saw him, would the months in between have changed her? Would she want him dead now? Krang shuddered to think it. He didn't mind the thought of being killed, in fact he expected it, just as the soon-to-be-dead husband had expected his punishment, calmly waiting beside the bodies for the villagers to take him, but Krang didn't want his death to be because of Sarah. He didn't want to force her to compromise herself, or her act. Because when Krang thought about it, nothing that he had seen or heard or read about had ever come close to what Sarah had done. It was an act beyond this world. Krang shook his head. He didn't think he would ever truly understand what it meant to forgive.

When the villager's brought him the husband's body, fresh from the hanging tree, Krang buried his dead, taking special care with the husband's body. He whispered a prayer to God to help the man's soul forgive itself, for he knew that was the hardest thing of all. He left the village at dusk, three apples in his pocket as payment for his work.

Krang walked south, as the sky darkened from blue to purple to black. Clouds hung to the west, false mountains that broke up the barren flat lands. No moon would rise tonight. He liked the dark because it was the one time he felt like he didn't exist for the rest of the world. He was simply one more ghost in his entourage of ghosts, insubstantial and unable to impact the world around him.

As he walked, he thought about Katie. He had built a wall around his memories of Katie, to keep them from coming back to him when he wasn't prepared. He never fantasized about having her back in his life. He had given her up to protect her, the only selfless thing he had ever done. He knew that if he thought, even once, that there was a chance of having Katie back in his life, he would throw away everything he had done to have it. And then she would die, and the baby, too. But in the darkness, when he was no more than a wisp of being blowing across the plains, it was safe to think of her for a few minutes. He had lost all track of the calendar, but he thought they had been apart for several months, but not long enough for Katie to have given birth. It couldn't be nine months. Was it two? Four? He shook his head. He should ask someone at the next town. He wanted to know how she was; to see how her body was changing as the baby grew, to see that she was happy. He did not worry about her safety, for he had a simple faith that she was fine. He daydreamed that she had found Sarah, and that Sarah had become her surrogate family. He knew in his head that wasn't likely, but the vision lived on in his heart. So he imagined her with Sarah.

As the night wore on, Krang found himself reflecting on his life since Katie left him. Since he had begun burying the dead, really. In the town of Kosca, he had buried a family that had died in a fire. He carefully placed the charred, unidentifiable remains in a single grave, and washed for an hour afterward trying to free himself of the smell. On the plains, in the little village of Hunder, there was the drunk killed when he had fallen asleep on the railway. He had help collect the mangled body from the tracks. The man was only identifiable because the village was small enough that they knew who was missing. He buried two children hit by truck while they chased a ball into the street; a young man who lost his arm in the sawmill and wouldn't let his friends use a tourniquet because he believed himself to be worthless without his arm; several widows who died of old age and loneliness; and more suicides than he cared to remember. Why did God let others end their lives, but refuse him?

He had also spent three days helping to dig a new well in a town of several thousand. The town had treated the digging of the well as a festival, with a calf roast and barrels of wine and Krang had felt buoyed by the good will. A widow, perhaps a few years older than Krang, had let him know her bed was available, and although she was beautiful he had gently declined. His heart was with Katie. He had dug drainage ditches, helped raise barns, picked strawberries on a farm, and done whatever other people had needed his help to do.

Krang realized, as he thought about the last weeks or months, that he knew what he wanted to do with his life. He had been toying with the idea that he should return to the camp, open up the pit, and re-bury the dead. It could become his life's work, for he imagined that it would take him years to empty the pit. But now he knew a way to honor Sarah. He could tell her story. When he reached Corabia, he would appear before the entire world, confess his sins, and tell of the one true act of courage that he had seen. All of the people he met had been beaten down by the war, whether they were Corabian or Montrovian. Their hearts ached at both the losses they suffered and those they had inflicted. Healing was needed, and Krang thought that telling of Sarah's act might provide that healing. Not that he expected to receive forgiveness from the rest of them. They could not do that, and he understood why. It was growing close to his time to die, but now he had a purpose to his life. Krang was ready to make his sacrifice. He would tell of an act of love that was the greatest since Christ himself had walked the earth.

Krang knew that he could not name Sarah personally in his story. There were many who would not understand, and would pervert what she had done. But he could tell her story publicly, keeping Sarah anonymous. When she heard him, she would understand that she had been right, and that he had never forgotten her or her family. That she had changed him. She had, with her act of compassion, destroyed *the guard*. It made Krang smile to think of it.

The abandoned hut had been carved into the side of a small hill, so that only the stone front was visible. A window and doorway had been framed in wood. The small window was covered with a sheer lace, the door with a heavy blanket. A garden gone mostly to weeds was crowded under the window, and a tree stump had been pushed up against the shack to serve as a stool. Across the narrow path, a few yards from the hut, a spring bubbled gently from some rocks.

Krang stopped first at the spring, drinking deeply from the pool of cold, clear water. Krang looked at his reflection in the pool of water and didn't recognize himself. Gone was the pink-faced baby, burned bald by the fire from the wrecked plane. An old man stared back at him, the face narrow and wizened, dark from the sun, with long, straggly hair and an uneven beard streaked with grey. Krang laughed to see himself. Grey hair? He looked like a wild prophet. He thought about taking an hour to cut his hair and shave, thinking perhaps he was scaring some people he met with his wild prophet look. But he had no scissors or razor, so a prophet he would remain. He filled his water skins, and then looked towards the hut. No one had stirred while he was drinking his fill.

"Hello..." he called out, not shouting.

Nothing. He nodded. The place was as empty as it appeared. He gathered up his skins and began to go, but something stopped him. Instead, he approached the hut, and knocked on the wooden door frame.

"Is anyone home?"

Nothing. And then a sound so faint he almost missed it. Krang pulled the blanket aside and looked into the gloomy hut. It was sparsely furnished and empty. Other than a small table, roughly fashioned from wood, and another tree stump for a stool, it was empty. There was an old fire pit in the center of the cabin, filled with ash, and a pile of rags that Krang assumed had been a bed. A rat moved in the bed and Krang started, and then laughed nervously. The rat moved again, only this time Krang saw it wasn't a rat but a hand.

Krang pulled the blanket down from the door to let light in, and slowly approached the bed. The old woman stared up at him with sorrowful eyes, not frightened, but silent. Krang knelt at her side, pulling his water skin from his back.

"Here, Mother," he said softly, "sip slowly." He gently filled her mouth with water, and she worked laboriously to swallow. Krang pulled a rag from her bed and wet it, and gently washed the grime from her face. The woman smiled at him, and he gave her another sip of the water. Her skin had drawn taut over her face, her breathing was shallow. She was close to death.

"What can I do for you, Mother?"

Her voice was deep and raspy, as if unused to talking. "Sit with me until I die," she said with a smile. "I thought I would die alone."

Krang nodded. "I would be honored to sit with you. And I will bury you when it is all over."

She nodded and sighed, and drifted to sleep.

When she awoke, Krang helped her from the bed. He had started a fire burning in the hut, and brewed a dark, bitter tea from a box of tea leaves that he had found on the table. The old woman sat by the fire and sipped the tea, and watched as Krang collected the rags on which she had lain and fed them to the fire. He laid his blankets on the ground for her bed.

"Mother, do you have another set of clothes?" he asked.

She pointed towards rough shelving in one corner of the hut. Krang found under things, a skirt, and a heavy blouse, and a cloth he could use for a towel.

"Who are you?" she asked him, as he warmed water for her bath over the fire.

"Just a traveler. I am heading south..."

"To Corabia?"

He heard the excitement in her voice. Was she Corabian? He nodded silently. When the water was warm enough, he gently bathed her. He started when he saw the tattoo on her left wrists, although he had guessed it would be there.

"You were in the camps?" he asked.

She nodded.

Krang had never buried anyone who had been in the camps. He could suddenly feel the remnants of his entourage crowding around him, joyful to see him serve one of their own.

"And where were you Mother? Down here by the plains, or west, near the sea?"

She shook her head. "I was in the mountains. The camp by Mountain City."

Krang sucked in a deep breath when he heard that she had been in his camp. He stared at her, trying to make out who she had been, but didn't recognize her. Was she one of the few to escape his attention, or had he forgotten her? Or was she so close to death she was no longer recognizable?

"How did you get so far from the City?" he asked.

"Like so many others, when we were freed we headed towards the Homeland. I so wanted to see the Homeland again. I had been many times, with my husband, and after the camp it would truly have felt like going home. I wanted to feel safe again, you know? There were maybe three hundred of us, crowded into the backs of the left over trucks from the camp. The rest stayed with the army, but we couldn't wait. It was amazing that no one minded the close quarters this time, though in some ways it was as bad as the trains coming in had been. The trucks broke down, or ran out of petrol, one by one, and that's where that group dropped out, making their way on foot, but the rest of the convoy would not wait. I was in the last truck, but we ran out of petrol after four days, so then we walked, too.

"One night, maybe a month or so after we started out, we were attacked outside a village by a group of ruffians. They were young men, either back from losing the war or possibly men who had just missed going. It doesn't matter, I suppose. I was injured." She paused, and Krang helped her take more water.

267

"The others went on without me. My husband went on without me. I do not blame him, really. We had grown apart in the camp. He was the leader of the group and they needed him. I believe they thought me too far gone to recover, but the villagers, ashamed of what had happened, nursed me back to health. I was well enough to travel within a few weeks.

"I set out on my own, but I only made it this far. I found this cabin, and I was so tired, and the garden was in, so I stayed. I don't know what happened to whoever planted the garden. I waited for them to return, but they never did. So I lived on what I could eat from the garden, hoping my strength would recover, but it never did. I just got weaker and weaker. And then I couldn't get up. I am almost done with this life. I have lost my husband and my daughters. I thought I would die alone before God blessed me with your presence."

Krang held her hand. "Is there anything I can do to help?"

"I beg of you one favor. Cremate me and take me to the Homeland. Bury me in the old cemetery in Corabia. My great grandparents are buried there. If I cannot have my daughters back, at least God can give me that."

Krang nodded. "I will carry your ashes to the Homeland and see them buried there. What is your name, Mother?"

"Katerina..." she whispered and lapsed into silence. Krang laid her on the new bed made with his blankets, and watched her sleep. He wrote *Katerina?* on a slip of paper, and found a small box in the cabin to serve as an urn. Her breathing grew ragged.

Krang drifted into sleep, and awoke to find her watching him. As tired as she looked, her eyes burned with passion. "Tell me your story," she said softly. "Why do you go to the Homeland? Are you looking for your family?"

"I am hoping to find someone who did me a great kindness," Krang said. "She was from your city, and was a prisoner in your camp. You may have known her, Sarah Jezek."

The old woman closed her eyes softly and nodded. "Yes, I knew her."

"And you do not know me, Mother?"

Katerina studied his face intently, then drew in her breath sharply.

"What is it? What do you see?" he asked apprehensively.

"I knew so many, and I thought I would remember them all. I felt like I owed it to them, to remember them all. We lost so much in that camp, but I vowed that I would not lose the memory of a single person who came into that camp. I would remember them, good or bad. But I don't remember you."

"Maybe we did not meet, Mother, for I do not remember you either. Maybe I know your family?"

"My husband was a teacher, as I said, a leader of our people. He was such a gentle man when we met. For most of his life, really. Benjamin Woerful."

"Woerful? The Elder? You're his wife?" Krang remembered Woerful and his wife. She had been quiet, but energetic. She always worked with the new arrivals to help them adjust. To warn them about him.

"The war changed me," she said with a soft laugh.

"The war changed us all," Krang agreed.

"Yes, it did. But few changed as much as my husband. My daughter changed as much, maybe more. It was strange to watch them. As the war enveloped us, he became more withdrawn and she more alive. He began to find signs that this was all a punishment of God, and that we must submit, and she grew in her conviction that we must never submit.

"When we were deported, she ran from the square, and my husband cursed her. That was the end of our marriage, really. At that moment, I was so proud of her for risking all to live, and he was so afraid of risk that he wanted her to go meekly to her death. Oh, how Katerina pleaded with us to let her sister go with her, and I froze. Bela was only eleven, Katerina fourteen. I held our youngest tight, and finally Katerina ran, and Benjamin cursed her. He called upon God to strike her down. How I have hated myself for that day, ever since."

Krang rocked back on his heels in shock. Could it be?

"Bela died on the train before we reached camp. She caught the flu, and there was nothing I could do for her. I held her body until we arrived, when a man took it from me, and carried her to the bed of a truck and threw her on it. The next day I saw the pit where she had been dumped. I think I began dying at that moment. My grief was such, I thought it would never end.

"But over the years I saw what happened to so many others, and I knew that I had not yet experienced grief."

Krang reached out and gently brushed the tears from the woman's face. Could it truly be? Had God intended for his path to cross with hers? He had never asked Katie enough about her family to learn who they had been.

"Mother, did your oldest daughter prefer to be called Katie?"

Katerina nodded.

"And she would be seventeen or eighteen?"

"Yes."

Krang felt a moment of joy that he had never felt before. Not happiness, nor something temporal or dependant on anything but what was burning inside him. To give this woman such a kindness. Why had God blessed him in this way? Why was he favored above others?

"Mother, I have news of your daughter."

"Yes?" He could see the hesitancy on her face, the fear hidden just below hope.

269

"She is alive and well. I last saw her on her way to the Homeland. By now she is there, living in freedom."

"How do you know this? You are not just trying to make an old woman happy?"

"Our paths crossed on the road, and we walked together for many weeks. She told me her story, but never her last name. She told of running away and leaving her sister Bela behind. The Katie I knew must be your daughter. You would be proud of her, for she is strong. Strong of will, and strong of faith. She let God guide her through her challenges. And she is with child, as well."

Katerina sighed. "She found love then? What gifts God gives us. I must write to her, a short note. There is paper and pencil on the shelf. I had always intended to write the names, but it exhausted me to think of it. But now I shall write a note to my daughter. You must give it to her, with this locket." She lifted a locket on a chain she wore around her neck.

Krang nodded, and brought her the paper and pencil. "I will find her, Mother, to give her your letter and locket." His mind was racing. Was this a gift of God? Was it a way for he and Katie to be reunited? Or was it a punishment, something to build his hope before God took it all away?

Katerina slept heavily, her breath coming in short ragged spurts. Krang was certain she did not have many more hours to live. He had the letter and locket wrapped in a piece of oilcloth in his hip pocket. He thought about the night he and Katie had parted ways. She had been so afraid that he had hurt her family, and he had been unable to tell her he hadn't. Could this change anything? Could it bring Katie back into his life? Might she forgive him?

He was not sure that Katie would see him to take the letter, but she would recognize the locket. It held a small photograph of two young girls, one of whom was clearly Katie. Krang knew there was a chance that the locket would change everything. If he could just see Katie, and give her the locket, she would know that he had not killed her Mother. And her Father was still alive as well, so perhaps there was hope after all.

Her father was Benjamin Woerful. Krang laughed softly at the idea. Woerful had been one of the elders on the camp council; in fact he had led it for the last year or so. He had argued with Commandant Bitmeyer about everything, but that was his job. And being on the council had certainly kept him alive, for the council was off limits even to *the guard*. Krang now understood Katie's descriptions of her father: he had been a man trying to build a wall around his people with only his bible for support.

Woerful had been obsessed with the rules. He enforced them more rigorously than the guards, not only as a means of saving his people, but because they were the rules. He seemed to think it was the will of God that the Corabians ended up in the camp. And when the camp fell, he was the one who thought it was God's will that power had come into his hands. He was the one Bitmeyer had negotiated surrender with, and then he had run Bitmeyer up the flag pole. He had ordered all the families of the guards held, and had sent prisoners out to arrest the local farmers who had supplied the camp with food. He had said it the will of God. And then he killed them all.

Krang laughed again. Who am I to feel moralistic? I would have killed them too. The only difference is I wouldn't have blamed it on God.

"What is it, Mother?"

"I will die soon. I want to thank you for your kindness."

"I have done nothing. I simply shared with you the truth. Although there is one favor I would ask?"

Katerina beamed. "Yes?"

"Would you tell me what you know of Sarah Jezek? Was she headed to the Homeland with your group?"

The old woman sighed. It was as if her own life drained away. Krang could see tears cloud her eyes.

"I wish I could repay your kindness with a kindness of my own, but I cannot. Sarah is dead."

Krang choked on his breath, feeling as if he had been hit in the solar plexus. He couldn't breathe. This can't be, he thought. She is mistaken. Krang shook his head violently, feeling trapped in the hut. He wanted to run outside, to breathe fresh air, to vomit. This couldn't be.

"No," he said, his voice soft and broken. "I saw her the last day. She wasn't sick."

Katerina nodded weakly. "I buried her myself. I wouldn't let them throw her in the pit with the others. We had lived in the same cabin. She became my daughter in the camp, and I her family. I had such love for her. And I was proud of her. Of whom she chose to be, in spite of what life had done to her. I was proud."

The old woman grew silent and soon drifted into sleep.

Krang rose from her bedside and walked bitterly away. He tried to tell himself that she could be mistaken, but he knew it wasn't true. How could Sarah have died? Unless she just gave up. Maybe she killed herself, to stay with her husband and son. Krang struggled to breathe, each breath a battle. Of all the people he had met, she was the most deserving of life, of happiness. He had somehow projected a life for her, remarried, with children and grandchildren and great grandchildren. Sarah's life was to be golden after the camp. He brushed tears from his face.

How could she act with such courage and strength and not be rewarded for it? Krang bit his cheeks to keep from crying out in anger. *What was the point of life if people like me lived and Sarah died? Even if she has gone to heaven, and if I burn in hell forever, what good is heaven if you have to suffer so much in life to get in? And what hell could be punishment enough for what he had done? What would ever be more punishment than this moment?* Sarah was gone to him. Katie had sent him away. His life was meaningless. He had tried to change, but life was better to him before he changed.

Krang returned to the hut, and sat beside the old woman. Her breathing was shallow, but peaceful. *Did it mean anything for you to know that Katie is alive? You won't see her, or touch her, or hold your grandchild.* He fingered the note and locket in his pocket. *Katie will never take these from me. She won't believe in them if she does. I will have to give them to someone to give to her, and leave her alone as I have promised. I cannot destroy her life any more than I have already.*

He found a cloth to wipe the sweat from Katerina's brow. He could see the shadow of Katie's face upon hers. Krang held her hand and watched her die.

Krang cremated her in the morning, and gathered her ashes in the late afternoon. He was angry; angry that God had taken Sarah and Katie from him. *Why did you show me a different path, if only to close it down?* Krang thought about sitting in the hut and burning it to the ground, but he knew that God would not let him die. And he had promised the old woman to carry her ashes into the Homeland. Maybe that was all that he had left to live for: keeping his word to the dead.

Chapter Twenty

Krang left the shack in the early morning, when the sun was just breaking the horizon. It had been three days since he had cremated Katerina, burning her body on a pyre he built from the dried wood stacked beside the shack. He had thought he would leave then, after collecting some of the ashes to take with him and spreading the rest behind the shack, but he hadn't. He had just felt numb and too exhausted to even think about leaving. He wasn't sure today was any better, but what was he to do?

The old woman's ashes were in a bowl, wrapped in oilcloth, in his pack along with the note and locket. Krang shook his head. Old woman? Katerina was not an old woman, just used up. She would be only a dozen years older than Krang. Maybe fifteen years older if she had waited a very long time to marry. He had had lovers who were the same age as Katerina. That was what he had done to her, what the camp had done. Even for those not directly killed by *the guard*, he had sucked the vitality of life away from them. And he had been proud of it.

Before he left Krang took a piece of paper from the shelf inside the hut, and wrote a short note:

> *Katerina, resident of Mountain City, Mother of Katie and Bela, died this November, 1949, at peace with herself and the world. She loved her daughters.*

Krang was unsure of the date. November was his best guess, but the weather felt like September. He was much further south than he had ever been, so it could even be late December or early January, not that it mattered. Nothing mattered anymore. He tacked the note to the wood table in the hut, and left.

Within a few miles the rolling hills had flattened into nothing. The road before Krang stretched endlessly across the barren plain. The grayness of the morning was unbroken. Except to the east, where the sun struggled to break through the clouds, everything was gray. The mist rising from the ground seemed to blend into the clouds hovering oppressively above him. He sighed. Life was fucked.

Krang shook his head as he walked, knowing that his thoughts of finding Sarah had been nothing more than fantasy. Finding her would have been a disaster for them both. He would have either forced her to act against him and negated all that she had done, or her indifference would have destroyed him. Some part of him had always known he would never find her. And yet that vision of standing before her had been what had kept him going.

Krang sighed. Sarah had never been real to him. He didn't know her from the camp. As horrific as his actions towards her had been, they hadn't been personal. Not to Krang. That was his real crime. That none of it had ever been personal. How do you smash an infant's skull, shoot his father, and forget? And it wasn't as if Krang repressed his memories to protect his psyche. He remembered much of what he had done in great detail. But he had forgotten the three of them until Sarah reminded him.

In spite of everything Sarah had forgiven him. And had even asked Krang to forgive her for hating him. Why had that changed him? He had resisted changing, but somehow couldn't stop it. Sarah had forgiven him and Katie had loved him, and he had lost them both. If only I hadn't promised Katerina anything, Krang thought, I could sit in that hut and starve myself. I could finish this business, and pay the only price I can. Not that my life is enough to pay for what I have done. And if hell is real, burning in those eternal fires won't be enough, either.

The sun had cleared the horizon, driving the gray mists away. The light breeze had broken the clouds up, letting the azure blue sky to show through. A small hedgerow ran along the road, and a flock of starlings wheeled and dove in a magical ballet to the symphony of their own cries. Krang drew in a deep breath, feeling the morning chill, and smiled. This would have been a fine morning for a smoke, if he had any cigarettes. A great morning to sit at a café with a coffee and the morning paper and pretend to look for work. What would it mean to return to one of those mornings and live it, instead of avoiding it? I could have loved Emma, and the children, if I had only known....

Known what? That I was a psychotic killer waiting for the freedom to act? I would have just killed them along with everyone else. But if I had known that the sky could really be as blue as it is right now, if I could have seen that Emma was merely trying to survive as well as I, if I could have known that God wouldn't leave me where I was, then could I have loved them? Krang sighed. What useless questions. Useless like him.

Do I love Katie? Krang saw her in his mind, heard again the squeal of joy when he told her he wanted her to have the baby. He had tried to forget her, but she was never far from his mind. I think I actually do love her, he thought. I saw something in her that I never saw in anyone else. A drive to live that wasn't based on fear of dying. I actually admire that girl, he thought. I don't think that's ever been true before.

Krang stopped in the road for a moment, and wiped his brow. He raised his water skin to his lips and took a long pull, enjoying the sweetness of the cool water trickling down his dry throat. He looked at the blue sky and at the endless road before him and smiled, then started on his way again.

"God," he said quietly as he walked, "I have to say thank you, for the wonder of this morning, and for the gift of service that I am able to give to Katerina, and hopefully, Katie. I will not beg you to bring her back to me, for I do not believe that you bargain with us, or at least not with one so foul as I. And I cannot think of anything that I can do that would ever justify such a happiness in my life. I am saddened and angry that Sarah is dead, but I hope that she has been reunited with her son and husband. And if life ends without such reunions, if it all becomes nothingness..." Krang trailed off, unable to finish his thought.

"According to Katie, I am a Divine Child of God. Everyone is. I think that perhaps I have glimpsed what she means, in Sarah and Katie. I am as far away from being like them as the moon is from being the sun. What Katie saw as my 'light' was nothing more than the reflection of her own, which shines so brightly and drives away darkness. I cannot promise you that I will live life as they would, but I will hold their memories as my guide to this life. I ask your forgiveness, God, not for what has been and is unforgivable, but for the errors that are to come. I will live the life you lay before me, Father...."

Krang paused. I have never done that, he thought. I have never used Father for God. Hell, before I met Katie, the only time the word God passed my lips was if I was cursing. Goddamn. Or you've been Godfucked. Or in some other bullshit phrase. He shook his head. And I feel happy in spite of everything, he thought. I can't stop it. I feel like someone who doesn't know any better.

Krang sighed, and started on his way.

The clouds overhead swirled and bumped against each other, threatening rain. The low clouds seemed oppressive, making the whole day feel gray. Lisle sat on the bench in the late afternoon and waited. She wasn't waiting for anything in particular. She had been at work all day, but wasn't ready to go back to the apartment she shared with Katie. Katie was probably napping, her big belly cuddled against a pillow. Lisle just didn't know what to do about the girl. Katie had let her know she was available every night when they went to bed, but Lisle hadn't been able to say yes again.

Lisle looked across the small square to the cathedral that dominated the street. The yellow stone face of the cathedral glowed golden in the weak afternoon light.

Two bell towers jutted into the sky, soaring over the square. The round stained glass window, the buttresses supporting the building, and the towers all had been copied from Notre Dame in Paris. The builders here had done a remarkable job of imitation on a building half the size of the original. Lisle hoped the war in Europe hadn't destroyed the original.

The crowds on the street, hurrying home after a day at work, or rushing to market to buy dinner, or out for a night on the town, passed by the church without a second thought. They didn't even turn their heads to glance at the church. Three priests stepped from the front door, their long gowns and headgear instantly marking them as belonging to the Montrovian church. But nobody noticed. To the busy crowds on the sidewalk, they were still Corabians.

Lisle knew there was a Jewish temple a few blocks from here, and a vibrant Jewish quarter in the city. There were Muslims and Africans and Sikhs in the city, and no one seemed to mind. Catholics, too. So why did she feel like such an outsider? Why did she dread going back to the refugee village?

She could feel the tears welling in her eyes and shook her head to keep from crying. Lisle was sick of herself. She felt out of place everywhere she went, yet had no reason to do so. She felt marked, as if each scar hidden under her dress was a vivid black symbol that everyone could see that screamed fraud or murderer or victim. And she didn't know which she was.

Krejci had died because of her. If she had ignored him, had let him be, he could still be alive. If she had really loved him, she would have known that their relationship wasn't safe, and let him be. She had pursued him as much as he had pursued him. She had been the seducer, the one who kissed first, and took off her blouse and bra first, and held his cock in her hand first, and swallowed him and fucked him. He had been such a good boy, so cautious and caring and unable to say no to her. She had killed him. Any other boy in the town, any Montrovian boy at least, would still be alive. And after Krejci was mutilated and hung from a tree in the school yard, what had she done? Nothing.

She had hidden her tears and her grief in fear that they would come for her. All she had done was to be scared. The villagers had revolted her, with their laughing and jeering about the deportations, but she had done nothing. Some had resisted. She knew a boy who had slipped away into the hills rather than be conscripted. His body had lain in the town square for days after he had been shot, but at least he had acted. Why couldn't she have had the courage to act?

Lisle thought of Katie, forced to her knees in some alley, sucking the cock of a policeman she had thought was a friend of her father's. I'd have died right then, Lisle thought. Even though I'd already sucked a cock, knew how to do it, liked doing it with Krejci, I would have been unable to in that alley and would have been shot or deported on the first day. I sat back and watched my people go to war against my friends and I did nothing.

Lisle looked at the church across the square. She had lied to Katie, had told her she was afraid to go into the church for fear that someone would see her. These people weren't going to do anything to her. As much as she felt like everyone could see her and know she was Montrovian, the only thing that gave her away was her northern accent. And that didn't really mean anything in this city, where people spoke in all dialects, accents and languages. Lisle couldn't go into the church because that's where God was. And she didn't deserve to be where God was.

Lisle wasn't sure if she thought she would be punished again if she entered the church. She already bore the marks of her shame, those hundreds of ugly scars that marred her body and would keep her from a lover's caress. That was the price she had paid for Krejci. Although whether the scars were punishment for fucking him or for abandoning him she wasn't sure. And if that's what God did to her for Krejci, what greater punishment waited her for her inaction through the rest of the war? Maybe her loneliness was punishment enough. Katie's burgeoning belly reminded Lisle everyday that she would never have a family of her own. And Katie's caresses, done from nothing more than her desire to prove to Lisle she was still beautiful and sexy, had reawakened a very dormant sexual hunger. Lisle found herself suddenly aware of men, of how they looked and felt when she brushed against them, of how they sounded and even smelled. That added to her guilt. Katie had made it clear she was available and all Lisle could think about were men, who didn't - couldn't - want her. But Katie's love hadn't convinced Lisle that anyone could ever love her or find her sexy. Not with these scars. Katie could fuck anyone to stay alive, no matter how repulsive, so her fucking Lisle didn't mean a thing. That was part of the problem. Lisle wasn't even sure if Katie really wanted her, or was just willing to try to make her happy. Katie really loved Walter, after all.

Lisle looked around the square, feeling panicked. She had already decided that she needed to leave the city, but she just couldn't decide where to go. She had looked at pictures in the atlas at the library, and wondered how much was really left in Europe. So much of the continent had been destroyed by the war. Katie had suggested they go to America, where the kind of prejudice that had caused this war didn't exist, but she didn't think American men would like her scars any better than the men in this city. She didn't think men anywhere would like her scars. She would even be ugly to a blind man, she thought, a sad grin on her face, as she imagined a blind man feeling her body and dismissing her.

She sighed, and stood up. It was time to go. She had weeding to do in the communal garden behind their building. She hated weeding. She hated Corabia.

Lisle climbed the stairs to their apartment, her back aching from the work she had done in the garden. Who gardens in the winter? Gardening wasn't even the term. Today they had been turning the soil with shovels, prepping it for next year's planting. She hoped to God she wouldn't be here next year. Lisle was ready to soak in the tub. At least she no longer felt she had to hide from Katie. It seemed like one of those normal things, to have a friend talk with you while you soaked in the tub.

When she crested the top step, Lisle could see the corner of an envelope peeking from under their door. Lisle frowned. Katie should have been home to answer the door. Lisle unlocked the door and pushed it open, reaching down to pick up the envelope. It was addressed to them both, "Lisle Woerful and Katrina Woerful." The envelope had an official seal on it. There must have been a decision about their request for asylum.

Katie was napping on the floor of the little living room, sleeping in the same spot where Lisle had found her for the last several afternoons. A weak ray of sun had broken through the clouds and bathed the girl in a golden light. Katie's ability to curl up on a sunny spot on the rug and fall asleep reminded Lisle of a kitten. When she woke, Katie would yawn and stretch in a way that made the comparison seem even more real.

Lisle was torn. She knew Katie would want to know immediately what was in the envelope, but it held bad news for one of them.

Watching Katie sleeping, Lisle was overcome with feelings. She felt a rush of joy every time she saw her friend. It was that feeling of safety, of knowing that here was someone who would protect Lisle, and who would be there for her. And of course, the joy was immediately mingled with the fear that something out there could tear them apart. The fear that Katie would leave her when she found her family or that Lisle would abandon the girl because she couldn't risk accepting responsibility for her. Because she was afraid Krejci would happen all over again. Whatever was in the envelope would determine what happened.

Lisle sat down next to her friend. "Wake up, Katie," she whispered, lightly stroking Katie's shoulder and cheek. Katie stretched lazily and rolled onto her back, slowly fluttering her eyelids as she woke up. She looked up at Lisle with a grin, and slowly sat up.

"It came," Lisle said, holding up the envelope.

"What came?"

"The notice from the relocation center."

Katie nodded slowly, suddenly grave. "Open it."

Lisle tore the envelope open and pulled out the single sheet of paper.

Located Father in Olive Hill. Requests Katrina relocates immediately. Send details of arrival as soon as possible. Train daily.

Lisle folded the paper and put it in the envelope. She felt as bleak as she had on the train, the moment she was going to throw herself under the wheels, just before Katie had found her.

"You'll have to relocate," she said. "I'll go back to Montrovia."

"You'll do no such thing!" Katie snapped, anger under her voice. "Why do you want to leave me?"

"He doesn't want me there," Lisle said. "He wants you. He knows I'm not his daughter…"

"You may not be his daughter, but you are my sister," Katie said. "And you could be more than that, if you chose. He doesn't get to decide this."

Lisle shook her head. "I won't go. I won't get in the way of your family."

"Then I won't go," Katie said.

"You have to go," Lisle said. "We've been waiting for months for this moment."

"No," Katie said. "You've been waiting for months. I've been happy just living with you. I'm home now."

Lisle nodded. "I know that, but I'm not. I've tried to make it work here, Katie, but I don't think I can. Maybe I'll never feel at home anywhere, but I can't stay here."

"Then let's go away," Katie said. "I'd rather have you in my life than not have you in my life. Let's just pick a place and move there."

"You'd really do that for me?" Lisle started to tear up.

"Of course I would. You're my family now. I don't know my parents anymore, or Bela. I can't be the child to them that I was before I ran away."

"I'll tell you what," Lisle said. "You need to have this baby before we could travel anyway. Why don't you go see…"

"We. Why don't we!"

"Why don't we go see your Father? We can move to Olive Hill until the baby comes and then decide what we want to do."

"You'd do that for me?" Katie asked.

Lisle nodded. She wasn't happy about it, but she couldn't keep Katie from her family. "I do have one question," she said. "What happens when Walter comes for you?"

"He can't come for me. This place is death for him."

Krang lay on his blankets on the top of a small rise, his pack nestled under his head as a pillow. It had been three days since he had left the little cabin. He had no idea how much further he would have to travel to reach the Homeland, or what he would do once he finally reached it. He would need to arrange to bury Katherine's ashes, and to get her locket and letter to Katie. Would there be a way for him to see the girl? Not meet with her, or talk to her, but just to see her. Reuniting with Katie was as much a fantasy as finding Sarah had been. Men like Krang didn't deserve to be loved. So he would not step back into her life, or even let her know that he was still alive. But he would like to see her, to know that she was well. To see how big she must look with the baby. Had the baby been born yet? It must be getting somewhat close.

Krang sighed. His life had taken such a turn that he didn't recognize himself anymore. Was he really different? Did it even matter? Could you look at his life as two separate parts? Two separate people?

Krang rolled up in his blanket and watched the stars overhead. The night was clear, and the moon had set hours ago, leaving nothing to challenge the brilliance of the stars. Krang hadn't eaten that evening, in fact he had eaten nothing but a turnip earlier in the day, but he wasn't hungry. He had lost so much weight in the last few months that he now looked like one of the camp survivors. He was grinning as he looked up at the stars.

I feel like a fucking moron, he thought. Like I'm too stupid to realize the gravity of my situation. I have no food, no money, no place to go, and if anyone ever finds out who I am they will kill me. And yet.... He shook his, still grinning. So this is joy. The absolute inability to accept reality. A shooting star streaked across the sky like an exclamation point.

Chapter Twenty-One

Krang stood in the line of people waiting to cross the border into Corabia, alone. He wasn't sure when the last of the entourage had evaporated, but for the first time since he left the cave after the camp, Krang didn't feel their presence. He had come to depend upon them to be the reason he kept moving forward, towards the Homeland, every time his resolve failed. And now the last of them were gone.

The border crossing had materialized before him like a mirage in the desert, a line of trucks and cars parked by the side of a road outside a cinder block building. It had taken him twenty minutes to even realize what he saw, as he trudged across the dry, dusty landscape, trying to understand why the vehicles had all stopped. His first thought was the place must be a bar, and he wondered if he might be able to buy a beer, although he had no money. Then, as he got closer, he saw the soldiers and he knew.

Krang felt his heart begin to race. Sweat was trickling from his brow, but the late morning sun wasn't particularly hot. The people in line around him complained about the wait and the idiocy of bureaucrats. Before the war, no papers were required to cross the border. Krang felt vulnerable. He could feel the other staring at him. He hadn't bathed in more than a week. His hair and beard were dirty and tangled. The handles of the shovel and pickaxe stuck up above his thin shoulders. He was out of place in this line of ordinary people.

Krang looked down at his feet. His boots were falling apart. His pants were shredded around his ankles. His shirt was worn so badly he couldn't button the sleeves around his wrists. His gaze fell upon the half-obliterated tattoo on his left wrist. He wasn't here to pretend anymore. He casually covered his left wrist with his right hand. He would face the border guards without pretense.

I am no longer protected, he thought. I have reached the end of this journey that God required and can now suffer the retribution of these people. Krang had a moment when he wanted to step out of line, to turn around and walk away, but he couldn't. It was as if he were paralyzed, being shuffled along by some giant hand that pushed him one or two steps forward every few minutes as the line advanced.

I will not let fear rule me, he thought. I have been delivered here for a purpose, and I must let that purpose be. He looked at the hundreds of small clouds scudding across the brilliant blue sky, and drew in a deep breath. To his left, barely visible on the horizon, mountains broke roughly against the sky. He could smell the hint of the ocean some miles to his right. Krang smiled, feeling that deep joy welling in his chest. It did not matter why God had brought him here. It only mattered that he was here.

The line moved slowly, snaking its way up to a small, unpainted, cinder block building alongside the crossing. Each supplicant disappeared inside the building, to return a few minutes later to show a piece of paper to the guards on the crossing and then be waved through. The guards raised a double crossbar and the men walked or drove their trucks across the border. Although the line moved slowly, everyone seemed to pass through.

When it was finally his turn, Krang slowly entered the low building, his eyes struggling to see in the dim interior after the harsh glare of the sun. The building was cool. Once his eyes adjusted, he could see a small fan on the corner of a desk, blowing cool air. Krang leaned his shovel and pickaxe against the wall next to the door and moved to the desk. He sat in the open chair.

The man behind the desk was older than Krang. He appeared bored with the stories and complaints of the men who had come before Krang. He was studying some papers on the desk and never looked up at Krang. This was a bureaucrat in a uniform, not a soldier.

"Papers?" he asked, holding out his hand. Krang shrugged.

The man looked up from the papers on his desk, his eyes widening in disbelief when he saw Krang. Krang knew he looked like a scarecrow, or a mad man. The man studied him, shaking his head softly.

"I am a gravedigger," Krang said to the man who was questioning him, "and these are my tools." He indicated the pickaxe and shovel across the room.

"Your papers?"

Krang shook his head. "I have no papers. I am a gravedigger."

"I thought we'd seen the last of the likes of you," he said, more to himself than Krang. He cleared his throat. "Where are you from? Which camp?"

"Mountain City, in the north."

"You walked from Mountain City?" he asked, shaking his head again, as if he couldn't believe it.

"Mostly," Krang said.

"And how did you come to be a gravedigger?"

"The dead needed burying. They implored me to help. It became my work. I owed them, you see, because of the camp."

The man nodded quietly. The look on his face told Krang that the guard thought he was mad, thought he was out of touch with reality. It didn't matter as long as he was allowed to cross the border.

"What did you do before the camps?"

Krang shrugged and shook his head. "As little as possible," Krang said with a laugh. "I was a worthless piece of shit. But now, I am a gravedigger."

The guard nodded.

"Do you have any family here? Any friends?"

Krang closed his eyes and saw Katie. He shook his head. "My family and friends are dead."

"And where in Corabia do you want to go?"

Krang shrugged. He hadn't actually thought of where he would go.

"Where all the other refugees have gone," he said, hating how the words sounded. Words that marked him as one of the uninitiated. He reached into his pack and pulled out the wooden bowl holding Katerina's ashes and gently set it on the desk before the guard.

"I have been carrying the ashes of this old woman for some time. I promised her I would see that she was buried in the Homeland."

The man leaned back, a look of amusement on his face. He pushed the bowl back to Krang.

"We have a resupply truck coming in this afternoon, and taking the boys into Corabia for a weekend pass. You can ride with them. They will drop you at the relocation center. In the meantime, you will need to shower and burn those rags you are wearing. We don't need lice here. We will give you something clean to wear. You wait outside, and one of the boys will come get you."

Krang sat in the back of a truck, his pack on his lap, the pickaxe and shovel at his feet. He was surrounded by soldiers, but none carried a weapon. The soldiers watched Krang indifferently. To them, he was just one more used up refugee seeking asylum, and therefore unimportant. He certainly wasn't more important than the prospect of a weekend pass in the big city.

He was wearing an old Corabian army uniform that was slightly too big for him. The sleeves were worn bare at the elbows and pants were too short. Krang had balked at putting on the uniform. He was sure the soldiers thought he was just a crazy old coot who couldn't give up his rags, but it had been the fear of what the uniform meant that had made him hesitate. But his fear had been meaningless. The uniform held no power, nor the pretense of power. It was just a hand-me-down.

Krang had been sure that stepping up to the border crossing would be the end of him, but once again death had been kept at bay. Even without seeing his fake tattoo they thought he was a camp survivor. He knew it was time to end the charade. When he got to the city, he needed to them the truth: he was Walter Krang, *the Guard*. All they would need to do is read one survivor's account of the Mountain City camp and they would understand the enormity of his crimes.

The truck crested a rise and Krang could see the ocean. The blue-gray swells seemed to go on forever, like miniature receding mountain ranges, until they met the sky at the horizon. The immensity of it was strangely pleasing to Krang. It was so much more than he was, and he took a delight in acknowledging his own insignificance. Growing up in the mountains, he had never felt the power of their beauty, but this first sight of the ocean forced Krang to reorder all of nature. He was suddenly aware that over the last several months, he had slipped out of the center of his own life. No longer did the sun, the moon and all the world orbit around Walter Krang. Instead, he was no more than a comet, passing through and leaving the universe untouched.

Krang smiled. It was better this way. Being the center of the universe had cost him too much. And he hadn't even known he was paying.

Along the coast a city nestled against the ocean. Scores of buildings taunted the clouds. A busy port dominated the bay. An old walled city stood in stark contrast to the modern towers, offering the safety of tradition. Neighborhoods of small homes surrounded the city, stretching outward for miles. Krang knew this would be an easy city in which to get lost. He could disappear here and live his life out in anonymity, never having to take responsibility for what he had been. He could let *the guard* disappear as completely as his entourage had. It was a tempting thought, but an empty one. Krang was ready to pay for what he had done. He wasn't sure exactly when he had truly accepted that he was responsible, but at that moment there had been only one outcome. Had Sarah known she was sentencing him to death? Or had it been Katie, who had loved him, who had driven the stake through his heart?

The truck stopped short of the modern downtown, in a university-like setting that was the refuge village. A soldier pointed out the low brick building that was the relocation center. Krang collected his things, and then watched the truck pull away. His heart was racing. Once he entered that building, his life was over.

Krang looked around, trying to slow his racing heart. He needed a moment to collect himself, that he might do what was his to do. He walked for a minute, away from the relocation center, steeling himself to his task. The cemetery, headstones rising in caricature of the city around it, beckoned him from a few blocks away. Krang thought he might find a moment's peace among the dead, so he walked down the street to the burial ground.

The cemetery was old and huge, with many additions over the years, walled sections having been added again and again. Krang stood before the iron gates and looked at the endless rows of headstones, tall and short, plain and ornate. A city of the dead. This would be a good place to dig graves, he thought, wondering why he had never sought work in the cemetery at home as a young man. He grinned, because he knew the answer: too damned much work.

Krang walked through the gate into the cemetery, looking at the grave stones. He paused to steady himself, resting his hand upon a tall marble monument. The contact produce a charge in him, almost an electric shock, and he knew that he was not alone. The dead were here, in numbers. Some at peace, some angry, some lost. Krang knew that he would have much work to do here. He felt that charge run through him. A calling. He was to be here, in this place of the dead. He had more work to do before his time was ended. More dead to care for. He had been wrong to think that the fifty or sixty people he had buried on his way to the Homeland repaid the debt he owed to the hundreds he had tossed in the pit. He might have a lifetime of burials to complete before it would be time to turn himself in. Or it might just be a handful, a few extra to sow harmony in this country. To let the dead know he was their ally in this place as well as in the hell he had helped to create in Montrovia.

From where he stood, Krang could see a medieval stone chapel with a tall tower and a small nave near the center of the cemetery. He headed towards the chapel, wandering among the headstones, running his hands over them as he passed, each contact producing a similar charge as the first. The power of the dead boiled under the calm surface of the lawns, calling him.

A long, low block building squatted behind the chapel. A backhoe was parked outside the office, the ugliness of the present tearing a hole in the fabric of antiquity. A man, about Krang's age, dressed in a dark blue coverall, leaned against the backhoe, smoking. Krang nodded to him, jealous of the cigarette.

"The boss?" Krang asked.

The man eyed Krang suspiciously, and after a moment pointed to a set of double doors.

Krang nodded his thanks.

"He ain't hiring. He's got all the help he needs. I'm the grounds man here."

Krang nodded again, and entered the low building. A bell on the door announced Krang's presence. It was cool inside, and dark. Krang paused in the doorway to allow his eyes to adjust to the gloom. He was standing in a large equipment room that took up much of the building. He saw a young man sitting at a small desk against the wall. The tall, narrow windows did not catch the late afternoon sun, so the man's desk lamp was the only light in the room.

The young man looked up, ran his eyes over Krang and dismissed him, returning to the papers he was reading. "Yes?" he asked, distractedly.

Krang paused where he was, and waited.

The young man looked up, annoyed. "Yes?" he said sharply.

"Are you the boss?"

The young man nodded. "I'm the superintendent."

Krang cleared his throat. "I dig graves."

The young man shook his head. "I'm not hiring." He looked down at the papers.

"I did not ask you to hire me," Krang said.

The young man looked up. "I'm sorry," he said. "I thought you were looking for work."

"I am a gravedigger. I have come to dig graves."

The young man frowned. "I already have a grounds man who operates the backhoe."

Krang shook his head. He felt powerless to say the right thing. "I am not a backhoe operator. I am a gravedigger." He slipped his pack off, pulled his shovel and pickaxe free and laid them gently on the floor. "These are my tools. I have felt this place, it called me. I am needed here."

The young man stood up from his desk and walked over to Krang, a grin on his face. "You dig graves by hand?"

Krang nodded.

"You dig them squared, and regulation depth?"

"Yes."

"And you can prepare the dead?"

Krang nodded again. "I will wash the bodies, and wrap them in linens."

The man laughed. "We have more and more families who come to us wanting a traditional burial, no backhoe, no elaborate caskets. The want to be buried as their forefathers were. And no one here will dig a grave by hand, or wrap a body."

He stuck his hand out and shook Krang's hand. "My name's Tesare. I can't pay you much. Hell, I can't really pay you at all, but you can live here, in a room in the back, and I'll see to it that you have enough to eat every day, and that you get something from each funeral that you do."

Krang nodded. "Thank you, Tesare. I am Kr.... Werkamp. Walter Werkamp."

"Welcome aboard, Walt."

Tesare led Krang down a narrow hall to the rear of the building. There was a room with several long tables that could be used for preparing the dead for burial. The room had not been used for some time and was covered in dust and mold.

"You will need to scrub it clean," Tesare said, as they looked into it. "The city has to inspect it before we can offer burial services through the chapel. The mortuaries in the city have all modernized. The last of the traditional undertakers, down in the old city, closed last year when the old man had a stroke. His sons moved out into the suburbs. That's where all the money is. But with the war and all, there are many crying out for a return to the old ways. We can truly meet a need, if we can offer a traditional burial service. That means picking up the body, washing and wrapping it and completing the burial by sundown of the day following the person's death."

"I can do it."

"Great," Tesare said. "Let me show you where you can stay."

Krang's room was small, jutting off the rear of the building like the afterthought of a crazed architect. It had large windows that faced east and west, so it would catch both the morning and afternoon sun, and entrances both through the building and directly to the cemetery. It was clearly the brightest room in the entire building. A narrow bed was pushed against one wall, a chest of drawers against another. A small writing desk was set against the third wall. The windows came with interior shutters, although Krang couldn't think of why you might want to close them. A naked light bulb hung in the middle of the room.

"This was the caretaker's room, back when we had someone on site twenty-four hours a day," Tesare explained. "It's only used now when Lomy, you met Lomy, the grounds man, right? It's only used when Lomy sneaks his girlfriend back here. He thinks I don't know." Tesare laughed. "I'll make sure we get you some clean sheets.

"It's not heated or air conditioned, but that shouldn't matter. The stone exterior keeps us very comfortable, and you get quite a breeze back here. You'll be able to wash your clothes in the body prep room, and can hang them out to dry after dark, when no one will see them.

"There's a lunchroom at the end of the hall. It has an icebox and a small stove. You can eat in there."

Katie climbed awkwardly up the wrought iron steps into the train carriage and followed Lisle to their seats. They were leaving from the same platform they had arrived at months earlier, but everything was different. Their belongings had been loaded into the luggage car. The trip to Olive Hill would take a little less than two hours. Katie felt more nervous than the day they arrived. She knew Lisle was on edge as well; they had been fighting all morning.

The train pulled slowly away from the station, heading south, running along a ridge a few hundred yards from the ocean. Katie shifted uncomfortably in her seat, watching the waves as they crashed into the shore. Lisle squeezed her hand gently.

"I'm still not sure I should be coming," Lisle said softly. "I feel like I'm crashing your family reunion."

Katie looked at her friend, wishing she understood why Lisle was so afraid.

"How many times do I have to tell you that you are my family? I've heard nothing about mother or Bela, so I don't think they made it..."

"But your father?"

"I want to see my father, I really do...."

"But?"

"It's just so complicated. My last memory of him is when I ran away and he was cursing me. When I was living on the streets, I blamed him for everything that happened. I don't know if I can get past that, or if he can. Will I ever be anything more than the rebellious daughter?"

"I'm sure he loves you."

"I'm sure he does too, but that doesn't mean anything. I wondered last night if I knew for sure about mother and Bela if I would even be going to meet him. His cable said nothing about them, so I have to go, but I would have been happy staying right where we were."

"Once your father was found we couldn't stay in the refugee village any longer."

"Don't be an idiot," Katie snapped. "I know that. What I'm saying is I love you and I'm happy with you and I don't want my father to mess it up."

"I doubt..."

"I don't want you to mess it up," Katie said. "I don't want you running away in the middle of the night because you're unhappy. I'll go anywhere with you, once I know what's happened. Father doesn't know I'm pregnant, doesn't know I live with a Montrovian, doesn't know me. There was a time when none of that would have mattered to him, but I don't know any more. We might get right back on the train and ride away."

The rest of the trip was spent in silence, watching the landscape sliding past. The baby seemed to like the rhythmic swaying of the train, as it began kicking and rocking in time to the train's gentle motions. Katie felt the baby kicking and wondered what had happened to Walter. Was he still alive? She thought she would have felt it if he had died, but immediately realized the childishness of that. She had no more idea what was happening with her mother or sister than a stranger, so to think she would know if Walter died....

She felt a hole in her life where he belonged. And if he showed up today, she thought, I would take him back without thinking about it. I don't care what he did in the camp. I don't care what he did in front of mother or Bela. That part of him was dead before I met him. And yet she didn't think she could touch him again. She was afraid she would recoil away from him like she had the night he told her the truth. She was afraid her body was less tolerant than her heart.

She glanced guiltily at Lisle. She could spend the rest of her life with Lisle, as her lover, if Lisle let her. She had filled a void in Katie's life that Katie had thought was never going to be filled. But what if Walter came back? How could

288

she be in love with both of them? What was wrong with her that both of the people she gave her heart to were off limits?

It doesn't matter about Walter, Katie thought. That he could somehow come back into my life is an empty fantasy. Lisle is the most important person in my life right now. And when Lisle finds a man who loves her and doesn't care about the scars, well, that's okay too. Nothing is forever. I will have my baby, and we will make a life together.

The train circled down into the town along the same ridge that they had been following since they left the coast. Lisle and Katie watched Olive Hill unfold beneath their eyes. It stretched along the intersecting floors of two shallow valleys, spreading out into a soft x shape. The olive trees that gave the town its name covered the land as far as the eye could see. Stone houses dotted the hillsides surrounding the town. Katie felt a moment of hope. It reminded her in many ways of Mountain City before the war, when it was more a sleepy backwater than an important place. She liked the idea of returning to that kind of anonymity. She could see the train station a mile or two down the track and wondered if her father had come to greet them.

"I'm scared," Katie whispered to Lisle. "I don't know what I want from this. I wish we hadn't come."

"Nonsense. You want to find some part of your life from before the war. Don't we all? That is nothing to be ashamed of."

"But why am I so nervous?"

Lisle squeezed her hand. "In some ways you are still the fourteen year-old who saw her parents carted off to the death camp. You had put that part of yourself away, and now she is slipping out. It's okay. I'll be here for you."

The train began slowing on the gentle grade into town. Katie scanned the crowds on the platform, looking for her father, but couldn't find him. As the train stopped before the platform, she turned to Lisle.

"I don't think he's here."

"I'll go see to our things," Lisle said. "You wait on the platform. See if you can find him."

Katie waited until the train car was empty before rising and making her way along the narrow aisle. She could feel her heart pounding and she thought she might throw up. She couldn't stand how nervous she felt as she scanned the crowds on the platform for some sign of her father, but as she made her way to the entrance, she saw nothing of him. She knew she was on the verge of tears. Some part of her felt like she was being abandoned by him again.

Her pregnancy made climbing out of the train difficult. She stood on the last step of the car trying to figure out a way to step down to the platform without falling. A young man saw her predicament and came over and offered her his hand. Grasping it firmly, Katie swung herself down onto the platform.

"Thank you," she said to the man, who nodded in return.

"Katrina."

Katie spun to her left, and losing her balance, grabbed the young man's hand for support.

Her father stood a few feet away, a faint smile on his face. He had let his hair grow, and a beard, and was dressed in all black, but he was her father. Her father. Thinner than she remembered.

"You didn't say anything about being married," he said gruffly, pointing at the young man.

Katie turned to the young man who was blushing furiously. "Thank you," she whispered again, and then steadied herself and let him go.

"No, Papa," she said with a curt shake of her head. "I am not married."

Katie, ignoring the look of disapproval that swept across his face, stepped forward and hugged him. He stood stiffly for a moment, then wrapped his arms around her and squeezed her tightly. Katie could smell the lingering sweetness of his pipe, and she closed her eyes and knew that she was home. For a moment, at least, the war had never happened. As he hugged her, he began to shake, softly, and hugged her even more tightly in his arms. Katie was shocked when she realized he was crying.

Katie pressed her lips to her father's ear. "What of Mother and Bela?"

Her father shook his head mutely.

Katie felt her tears joining his. She was not shocked to hear they were dead, she had suspected it for some time, but now she had to grieve. She stood in her father's arms and cried. Finally she was home.

Lisle stood silently behind them, a smile on her face. She had seen the young man help Katie from the train, and had thanked him again. She felt a guilty surge of jealousy flash through her breast, knowing that she would never have a reunion with her father. If only her family was just lost in the chaos of the war, rather than having banished her, she might hold some false hope of renewal. But there would be no renewal. For all she knew, her father had been one of the ones who attacked her.

I should leave, Lisle thought. If I get back on the train now, it will be gone before Katie realizes it. She doesn't need me anymore, now that she has her father. I can go back to my village and let them finish what they started. And then I will be at peace.

She stared at Katie, wrapped in the arms of her father, disappearing within him. "I wish I could have loved you," Lisle thought. Katie deserved to be loved, and Lisle was sure that someday she would be. She deserved someone without taint, not Walter nor Lisle, but someone worth being loved by Katie as well.

Lisle turned and went back along the dock to find their luggage. It had been stacked on the platform by a porter, who was now looking for a wagon to send it on to where ever they would be staying. Lisle began looking through their luggage for her valise. It would have enough clothing and toiletries to get started. She didn't need much. A day or two would get her out of Corabia and she could finish what Katie had interrupted on the train. It would be so easy now, knowing that Katie was safe. She had some sleeping pills, prescribed to help her get through her nightmares; that would do the trick.

"Don't think you can sneak away now," Katie said from behind her. Her voice was light and joyful.

Lisle stood up guiltily, and nodded to Katie's father.

"Papa," Katie said proudly, "this is Lisle, my best friend. Lisle, this is my father, Benjamin Woerful."

"Pleased to meet you, sir," Lisle said. She felt intimidated by his stern visage. "Katie has told me so much about you." She stopped, unable to find anything else to say.

Woerful eyed her coldly. "I have to say that you don't belong here. It was wrong of you to pretend to be one of us to escape your own troubles. You will have to learn our ways, and of course, convert, if you wish to stay in Olive Hill."

"Papa!" Katie said angrily. "Lisle saved my life. She was almost killed by her own people."

Katie's father nodded. "Katrina, I realize that she is your friend. But the world is different than it was before. I want no trouble here."

"Then we will go." Katie stepped away from her father and stood next to Lisle.

"No," her father said. "That's not what I want. I just urge caution. Let us gather your things together and come to the house. We will find a rooming house for your friend in the morning."

Katie shook her head. "I will not stay with you Papa, and have Lisle carted off to a rooming house. We will find a place to live in the morning."

Woerful sighed, and shuffled his feet. "You must stay with me, Katie. I will not have my daughter living alone. Your friend can stay in the attic with the serving girls."

Katie linked her arm through Lisle's. "No, Papa. I am not the little girl that you lost four years ago. I may be young, but I am an adult now. I have seen too much to be treated like a child. We will find a place where we can live together and not disturb you."

"That is why you must take your place as my daughter, in my house. You were forced to grow up too quickly. You need time to regain your childhood, that you have a chance to become an adult properly."

"How much time would I have, Papa? My baby will be here in less than two months. Is that enough time to make up for years of hell? Nothing can give me back those years. Nothing can bring back Mother, or Bela. I am here because I am your daughter, but I am your adult daughter."

Lisle grinned in spite of herself. How she wished she had ever told her father what she really thought. She let her hand intertwine with Katie's, giving her a gentle squeeze.

"Young women of good standing don't live alone..."

"I'm pregnant and unmarried. I'm not pretending to be a virgin, hoping to snare a husband."

Woerful nodded his head at Lisle. "And your friend? Is she as loose with her morals as you? Will you be seen by my congregants as women of scandal?"

Katie laughed, clear and loud. "Lisle is a scandal-free as you could wish for, Papa. She doesn't even talk to boys, let alone do anything else with them. I'm the one with the bad reputation. I'm not ashamed of who I am. If you are, just don't admit to knowing me."

Her father was slowly shaking his head. "It's difficult to see you. To know all the loss our family has suffered. I can see your mother on your face and know that she is gone to me forever. And sweet Bela..." He shook his head. "The world is different now, and nobody understands the rules. Forgive me for loving you too much. For missing you too much."

"Papa, I love you, too."

Krang took two days to clean the prep room, scrubbing the tables, floor and walls with steaming hot water and lye soap. Tesare found him several pairs of coveralls to wear when on duty. He was there for almost a week before he was needed to dig his first grave, which he did under the watchful eye of Tesare and taunts of Lomy. Krang, as was his practice, laid out the grave with string. He removed the top layer of sod and set it to one side, and then used the pick to break up the soil. Digging no longer made him hurt, as his muscles were now very comfortable with the repetitive motions. He loved the gentle ache in his shoulders and back as his muscles loosened, the steady intake of breath, and the growing pile of dirt that marked his progress. The grave was situated in a family plot, with headstones all around. Krang was careful not to cover any of the other headstones with loose dirt. Tesare brought out a tarp which was used to cover the mound of dirt, and a canopy was raised to create shade next to the grave.

The body of an elderly man was delivered to the prep room early the next morning, and Krang gently stripped it, setting aside the clothing and possessions for the family. He washed the body on the long steel table that had a deep sink attached at one end. The same sink where he washed himself each morning and evening. Krang wrapped the old man in clean white grave linens, and using a narrow cart took the body into the chapel.

The little stone chapel was dominated by a beautiful stained glass window of the resurrection, showing the stone rolled away from the tomb, and a white robed figure in the garden outside. The body was laid on a narrow table under the stained glass window. Krang found the stillness of the room to be very peaceful. He stood in a corner of the room, at attention, to honor the old man he did not know.

The funeral was in the early afternoon. After a short and emotional service, the old man was carried to the grave on the shoulders of family and friends. The minister led a long prayer at the graveside, almost as long as the service had been, and the body was lowered into the grave. Once the mourners slipped away, Krang was left to fill in the grave.

A middle-aged man sat stiffly against a neighboring headstone, outside the canopy, watching Krang shovel the fresh dirt back into the grave. He watched quietly, without tears or words. When Krang was finished, he nodded to the man and left him alone in his contemplation. Later the man stopped by the work room.

"I have to say thank you," he said quietly. "I am not an overly sentimental man, and Father and I had our arguments. There are things about him I won't miss. But when I saw that machine that is used to dig the graves I couldn't bear the thought of it dumping loads of dirt on a coffin with him in it. I know it's silly. He wouldn't feel a thing, but I would have."

Krang nodded and shrugged. "I didn't always respect the living, so now I try very hard to respect the dead."

"That is how I'm feeling about my father," the man said, nodding.

Krang patted him on the shoulder. "Your father is comfortable here, and he is at peace. The dead come to me when they have grievances, and he has none."

The man brightened. "I bet they do come to you, don't they?" He shook Krang's hand and left. Krang went to bathe. He caught his reflection in the one mirror in the workroom: his beard had been trimmed but was still several inches long. His hair fell to his shoulders. Both were streaked through and through with gray. He was eating more regularly than when he had been on the road, but only small amounts, so he hadn't put on any real weight. Without his shirt, he was wiry and thin. Not quite frail looking, but certainly not like he was healthy. Krang laughed. He felt more physically fit than he ever had before in his life. The man who had buried his father was at least fifteen years older than Krang, but he had thought Krang the elder, because of his appearance.

Krang settled into a comfortable routine. He found that he dug most of the graves in the oldest sections of the cemetery, where the backhoe was too big and destructive to be used. When he wasn't digging a grave or preparing a body, he spent his time caring for the headstones, cleaning them and repairing them. He learned how to buff and shine marble, how to cut limestone, and how to use acid putty to add names and dates to existing headstones. He loved caring for the dead and their graves. He was at peace.

Early one morning, as the sun was just breaking the eastern horizon, Krang buried Katerina's ashes. He had been at the cemetery for three weeks and had searched for several days to find the perfect spot. He buried her under a beautiful cedar tree, on a small rise in the oldest part of the cemetery. Under the tree, on the hill, she had a view of both the ocean to the west and the distant mountains to the east. Krang dug the grave quickly, a small deep square. He knelt and set the bowl of ashes into the grave, and laid the letter and locket, still wrapped in oilskin on top of the bowl. Krang began to brush the soil back into the grave. The clumps of dirt pattered onto the oilskin, and after a second Krang reached in and pulled the letter and locket free, brushing the dirt back into the grave. He had promised Katerina. He would find a way to see it was delivered. He filled in the grave and placed the sod on top, gently tamping it into place.

Krang sat next to the grave and watched the sun rising. He would not look for Katie himself, for he could feel his longing for her boiling beneath the surface of his being. He had freed her, and free she must remain. He was sure she was in the Homeland, possibly even in the city which rose right outside the walls of his cemetery. He wasn't sure if the baby would have come by now, or if it was just due. He had never gotten a real time line from her the night she left. She had simply said she was due in the spring. And spring would be here before he knew it. He could hardly believe that almost a year had passed since Sarah had freed him.

Krang resolved again not to look for Katie, but simply to wish her well. His hope for her was simple: that she meet a man who could help heal the terrible damage done to her soul by the war. Someone who would love the child as much as he loved Katie. Krang closed his eyes and began his morning prayer. As usual, his only request was peace and health for Katie.

When he returned to the office, he joined Tesare and Lomy for a cup of coffee.

"How would I find someone who had come to the Homeland after the war?" he asked, explaining briefly about finding Katerina in the cabin, but never mentioning that he knew Katie personally.

"The daughter is young?" Lomy asked, a cigarette hanging from his mouth.

"Seventeen or eighteen."

"I will help you with this. Let me see the picture. Then I will go door to door

294

through the city and interrogate all the young women until we find her." He said it with such a leer that even Krang was offended, although he found himself laughing. He knew he was laughing at himself. In Lomy he had found exactly who he had been before the war.

"I would try the relocation office," Tesare suggested. "You know, in the refugee village, where you were checked in when you arrived in Corabia. They will have a record if the woman's daughter entered the country. If she has been sent on to another city, they will know that as well. I am sure they would see to it that a personal item like that was delivered, if they have any record of her."

Krang liked that idea. He would say that it had been in the possessions of an old woman recently buried in the cemetery who had never found her lost daughter. It need never lead back to Krang. So he prepared to leave the cemetery.

Krang had felt like an idiot asking Tesare to address the large envelope he had purchased from his meager earnings, but he was afraid Katie might recognize his hand writing, not that he could remember having ever written anything in front of her. He told Tesare he had hurt his hand, but he was sure Tesare thought him illiterate. He asked Tesare to write her name as Katrina Woerful, rather than Katie, just to make sure it didn't lead back to him, for he had never called her Katrina. Tesare had then given Krang directions to walk to the relocation center, about a half mile from the cemetery.

Krang stepped through the gate of the cemetery. To his left, the stone wall of the old city beckoned, but he turned to the right, and headed towards the modern city. The relocation center was easy enough to find. Krang never had to enter the maze of skyscrapers that taunted him from the heart of the city, since the refugee village lay between the old walled city and the modern downtown. He was surprised how close it was to the cemetery, with most of the dormitories actually backing up on the cemetery. Katie might have a view of him at work every day, and not even know it.

Krang entered the low brick building. A soldier sat at a desk that blocked access to the building. Krang was still nervous around soldiers. He had met several in the weeks he had been in Corabia, after burying their fathers or mothers, and found most of them to be pleasant enough, but the risk of exposure was always on his mind. He shook his head, knowing that he would never be found out until God decided it was time, and once that happened, nothing he could do would prevent it. His being discovered was just like death. You knew it was going to happen, in its own sweet time, so there was no point in worrying about it.

"I've a package..." Krang said, holding up the envelope.

The soldier looked up, irritation flashing across his face.

Krang straightened his shoulders and spoke again, in a louder, more certain voice. "I buried an old woman a few weeks ago, and she had this envelope in her possessions. It's for her daughter, who was relocated here before her. They were separated in the camps..."

The soldier raised his hand, cutting Krang off. "What's in the envelope?"

Krang stared at him.

"Do you want me to open it?"

"A letter and a locket. She wants them to go to her daughter, who she knows was processed through the center."

"Okay," the soldier said. "If she's been through here, we'll be able to deliver it to her." He held out his hand for the envelope. Krang felt reluctant to give it up.

"We're delivering several pieces of mail a week to relocated refugees," he said.

Krang nodded and handed over the envelope. He stood before the desk, feeling suddenly emptied of hope.

The soldier glanced at the envelope. "Do you want to put a return address on it, in case there is a reward?"

"No," Krang replied, "it's a letter from her dead mother. Do you think I want to be rewarded for that?"

The soldier shrugged, the look on his face telling Krang that's exactly what he thought Krang wanted. Krang turned and walked away, understanding that he was fleeing. The sidewalk was his refuge. He put his head down and trudged away, feeling the hatred of the soldier boring into his back like the look of a malevolent teenage girl. Krang hated himself for walking quietly away; hated himself for his sudden lack of attitude and confidence. He didn't know how to live now. He wasn't *the guard* anymore, and he wasn't the Walter Krang from before the war. Neither of those versions of himself would have taken any shit from a soldier of no account sitting behind a desk. But he was trying to figure out how to treat people like people, which was hard enough to do with someone like Tesare without having to deal with assholes on top of it all.

Krang looked up and realized he had no idea where he was. Instead of turning back towards the cemetery he had walked into the heart of the city. The streets were clogged with traffic, trucks and cars fighting for the same spaces, horns blaring at the pedestrians who stepped from the curb without looking. People scurried by without noticing him, as if late for something very important. The sidewalk was packed with people. It was lunchtime and Krang felt as if every building in the city must have emptied out onto the sidewalk. He turned around but couldn't see the relocation center from where he was. He had walked several blocks into the city. Krang had no idea how he had gotten where he was. He would have had to cross several intersections. He was lucky he hadn't been run over by a truck.

He looked at the buildings on the street, soaring upward. He craned his head back to follow them up into the sky, and immediately felt a sense of vertigo. He swayed, wondering if he was about to fly upward from the face of the earth, the first person in the world to lose gravity. Krang shook his head and looked back down to the sidewalk. At least the sidewalk was safe. He trudged forward, buffeted by the crowds of people. It seemed impossible to take three steps without someone brushing against him, bumping him, or stepping so closely in front of him that he had to stop to avoid running into them.

The woman were as bad as the men. Wrapped in light overcoats against the cooler winter air and light rain, they flashed past on high heels that looked like they could kill. Their faces were set into grim caricatures of the men around them as they tried to be women and men all at once.

Panic rose up in him like a wild animal. He couldn't breathe, couldn't feel his feet upon the ground. His heart was hammering in his chest, the blood pounding in his ears. He needed his cave, a complete withdrawal of all sensation, so he could be safe again.

Krang turned a corner, hoping to see some recognizable shape to orient himself. Instead he saw a low stone wall, waist high, and the beautiful expanse of trees and grass that lay beyond it. The park was a beautiful refuge. He walked under the wrought iron arch at the gate and immediately the noise of the city seemed dulled. The people in the park moved at a different pace, not rushing from one place to the next, but clearly seeking refuge from the circus around them. Krang found himself able to breathe again. He found a bench and sat, taking a few moments to recover.

The sky had cleared, and the sun was shining brightly. For some reason, it reminded Krang of his last day in the camp, when he had been on the barrack roof with Gerri and Willi. It was the warmth of the sun on an otherwise cool day that brought the memory back. It was late February here, but the weather was similar to that late March afternoon. He hadn't thought of Gerri, or the boy Willi, in such a long time. Gerri would have loved the energy of the modern city, as the old Krang would have. Willi would have loved the park. Do you haunt Woerful they way my dead haunted me?

Krang rose from the bench and explored the park. It was six blocks on a side, with neatly manicured gravel paths that ran along the edges and criss-crossed the center. All of the trails converged in the center of the park, at a beautiful memorial that was under construction. It was almost finished, but workers still scurried around the site, making last minute fixes. A pond had been built in the middle of the park, with a fountain at one end and a gas flame at the other. A marble retaining wall, waist high, ran round the outside of the pond. A marble podium was built on a small rise overlooking the pond, reminding Krang of a pulpit in front of a church. A wooden sign announced a ceremony to open the memorial on the first day of March. Krang felt a shiver run down his spine, remembering how angry he had felt when he had seen the camp bulldozed flat, as if that could somehow change what had happened there. He had thought the place deserved to be saved, to be remembered forever. They had built that memorial here, instead. Each of the marble panels surrounding the pond, perhaps a hundred of them, had been inscribed with the names of the Corabian victims of the camps.

Krang circled the pond, staying far enough back to keep out of the way of the workers. Each camp was named and described in a marble panel, and then in the panels that followed were the names of the dead from that camp. A blank panel sat between each camp's display, clearly intended to allow them to add names as necessary.

They must have started on this before the war even ended, Krang thought. The minute they knew about the camps. Where did they get all the names? Krang had never seen a list of the dead among the inmates. Everyone knew such a list would have meant instant death. There must have been hundreds of Katerina's who had written down the histories of each camp, quietly documenting the destruction wreaked by Krang and the others like him. Or they had taken the files before they destroyed the camps, in which case they had the names of all the guards as well as all the prisoners.

People walked past the memorial like it was invisible to them. Krang watched them wander past, not too hurried to take the time to see what it was, but indifferent. Even before the memorial was dedicated, most Corabians didn't care about it. He approached it slowly until he was standing before a marble panel, far away from any of the workmen. He ran his hand over the marble, his finger tips catching as they ran over the engraved names. He crouched before the panel, his hand on the marble, taking deep breaths. He knew he was crying, but didn't care. No one passing by asked how he was. He had become as invisible as the wall.

Krang could feel a charge in the marble just like at the cemetery. Now he knew why his dead had left him, for he was sure that they had come here. All of the dead had come here. He raised his head and let his eyes circle the pond. A hundred panels, maybe more. Hundreds of names etched upon each panel. How many had died in the camps? A hundred thousand or more, and Krang felt the weight of each soul upon his body.

Krang stood, reluctant to break contact with the wall, but he knew what he needed to do. He walked around the pond, trailing one hand along the marble, stepping away only when a worker was in his way, until he found the panels for his camp. He crouched again, raising his hand to the first of the names. His fingers tingled as if an electric current ran through the marble panel. They were all here. He knew them all. He closed his eyes and slowly traced his fingers over every

298

name. Each name he touched brought a face unbidden from his memory. These were his dead, even the ones who had not died directly by his hand. Many of them had been in his entourage, and were old acquaintances. Some he had forgotten entirely until he felt their name upon the wall. Of course, he hadn't known all their names in the camp. It amazed him now that every name on the wall brought a face to mind, for he hadn't purposely tried to learn their names.

When he had touched every name, Krang sank to his knees. He was sobbing, trying to catch his breath, overwhelmed by this experience. He couldn't escape the enormity of what he had done. And in spite of all that he had done, an even graver crime had been revealed to him. Sarah was not among them. His fingers had not found her name. Her face, with that beautiful smile, had never appeared before him.

Krang went back to the first panel for Mountain City Camp and read each name. He had thought his fingers had jumped her name, avoided her somehow, because of the debt he owed her, but she wasn't there. Krang looked again and again. He sat on the ground before the panel that should have listed her and read each name ten times or more. Abraham Jezek. Capek Jezek. Ruza Jirina. Tonda Jirina. No Sarah Jezek.

Krang got to his feet and went from panel to panel, circling the entire memorial to make sure that someone hadn't carved the name under another camp. No Sarah Jezek.

Krang walked to the podium on one side of the memorial. The podium had two books, bound in plastic covers, with thousands of pages each, tissue paper thin. The first book listed each victim by camp, the second was an alphabetical listing of all persons, regardless of camp. No Sarah Jezek. Krang sat on a bench near the memorial, getting up periodically to look again, but he couldn't find her name. He didn't leave until after night had fallen, and it had grown too dark to read the names. He would come back tomorrow and find her. He needed to find her.

It was after lunch before Krang could get away from the cemetery and he came straight to the park. The workers were laying sod around the outside of the marble retaining wall, so Krang was unable to approach the memorial, but he didn't need to touch it today. He went back to the podium and looked through each page of the book, making sure her name wasn't listed incorrectly, or spelled wrong. Sarah was still missing.

Krang wanted to tear the books apart, shred the fragile tissue paper pages and punish whoever had forgotten Sarah. He wouldn't take his rage out on the monument, adding even more injury to the memories of those he had harmed. He would find another way. On the inside cover of the book was a listing for the

299

Corabia Parks Division, 1501 Oceanview Blvd. Krang glanced at his watch. Three o'clock in the afternoon. He left the park, disoriented immediately by the chaos of the city, and tried to guess where he would find Oceanview Blvd. Krang turned to the west, towards the ocean, and then stopped. Not right by the harbor, he thought. He glanced around, and followed a street that ran north, towards a small rise that dominated the bay and the cluster of buildings that towered over the city from that high point. He smiled to himself when he found it. Oceanview meant far enough away to be free of the gulls and pelicans, free of the stench of the fishing boats.

The parks division was housed in a twenty story glass and steel building that stood right on the edge of the city. In addition to housing the parks division, it housed several other city offices, and leased the top ten floors to private companies. According to a sign out front, the top two floors were a restaurant called the Oceanview.

The parks division was on the third floor, on the ocean side of the building. A row of windows offered a wonderful view of the sea stretching away to nothing. The sky was clear and blue, with a handful of cottony clouds drifting high above the water. Krang stopped a moment and stared out the window. He would never tire of the sea.

Krang stood in a line of people who were signing up for various activities and organizations offered by the division. He felt dirty and out of place in his coveralls. The counter was staffed by a young woman, a girl really, whose main purpose seemed to be cheering each customer's request for an activity. When she finished with the woman ahead of him, she glanced up at him. She looked Krang up and down, with an uncertain smile on her face.

"Next?" She eyed him with amusement as if finding out what activity he wanted to sign up for would be the funniest moment of her day.

Krang shuffled forward uncomfortably. He was unsure how to proceed. "I was looking at the monument, for the camp victims?"

"Yes?"

"Well, I think there may be a mistake."

"Yes?"

"It's wrong…"

"Is there a name missing?"

Krang felt a moment of relief and nodded.

The girl laughed gently. "Don't feel bad. Since they began construction on it, hundreds of names have been added to the panels. They published a list of the names and asked anyone who had information of others to please share it, so they could engrave the panels before they went up.

"Oh, don't worry," she said when Krang frowned. "They have a process to add more names to the panels after they're up. I mean, that's what we've been told. We have a form that you can fill out." She reached under the counter and brought out a three piece form and handed it to him. "Next?"

Krang stepped aside and looked at the form. It asked for the name of the missing person, the camp they were sent to, the date and circumstances of their death, the relationship of the claimant to the victim, and current contact information. Krang put the form on the counter and started to walk away.

"Sir!"

Krang stopped and turned to look at the young woman.

"You didn't write anything down."

He gestured towards the form and shrugged. What could he say?

"Don't worry about the form, most people can't fill it out. I'll help you."

Krang shook his head. "It's too much."

"Let's try it," she said with a smile. "We can always throw it out if I don't get enough info."

Krang returned to the counter.

"Is this a relative who can't be located?"

Krang shook his head. The young woman looked surprised.

"Name of victim?"

"Sarah Jezek, at the Mountain City camp."

"How did she die?"

Krang shrugged. "I don't know. I had already escaped. The camp was liberated the very next day."

"Maybe you should be at the relocation office, instead of here?"

"No," Krang shook his head. "Another inmate saw her die and told me."

"Then you should bring that person with you."

"She's dead now."

"Okay, let's list her on the form."

"Katerina Woerful, she died on the journey here."

The girl helped him finish the form, then asked for his name and address.

"I don't have an address."

"We just want to send out the results of our investigation. Who can we send it to?"

Krang shrugged.

"Are you in the refugee village? Or do you have a job?"

Krang brightened. "Send it to the cemetery..."

301

Chapter Twenty-Two

The package lay unopened all afternoon. It was a larger envelope, with a bulge in the middle that suggested something more than a letter was inside. Katie's father had brought it to her apartment a little before noon, after it had been delivered to his home by someone from the refugee center in the city. Katie would have opened it at once, except that she and her father had argued again. It was the same argument they had had almost every day since she had arrived in Olive Hill. He thought she was disrespecting him and his position by living with Lisle instead of being a dutiful daughter and living with him. There was no real scandal – everyone assumed she had lost her husband – but he seemed shamed by her presence.

She had tried to love him. In truth, she did love him, but he wasn't the man she remembered from her youth. He was still the man who had shouted at her as she ran from the wagon to avoid being sent to the camps. Katie couldn't imagine the sorrow he carried in his heart. He had lost his wife and daughter, lost both daughters in a way, and presided over the slow massacre of hundreds of his followers at the camp. She tried to forgive him his rigidity, his need to have things just so, but couldn't forgive him for not seeing her as an adult with a right to live her own life.

She had never told him how she had survived the war and he never asked. When he looked at her she could see the unspoken accusation on his face, that she was some kind of collaborator or worse, but he didn't have the strength to ask her for the truth. Maybe that, more than anything, kept her from seeing him as a father any longer.

He had waited awkwardly for Katie to open the package, but she hadn't wanted to, not with him in the room. They had argued and he had left. Now she was washing laundry and hanging it on a line outside the window to her small apartment. Nesting, Auntie Zophie, the midwife who lived across the hall, had said. It meant the baby would come any time now.

Who would send her a package? Katie couldn't imagine who even knew she was in Corabia. Could it be from Walter? It wasn't addressed in his handwriting, which meant that it might be about Walter, rather than from him. She realized she was scared to open the envelope, afraid to find out what it was and who it was from.

Katie washed the dishes lying in the sink and cleaned the kitchenette. She straightened up the small living room, and folded the laundry, leaving the windows open to catch the breeze. She felt an incredible restlessness, and fought an urge to scream and kick her heels. Open the damn package, she finally told herself. You cannot change what it is by waiting.

Katie entered the dining room and picked up the envelope. She ran her hands over it, feeling the hard lump in the center, and hearing the crackle of paper inside. She carried it out into the other room, and sat in the rocking chair. Her hands trembled as she opened the envelope, only to find another envelope inside. This one was addressed in pencil, in a hand that looked vaguely familiar, but still not Walter's.

Katie tore open the second envelope. A gold locket and chain fell out. Her heart pounding, Katie set the locket aside. Her entire body was buzzing. Somehow she knew what this was, but couldn't get her thoughts clear enough to put it all together. She pulled the letter from the envelope with trembling hands. The letter was barely legible, the pencil markings so soft as to seem to disappear on occasion. The paper was filthy. Katie's heart jumped.

> *My Dearest Daughter,*
>
> *I met an angel today. An angel who told me that you were alive. Not only alive, but pregnant with my grandchild! I prayed for you every day I was in the camp. I couldn't mourn for you, because I always hoped that you were in a better place than we were, but I missed you so much.*
>
> *Bela died of influenza before we even arrived at the camp. Your Father and I survived the war, so if you haven't found him, please don't give up hope. Forgive him for his fears, for I know he loves you.*
>
> *I am close to making my transition. Do not be sad for me, for I leave this world filled with joy knowing you are alive. Tell my grandchild that I am filled with love for him or her. I am including the necklace that you always liked, so that you will know this is truly from me. Even though I die far away from the Homeland, my angel has promised to carry me home.*
>
> *Your Loving Mother*

Katie stared at the letter, reading it again and again until the words blurred over and she couldn't see anything. She set the letter on the table and wiped the tears away with the back of her hand. She didn't stop crying, but at least she could see again. Katie picked the locket up from the table and now knew it exactly. She smiled, knowing what pictures she would find inside. She opened the locket, and inside was a miniature of two girls, herself and her sister, Bela. They were ten and seven forever in the locket, and Katie wished she could return to the day the photo had been taken.

"Oh mama, I miss you," Katie whispered, crying again, but the tears were not from sorrow.

Krang went to the park every day, whenever he was free, sometimes first thing in the morning, sometimes so late at night that he couldn't read the inscriptions. He always sat in the same place, on a bench before the panels devoted to the Mountain City camp. These were his people, the ones to whom he owed a life. He would read the names from beginning to end, and even could continue when the light had grown too weak to see. And every time, when he reached the place where Sarah's name should be, his heart would break. How could they have missed her?

Krang would look at the panels and remind himself that Sarah was dead. Katerina had no reason to lie to him. He tried hard to protect himself from the faint sliver of hope that burned in his chest. What if Katerina was wrong? Could Sarah be alive? He couldn't stop himself from thinking it. *What if she hadn't died?* What would that mean to him, if they told him she wasn't listed on the panel because she was still alive? Every day he asked himself the question. It never left the back of his mind, whether he was in the park, or working at the cemetery. He waited for an answer to his inquiry with growing impatience.

The workload at the cemetery slowly increased. He was doing a burial several times a week. They were mostly in the older sections of the park where it was difficult to use the backhoe. He buried the very old and the very young, but very rarely young adults. They were too modern to want his services. Family members often stayed behind after the burial service was over to let him know the comfort they had received from his work. Their presence had originally made Krang uncomfortable, but he had come to enjoy their company. Not their grief, but their need to reach out to someone. He wasn't supposed to talk with anyone if they didn't approach him first, but he made sure he was available for anyone who wanted to talk after the burial. Mostly they wanted to share a story about the deceased, and explain through that story why a traditional burial was the right thing to do. Krang just liked hearing the stories. The more he knew about the people he buried, the better.

One half of the grounds building was devoted to stonework. They didn't make the granite or limestone monuments, but were responsible for maintaining them once they were installed. Krang had become very adept at caring for the headstones, buffing out nicks and cuts or using acids to etch new names and dates into existing stones. He found the work very pleasant, both exacting and relaxing.

Krang made a small granite headstone and erected it under the cedar tree where he had buried Katerina. It was nothing special, made of a cast-off chunk of granite, and the lettering was crudely done, but he was proud of it nonetheless. He liked to bring his lunch or dinner out under the tree, and talk freely with Katerina about his day. He never saw her manifest the way he had seen his entourage, but he always felt like she was present and listening.

Lisle sat quietly in the room, starting at her friend. No lights were on in the apartment, and the gathering darkness was so thick she could barely make out Katie's features across the room. Katie had been talking about her mother ever since Lisle had come home from work. They hadn't even eaten yet. Lisle felt jealous, knowing she would never talk this way about her own mother. She was happy for Katie, but knew in her heart that their life together was coming to an end. Katie hadn't realized it yet, but the locket and letter resolved everything. Lisle wasn't sure how Walter had managed it, but she knew it must have been him.

Katie finally fell quiet. Lisle stood up, walked across the room and gently kissed Katie on the forehead. "I'll always love you. It's okay to do what you need to do."

"What?"

Lisle shrugged and shook her head, and sat back down where she had been before. Katie, her belly huge, struggled to her feet and knelt in front of her.

"What is it?" Katie took Lisle's hands in her own, holding them tightly.

"This means he didn't kill them," Lisle said.

"What?"

"The letter means that Walter didn't kill your mother or your sister."

Katie nodded. "I thought of that."

"So now you have no reason not to love him."

Katie sighed. "I think I always did love him, secretly, in spite of everything. And I hated myself for it."

Lisle reached out and gently stroked Katie's face. Oh my God, she thought, when did I begin to need you in my life? I never thought I would have to lose someone I loved again, so soon after Krejci. "Now you have no reason to feel guilty."

"He killed all those other people..."

"But that was before you met him. He changed."

"And that should matter?"

Lisle nodded, feeling the tears running down her face. She felt ashamed of herself. She was scared to give herself to Katie, scared of the love and passion the girl had offered her again and again, but she didn't want to lose her to Walter. What should she do?.

"According to everything that you have taught me, it should." Lisle could barely get the words out.

Katie began to cry very softly. "Why do you want me to love him? Why do you want to send me away?"

Lisle shrugged, feeling everything falling apart. "I don't want you to love him, Katie, but you do. I can't be what keeps you from him. This life, this apartment, the idea that we could somehow live here until we grow old and die together.... That's just a fantasy. A beautiful fantasy that you created, but you didn't check in with God. My life isn't meant to be. I should have died with Krejci or when I was attacked. I'm not supposed to be here, in your life. Walter will come and find you, and the baby. And I think that's a good thing. And I'll be alone, but that's what God wants."

"I'll never choose Walter if it means leaving you alone," Katie said. "He healed me in one way, but you have healed me in another. I won't let you slink back to Montrovia. After the baby comes, we leave together. We can go to America. Walter will never find me there."

"You can't..."

"I can, and I will."

"I won't be what keeps you from Walter. I can't live with that."

Katie stared into Lisle's face, until Lisle had to look away. "Look at me," Katie said, an edge of anger in her voice. Lisle looked up at her.

"You need to understand two things. Separate things, but connected. The first is that I love you. I would be your lover if you let me. I want to spend my life with you, even if I can't be your lover. And I worry that someday you will leave me, when you fall in love again, but I will take that risk.

"The second thing is that I will always love Walter, but I cannot have him in my life. A part of me wants him too much. That part of me would be with him, even if he were still at the camp, and it scares me. It's not that I can't forgive Walter for what he did. I know that I forgave him even when I thought he had killed my family. My problem is that I can't forgive myself for loving him. I can't accept that part of myself. If I gave into it, it would drive me mad. I think I'd kill myself. So we can go as soon as our baby is born."

"What about your father?"

"He isn't the man I used to love, and I can leave him behind. I've been saving money. I checked on what it would cost to sail to America, and I already have enough saved up for the both of us."

Lisle saw the look of love on Katie's. Katie really does love me, she thought. I wish I could give her back what she is willing to give me. She leaned in and kissed Katie, more passionately than she intended. A promise? She wasn't sure.

It was unseasonably hot for early April. Krang was covered in sweat. He had just finished digging a grave in one of the oldest sections of the cemetery. The grave had been very tight, squeezed into a family plot between several older monuments, forcing Krang to carry the dirt away from the site as he was digging. He was exhausted, and needed to clean up for the service later that afternoon. He was still washing when Tesare came into his room.

"Walt," Tesare said, looking uncomfortable, I accidentally opened a letter for you today that came in the mail. I apologize. I didn't look at the envelope before I opened it."

Krang felt puzzled. Who would write to him?

"From the Parks service."

Krang felt his heart jump in his chest. He nodded slowly. It had been more than six weeks since he had submitted the request to add Sarah's name to the monument. "I made a request. The monument was missing a name."

"We've never talked about your life before you came here." Tesare nodded towards the partially obliterated tattoo on Krang's forearm. "Obviously, I assumed you were a survivor. Do you want to tell me about your request?"

Krang shook his head. "There's nothing to tell. I sit in the park and study the monument every day. A name is missing. Someone I thought she had survived, until just a few months ago. I just want to make sure everything is right."

Tesare sighed, and held up a letter in his hand. "Everything isn't right."

"What?"

"They've refused your request."

Krang nodded his head slowly. "The girl at the counter who helped me fill out the application said it might be turned down. The eyewitness who should have filled out the form is dead."

"That's not it. They agreed with your claim that she died the day the camp was liberated."

"Then what's the problem?"

Tesare reached out and touched Krang on the arm. "I like you, Walt. I'll do anything I can to help......"

A feeling of dread settled around Krang's chest. "What is it?"

"They have her listed as a war criminal."

Krang felt as if someone had stabbed him in the chest. He leaned heavily against the edge of the steel sink, trying to clear his mind and understand what the other man was telling him. "What?"

307

"The letter says Sarah Jezek was executed for aiding and abetting the Montrovian government..."

Krang was on his feet, one hand grasping the front of Tesare's shirt, the other balled into a fist ready to strike. He let out a howl of rage. Tesare wrapped his arms around Krang, not to stop him, but just to hold him. To comfort him. It brought Krang up cold. He let go of the younger man, shrugged his arms to break his grip and stepped back. He walked to his cot and sat down. It took a minute for him to catch his breath and speak.

"They executed her?"

Tesare nodded. His confirmation was like a blow to Krang's chest, a fist in his heart.

It was like learning of her death all over again, except this time Krang knew it was his fault she was dead. He might as well have killed her on the first day, with Abraham and Capek, as let her help him escape. He remembered the cold of that March morning, as he ran naked through the tall grass to get away from the camp. The screams started before the guns. Sarah would have been alone, truly alone, neither Corabian any longer nor Montrovian. Such fear she must have felt, to not have the comfort of another's hand. Did she already hate him again at that moment? Did she hate herself for her weakness that freed a killer and cost her life? Or had Krang been her suicide?

And what of Katerina? To watch the one you adopted thrown to the dogs, brutalized? How hard it must have been to pick Sarah's body up after the massacre and take her away, to her own grave, to be free of the pit. Is that why they left you behind? Did I kill you too? Were you contaminated by your love for her?

Krang turned from his boss and wandered from the building. He went to be with the dead. They were truly his family.

"Mother," Krang whisper. He was lying under the cedar tree, his face pressed into the ground against Katerina's headstone. His face was wet with tears. It had taken him an hour to find his way to her grave. He had wandered through the cemetery, sitting among the dead, feeling them more present than ever. They were alive to him. He had been afraid to come find Katerina, until he realized that she had always known the truth. He had been the one in the dark.

"Forgive me. I killed one you loved as a daughter. In truth, I may have killed all your daughters. But I know that I killed Sarah. I took her kindness, her act of incredible courage, and I walked away with her life. I could have accepted her gift of grace, accepted her forgiveness, and still stayed with my comrades. I could have accepted the death that was mine."

Krang rolled onto his back and stared up at the sky. He knew what he would

308

do. He would find whoever was responsible for Sarah's death and kill them. And then he would kill himself, and this game would be over. Tesare kept an old rifle in the office for killing rodents. It would do the job.

I'll have to find out who killed her, Krang thought. I can call upon the dead and find out who was responsible for Sarah's death. Katerina won't tell me, for even in her grief and pain she doesn't want to see more death. She is so like her daughter. My dead won't tell me, for they are one with the men who killed her. They see her act of kindness as an aberration. As an abomination.

"How could I think that anyone could forgive me? All Sarah did was trade her death for mine," Krang said bitterly. "How could they pervert what she had done and make it a crime? Did they not examine how much pain I caused her? I destroyed everything that was precious to her, and yet, she forgave me. And they call that a crime?"

I know who can tell me, Krang thought. Abraham. I will go to the memorial and call him back. He will tell me the truth.

Krang sat on his favorite bench in the park, staring at the monument. It was late. The city that surrounded the park was quiet. Traffic outside the park was very light. The park itself was almost empty, except for the occasional couple or small group strolling in the park near the gates. No one came to sit by the monument. Krang felt peaceful, at one with the quiet night.

The moon struggled free of the clouds, bathing the monument in silvery light, revealing Krang's handiwork. He laughed as the letters seemed to glow in the weak light. Krang glanced down at the gallon of white paint that sat at his feet. He had found it in a storage room at the cemetery, unopened.

The letters were as tall as the marble wall itself, almost forty-eight inches high. Krang had worked carefully, so that none of the paint had run. The name Sarah Jezek was painted across all six panels devoted to the Mountain City camp.

The moonlight illuminated Sarah's name. Krang knew the park staff would have a work crew out here before the end of the day tomorrow to scrub it off, but that was all right. The paint had only been a test. He needed to make sure that stencils worked. The real name would be permanent.

Krang rose from the bench with a sigh. He had let go his desire to avenge Sarah. Not easily, but he had let it go. He had sat in this place for days, willing Abraham to appear, and thinking of Sarah. His thoughts always returned to her act. Why had she forgiven him? He hadn't deserved forgiveness. Maybe it didn't matter so much if the person really deserved forgiveness. He knew in his heart that if she could forgive him what he had done to her family, then he must let go what had been done to her. She would not want him to kill another in her name. Krang felt empty. He longed to purify the pain he felt, to wash it away, to reduce

309

it to the simple joy of hatred. But Sarah wouldn't let him do that.

No, he corrected himself. I won't let myself do that. I won't trade the truth of my pain for the narcotic of blind rage. I've lived my life that way, and now it has to stop.

Krang felt raw as he made his way out of the park.

Chapter Twenty-Three

Tesare dropped the newspaper on his desk and glared at Krang. He pointed to the story on the front of the second section. "Walt, I won't report you for this, but I know that you did it. I understand that you were angry, but vandalism? That's not what I expected of you. There's got to be a better way for you to fight this than defacing a national monument."

Krang shrugged. "The paint wasn't permanent."

"I don't care," Tesare said. "You've been better for this cemetery than I ever thought you could be. I thought I was doing you a favor when I hired you, but in truth, you were doing the favor for us. And you won't even let me really pay you. I've got to sign you up as a public employee to do more than give you petty cash and you refuse. I know your needs are simple. But hear me when I say this: I will turn you in if this happens again."

Krang nodded, his eyes downcast. He looked up at Tesare. "I won't paint her name on the monument again. I was just feeling crazy."

"Let me help, Walt. I trust your judgment. If you think they were wrong to execute her, I believe you. Let's fight this. I'd like to help you clear her name."

"There's really nothing to do," Krang said. "It was just such a shock." He felt bad that Tesare was so concerned. His eyes fell on the article in the paper and he smiled. Sarah's name had been scrubbed from the marble before lunchtime, but not before the newspapers had all sent reporters. One of the papers had even run a picture under the caption "Who is Sarah Jezek?" People were asking questions. Krang stood to leave. There would be no paint next time.

Krang went back to the park that afternoon. He sat on his regular bench, but instead of studying the monument, he studied the people who came to see it. If nothing else, the articles in the papers had made people curious enough about the monument that they came out in the hundreds to take a look at it.

Two policemen stood on duty, one on each side of the pond. They stood at attention, their backs to the memorial, standing as stiffly as if they were created from the same marble as the rest of the monument.

Krang looked at the police and laughed. Did they imagine he would make a

311

crazed attack on the monument in broad daylight?

Krang sat on the bench in front of the monument and watched the sun set behind the city. A knapsack sat at his feet. It had been ten days since he had painted Sarah's name on the monument and he was ready to do it again. A police officer was walking a random circuit through the park, one that brought him past the monument every twenty minutes or so. He nodded at Krang as he wandered past, then came back a few minutes later.

"I see you here every day," the officer said.

Krang nodded.

"I've come to love the beauty of this place and I didn't lose anyone in the camps or the war," the cop said. "It must be even more meaningful to someone like you."

Krang knew the cop thought he was a survivor. He looked the part, still thin, with his long beard and wild hair and the ever present partial tattoo.

"I lost several people I cared about," Krang said. "This is a place to come and remember them." Even Katie was lost to him. It was an apt term.

"If you ever see anything suspicious, let us know," the officer said. "Personally, I think it was a boy, putting his girlfriend's name on the wall. You know, to impress her."

Krang smiled. "Someone with a crush," he said, "that makes sense."

"You have a good night," the officer said. He glanced at his watch. "I'm about done for the evening. I'll see you tomorrow night." He made one more circuit of the park before giving Krang a wave from the other side of the pond and leaving.

Krang waited patiently as darkness enveloped the park. The streetlights for the park were the new electric lights rather than the gas lights that were found throughout the city. They came on all at once, the ballasts humming softly as they blinked into life. The sidewalk that surrounded the park was brightly lit, but only a few lights burned within the park and none very close to the monument. Krang was left enfolded in darkness, but anyone who approached the monument would be brightly lit from behind. The park slowly emptied, but he waited another hour for the sidewalks around the park to quiet.

Krang unfolded the cardboard stencils that he had used when he painted Sarah's name on the monument, and attached each one to the marble face of the monument with pieces of putty. He reached into his backpack and brought out a large glass jar and a metal spatula. The jar held a blend of gray putty mixed with acid that was used in the cemetery to etch additional names onto headstones already marking a grave. It did not etch the marble with the speed or power of the full strength acid, but it did the job if you let it sit long enough. Lomy was an expert in using the acid-putty mix, and Krang had learned enough from him to do the job he wanted to do tonight.

Krang quickly applied the acid-putty to the marble wall that showed through the stencils, right across the names that had already been etched into the stone. Then he sat back on his bench and waited, the silence of the night broken by the soft sibilance of the acid working on the marble, the occasional cry of an owl, and the faint sounds of a couple's passion rising from the darkness of the park.

Krang thought about the woman he was honoring. Sarah had sacrificed her life to free him. She had latched onto an ideal that was so powerful that it simply overwhelmed reason. He could imagine her standing before the council of old men who had been running the camp those last few days and trying to explain to them what she had done. For all their learning, all their years of living, they would not have understood that the only way for Sarah to be free of Krang was to forgive him. Complete and full forgiveness. In a way, Krang couldn't blame the old men for their response. Who could? What Sarah had done was foreign to reality. Everyone talked about forgiveness, but who ever practiced it?

Krang felt like he should be on his knees praying, humbling himself before a God that was greater than he. A God somewhere between the angry God of his mother and Katie's God of love. He was still too stubborn to submit, though, still too angry at himself and God for the atrocities he had committed to humble himself in such a fashion. Give me courage, you bastard, he thought, to see this through to the end. Give me the words to speak only truth.

He walked around the pond while the acid ate at the marble. A thin wind rustled the budding leaves in the trees. Bats swooped and whirled in the faint light of the streetlamps, chasing down the moths drawn to the light. Krang felt more alive than he had ever felt, even in the camp. He knew it meant his time here was coming to an end, but he wasn't afraid.

The sun was rising behind the skyscrapers to the east of the park before Krang finished removing the stencils and could admire his handiwork. Sarah's name was superimposed over the listing for the Mountain City camp, etched an eighth of an inch deep into the face of the marble.

"Sarah," Krang said softly, staring at her name, "I will tell your story until the entire world understands the sacrifice that you made. It is the only thing I can do to repay you for your gift."

He picked up his knapsack and walked away. The couple he had heard making love was still in the park. They had spent the night on an old blanket under a maple tree with widespread branches. The woman had just finished pulling on her long skirt, but was naked from the waist up. She stopped when she saw Krang and straightened up, unfazed by her nudity. The young man, embarrassed, stepped behind her. Krang nodded at her, not staring, but making sure she saw his features and could describe him later. She nodded back, and then bent down to pull on her shoes, leaving her breasts free. Krang left them, amused with her boldness.

Janos Lev, the city attorney, turned away from the old man in shackles, and walked back to his office, followed by his assistant attorney. A secretary smiled at him as he walked by her desk. Lev smiled back. He knew he cut quite a figure in his new suit, which probably cost twice the secretary's annual salary. A year ago he would have bedded her, but not now, with the election just six months away.

Once in his office he turned on his assistant attorney. "Why in God's name do I want to be involved in a case against some vagrant? Don't waste my time."

Maxwell Lev was his cousin, at forty-eight, younger by two years. "Janos," he said, his voice thin, "you're not thinking. The monument hit a nerve. People are angry."

"It's an act of vandalism! How is prosecuting a vandal going to make me look like I should be the next Prime Minister? We agreed I'd run on my war record."

"Which would be fine, except your opponent is also a hero, and maybe more of one than you. This is more than a simple act of vandalism. He caused more than ten thousand in damages. It's a major crime."

"How is sending an old man to prison, a survivor no less, going to help me win this fucking election?" This election which shouldn't have been a contest, he wanted to add, if we had done what I suggested and discredited that asshole Andross before he declared. Andross, known as the fucking Lion of Corabia for surviving a three month siege that ultimately turned the course of the war. It wouldn't have been a three day siege if he had trusted the fucking Intel and moved his troops into a blocking position to the north, but who the fuck understood that? Ten thousand unnecessary dead and they were calling him a fucking war hero? Anything that came out now would seem like politics.

"That's the best part," Max said. "You're not going to prosecute him for a major crime."

"Then why the fuck did you bring him over here?"

"Look," Max said, grinning, "you need something that lets you look strong, but not like you're such a big prick. Something to humanize you. You crushed Montrovia. Everyone knows you're strong. So you have this case, which qualifies as a major crime, with ten years on the line, but you refuse to prosecute him. Instead, when we get to court, you ask for a competency hearing. We acknowledge the man's a survivor, he's mentally unbalanced, we can't have him going around destroying public property, but we just want to get him help. You look human for a change."

Lev considered the tactic. It could be a way to soften his image.

314

"What happens to him? He goes free?"

Max shook his head. "No fucking way. The man's a nutcase. Says he'll keep doing it over and over until they add a name to the monument. He's declared incompetent and we lock him up in a dark hole until he dies."

"And we're sure the public will support this?'

"Absolutely," Max said. "That's the beauty of this case. The woman he's so upset about is a monster. She helped one of the worst criminals of the war escape when her camp fell. No one is going to feel any sympathy for him once the story comes out, and you will look like a real moderate for a change."

Janos Lev nodded. He thought about this Walter Werkamp. Werkamp had looked at him across the room and Lev had recognized his power in spite of how he looked. He wasn't harmless, that much was clear. Was it right to build his campaign on the back of some miserable man who was fighting his own lost cause? Lev dismissed that concern immediately. It was no different than the war, sending men to die for a greater good. His country needed him and this was a clear path to that greater good. Something about Werkamp had seemed so familiar, though. Lev had a sudden image of a soldier, a non-commissioned office, in a battle outside of Corabia in the early days of the war. He needed a man for a suicide mission and this man had stepped forward. He had this look in his eyes. Not peace, but resignation. That's what Werkamp had looked like: resigned to a cause. A volunteer if you will.

Lev smiled. He wondered if he could take the secretary for a drink. "Okay," he said. "Let's do it."

Krang sat at the table in the interview room, hands and feet shackled, and waited for the door to open. The room was bigger than his cell. He had been confined in a tiny room, seven feet by nine feet, with a pit toilet in one corner and a cot against one wall. He had been in jail for two weeks and this was his first opportunity to learn about the charges against him. He was nervous, for he didn't know if they had figured out who he really was.

Tesare had come to see him once since his arrest. He had stood uncomfortably outside the cell and lectured Krang.

"I told you I'd have to turn you in," he had said, sounding hurt.

Krang smiled at him. "I know. We both did what we had to do. We both did the right thing. You've given me a lot..."

"Then why throw it away?"

"Because Sarah gave me more. She gave me my soul back."

It had been clear that Tesare hadn't understood. He let Krang know that he wouldn't be back, and that no matter the outcome, Krang no longer had a job at the cemetery. Krang had thought he saw tears glistening in Tesare's eyes as the younger man left.

Lomy had come once, too. He had smuggled in a dozen cigarettes and a box of matches and left without saying a word. His visit had shocked Krang more than Tesare's. The cigarette's had been smoked, one a day, until they were gone.

The door to the interview room opened and two police officers and a man dressed in a suit swept into the room. The man sat at the table opposite Krang.

"Janos Lev," he said, by way of introduction. "I am the city prosecutor, and I will be handling your case personally." He reminded Krang of Commandant Bitmeyer: full of himself, but still dangerous. A man who had grown too comfortable with the power he held.

"Your little act of vandalism has created quite a stir in our city. Do you have anything to say for yourself?"

Here we go thought Krang, studying the man before him. He wished he didn't have to make his confession to such a pompous ass, but you played with the hand you were dealt.

"I..." he began, and then stopped, at a loss for words. As many times as he had told the story in his head, he still didn't know how to begin it. Do you start with being at the camp and all that happened there, or with Sarah's story in particular? He didn't want the horror of the camp to drown out the wonder of her actions.

"Never mind," Lev said with a wave of his hand. "You can tell us all in court tomorrow."

Krang smiled. That would be better.

"We know who you are," Lev said. "I've had quite a bit of success prosecuting men like you, who somehow managed to get into our country without a record. If you went through the relocation center at all, you lied about who you are, but I don't think you did that. I think you're one of the thousands who walked across the border, probably at the height of the war, believing we owed you sanctuary, and hid here instead of doing your part."

Krang shook his head at the accusation. If only his crime was so insignificant.

"It doesn't matter," Lev said. "You are not going on trial for your act of vandalism, even though it will cost thousands of dollars to replace the panels that you defaced. Tomorrow is a competency hearing. My team thinks you are a danger to yourself and others. They want to see you locked up in an asylum where you can't hurt anyone."

"Will I get to tell my story?"

"You'll get your chance to deny everything, but it won't matter. We can prove you destroyed the monument, and with malice."

"I did it," Krang said. "I knew exactly what I was doing. I added Sarah's name to the monument. And I'd do it again if I got the chance. I want to tell why."

"Good. That will make this interesting." Lev stood and left the room.

Katie sat on the sofa in her apartment waiting for the mild contraction to finish. She had been having contractions for almost twelve hours. Auntie Zophie had been in several times to check on her. She would run her hands along Katie's buldging belly, feeling the placement of the baby and how it reacted to the contractions, and then smile and nod and tell Katie to keep walking while she could. Auntie Zophie had said she wasn't in full labor, yet. That Katie might have a day or more of these mild contractions before things really got started. She told Lisle to be sure to come get her if Katie's water broke.

Katie had been feeling more and more nervous as the day went on. What was she going to do with a baby? She smiled to herself, knowing it was much too late to ask that question. She wondered where Walter was, and hoped that somehow he knew his child was about to be born.

The knock at the door was loud and abrupt. Katie and Lisle both startled at the noise. Lisle got up to see who it was. When she returned, Katie's father followed her. He was dressed in a long black overcoat and carried a valise. He smiled at Katie.

Seeing her father made Katie feel sad, and she hoped he wasn't planning on staying with her for the birth. She didn't feel like she had the energy to deal with him for more than a few minutes. She knew he was trying to be loving and kind to her. He even seemed to like Lisle. But so much remained unsaid between them. It was like there was a dead space around him, a wall that kept the world away. They had never spoken of the day she ran away, never spoken of their time apart, never spoken about her mother or sister. Her father was as awkward around her as he was rigid around everyone else. She could tell he wanted to love her, but he seemed unable to allow himself to do so. She sighed. She imagined he felt the same way about her. So many secrets kept them apart.

"How much longer?" he asked hopefully.

Katie shrugged.

"The midwife says it could be another day," Lisle said. "The contractions aren't doing much other than keeping Katie from resting."

Woerful scowled. "I had hoped to be here for the birth of my grandchild," he said, "but I've been called away."

Katie could see a smile spread across Lisle's face at the news. Lisle was standing behind her father, who didn't see a thing. A contraction kept Katie from laughing out loud.

"What calls you away?" Katie asked. She pointed to a chair for him to sit.

Her father shook his head. "I've a train to catch in half an hour."

"Where are you going?"

317

"To Corabia city. I'm out of sorts about it, really, and it's more than just being called away from you. I have to testify at a trial about something that happened in the camp."

Katie felt for her father. His face looked older when he spoke of the camp. She wished he could be more open with her, rather than trying to keep everything hidden away.

"It must be hard to remember the camp," Katie said.

Woerful nodded. "It is. The trial is a strange thing. Some lunatic has defaced the monument that was built to remember those we lost. You may have seen it when you were there?"

"It was still under construction," Lisle said, "not far from the library where I worked."

"Lisle took me to see it once. It looked like it was going to be beautiful, but I found it too sad to stay." Katie frowned. "What has the monument got to do with you?"

Woerful reached out and touched her hand. It was an unusual gesture for him. "The part that was vandalized was the section for Mountain City camp, and since I was there, and in a position of power among the prisoners, I've been called to appear. To answer questions about what happened at the end, as the camp was liberated." He paused, looking at the floor, lost in thought.

"I've been thinking about your mother, almost every day since this came up. I'm sorry that she never knew that you survived. It would have made her time easier."

Katie could feel the locket she wore around her neck laying against her skin. She had never told her father about the letter. It was part of that dead space between them. She said nothing.

"I've never told you anything that happened in the camp. It was a terrible time, and the stress of the camp slowly tore us apart. As much as having someone to love was probably the best way to survive that place, we began to realize that we couldn't love each other anymore. Your loss and Bela's death were just too much."

Woerful paced back and forth uncomfortably in the small room. "I hoped, as the camp was liberated, that we might have a chance to start over, but then something happened that made any reconciliation impossible."

Katie groaned softly as another contraction wracked her body. "What does this have to do with the monument in Corabia city?"

"A man carved a name into the monument, a name he felt had been left off. It damaged the monument and caused quite a stir. The man is on trial."

"So why do you need to testify?"

"There are some here in Corabia, with no knowledge of what really happened

318

in the camps that seem to feel that the lunatic is right. That simply because she was in the camp, her name should be on the monument. They don't understand the woman was a collaborator and as bad as the Montrovians."

"I still don't understand what this has to do with you."

"As the highest officer of God who was there, I have been asked to tell the truth about Sarah, so that no one ever forgets."

Katie felt her heart pounding. She couldn't have heard him correctly. It just couldn't be. "Sarah? The woman's name is Sarah?"

Her father nodded. "Sarah Jezek. Did you know her? She was about ten years older than you. She tore our family apart."

"What?"

"Your mother never forgave me, after the tribunal. She hated me, but I only did what was necessary. Your mother couldn't see the truth."

"What tribunal?"

"Sarah was accused of the most heinous of crimes. She came before our tribunal..."

"What did you do?" Katie's voice had an edge of panic to it. A part of her wanted to send him away now, before he said another word. Before he took away what was left of her family, but she couldn't. It was like that moment just before an accident, when time slows down, but there is nothing you can do to stop what is going to happen. Like the moment when Krang told her who he really was.

"After everyone testified, the council of elders found her guilty. I was the chief elder, and I ordered Sarah's execution. She had betrayed us. She freed *the guard*. I had no choice."

Katie doubled over in pain, letting another contraction dull her mind. Walter had been sure that Sarah was alive. It was Walter's search for Sarah that had changed him, and allowed him to find himself and now she was dead. My father killed her, Katie thought. My father had killed the woman who had healed Walter. The woman who had the courage to live the faith, not just recite it in church on Sunday mornings. My father had done that. The spasm passed.

"You killed people in the camp?" Katie asked

"No, I never killed anyone myself."

Katie corrected herself. "You ordered them to be killed."

He nodded. "It's very complicated. When our camp was about to be liberated, the Commandant, in an effort to win his freedom, turned the camp over to us. Commandant Bitmeyer was willing to give up the guards who worked there, the ones who tormented us, in exchange for his own freedom. He and I had been working on a plan for days, but I had no intention of ever allowing him to escape. Justice had to be served. He surrendered and within minutes was hanging from the flag pole in the center of the camp. The council of elders promised everyone that the guards would pay, but that we wouldn't allow individual acts of retribution. Judgment must be done without passion, in order to be just. So we agreed to execute the guards."

Katie's mind was screaming at her. She was struggling to comprehend what her father was saying. This man who had held her on his lap and read to her had ordered men executed. In some strange way, that bothered her more than what Walter had done.

"How many?"

"Does it matter?" He studied her face. "Perhaps thirty or forty guards, and their families. And some local farmers that made a living off our misery. Maybe one hundred total. It was done as quickly as possible, so that they wouldn't suffer. We put them together in a field and shot them with machine guns. God let us be merciful."

One hundred people! You ordered one hundred people killed! Katie shook her head, trying to gather her thoughts "But Sarah was a Corabian. You executed Corabians, too?"

"Only the collaborators. And I've struggled with that since the day it happened. I've come to think that I made a terrible mistake, putting Corabians, Sarah in particular, on that parade ground with the rest of them. I saw her at the end. She was holding hands with an old couple, farmers. She was staring up at the rising sun, with a smile on her face. She never understood that the wrath of God was being visited on her. She never felt alone, never seemed to feel judged. We should have executed her separately. One of the elders had suggested stoning her, and I was against it. I thought it too barbaric. Now I wish we had. She should never have died feeling cared about by anyone. She should have felt abandoned, and spent her last moments contemplating the wickedness of her actions." His words came out in such a rush that he was left breathless.

"You..." Katie felt crushed by his words. How could he have done this?

"You don't understand. You weren't in my place. I had to bring some order to what had happened to us. And I gave everyone the chance to explain themselves. The story that Sarah Jezek told was unimaginable. She defiled the memory of her husband and son and all of the people we lost. She put herself in God's place. We couldn't allow that."

"And now? This trial?"

"I go to represent the camp. Many in this country have no idea of the true horror of our experience. They believe Sarah should be on the monument, simply because she was at the camp. We can never forget what happened there. And we cannot forget that she freed the worst of our tormentors..."

"Papa, what about forgiveness? You taught me to forgive."

Her father nodded and picked up his valise. "I was wrong. Our people have

320

never faced such a terrible challenge before. We lived in a fantasy, Katie, to think that God imbued the world only with good. We ignored half of the Bible, to be able to ignore the Truth. We preached the Gospels of the New Testament, but ignored the warnings of the Old Testament. Like all Christians, our story is also told there. God judges and punishes us, without mercy. You cannot forgive those who hurt you."

"And what about what Jesus teaches us?"

"Jesus is dead. He was humiliated on the cross. I can't risk letting my people give their lives for an idea. There were no moments of Glory in that camp, Katie. No moments when I saw someone going to heaven. It's a hard world..."

"But our Faith is founded on principles, Papa. Not as you say it now, but as you taught it to me as a child. Your ideas don't fit with our Faith. You ignore the teachings of Jesus."

Her father shook his head. "I am too caught up in my emotions to explain this well. I don't want to leave behind the teachings of Jesus, but I need to temper them with the divine words that came before him. We teach that Jesus is a divine man, as we all are. And we all make mistakes, even Jesus. You will understand when you are older."

"Papa, you're wrong. The council of elders had no right to kill anyone."

Her father stared at her. "I don't know what you did to survive the war. I don't know who you collaborated with, but you have no idea what a struggle it was, for those of us who were righteous."

Lisle caught her breathe across the room. Katie loved her for the look of anger that came over her face, but she held up her hand to stop Lisle from saying anything.

Katie took a deep breath. "You've always been afraid to ask, haven't you, Papa? Afraid that whatever I did will somehow embarrass you. That if the world knew, you would be humiliated on my account. Well, you don't need to worry Papa. I did nothing of which I am embarrassed. I lived as righteously as possible for a fourteen year old girl during a war." She paused, letting her words sink in. Her father stared at her.

"I sold myself, Papa. I degraded myself to anyone who would take me for a place to sleep or a bite to eat. I lived on my knees in the gutter, in bathrooms, in train stations. Wherever anyone would have me. The very first time, not more than a couple of hours after you climbed on that bus to go to the camp was with one of your friends, Papa. I've lost his name, now, but I'm sure you remember him. The policeman? Who stopped in your church every day while he walked his beat, just to chat theology? Who you said had the soul of a righteous man, even if he was confused about the bible? Do you remember him?"

Her father nodded, his face drained of color.

"And I blamed you every time I was sucking or fucking someone. I blamed you for not protecting me. I hated myself for being braver than you were. I hated you for your weakness."

Her father stood, a look of pain and disgust on his face. "I have to be going. You think that you can drive me away with your words, but you can't. I will soon have a grandchild that must be raised to be a child of God. You cannot think I would abandon this baby?"

"You abandoned me, Papa." Katie watched as her father turned away from her, towards the door.

"Who is on trial for this act of desecration?" Katie could barely form the words.

Her father stopped at the door and looked at her. His eyes were dead. "That's one of the strangest parts," he said. "It's not anyone I remember from the camp. I don't know how he even learned of Sarah Jezek."

"Maybe it's her family?"

"Her family is dead. The name they gave me was Walter somebody or other."

"Walter?" Katie thought her heart would burst from her chest.

"Yes, that was the name. Walter Werkamp. I don't remember him. Do you remember a Werkamp family from back home?"

"I don't think so," Katie said, praying her face wouldn't give her away. "I met a Walter, once, but his last name wasn't Werkamp." Her father nodded absently, and then was gone.

Katie got up from her seat and went into the bedroom, Lisle trailing behind her. She pulled a valise from the closet. "We have to leave," she said, a look of desperation on her face.

Lisle took Katie by the hand and led her back to the bed. "You have to have a baby. Then we can talk about leaving."

"I won't let him around my baby. I told you I've been saving money, Lisle. It's in the second drawer of my dresser. In the morning, I want you to book passage to America. Somewhere my father can never find us."

"What about Walter? It is your Walter, isn't it?"

Katie nodded, tears beginning to trickle down her face. "He's killing himself."

"What?"

"He always felt he needed to make amends for the camp. That's why he carved Sarah's name in the monument. Now he can take responsibility for what he did. He'll never survive this trial. Once he tells his story, his life is over."

"Why didn't your father tell us who it was?"

"Father doesn't know that Walter is *the guard*. Apparently he hasn't told anyone the truth yet. Walter would wait until the attention of the entire world was on him. A trial would be the perfect place. He's been planning something like this for as long as I have known him. He always told me he wouldn't survive. He always worried that if I was with him when the truth came out, then I would be punished with him. Even when he thought he was hunting Sarah down to hurt her, he was trying to figure out how to punish himself for what he had done. He believed that he should have been killed with the other guards. He could never understand why that hadn't happened." She stopped, catching her breath. "I wish I could see him one more time. Just to let him know that I don't hate him."

"Maybe we could go after the baby comes. Maybe you could stop in and see him before it's all over. To say goodbye."

Katie smiled at the idea. "Maybe we could," she whispered. To show him his child before he dies. She nodded. That could be the right thing to do. She smiled as another contraction began low in her abdomen.

Chapter Twenty-Four

Krang stood silently while the guards shackled his arms and legs. It was morning, but the sky was still dark outside the small window of his cell. They had brought him cold porridge to eat, telling him it was the best they could do this early in the morning, since the cooks weren't in yet. They wanted to move him to the courthouse as early as possible.

Krang shuffled after the guards. The jail uniform, rough blue pants and shirt, were too small. He had not been allowed to shower, shave nor cut his long, tangled hair. Janos Lev was doing everything in his power to make Krang look like a madman. Krang knew that Lev was trying to humiliate him. To break his spirit. Unfortunately, Lev didn't understand that Krang knew the psychology of degradation better than anyone. None of this hurt him. It just reminded him of what he had done and strengthened his resolve to tell the truth. Krang smiled. As strange as it sounded, he was looking forward to having time to tell Sarah's story, and his own. He was looking forward to being free of what he had done.

He shuffled from his cell down a long hallway to the loading dock at the rear of the building. Krang guessed it was maybe five in the morning. The sky was beginning to lighten to the east. A small crowd, perhaps thirty or forty people, stood outside the jail between Krang and the small car the guards indicated he would travel in. The crowd began screaming when they saw him. Krang smiled. Lev had tipped them off, if he hadn't actually paid them to be there. A couple of men with cameras were taking photos. The guards motioned him forward. The crowd was screaming and spitting as he walked past, bumping him. Someone threw a punch, but one of the guards blocked it with his club.

Krang looked for anyone from the camp, but didn't see anyone he recognized. He didn't think that any of these men had been in any camp. These zealots didn't have the haunted gauntness that you still saw with survivors. Their anger was real, however. Krang slipped into the back of the car. The crowd swarmed around it, rocking it and pounding on the windows. A rock struck the windshield, cracking it. The driver began blowing the horn, rolling the car slowly forward, parting the crowd. In a few seconds they were free. You think you hate me now, Krang thought as he was driven away. Wait until after I tell my story.

324

Katie lay back on the pillow, exhausted. Her brow was covered in sweat, and she began to shake from chills brought about by her exhaustion. Her water had broken about ten last evening, and the contractions had suddenly become very strong. She had been in heavy labor all night, and the baby wasn't coming. Lisle wiped her face with the warm wash rag and looked helplessly at the midwife.

The old woman shrugged her shoulders. "We must give her another hour or so, and if we don't have the baby, we will call for the surgeon. She is young, and first babies can be hard. She doesn't have the hips for birthing yet. After this one, her babies will come very quickly."

Lisle nodded. "What can I do?"

"More water for Katie," Auntie Zophie said. "And tea, for you and I."

Lisle headed to the kitchen to make tea. She was so grateful for Auntie Zophie, who was as implacable as a rock. Nothing seemed to ruffle her. Every time Lisle felt scared, Auntie Zophie would tell her that this was normal, and that Katie was doing great. She was the only thing forestalling the feeling of impending doom that seemed to be swirling around Lisle tighter and tighter.

The courthouse was a majestic stone building, rising from a low plateau about a mile east of the ocean, with a panoramic view of the city and port. It had been built nearly two centuries ago, long before society ever knew it might want to have several trials ongoing at once, in a time when petitioners still pled their case before royal judges.

The marble glowed pink in the early morning sun. There were no raucous crowds here. The car stopped on the street, dropping Krang and one of the guards. The morning air was chilled, but the gentle breeze blowing off the ocean felt good to Krang. He felt peaceful as he walked up the steps to the courthouse. Krang could feel the promise of justice about to be delivered.

The guard debated whether to put him in one of the small holding rooms for prisoners down in the basement, but decided they could wait in the courtroom. Krang was glad. He didn't want to be forced out of the light. His days were numbered now, and rightfully so, but he wanted to enjoy the beauty of them, all the same.

Krang shuffled into the courtroom. The guard walked him to a table near the judge's bench at the front of the court room. This allowed him to survey the court room. It was a big room, with an observation deck that ran along three sides of the second floor. It could hold two hundred people, Krang guessed. Next to the jury box was another small platform, labeled with a small sign that said it was for members of the press only. Krang smiled. He hoped that box would be fullest of them all.

While he waited, a young man dressed in a suit came into the courtroom and set up three wooden easels in front of the jury box. He had three large pictures he set up on the easels. One was a diagram of the camp, drawn from above, that showed the location of the barracks, offices, fence, guard posts and the pit. The second was a photo of the camp after liberation, only the concrete pads from the former barracks visible. The third was a photo of Commandant Bitmeyer. Krang was shocked to see the photo. It was from before the war. Bitmeyer was sitting in a chair in a library, pipe in hand, his round face and receding hairline making him look like a gentle grandfather. Once the photos were up, the young man covered them with sheets and left the room. He never looked at Krang.

"I can't help. I must get the surgeon. It is the only way to save the baby." Auntie Zophie shook her head nervously as she spoke.

Katie nodded. "Please go," she said, her voice so soft Lisle saw her lips move but didn't hear the words.

The midwife took Katie's hand in hers. "When he comes, he will take the baby. I don't know if you will survive. You are already so weak, and the surgery will cost you blood. But if you want this baby to live, it is what we must do."

Katie nodded.

"The surgeon has another choice. You would live, but the baby will die."

Katie shook her head. "My baby must live."

"No!" Lisle said, louder than she wanted. Katie looked up at her, her face pale.

"You can't do this," Lisle said to the midwife. "You have to save her."

The old woman looked at Lisle, sadness on her face. "We will do everything we can, my darling, but there is no guarantee. Only God can give us guarantees, and he chooses not to. I will be back within the hour."

Katie grabbed Lisle's hand, and held it tightly in her own. Lisle could see how tired Katie was. Lisle hoped that Katie couldn't see the terror she felt. She tried to convince herself that everything would be all right. But how could God do this? Lisle took a deep breath, trying to quell her own fears.

"Lisle, you must have faith," Katie said, giving her a weak smile. "God loves me and all is as it should be. I am not planning on dying, but if I do, this new life will be worth it."

Lisle shook her head. "No," she said softly, the tears falling.

Katie squeezed harder on her friend's hand. "I need you, Lisle. You must promise me, if I die, to take this baby and flee. My father will expect to raise this child, and that can never happen. Do you understand me?"

Lisle nodded numbly. How would she survive, alone and with a baby? She couldn't even take care of herself.

326

Every seat in the observation area behind the prosecutor's table was taken. The observation deck that ran along both sides and the rear of the second floor was also packed with people. The crowd was raucous, more like what Krang would expect to find at a rugby tournament than in a courtroom. To Krang's left, the judge's bench and the jury box were empty. There would be no jury, since this was not a real trial. The judge would listen to all the facts revealed during the inquiry and then determine if Krang were to be committed to a mental institute.

Janos Lev had stopped by Krang's seat when he arrived, to assure Krang that by the time he was through presenting the case, Krang would be committed for life. Of course, thought Krang, after I tell my story they'll want to have a real trial. If I even make it out of here alive. He smiled and brushed his long, dirty hair from his eyes.

Katie's daughter was born mid-morning. The surgeon decided against the caesarian section, instead making an incision in her perineum to allow the baby to pass. He repaired the damage while Katie held the infant to her breast and left, confident that all was well. Katie was exhausted, but content. When the infant fell asleep she handed her to Lisle to hold.

"Her name is Sarah," Katie whispered. "Her middle name is Katerina, for my mother." She looked up at her friend. "I thought about Lisle for her middle name, but I will find another way to honor you for your friendship."

Lisle blushed. "Sarah Katerina is the perfect name," she said. She lay the sleeping infant in the bassinet in the corner of the room.

"I need paper," Katie said. "I need to send a message to Walter. I need to tell him his daughter was born."

"Why don't you tell him yourself?" Lisle asked. "Tell him in person. In a few days you'll be strong enough to travel to the city and show him his daughter."

Katie shook his head. "I can't go see him," she said. "I can't watch him throw his life away, even if it's the right thing for him to do."

"Maybe he won't," Lisle said. "Maybe if he sees you and Sarah, he will realize what he has to live for."

"It would be a lie," Katie whispered. "I know I love him, but I can't go back to him. He was *the guard...*"

"But he changed..."

Katie smiled weakly. "That's what the selfish part of me says. He did change. But what about the Corabians who were in that camp? I owe them something too. I don't have the courage that Sarah had, to just forgive him. I wish I did. I have prayed for hours, every day, for God to open my heart, to let me know that loving him is okay. God knows, Walter needs to be loved. He is as scarred on the inside

327

as you are on the outside. Which means he's also as beautiful as you are. He's earned the right to be loved."

Katie started to cry. "But I'm too afraid to do it. My father already disapproves of me. What would he think if he knew the truth? He would hate me. As much as I don't want him around my baby, he is still my father. I don't want him to hate me again."

Lisle took Katie's hand in hers. "Like my family and village hate me," she said. "Maybe that is why we found each other."

Katie nodded. "I'm not as strong as you, either. I would have thrown myself from that train at the first bridge..."

Lisle laughed, and wrapped her arms around Katie. "That's the biggest lie I've heard all year. You are driven to live, girl. Write your letter. I'll take it. You're just feeling down because you're exhausted."

Katie shook her head. "I feel like I've failed him, Lisle. Walter needs me and I can't give myself. I've never seen another person change the way he has; I'm not sure it's really possible for most of us. But as strong as Walter is, he is just a lost child. He needs someone to hold his heart in theirs and help him continue to Become. And it should be me, but I can't do it..."

"Hush now," Lisle whispered. "You may feel differently tomorrow."

Katie looked up at her friend and smiled weakly. "He needs someone like you."

Lisle laughed nervously. "So now you want me to abandon you for your old boyfriend? Even I'm not that desperate."

Lisle brought the pen and paper, and Katie worked silently for almost a half hour. Then she sealed the envelope and gave it to her friend. "Tomorrow?" she asked quietly. Lisle nodded, pulled the covers up and watched her friend drift into sleep.

"All rise," the bailiff intoned. It was almost noon. Krang had been sitting in the docket, listening to the jeers of the crowd, for hours. The hearing had been scheduled for ten, but had not started. No one explained anything to him about the delay.

The judge swept into the courtroom, his black robes flowing behind him. He was young, in his mid-to-late thirties, and had a look of anger on his face. He glanced at the docket and saw Krang, shackled and in his prison uniform and grimaced.

"The honorable...."

The judge rapped sharply on the podium with his gavel, cutting the bailiff off mid-sentence.

"Please be seated," the bailiff said with a sigh and shake of his head. He appeared to be at least twenty years older than the judge.

"Mr. Prosecutor," the judge said.

Janos Lev stood from behind his table. "Your honor?" he said, contempt in his voice. "It was nice of you to join us."

"Approach the bench."

Lev walked slowly to the front of the courtroom. He had a tight grin on his face.

"Why are we here?" the judge asked.

"I thought you'd wait at least until after my opening arguments before you did this..."

"Why are we here?" the judge asked again.

"I would have expected you to be aware of the facts in the case..."

"Don't push me," the judge said. "The man has already admitted he vandalized the memorial. Convict him. Other than your upcoming bid for Prime Minister, why are we here?"

The crowd in the courtroom tittered anxiously at the accusation.

Lev glared at the younger man. "If you have a problem with the prosecution in this case, you should recuse yourself from the case," he said bitterly.

The judge laughed. "You'd like nothing better," he said. "I won't forget what's really going on here."

"Your own election doesn't escape me, your Honor," Lev said with a sneer.

"I'm unopposed for re-election," the judge said with a smile. "I've nothing to prove. Step away from the bench."

Lev returned to his table.

"Why does Mr. Werkamp not have an attorney present?" the judge's voice carried throughout the courtroom. Lev looked surprised.

"Your honor, this is not a trial, as you know. It is a simple competency hearing..."

"So we don't allow counsel at such an important hearing?"

"The state doesn't provide counsel for free at competency hearings, your honor. And he can't afford one. He's a vagrant who lives at the cemetery."

"And why is he dressed so poorly, and unwashed?"

"There is no jury here to be swayed by his appearance. He wears his hair long. I don't see a problem."

"And the shackles?"

"He's dangerous."

"How so?"

"He used acid to desecrate a state monument. He obviously hates the Homeland, and we can't have him flinging acid about in the courtroom."

"Did he 'fling acid about' when you arrested him?"

"No," Lev said. "He seemed to be waiting for us."

The judge banged his gavel on the podium. "Guards, release Mr. Werkamp from the shackles."

"I object..."

The gavel rapped sharply again. The judge grinned at Janos Lev. "Mr. Prosecutor, I will have you present your case in the very shackles Mr. Werkamp is wearing, if you don't withdraw your objection. And don't ever come into my courtroom with such a stunt again."

The courtroom exploded with gasps and laughter.

Janos Lev cleared his throat, angrily. "I withdraw the objection, your Honor, and beg your forgiveness."

"Mr. Werkamp, the state will order the prosecution to provide you an attorney at their expense if you desire counsel. Do you wish to be represented?"

Krang shook his head.

"Please speak your answer aloud."

"No. I only wish to tell the truth."

"A commendable objective. I order this hearing into recess for one day to allow the defendant time to have a shower, have his hair cut and shave, if he so desires, at state expense. We'll return tomorrow morning." The judge banged the gavel sharply, and grinned at Janos Lev's shocked expression.

Lisle never knew exactly when Katie died. Katie had taken Sarah to breast again, smiling weakly at her daughter as the infant noisily sucked at her nipple. Katie had drifted off to sleep as the infant did, a wide smile on her face. The midwife had been unable to wake her an hour later when she went to check on her.

Lisle stared at her friend's body, her mind shrieking, unable to say anything. The vitality that had been Katie was gone. The body was diminished in some way, Katie's hands suddenly flat and unreal. Lisle could only stare. In some strange way, it felt like Lisle was staring at her own body. She had been diminished as well. Some part of her being was suddenly gone. Lisle shook her head. It was the world that was diminished. The textures were all wrong. Nothing had the right depth, or feel, or color.

Lisle sat on the edge of the bed, the baby held in one arm against her breast, Katie's hand in her own, rocking numbly and watching as the midwife took over. Auntie Zophie knew a young woman who had just lost a child that she would bring in as a wet nurse. She contacted the cemetery about burial, she prepared a telegram for Katie's father.

Lisle sat through it all, unable to move. She didn't know what to do. She didn't say a word when a young woman about her age showed up and took the baby from her arms. She watched for a moment as the woman placed Sarah at her breast, and then looked away. She stared at her friend's face. Katie looked so happy, so peaceful. She had found some kind of joy that made her own death insignificant. Lisle couldn't figure out what it might have been.

Later that afternoon, the surgeon returned to check on Katie. He was saddened by her passing. He sent everyone from Katie's room so he could examine the body. After ten minutes or so, he came into the living room.

"I think it was her heart," he said. "She did not bleed excessively, the afterbirth was fine. As difficult as the birth was, she should still be alive. So she may have had a heart defect that no one ever knew about. Or perhaps, the shock of birth was simply too much for her body to stand, after her last several years. It was the will of God."

The will of God? Lisle wanted to grab the surgeon by his jacket and shake him hard, make him take back those words. It could not be the will of God for Katie to be dead. Instead she left him talking with Auntie Zophie and returned to her vigil at Katie's side.

Lisle had to be restrained when they took Katie's body away. She fought, yelling for them to stop, to leave Katie be. To just give her another minute, another hour with the only person who mattered in her life. In the end, they gave her the locket Katie was wearing around her neck, and took the body from the apartment. Katie was to be buried in the morning.

The wet nurse was the only one who understood. Late in the evening, after all the others had left, and she had nursed Sarah once again, she came and sat next to Lisle on the floor of Katie's room.

The young woman nodded to the empty bed. Someone had stripped the sheets away.

"It doesn't make any sense to me," the woman whispered. "Why do these things happen? How could my son die, when he was all I had left? My husband," she paused for a moment, gently taking Lisle by the hand, "Forgive me my lie, we weren't married yet, but we were planning on it. My husband died celebrating the news he would be a father. He got drunk and stepped in front of a car. I moved here to be with him, my family disapproved. But I had my son to live for.

"And then he's gone too. He lived for six days. In six days he took up all the room in my life. He became my life. It was like he had always been there. In six days I had forgotten what it was like to be alone. And on the seventh day, the seventh day, you understand? He laid down for a nap and never woke up. That was three days ago. I know what alone is again."

Lisle looked at the woman, something in her tone breaking through the numbness in her soul. "Why did you come, when the midwife asked you?"

The woman looked at her, tears streaking her face. "What else am I going to do? I can sit in my room and pray for God to take me, or at least to stop the ache in my soul and know that God won't do either, or I can come here and do the same thing. At least now, I'm giving someone a chance at life.

"I just don't understand why God needed my son. Or your friend. That's what doesn't make sense. Why not let me die, and let your friend live?"

"Katie wouldn't have seen it that way," Lisle said quietly.

The woman smiled. "She would have if her daughter had died and my son had lived. I don't doubt her faith, mind you. I just know that grief can drive a wedge between a person and God. I imagine some day, faith might come back. I hope it does, actually. Maybe that's what hurts the most. The feeling that God left me."

Lisle squeezed her hand tightly.

"I hate God," the woman said. "I hate God. And I hate myself for feeling that way. It would be so much easier if I didn't believe God existed. If everything was random, then what would I have to feel hurt by? Things happen. But to know... to know that God is all powerful and this happens. What am I to do with that?"

Lisle searched the woman's face. Her grief was visible. Lisle squeezed her hand again. "Katie told me that we need to learn to forgive..."

"Forgive God? Never. How can I forgive what has happened?"

"Not God. God doesn't need to be forgiven. You have to learn to forgive yourself. It's okay to hate God, you just can't hate yourself."

"Your friend was awful young to think like that," the woman said.

"Have you ever wanted to go to America?"

Krang walked into the courtroom, his legs and arms free of restraint. He was dressed in new clothes: a white shirt, tie, dark pants and shoes. He had showered that morning, and his long grey-streaked hair had been combed. His guards lead him to the docket near the judge's bench.

"All rise," the bailiff said, as the judge swept into the room. He glanced at Krang and nodded, apparently more pleased with his appearance than he had been yesterday.

"The Honorable Judge Belthus presiding," the bailiff said. "Please be seated."

The judge looked over at the prosecutor. "Mr. Prosecutor, please approach the bench."

Janos Lev scowled, but quickly crossed the courtroom. He stood silently before Belthus.

"I thought I told you to get him a haircut and a shave?"

"Your Honor, we got the clothing you requested and removed the manacles. We couldn't get a barber to come to the jail to take care of his hair."

"If you don't want me to summarily dismiss this hearing, you will make sure that he gets a haircut this evening. Do you understand me?"

Lev nodded. From the look on Lev's face, Krang knew that he was thinking that he hated judges.

"You may begin."

Janos Lev crossed the room and stood next to his table. "Your Honor. The story we tell today is one of murder, lust and betrayal. It is not for the faint of heart." He nodded to his assistant who rose and removed the sheet covering the first easel, revealing the diagram of the camp.

"The setting of this sordid tale is Work Camp 361, known as the Mountain City camp. It was located in Northern Montrovia, about twenty miles outside Mountain City, a mining and manufacturing site. There were approximately one hundred similar camps in Montrovia..."

Belthus rapped his gavel. "Mr Prosecutor, we do not need a history of the detention camps in Montrovia. Stick to relevant facts in the case."

Janos Lev gave a curt nod to the assistant, who removed the second sheet. "The camp was so brutal and hated that after it was liberated, the survivors obliterated any sign of it. A place of horror and murder, with crimes too numerous and heinous to recount..."

Belthus raised the gavel , but Lev waived him off with a quick nod.

"The cast of characters in this sordid tale include a young woman, lost and alone, who turns her back on her own people, a man so violent that the survivors still won't refer to him by name, but rather by the nickname they created for him, *the guard*," he nodded and the assistant removed the last sheet, "and evil so normal looking it could fool anyone."

Many of the observers in the room pointed at Bitmeyer's large photo.

"This is Krang, the one they referred to as *the Guard?*" Belthus asked.

Lev shook his head. "When the camp was liberated, the survivors destroyed everything, including the files on all the personnel. We don't have any photos of *the Guard.* We do have descriptions from the survivors. This is a photo of the man who ran the camp. He was a professor before the war, and had published a number of academic works. The photo is from one of his books."

"And his relevance to this case?"

"He was ultimately in charge," Lev answered. "I wanted everyone to see that people's behaviors aren't controlled by appearances, whether a kind grandfather who turns out to be a vicious killer or a young widow who turns out to be a collaborator, and thus a murderer in her own right."

Belthus nodded. "Please continue."

As I have already stated, this is not a criminal trial, but simply an inquiry into the mental state of Mr. Werkamp. You will find that the defendant does not dispute the charge that he defaced a national treasure..."

"Then why are we here?" Belthus interrupted. "Do we try to institutionalize someone for vandalism? Fine the man, or put him in jail for a month and be done with it. This is a waste of the limited resources of our city, and nothing more than a grab for headlines by a man running for office."

Janos Lev laughed, unfazed by the judge's outburst. "Your Honor, it's not that simple. The defendant does not deny carving the name Sarah Jezek on the monument. He originally put in a request with the park service to have the name added. The request was refused."

"Why did the park service refuse an official request to add a name to the monument?" Belthus asked.

"Sarah Jezek was executed for aiding and abetting Montrovia while a prisoner in the Mountain City death camp."

Krang winced. It still hurt to hear what had happened to Sarah. What had happened because of him. Her death was the one about which he felt the most guilty.

Lev continued. "Mr. Werkamp refuses to accept this. He simply says that we are wrong, over and over again. He also says that every time we repair the monument he will add her name to it again. The state sees no alternative to confinement."

"What if he is right?"

The prosecutor nodded. "The state is aware that life in the camps was chaotic, and that much misinformation exists. So I assigned staff to the case who went out and found the primary witnesses against Sarah Jezek, and the judge who sentenced her, and have brought them here to testify. We have also brought in several witnesses from the Mountain City camp who all will tell you that they do not know a Walter Werkamp. No such person is listed on the prison roster."

"You are saying that the defendant was never a prisoner in the Mountain City camp?"

"That is correct."

"Then how does he know Sarah Jezek?"

"We're not sure, your Honor. Mr. Werkamp hasn't said. You have ten affidavits before you that all swear to the fact he was not an inmate at the camp. Can I call my first witness?"

Belthus picked up the stack of statements and leafed through them. "I will accept the affidavits without needing to hear individual testimony from all of them. The court accepts these affidavits that none of these witnesses remember Mr. Werkamp. For the sake of your argument, until challenged by other testimony, the court accepts that Mr. Werkamp was not a prisoner at Mountain City camp, at least not under that name. You may call your first witness."

"If it please the court, the state calls Mrs. Krasna Otka."

The bailiff opened a door on the side of the courtroom. A slight woman entered, dressed in a dark skirt and blouse. She looked very uncomfortable. Krang did not remember her from the camp, but she had that survivor look. The woman walked across the courtroom and sat on the single wooden chair on the judge's left, opposite Krang. She never looked directly at him as she crossed the room.

"You have sworn before God to tell the truth," the judge said. He nodded to the prosecutor. "You may begin."

"Please state your name for the court and your relationship to Sarah Jezek."

The woman's voice was weak, and quavered as she spoke. "My name is Krasna Otka. Sarah Jezek was my sister-in-law. She was married to my brother, Abraham."

"Do you know anyone named Walter Werkamp?"

"No," she said forcefully. "No one."

"Do you know the man sitting in the docket by any other name?"

The woman leaned forward and craned her neck to study Krang. She had a look of puzzlement on her face. After a moment she said, "No, I don't believe so."

"Do you or don't you?" The prosecutor sounded irritated.

"No, I don't," she replied meekly.

"Have you ever seen him before at all?"

"I don't believe so."

"Not in the camp?"

She hesitated for a moment. "No."

"Not on the roads after the camp?"

She leaned forward and looked at Krang again. "No."

"Can you tell us about Sarah?"

The woman nodded. "As I said, she was my sister-in-law. We were always very close. She was my friend and schoolmate before she began dating Abraham. I was so very happy when they became engaged. She was in my wedding party. I still can't believe that she betrayed him."

"What happened when you and your family arrived at the camp?"

"It was horrible. The train had been overwhelming. People had died from lack of water and some had suffocated because it was just too crowded. Children and the very old suffered the most. Abraham was wonderful, however. He risked his life to smuggle on a water skin and made sure that Capek, his son, had enough to drink.

"When we arrived the train was unloaded in the middle of the night. I've never been sure what Sarah did to anger the guards, why she just didn't do what she was told. She got off before me. All I know is that as I got off, I saw her arguing with the guards. Arguing! And then he stepped forward and shot Abraham and killed Capek before my very eyes."

"He?"

"The one we referred to as *the guard*. He was the most terrible creature imaginable. In all our time in the camp, it was *the guard* who truly frightened us. He was the one who would pull you out of line for walking the wrong way and kill you. Or for breathing too loudly. Or for any reason he could think of."

"And did this 'guard' hurt Sarah as well?"

"I..." she paused, looking at Lev, "I guess not."

"Please explain what you mean."

"She became his lover..."

The audience exploded with gasps and commentary, cutting the woman off. The judge wrapped sharply with his gavel. "I shall clear the courtroom if I do not have quiet."

"His lover?"

"That very night he came for her. I was blind to it, you see. I thought he picked her at random. Maybe he did that night. I remember we were all afraid he would take us, all but Sarah. She said she didn't care. I thought that he raped her. But afterwards, when I spoke with my cousin, Rybar Vrba, I realized that they had been lovers since that very first night."

"So they continued their liaisons throughout your internment."

"I assume they did. I did not see anything, mind you, or I would have reported her. I still thought of her as family. But at the end, it all became apparent."

"Can you tell me about what happened on the day Sarah was convicted?"

"I was in our cabin looking after a sick woman when Sarah came in. She was acting strange. Everyone was so excited about the camp being liberated. It was only going to be a few more hours until the Corabian army arrived. We could hear the tanks in the woods, so we were all a little giddy. Everyone except Sarah. Sarah was... calm. She said she was tired and wanted to lie down and sleep forever. She went back and sat with Mrs. Woerful and talked. I wasn't close enough to hear what they were saying, but clearly she was upset. Mrs. Woerful was hugging her and comforting her. They were still talking when the men broke in and took her. When Rybar told me what she had done, I went right to the tribunal council to tell them what I knew."

"What had she done?"

"She had let that bastard..."

The judge slammed his gavel on the podium, cutting her off in mid-sentence. "Speak of only what you saw, nothing more. Since you did not see the acts that Sarah was accused of, you cannot speak of them as fact."

The prosecutor raised his hand. "I apologize. Let me rephrase the question. Who told you what had happened?"

"My cousin, Rybar. He had tried to be nice to her since Abraham was killed. I think he wanted to marry her."

"And what did he tell you?"

"That she had kissed him and let him go."

"Kissed who?"

"*The guard.* She kissed him and let him go. And she never denied it. At the tribunal she admitted to it."

"Did she say why?"

"She said she needed to forgive him, for Abraham. As if anything he had done could be forgiven."

"Do you think Sarah's name should be on the monument that was erected here in Corabia?"

"Absolutely not. She was no better than one of them. No better than *the guard.* It's odd, because there are moments when I miss her. She was my friend. But then I think of Abraham, and of their beautiful boy Capek, and I don't understand how she could have done it. How could she betray them? She deserved to die, and she did."

"Thank you. No further questions, your Honor." Krasna Otka stood up from her seat.

"Wait, please," Judge Belthus said. "I have questions." Lev glared at him as the woman froze.

"Your Honor," Lev said, "this is most irregular..."

"Not in my courtroom," Belthus snapped. "I will not allow testimony with no chance of rebuttal. Since you have not provided an attorney for Mr. Werkamp, I will ask the questions that are on my mind, or else I will dismiss this hearing now."

Janos Lev nodded curtly to the woman to sit down in the witness seat again.

"Am I to understand that the only proof you have of this affair is the statement by Mr. Vrba that Sarah Jezek kissed *the guard?*"

"That's when everything made sense. It was Rybar who made the connection about the affair. I didn't think that, even when I heard about the kiss, but after he said it, I saw the truth of it."

"The truth of it?"

"It made her other actions understandable, your Honor. No person would do the things Sarah did unless they had a reason. She kept *the guard* from hurting any of the woman in our cabin that first night. Every other woman in that cabin was afraid for her life, except Sarah. That doesn't make sense. And who forgives the man who murdered your husband and son? There are limits to what could be true."

"And why would you believe Mr. Vrba's claim that he saw her kiss *the*

337

guard?"

"He's my cousin. Why would he lie?"

"But Sarah was Abraham's wife. Why would she lie?"

"Because she was guilty."

Belthus sighed. He glanced at Janos Lev. "I don't recall seeing Rybar Vrba on your witness list."

Lev shook his head. "No, your Honor. Unfortunately, we haven't been able to locate Mr. Vrba."

"That is unfortunate," Belthus said.

"Mrs. Otka, why did it matter that one man escaped justice?"

The witness cocked her head to the side as if she hadn't heard what he had said. When she spoke, her voice was very soft.

"You can't understand, because you weren't there," she said. She nodded towards the oversized portrait of Bitmeyer. "He was a bureaucrat, only concerned that the camp run smoothly. He could be cruel or generous to get what he wanted. Other guards could be read. A smile was good, a frown bad. Some of them got excited, aroused, you know?, but you could see the signs.

"*The guard* was like a shark, not human at all. He would circle you and attack, or not, at his will. You never knew where you stood with him. He wasn't human. No emotion at all. We hated the sight of him, but if you couldn't see him you were even more afraid. He was the proof God had forsaken us."

Krang nodded at her words. That was the truth.

"You may step down," Belthus said to her.

Krang watched as she left the witness box and walked to the rear of the courtroom. He remembered her now. She had lived in the same cabin as Sarah. Listening to her testimony, he had wanted to scream at her to wake up. He bit his lip instead, knowing that any outbursts on his part would simply weaken Sarah's story when he told it. Let them all have their say, he thought. The truth will win out.

The funeral was plain and simple. Katie was gently wrapped in fine white linen and carried through the streets to the cemetery. There was no coffin. Fifty or sixty people turned out. Even people Lisle hadn't thought of as friends. It made her feel comforted, to know that even in the few weeks they had been in Olive Hill Katie had touched so many people.

Katie was buried in a small cemetery on the western edge of town, in a spot that would get the afternoon sun. Lisle, reminded of Katie's naps on the floor of the apartment, found the site fitting. She was numb, unable to put her thoughts together. She had had no word from Katie's father, but the midwife assured her that the telegram had been sent. The funeral would not wait for his return. Lisle would have been happy to wait for Woerful to return, simply to have an excuse not to bury her friend.

Lisle had spent part of the night packing. She was going to catch a train to the city in the afternoon. She had Katie's letter to deliver. Then she was going to book passage on a steamer, to Europe or America, and disappear from this place forever. The young woman who was nursing Sarah, Jana Cermak, would not go to America with her. She was going to go back to her family in the city. She would stay with Lisle for a few days, to be sure Sarah was eating well, and then Lisle would have to move her from breast to bottled milk. Lisle hadn't really expected Jana to want to go to America. She didn't know what she would have done if the woman had said yes. How do you move to a new country with someone you just met?

Lisle watched as the priest shut his Bible and lowered his head to pray. I've got to stop calling them priests, she thought. They're teachers here, not priests. She realized she hadn't heard a single word of the service, and she wasn't following his prayer, either. What good would it do to pay attention? He could say nothing that would take the hurt away. Nothing that could remove the film that seemed to be separating her from the world around her. Will I ever remember this day? Is my memory getting it, even though I don't feel present myself?

She watched the two young men shovel dirt into the grave. She felt a sense of panic, an irrational fear that Katie would awaken alone and lost. Lisle made herself stay until they were finished and everyone else had left. She sat on the ground beside the grave and dug her fingers into the loose dirt.

"I promise you that I will raise your daughter as if she were my own. As if I were you. I want her to know everything about you, about your faith and what you believed in. And I'll be sure that she knows about her namesake as well.

"I'm scared that I will never have your strength. I don't see the world as you see it. But I'll do my best to raise her in your frame of mind. I promise this." Lisle began to cry, great sobs wracking her body. "I love you, Katie. I'll never know another person like you..." She stopped. She had no more words to say. When she was cried out she stood and headed back to the apartment. She had a train to catch.

Krang shifted in the hard wooden seat in the docket, anxious for his turn to speak. It was late in the afternoon and he didn't think he would get his chance today. The day had been filled with a parade of similar testimonies: men and women who had known Sarah in the camp, but who loathed her now because they had heard what she had done. Not one person stepped forward who could explain why Sarah had freed *the guard*.

Krang recognized almost every witness. He was surprised that his heart gave a little jump every time someone new came in to testify. He was glad to see that they were alive, and apparently doing well. Krang had expected to feel animosity or fear or some other emotion when his former prisoners testified, but all he felt was a sense of well being that they had made it. He was terribly sad that they all hated Sarah, but he couldn't blame them. In their eyes, she had betrayed them. As he listened to their testimony, and heard the anger and pain in their voices, he realized that Sarah's act of forgiveness was even more miraculous than he had understood. None of these men or women were at a place where they could forgive anything about the camp.

Krang was also disappointed that Belthus carefully steered the testimony away from the camp itself. Witnesses were allowed to tell how they knew Sarah, and for how long, and how they had heard of her betrayal, but nothing of the camp in general, and he asked no more questions about *the guard*. None of the witnesses had been first hand observers of her act of forgiveness.

When asked about Walter Werkamp, the witnesses would peer into Krang's face and shake their heads. They did not know him. Krang wondered how it was that he could look so different. Certainly, his hair was much longer, for he had not cut it since it had been burned off on the plains, several months ago. And he had lost weight, maybe as much as fifty pounds. And he wasn't dressed in a uniform, or carrying a gun, but he had expected to be recognized. He needed to be recognized in order to prove that Sarah was no collaborator. He worried that Bitmeyer's photo was influencing the witnesses. It was hard not to expect *the guard* to look like the round-faced man in the photo.

One young man, no more than fifteen or sixteen, had stared at him especially hard as he walked to the witness stand. Krang remembered the boy slightly; his father had done a wonderful job of keeping the boy out of sight and out of trouble. Krang thought at last someone was going to tell the judge who he was.

Marek Gareg didn't say a word about *the guard*. He had stared at Krang because he wanted to see who had the courage to do what he had always wanted to do: recognize Sarah.

"She was like an older sister to me," the young man said, then he blushed. "I wanted her to fall in love with me. I had such a crush."

The prosecutor seemed annoyed at the boy's testimony. "You said nothing of this when we interviewed you," Lev snapped.

Marek nodded. "I know that I wouldn't be here if I had told you this. I don't care what she did the last day of the camp. She was my friend, and friend to many. She took care of people, made sure they had food, found extra blankets. I'm sure many of us survived the camp because of her caring."

"Which has what to do with her crime?"

"Her crime?" the boy said, his voice rising above the noise from the crowd. "What was her crime? Even if she did as they said, then I would accept her story

340

of why. There was so much death in that place, how were any of us served by the death of one more? Even if it was *the guard?* When I saw her on the parade ground the next morning, saw her gunned down with the others, I died that morning."

"A school boy crush can overwhelm the most..."

"My love for her may have been no more than a crush, but that doesn't change the truth. My father cheered when the tribunal sentenced her to death," Marek said. "Do you understand? My father, who worked so hard to keep me alive, cheered when those useless old men sentenced Sarah to die. He made me watch them kill her, and all the others, and he cheered that too. I survived the camp, only to lose my friend and my father on the last day. I hurt so much, I tried to hang myself in the barrack, but someone found me and cut me down before I was gone. What right did we have to act like those who had tormented us?"

Lev was taken aback by the boy's testimony. After a moment's silence, he released the boy from the witness box.

"Do you agree with what Sarah did? Do you forgive *the guard?*" Belthus asked him.

Marek shrugged. "It doesn't matter what I think," he said. "It mattered that Sarah forgave him. I believed what she said: she forgave him."

Belthus nodded and released him.

The late afternoon sun was shining through the courthouse windows, the stultifying heat on the verge of overwhelming the fans lazily spinning on the ceiling, when Benjamin Woerful was called to the stand. Krang watched him walking slowly across the courtroom in his dark suit, his hat clutched in his hand. He walked hesitantly. Krang felt rage flair in his breast at the man who had led the tribunal. He couldn't see how this man had given Katie to the world.

Krang had no trouble recognizing the man. Woerful had spent most of his time interacting with Commandant Bitmeyer, not with the guards, but Krang had seen enough of the man to never forget him. Woerful had been the de facto second-in-command of the Corabians for much of his tenure in the camp, and had risen to the top position upon the death of his predecessor. Woerful, in his role as chief negotiator, protector, and enforcer had more power than anyone in the camp except Krang. He decided when to intervene on behalf of the other prisoners. He had been the one person in the camp who could make a guard stop whatever abuse he was committing and take the situation to Bitmeyer for resolution. He had used his power sparingly, but successfully. When he intervened, he had almost always gotten what he wanted.

Only *the guard* had been free of his interference. Krang had known that Woerful and the other elders were off limits, even to him, but his actions had seemed so random and chaotic to them that they had never dared to find out.

Woerful seemed reduced from the camp. He had held such a position of power in the camp, and Krang wondered if he had struggled to find himself in the post camp world. He looked old, pale and tired, as if life had been even more unjust to him after the camp. He carried a handkerchief in one hand and continually wiped his eyes and face.

"State your name and occupation for the court."

Woerful sat upright, rigid, in his seat. His voice was so soft Krang strained to hear it. "I am Benjamin Woerful, mayor and spiritual leader of Olive Hill."

"I'm sorry for your loss," Lev said softly. "We could recess for a few days, if that would be better."

Woerful shook his head. "She was a wonderful daughter and her death a shock. She would understand why I am here. Let's continue."

Krang recoiled. Daughter? Was it Katie or her sister? But her sister had died of the flu. No, Krang thought, it cannot be. He gripped the arms of his chair.

"And the child?"

"I have been assured that my granddaughter is in excellent health. I will return home this evening to take possession of her."

Krang wanted to scream. Katie was dead? How could that be? God had finally stripped everything from him. He was reduced to nothing, as blank a soul as the day he was born. He could feel his blood rushing through his body, could feel his pulse pounding in his ears. The tears began before he could stop them. The prosecutor was talking, but Krang couldn't make out what was being said. He could see her face, one moment the look of joy when he told her to have the baby, the next the look of horror and revilement when he told her his truth. Oh God, forgive me, Krang thought. Forgive me for ever causing her a moment's pain. Forgive me for having the audacity to love her, especially after proving I was so unworthy of love. Take her home Father, and let me join her shortly.

"Do you know the man sitting to your left?"

Krang blinked, wiping his eyes on the back of his sleeve. He caught his breath. This was the moment he was to be revealed.

Katie's father turned in his seat and stared blankly at Krang for several minutes before shaking his head. He looked like a blind man, like everything that he saw with his eyes simply didn't register in his brain. "No."

Krang wanted to jump from his seat, to grab the old man and shake him until he saw the truth, but he couldn't move. Katie was dead?

"He was not at the Mountain City camp?"

"No."

"Do you know anyone by the name of Walter Werkamp?"

"No."

"Did you know Sarah Jezek?"

342

"Yes. I condemned her to death for collaborating with our tormentors and betraying her husband and son."

"And you had proof of this liaison?"

"Her sister-in-law testified before the tribunal about the relationship. She never denied it."

Krang shook his head. How lost you all are, he thought. I took what I wanted. I took everything I wanted. Who would ever think I would want a relationship? I would just take.

"What did she say about the allegation?"

"She spoke in gibberish. She would tell us that she was tired, and just wanted to sleep forever. And then she would say that she had done it for her husband. Imagine that! She blamed her infidelity, with her husband's murderer, on her husband. I had no choice but to order her execution."

"I caution the witness," Belthus interrupted, "to speak of only what you had direct knowledge of. To speak of only what you witnessed. Did you witness this affair?"

Woerful sighed, and slowly shook his head. "It was reported to the tribunal by Abraham's sister and his cousin."

"How long did they say this affair had been going on?" Lev asked.

"From the very first day. The day her husband and son were killed before her eyes."

"I understand that in other camps, when an inmate had an intimate relationship with a guard, they were often killed by the other inmates. Why did that not happen in this case?"

"She was very careful. No one had any clue about this relationship. Abraham's sister and cousin only put it all together after she was arrested. And then it all made sense. Much more sense than the lies she tried to pass off in her testimony."

"What did she say?"

"She testified that she had forgiven him. Forgiven *the guard.* Can you believe that? She said that she had to, in order to free the spirits of her son and husband from the camp."

"So you discount this story?"

"I have been a spiritual leader for more than thirty years. I have preached to my congregation lessons on forgiveness, more than I can remember. We are, as a church, required to practice forgiveness. But not of this. Some acts are too heinous to be forgiven. God may be merciful, and may have unlimited understanding, but even God cannot forgive certain things.

"In fact, it would be a sin to forgive something of this magnitude. The idea of forgiveness is to remind us that we are not to judge one another, but to leave

343

judgment with God. I cannot tell you how often I have had a congregant come to me with some petty complaint about another member of our community, and I would talk them through the process of forgiveness. I would help them see that they were judging another human being. But God does not expect us, or want us, to forgive something of the nature of what happened in that camp."

"So forgiveness is limited to minor wrongs?"

"Oh no. Please don't misunderstand me. I have counseled wives to forgive their husbands for an infidelity rather than seek divorce. I have counseled an employer to forgive an employee a debt, rather than seek prosecution. I myself have forgiven my daughter for failing to heed my authority and running away in the middle of a crisis. God expects us to forgive."

Krang rocked in his seat when he heard Woerful mention Katie. You lying bastard, he thought. You forgave nothing. You would have been happiest if she had been at your side in that hell, at the mercies of any guard strong enough to take her from you. And I would have. Don't you understand that, you old bastard? You were never strong enough to protect her. You were never as strong as she was.

"But also understand that some acts are an abomination before God's eyes. God does not forgive everything. Imagine if God did. There would be no consequences to any of your actions. Society would fall apart. We hang murderers to keep them from killing again. God does not come down from Heaven to pardon them from their crimes and set them free, does he?"

"You teach a literal heaven in your church? That is not what is taught on Sunday in my church." Lev asked the question deferentially.

"I speak metaphysically, sir. We all know that heaven is the mind of God. And we all know that God is love, and that that love is responsible for a multitude of miracles and blessings every day. I have seen men and women on their deathbeds suddenly healed by the love of God. But I have never seen, nor heard, of a condemned murderer, once hung for his crime, being resurrected by God as an act of forgiveness.

"Some transgressions are too horrible to be forgiven. You explain to me how this young woman Sarah, having seen her husband and son killed before her very eyes, could forgive the man who had done it? Not unless there was something else going on."

"And what happened when you ordered Sarah's execution?"

"That is when I was most sure of my actions. Her guilt was clearly weighing on her at that time."

"How so?"

"She thanked me. She smiled, and nodded her head and thanked me."

"Anything else?"

344

"She did not say that she forgave me."

Chapter Twenty-Five

Lisle sat by the window, the infant Sarah sleeping in her arms, as the train pulled out of the station beginning the trip to the city. Jana Cermak, the wet nurse, sat silently at her side, staring at the floor, lost in her own grief. It was late afternoon.

Lisle studied the infant cradled against her breast, looking for some sign of Katie on her face. She didn't see it. Lisle wasn't looking just for Katie's features, but some sign of her extraordinary strength. Lisle had hoped that taking Sarah would mean that she would have some part of Katie with her forever, but now she understood that wasn't to be. She had a terrible thought: she could leave the infant with Katie's father and just disappear. She could still finish what Katie had interrupted on the train.

Lisle felt the tears begin to slide down her face. She felt so guilty. She should want this child fiercely, because she was Katie's daughter, but all she felt was this overwhelming bleakness. If she were honest with herself, she had to admit that she had been a little jealous of the baby growing inside Katie. The baby was one more thing that would come between them, just like Walter would. And now she had lost Katie, but had been given the child and was going to see the man. What did I do to deserve this?

Lisle knew she would be dead if it hadn't been for Katie. She had been planning to throw herself under the train when Katie found her. When Captain Aesop had picked her up in his jeep, some school girl part of her had hoped he was going to claim her for himself, but he had just taken her to the checkpoint and handed her over to the Albanians. He had seen her naked in the hospital and had proven how ugly she really was.

The Albanians had put her on the empty train without saying a word. The Corabian survivors came later that day, and she had sat silently in her seat, afraid for her life as they shuffled down the aisles and spilled into the seats around her. That was when she had known she was going to kill herself. She wasn't going to let anyone hurt her again. She had fallen asleep thinking about how to do it.

Lisle had woken up with the train in motion. She remembered the couple sitting across from her: the woman had been huge with a baby and the man small and diminished. The person next to her had been asleep, leaning against her shoulder. Katie. Lisle hadn't even looked at her, not enough to really see her. Katie had been invisible to her. As soon as the train had stopped to take on water and coal, Lisle had slipped away from her seat and made her way to the open car. None of the guards had noticed her.

She had been waiting for the train to gather enough speed that she could be sure to die quickly. But within five minutes of pulling out of the siding, Katie had joined her on the tender car and changed Lisle's life. Katie, in the midst of her own grief and loss, had still had enough love within her to seek out someone else that was in pain and needed help. Her love had made it okay for Lisle to keep going. Somehow Katie had known what Lisle was planning to do and what was necessary to stop her. It was just like that day in the bathroom. Katie had known exactly what boundary to cross to give Lisle back her life. To give her back the hope that someday someone would love and desire her.

Why did God take you from me?

Lisle knew what Katie would say: God had nothing to do with it. That if Lisle just opened her eyes to God, she would see the good all around her. Lisle glanced around the train, looking at all the people. Some together, talking or arguing. Others, whether sitting together or not, lost in their own thoughts. She saw weariness, not joy. There didn't appear to be a Katie among them.

Sarah began to squirm in her arms, and angry sigh escaping her lips. Lisle looked down at the infant. Her face was getting red as she squirmed. She was going to hand her off to the wet nurse to feed, but Jana was asleep. Lisle stroked Sarah's lips lightly with her finger, as Jana had taught her. Sarah sucked the tip of Lisle's finger into her mouth, her mouth moving around it, and settled back into sleep. Her mouth continued to work the tip of Lisle's finger, warm and wet and full of need. She sighed and her mouth slackened.

When Sarah was peaceful again, Lisle pulled her finger away, suddenly awed by the infant in her arms. That this child could become someone else's Katie seemed such a preposterous idea, but that was the truth wasn't it? Had anyone noticed Katie's greatness when she was two days old? She imagined Katie's mother had. And maybe my mother saw the same thing, Lisle thought. Maybe all parents see the potential greatness in their children, before we grow up to disappoint them.

Woerful's testimony dragged on late into the afternoon. Krang grew bored with it very quickly. He felt that Woerful and Lev were serving each other, not the truth. Lev kept bringing Woerful back to the sordid idea that Sarah had been fucking Krang and that was why she had released him.

"Do you have anything else that you want to add about this case?" the Lev asked Woerful.

"Sarah represents the very worst of our people. That she could work with *the guard*, against us, forgetting her own people, is unforgivable. If this vagrant is unable to see that, then he is a danger to us all. He should be locked up or worse. He is no better than Sarah."

Krang let his rage wash over him as Woerful testified, consuming him until nothing but hatred was left. Woerful was the man who had killed Sarah. He had killed her from fear, arrogance and the pleasure of his own power. And Katie was dead, so Krang couldn't hurt her if he killed Woerful now. He knew that he could jump Woerful as the old man left the witness box, and snap his neck before anyone could react. And then the guards would shoot him, and everything would be complete.

The idea of killing Woerful had a perverse pleasure and symmetry to it. Krang smiled at the thought of it. He would die truthfully, as he had lived. He stared at Woerful, feeling the adrenaline flowing through him as it had in the camp when he was *the guard*.

But that was the problem. *The guard* was dead. Sarah and Katie had destroyed him and Krang wasn't willing to resurrect him now. He owed a debt to those women, a debt he was willing to pay with his life, and violence couldn't be part of it. So Krang let the thrill of his rage slip away. He slowed his racing heart, he turned his head from his quarry. He bent his head down to hide his tears. He would honor Sarah and Katie. Krang took a deep breath, and willed his body to relax. He had almost done what the world wanted, but now he was safe.

After a minute he raised his head and refocused on the courtroom.

Belthus studied the man sitting in the witness chair. "Did no one speak in defense of Sarah Jezek?"

Woerful coughed, then slowly nodded. "Yes, your Honor. My wife spoke in her defense."

"And what did she say?"

"She accused us of losing sight of our faith and becoming no better than the Montrovians. She said Sarah should be honored for her action, not punished."

"And her words did not move you?"

Woerful looked across the room, lost in thought. After a minute, he responded. "Her words drove us apart. She loved Sarah. She had lost her daughters, and Sarah was a way to overcome the loss. I knew, when she stood before the tribunal in defense of Sarah that I was going to lose her. But I couldn't let my personal loss keep justice at bay. Even if everything Sarah said was the truth: that she freed *the guard* out of a sense of forgiveness, that didn't change the gravity of her own crime. She betrayed her people, your Honor. That is unforgivable."

"Thank you, Mr. Woerful. I'm sorry for your most recent loss."

Woerful rose from the witness stand and made his way out of the courtroom. Krang watched him go, his heart aching for Katie and the baby. And Sarah. It felt like an hour passed before Woerful was out of the courtroom. Krang breathed a sigh of relief. He had been so close to acting, but then he wouldn't have been able to tell Sarah's side of the story. Once people understood Sarah, they could deal with men like him.

"The court is in recess until tomorrow morning, when we shall hear Mr. Werkamp tell us why he carved Sarah Wilkins' name into the National Monument. Mr. Prosecutor, I expect Mr. Werkamp to have been given a shave and a haircut."

"Even against his will?" Janos Lev asked with a smile.

Belthus turned to Krang. "Would you like a haircut and shave?"

"Yes, your Honor," Krang said.

"Get the man a haircut." The judge pounded his gavel on the podium.

Lisle walked through the city at dusk. She had left Sarah at the hotel happily suckling at Jana's breast. Lisle didn't know what she would do in two days when Jana left to return to her family. She didn't feel that she could take care of the infant, but she had made a promise. She would keep it.

Everywhere she turned she saw Katie. Slipping around a corner, stepping onto a bus, pulling a door shut behind her. Lisle felt like she was losing her hold on reality. At least she wasn't chasing after any of the apparitions; she knew Katie was really dead. Somehow Katie had let Lisle play the role of older sister, when, in fact, Katie had been the one holding everything together. Lisle knew she was close to feeling like she had just before she met Katie. She was ready to throw herself from a train. But she couldn't. She had made a promise to her friend that she would never break. She would raise Sarah as Katie would have. And she had to deliver Katie's letter to Walter.

Lisle looked around to gather her bearings. She had set out from the hotel to book passage on a ship to America, but the offices had been closed for the day. It was too late to try to see Walter, but she would find the courthouse so she could return in the morning. She walked up the gentle rise from the docks to the city proper, and found herself on a small hill with the city laid out before her. It was a view she hadn't seen before. She had refused any attempt on Katie's part to explore the city. Katie would have loved the view from here. Lisle hoped Katie had found this place on her own. Had she kept Katie from so much? Lisle fought to keep the tears at bay.

People scurried through the failing light, unaware of Lisle's grief, caught up in the living of their own world. Somehow that was comforting. Her grief, as great as it was, didn't touch the world. She looked at them as they walked past. No one knew what was happening in her life, nor cared. That her grief was local didn't dull or mute it, but it gave her hope. All of these men and women had suffered in ways she didn't know, but today they could walk down the street and not even see her grief. Somehow they had survived.

Lisle saw a man slumped on a bench, his head in his hands. The crowd glanced at him, a few even stared, but no one stopped to ask him what was wrong. His body shook with tears. He slowly raised his head and wiped his eyes with a handkerchief, and settled his hat on his head. Lisle sucked in her breath in shock. It was Katie's father. He was barely recognizable. In some strange way, he seemed as diminished as Katie's corpse had been, as if the very life force had fled him. Lisle had never noticed how old and fragile he looked. His aura of power must have been all bluster, and when that was stripped away, all that was left was a man on the verge of collapse. Of all the people around her, the only one who understood her grief was a man she couldn't even acknowledge. She felt a moment's guilt, watching him rise and slowly walk away without saying anything to him, but she couldn't let him know she was here. She had made a promise to Katie that he wouldn't be allowed to raise Sarah.

It will kill him, she thought, when he discovers that we are gone. All that is keeping him alive is the hope of his granddaughter, and I am stealing that from him. What should I do? If I stay, I have no legal claim to Sarah, and she will be placed in his house. Lisle shook her head. She didn't want to raise the child. She hated her. Sarah had killed Katie. She deserved Woerful.

"Forgive me, Katie," she whispered, feeling the tears coming again. I'm not worthy of your trust, she thought. I can't do what you want of me. I've lived with fear so long, I don't know any other way of life. Your father has a certitude that will protect Sarah, and I can't.

Lisle turned and studied the courthouse beside her. She wondered if the trial was continuing to tomorrow. She could come, to see what happened. It would give her another day free of the baby before Jana left. She might even run into Woerful, and then she would have no choice but to give up Sarah.

Krang sat quietly in his cell. He had shaved, showered and had his hair cut short. They will recognize me now, he thought, a grim smile on his face. They will see *the guard* once again, and know that I tell the truth.

Krang had almost blown it in the courtroom. He had almost attacked Woerful. That would have been a betrayal of Sarah. It would have repudiated everything that she had done. She had acted to break a cycle of violence, and Krang had almost reinitiated it. Every time I think I have changed, I am challenged by something and see that I haven't changed at all. I must end this now, so that I am not a risk to the world any longer. I was so lost, before Sarah claimed me for God. Did she know what she was doing? Krang shook his head. I was always God's. I just didn't claim God for myself.

Krang settled back onto the cot in his cell. He was not confined to the cell, but free with his child. Free with Katie. Krang could see the sliver of a crescent moon through the small window of his cell. He was struck by the beauty of it. And by the fact that no matter what hatred and ugliness was going on around him, none of it changed the beauty of moon. None of it could change the joy of taking a deep breath and smelling morning on it. None of it could change the joy of knowing that his daughter had been born.

I will die tomorrow, Krang thought. But I will die filled with joy and at peace with God. I could not kill myself earlier because I needed to be here to tell Sarah's story. That is a worthy endeavor. The only worthiness in my life. So I will die, and if God wills it, I will be reunited with Katie. Or I will be nothing.

I wonder if Emma and the children are alive? Krang shook his head. I don't feel them in this universe any longer. Emma and I were a disaster. So incapable of loving anything beyond ourselves. And in truth, we didn't even love ourselves. We loathed ourselves. Each moment we spent together was an attempt to exorcize our own demons. To somehow scrape away what we hated and find something, anything that was worth loving. All of our fucking turned into fights, and all of our fights turned into fucking, until we gave up.

Krang laughed ruefully. The children loved us. Too young to understand how fucked-up we were, all they could do was love us, and it wasn't enough. Not even close. He thought of his son's face. I killed you the same day I killed Sarah's baby, he thought. Not because I didn't love you, you would have survived that. Because I couldn't let you love me.

It started off the same with Katie. She was nothing more than an easy fuck to me. She gave herself away to deny me the opportunity to take. I could play that game with her, but somewhere along the road, I realized that I respected her: her strength, her fearless determination. What happened to let me see Katie more clearly?

I think that Sarah forgiving me changed me.

I hated her when she did that. I thought she was stupid, letting me go like that. I would have killed her on the spot, just to prove to her how wrong she was, if I hadn't wanted to escape. Later on, I began to think that she had felt superior to me and I still hated her. How could she feel superior? I had owned her, damn it. And she acted like a Queen, granting me absolution. Krang brushed the tears away from his eyes. She knew they would kill her for freeing me, but she wasn't committing suicide. She was tired and alone, but she was ready to embrace life again. I know it. The courage it took to walk up to me and kiss me when she must have wanted to cut my heart out. I will never forget her. Never.

Lisle stood outside the courthouse, sipping coffee, a small roll in her hand. She had been told at the hotel to arrive early if she wanted to get a seat inside, and even two hours before the session began a crowd had gathered. The group was noisy and full of energy.

Two men argued about the case off to her left. The shorter man, much more stocky than his opponent, wagged his finger in the other man's face. "That Lev is a genius," he was saying. "He's got this thing wrapped up. I bet the bum gets put away for life."

"You're a moron," the taller man snapped. "Belthus clearly hates Janos Lev. He won't give the man jail time even if he confesses to everything. And we haven't even heard his testimony. I bet he's got a hell of a reason for doing it..."

"What kind of reason can he have?" the stouter man shouted back. "I had cousins in those camps and..."

"Oh, fuck off," said the taller one. "We all had cousins in the camps. You're a fraud, to make this personal."

"Bastard," the shorter one said, spitting at his companion's feet. "I should knock the shit out of you..."

A police officer appeared from the crowd, taking both men by the arms and pulling them from the courthouse steps.

Lisle had watched the whole exchange in shock. She took the opportunity, as the crowd surged around the men to hear what the police officer was going to do, to make her way closer to the entrance of the courthouse, to assure herself of a seat inside. She saw Woerful, standing alone at the back of the crowd, and kept herself away from him. Yesterday she had been weak, overwhelmed by her grief, but she had made a promise to Katie. A promise she meant to keep.

Krang stood patiently while the deputy removed his shackles outside the courtroom. He was wearing the same outfit as yesterday. He brushed his hands over his short hair. It was just like what he had worn at the camp: shaved on the sides and short on top. He expected the fireworks to start as soon as he walked into the courtroom. The deputy opened the door and escorted him inside.

Krang heard the murmurs run through the crowd like the buzz of an angry hornet. He walked crisply, knowing that he exuded power. *The guard* had returned. Krang sat in the docket and stared at the crowd. They didn't like the new Krang, he could tell.

Krang was disappointed, however. He had expected his entourage of dead souls to return in order to see him confess his sins, but they hadn't. Not a single soul stared back at him. He wondered if they were so filled with hatred towards Sarah that they wouldn't watch him confess if it meant freeing her memory. Or were they just so disincorporated that nothing remained to celebrate his coming death? Or in returning to God did they lose all worldly attachments, including their desire to see Krang pay for his crimes?

The bailiff rapped on the podium with the gavel. "All rise for the Honorable Judge Belthus..."

The judge pounded the gavel to quiet the crowd as he took his seat.

The judge turned to Krang. "Today is your opportunity to tell your story. Please approach the witness stand."

Krang rose and walked briskly across the courtroom to sit in the chair at the judge's left. He looked out at the crowd, searching their faces. They stared back intently. They were eager for his testimony. Were they ready for the truth? The men and women who had testified against him sat in the first row of seats, directly behind Janos Lev. They were clearly troubled by Krang's appearance, talking vigorously amongst themselves. Except Woerful, who sat on the end of the row and gazed off to his right, lost in grief.

One of the men tugged on the Prosecutor's arm, engaging him in conversation. Lev kept glancing at Krang and shaking his head. He turned to one of his assistant's and whispered in his ear. The young man ran from the court room. Krang smiled. The end was near.

Lisle sat in the observation deck and studied the man in the witness seat. This was Sarah's father. More importantly, he was the man that Katie had loved with all of her heart. Lisle was hoping to see what it was that had captured Katie's affections, but she couldn't. He looked hard and dangerous sitting at the front of the court room. As an undercurrent of tension flowed through the crowd, he smiled in challenge to them. She had no trouble imagining him doing everything that he had told Katie he had done, and she didn't see any sign of repentance.

"You may question the witness," Judge Belthus said to the prosecutor. Janos Lev turned around to look at the doors to the court room, clearly looking for the assistant he had dispatched ten minutes earlier, and then shrugged and approached the man in the witness box.

"Did you carve the name Sarah Jezek into the National Monument?"

Krang nodded. "I did..."

"Your Honor," Lev interrupted, "that is all you need to convict him. I move for a directed verdict of guilty, and an assessment that Mr. Werkamp is dangerous and should be committed to a mental institution immediately."

"Your motion is denied," the judge replied. "Do you have other questions, or are you releasing the witness?"

Lev scowled. "I have many questions, your Honor. We could be here for days."

Belthus smiled. "I doubt that will be necessary. Proceed."

Lisle wondered what the hell was going on between the two of them. It reminded her of some of the boys in secondary school, fighting over the same girl.

"You asked to have Sarah's name added to the monument, did you not?"

"Yes. My request was denied."

"Why?"

Krang shrugged. "I don't know."

"You don't know? Didn't you get an official report telling you Sarah Jezek was a collaborator? That she had been executed for collaborating?"

"They were wrong."

"You know this? That they were wrong?"

"Yes. I..."

"If we let you go, what will you do?" Lev smiled.

"Let me go?" Krang looked confused. "Why would you do that?"

Lev shrugged broadly, playing to the audience. "Who knows. But if we did, what would you do? Would you leave Corabia?"

"No."

"Why not?"

"I need to be here to be sure that Sarah's memory is honored."

"And how will you do that?"

"I'll put her name back on the monument. Again and again if I have to."

Lev nodded, and walked back to his table. He conferred briefly with a second assistant, before turning to Judge Belthus. "Your Honor, we have surely established Mr. Werkamp's guilt, which he admits, and his acknowledgment that he will never stop. That must be enough to see him committed."

"You would never leave the monument be?" the judge asked.

Krang shook his head. "No, your Honor. Not while an injustice is being done."

"Is having Sarah's name left off the monument such an injustice that you would risk your freedom?"

Krang turned and looked at the Judge. "The name means nothing. The injustice is that they murdered her. She survived the hell of the camp to be murdered by the people she thought were her community. I can't undo that murder, your Honor, but I can tell the world about it until someone listens."

Lisle was surprised by the emotion in Krang's voice. It didn't fit with his hardened exterior, or with the violence that he had committed. Maybe this was the part of him to which Katie had been privy.

"Tell us why you thought her name belonged on the monument."

354

Krang cleared his throat. "She was an inmate in the Mountain City camp, and she died there. Those are the only requirements that I am aware of. I asked at the Parks office and they told me that was the requirement. They said many names have been accidentally left off the monument."

The judge nodded. "I agree with your assessment. But surely, Mr. Werkamp, you can understand why the state might choose to keep off the name of someone who acted in collusion with our enemies."

"But Sarah Jezek did not act in collusion with anyone other than God. Her alleged crime was to forgive a far greater crime. And is that not what we are taught in our churches, whether we are Corabian or Montrovian? That forgiveness is the road to salvation?"

"Go ahead, Mr. Werkamp. You have proof that Sarah Jezek acted out of faith and not as a collaborator?"

The court room had fallen quiet. Everyone strained to hear.

"Sarah Jezek witnessed the murder of her son and husband on her first day in the camp. Babies and small children were routinely taken from their parents when they arrived at the camps. The parents were told the child would be taken to the doctor for an examination, or that they were being sent to the camp school, but they were just killed.

"When a guard started to take Capek from Sarah's arms, she tried to save her child. She argued with the guard, keeping the baby free from his grasp. The man in charge of the operation that evening was the one referred to as *the guard*. He was the most hated and feared man in the camp. The other inmates knew that to cross him was a death sentence, but not Sarah or her husband. They were too new. *The guard* walked up to see what was holding up the unloading of the transport, only to be implored by Sarah for help."

Krang stopped for a moment, taking in a deep breath.

"He reached for her son as gently as he could with one hand. He had to move his 9mm pistol to his left hand so he could take the boy in his right. He smiled reassuringly at Sarah, to get her to release the boy to him. *The guard* grabbed the boy by his ankles, and Sarah knew what he intended to do. She screamed in vain as he raised the crying infant over his head.

"Abraham rushed forward to save his son, and *the guard* raised his 9mm pistol and shot him at the same time he swung Capek down onto the concrete dock, crushing his head against the cement."

The crowd in the court room recoiled, as if they had been in the camp to see it. A woman let out a hysterical sob. Lisle had heard the story from Katie, but it had been told drily, with no emotion. She thought of the infant Sarah. Her heart broke to think of that child, her child, crushed against the loading dock. To imagine what Sarah must have felt to see her son brutalized. To see her husband shot dead before her eyes.

"In that one instant, Sarah lost both her husband and her son, simultaneously." Krang paused, and took a sip of water from the glass in front of him.

"Your Honor," Lev interrupted. "I have not finished questioning my witness. May I be allowed to continue?"

Judge Belthus looked surprised at the question. "You are right," he said. "Mr. Werkamp remains your witness."

Lev approached Krang in the witness box. "We're you a prisoner at the Mountain City camp?"

Krang laughed. "Good God, no," he said. "I was..."

"I know him!" One of the former inmates, sitting on the front row near Katie's father, stood up. "I know who he is."

Lisle watched as Krang smiled, nodding his head. He seemed to be encouraging the man to speak. The judge rapped sharply on the podium with his gavel.

"If you do not sit down, I will have you ejected from this court room," he told the man.

"But..." The gavel pounded again, and the man slumped back into his seat, whispering furiously to the prosecutor's assistants.

Lev turned away from the witness to join the hushed conversation. Lisle could see him shaking his head furiously, his face red. After a minute, one of the assistants grabbed the witness by the arm and pulled him from his seat. The man struggled, so one of the court room guards came forward and grabbed the other arm and they hauled the man from the room.

"I apologize to the court," Lev said. "The witness was overcome with emotion and very confused."

"You may continue," Belthus said.

"Your Honor," Lev continued with a nod. "He agrees he wasn't at the camp. I ask again for a directed..."

"I never said I wasn't at the camp," Krang interrupted. His voice carried throughout the courtyard, and Lisle felt chills run down her spine. This was the voice of *the guard*. "Let me finish telling Sarah's story."

The judge looked at Lev, who shrugged.

"You may continue." Belthus said.

"After *the guard* killed her husband and son, he left her kneeling on the platform, their bodies lying before her. He forced all the other new inmates to walk past them, so they would understand what would happen if they resisted anything. In his mind, it had been a wonderful lesson for all of them to see. To teach them the futility of resisting. To teach them that nothing they had ever experienced had prepared them for the camp.

"Later that night, *the guard* returned and pulled Sarah from her cabin and raped her. He frequently terrorized new arrivals this way. He made his way into her cabin, and all the women cowered in fear of him except Sarah, so he took her. He didn't have to beat her, or any of the women he took, because they saw everyday that resisting him meant death. So even though they acquiesced, it was still rape. It wasn't personal, you have to understand, because then he forgot all about Sarah. Two years later, on the eve of the camp being liberated, he didn't even remember who she was, or what he had done to her and her family."

The courtroom was absolutely silent. Lisle wiped the tears from her face again, and knew she wasn't alone in crying. She alone knew he was telling his own story, creating his own death. She could see the paradox that engulfed Katie. He was a monster, and yet here he was, honestly telling his story, trying to make the truth work. You've said enough, she thought, just let it go. They understand what happened now.

"The night before the camp was liberated, after control had been turned over to the Corabian prisoners, Sarah came up to *the guard* on the parade ground and she forgave him. And then she told him how to get away."

"Why would she have done that?" Lev asked. "If your story is true, tell us why she would forgive him."

"Krang asked her the very same thing: why not leave him on the parade ground to meet his fate? She was very honest, that she did it for herself, not for him. She was afraid that if he died in the camp, and was thrown into the pit on top of the bodies of her son and husband, that his guilt would trap their souls there for eternity. She was afraid that her own hatred for *the guard* would trap her husband and son in that place of pain forever. She couldn't reconcile what she had been taught all of her life with what she felt in her heart, so she acted on what she had been taught, not on what she felt. And she was afraid that leaving him there to be killed would mean that she hadn't forgiven him at all, that she had lied to herself and to her God.

"The crime that occurred that night had nothing to do with her act of forgiveness, and everything to do with the unwillingness of the camp to forgive her."

"Do you think she was right?" Belthus asked.

"Right? Probably not, but ask me was she righteous and I will tell you absolutely."

"Can you explain?" Lev asked. "How could she be righteous, but not be right?"

"How can anyone forgive *the guard*? If I ever met a man who deserved to die, it was him. If I ever met a man who deserved to be tormented in hell for eternity, it was him. He didn't just do what he was told to do. He searched for ways to make each day more demeaning and more horrifying than the last. He took his power from the camp, and from what he did to those people. Each new act of oppression made him more powerful and more in control. No one like him ever deserves forgiveness.

"But forgiveness isn't about how deserving the person is. Just the opposite is true. The less deserving of forgiveness the more divine and courageous an act it is. And Sarah acted in the most courageous and divine manner possible."

"So you believe that God wishes us to forgive the most heinous crimes?"

"No, I don't. I don't know what God wants from us, but as Woerful testified yesterday, God doesn't come down and save men who have been convicted of murder. I have buried enough of them on my way here to know that. I do believe, that for whatever reason, Sarah acted on what God wanted from her. He wanted something that we as a society are unwilling to do."

"Practice forgiveness."

Krang nodded. "Right. That's what cost Sarah her life. Only one single person in that camp, Katerina Woerful, believed Sarah was capable of forgiving the man who killed her husband and son. Even her family didn't believe her. So they killed her instead."

"How do you know all this that you've shared with us?"

"Sarah told me."

"You are saying that Sarah told you this, in the Mountain City camp?" Lev asked.

"Yes."

"You are aware that I have ten witnesses that swear you were never an inmate in the Mountain City Camp?"

"Of course. I've been here the entire time."

"How do you explain this discrepancy?"

"They're wrong."

Lev raised his hands in disgust. "This is why I am asking the court to place this man in custody. Even in the face of overwhelming evidence, he believes his own grandiose version of the truth. He's not sane."

"You can prove they are wrong?" Belthus asked, ignoring Lev's outburst.

"Of course," Krang said quietly.

"Please share it with the court."

Don't say anything, Lisle wanted to shout. Katie loved you. Let her soul protect you now.

"I know what I have told you because Sarah explained it to me before she told me how to get out of the camp. My name is Walter Krang. I am the man known as *the guard.*"

358

The courtroom erupted in a cacophony of shouts. Spectators jumped to their feet suddenly infused with passion.

Belthus began beating on the podium with his gavel.

Janos Lev was on his feet screaming for a mistrial.

"Quiet!" The bailiff shouted. "Order. Order."

It took several minutes before the courtroom quieted down enough for the inquiry to continue. The room was filled with a new energy, a dangerous dark force that threatened to sweep out of control.

"I told you I know who he is!" the old man shouted from where he had slipped back inside the courtroom.

The judge rapped his gavel.

"Your Honor," Lev shouted over the chaos. "I request a short recess. I have evidence that is important. My assistant should return shortly. It will address this question."

Belthus nodded. "That sounds like an admirable proposal," he said. "I grant..."

"I know who he is!" It was the old man again, walking up the aisle to the front of the room..

Shut up, Lisle thought. Just let it be. She could see Katie's father leaning forward, studying Krang, but he made no motion to indicate he recognized him.

"I would like to recall the earlier witness while we wait on your evidence," Belthus said.

Lev shrugged, then nodded. Lisle could see he was frustrated by the turn of events. Krang was sent back to his seat in the docket, and the old man brought forward and sworn in.

"You have already testified that you knew this man wasn't at the camp," the judge said. "Why do you change your mind?"

"I can see him now," the man said. "He is..."

"I haven't asked you who he is," Belthus interrupted. "I am more concerned with why you wish to change your testimony. Why do you think you recognize him now?"

"He looks different today, without the beard and long hair. Now he looks like *the guard*."

"He looks like *the guard?*"

"Yes."

"But looking like someone doesn't make it true. I look like my brother, but I am not him."

"I would never forget *the guard*. His image is burned into my mind."

"But you already told us you didn't remember this man."

"Because he didn't look like *the guard*. Now he does."

359

"Is that the only reason you think he is *the guard*? Because we cut his hair?"

"Yes. He was hidden before, but now he is not."

"Do you have any other proof to corroborate his identity? Do you know of a birthmark or other mark which would prove his identity?"

The man shook his head. "He says he is *the guard*."

Belthus turned to Lev. "Do you have any questions for the witness?"

"No."

"Thank you for testifying." the judge said. Belthus dismissed the man, who returned to his original seat in the front row. Lev's assistant had returned while the man was testifying, carrying a portfolio in one hand. Lev took it from him and held it up.

"I have items I'd like to place in evidence."

"Not yet," Belthus said. "I'd like to recall Mr. Werkamp and let him proceed with his testimony."

He turned to Krang, once he was seated in the witness box. "You claim to be *the guard*, one of the most hated and wanted men in this nation?"

"I claim nothing, your Honor. I simply tell the truth. I am Walter Krang. And Sarah Jezek was no collaborator."

"An admission like this is tantamount to signing your own death warrant. Do you understand?"

Krang shrugged. "I do what I must. The consequences don't concern me."

"Mr. Prosecutor, do you wish to hold this man for indictment on charges of crimes against humanity? He claims to be Walter Krang."

Janos Lev walked to the center of the courtroom, looked at Krang and shook his head in disgust. "Your Honor, this man is clearly not *the guard*. He would have been recognized by the others if he had been. None of the witnesses that saw him in line-up claimed he was Krang. None of the witnesses in this court claimed he was Krang. He is a desperate man, willing to throw away his own life to feed his psychosis."

"How easily you ignore his claims. Shouldn't you investigate them?"

Lev shook his head. "They are only more proof that he is a danger to himself and should be locked up."

"I caution you, Mr. Prosecutor, to think clearly on this matter. If you think to have him committed for insanity now, and later discover him to be *the guard*, I won't allow it. Either he is or he isn't. And if he is, then you and the state are very wrong about Sarah Jezek, and not only does her name belong on the monument, but she deserves special accord in our history."

"Look at him, Your Honor. Can a man of such power as Krang have fallen so far to have become a vagrant in a cemetery? And are we to believe that after the war, one of the most wanted fugitives in all the world would come to the very country that is so desperately trying to hunt him down? You heard his story of Sarah Jezek's first moments in the camp, a story that has been verified as true. Would a man of such viciousness just change? Would he suddenly throw away the life he has fought so hard to keep, simply because a confused, hurt woman said she forgave him? I can't believe it."

"Then why the charade?"

"He is a classic example of the worst kind of survivor. He is filled with self-loathing, and wishes to die. We see it all the time, especially in men. They carry an extraordinary guilt from surviving a situation which claimed their family and friends. This man simply doesn't have the courage to kill himself, so he concocts a story to force us to do it for him."

"A survivor of the camps? You have been arguing that he is not of the camps."

The prosecutor shook his head. "Nonsense. I have been arguing that he was never at the Mountain City camp. He obviously was in one of the camps. He has the tattoo."

"I have heard of fake tattoos."

"Just look at it. He tried to obliterate it, which proves that he escaped from a camp before the war ended. I have seen fake tattoos. They are always perfect."

"Show us your left forearm," the judge told Krang.

Krang shook his head. Belthus nodded to the bailiff who came over to the witness box and grabbed Krang's left arm. The bailiff unbuttoned his shirt at the wrist and rolled his sleeve up, then lifted his forearm high in the air. Janos Lev pointed to the partial tattoo and the burn scar beneath it. The audience in the courtroom strained forward to see.

"You would have us believe that he knew that he would be in this docket some day, so he gave himself the tattoo, and then tried to cut it out? Look at that scaring. He was in a camp."

"But not the Mountain City camp."

"Correct."

"Which camp was he in?"

"I don't know your honor. We have no record of Walter Werkamp."

"At any camp?"

"No, your Honor. We believe he is lying."

"Lying? You just said…"

"About his name. We believe he is lying about his name to hide his true identity."

"And yet you believe that he was in a camp."

"I know he was in a camp."

"What is the number on his arm?"

"All that can be read is 361.... The rest he destroyed."

"And which camp is referenced by that tattoo?"

"It's hard to say with a partial number, your Honor."

"I can have you thrown in jail on contempt charges for lying."

Janos Lev nodded slowly. "The 36 references the Mountain City camp, but we know he wasn't there."

"So you claim that the tattoo proves he was in a camp, but not Mountain City? Even though he has the Mountain City number?"

"Yes."

"And he's crazy?"

"Yes."

"But if he was in a camp..."

"He was your Honor."

"And the tattoo is the only evidence we have of that..."

"It is, your Honor."

"It seems logical to me that he could have been in the Mountain City camp. I am sure there are other inmates from the camp whom no one would remember, either they came late, or they hid, or they simply made themselves nondescript enough to survive by being invisible. And if he was in the Mountain City camp, then I must believe that he knew Sarah Jezek. In which case, I must believe that his story is true, for as you say, who would willingly throw away his own life?"

"But he's crazy..."

"Crazy? Possibly. But if you knew the truth about Sarah Jezek' life, wouldn't that make you a little crazy? If you knew what she had done, and that she had been murdered by our own people for it, wouldn't that make you a little crazy? If you knew that the spiritual leader of her camp, the man who should have held her up as a blessed example of how we live was responsible for her death, wouldn't that make you a little crazy? If you had told your story to the parks commission, only to have them deny you, wouldn't that make you a little crazy?"

"Your Honor..."

"Might you not be desperate enough to masquerade as a hated man, if you thought it would make a difference? Especially if you didn't care if you lived or died?"

"You Honor..."

"Why is the state pursuing this? Why is it so important to deny Sarah's story?"

"She freed *the guard*. One of the most notorious criminals in all the war, and she decided to let him go. She had no right to do that for any reason. Certainly not because she forgave him."

"So the state has more authority than God?"

362

"I beg your pardon?"

"Are you saying that the state has more authority over her than God?"

"No, not at all. I'm saying that she had no right to free Walter Krang from a death sentence. She could have forgiven him and walked away."

"I forgive you, but I still seek your death?"

"Yes."

"But aren't we taught that with forgiveness comes freedom from judgment?"

"She wasn't judging him, society was."

"And she should have acquiesced?"

"Yes."

"But if God told her to forgive Krang in order to be free of him, and if God told her that meant freeing him, how can we supersede that?"

"God wouldn't have told her that."

"So now you speak for God?"

"She let Walter Krang go. That was treason."

"Treason? Against whom?"

"The Homeland. Corabia."

"She wasn't a citizen of Corabia, so your argument is nonsense. If this man isn't *the guard*, where is Krang today?"

"I am here, your Honor," Krang said. He looked bewildered by the conversation between the two men. Lisle knew that Katie was the architect of it all. Somehow, even after she died, she was saving the man she loved.

"Your Honor," Lev said angrily, holding up the portfolio. "I have tried to enter this report in open court, but you have stayed my hand. The world has waited to capture Krang and bring him to trial. You are keeping this evidence from providing comfort to those who suffered most under Krang's hand."

Belthus shook his head, an irritated grin on his face. "By all means, Mr. Prosecutor, please share your evidence with the court."

"We have a report that claims Walter Krang was killed at a road block outside Mountain City in the waning days of the war. There are reports that he was caught with his youngest son. Unfortunately, the son was freed and disappeared, but Krang was executed and his body thrown into a mass grave with others trying to slip out of our net."

"How old was the son who escaped?"

"A year, eighteen months, we're not exactly sure. A man took the child from Krang just minutes before he was killed."

"And you're sure this man who was executed was Krang?"

"Yes. We had a witness who told us he had seen him in the detention area carrying a child. When they returned with our soldiers, the only man with a child had just been executed by firing squad. Several other witnesses agreed with the description, so we are confident that was him. It was very unfortunate that he wasn't recognized early enough to be put on trial, for we believe the world deserved the right to see him in the docket, as they saw the Nazis at Nuremburg."

"So this man cannot be Krang?"

"No, your Honor, he cannot. *The guard* is dead, his body rotting in a pit similar to the one he used at the Mountain City Camp. It is ironic, isn't it? But God always brings justice to those who deserve it. As he did to Sarah Jezek as well."

The crowd in the courtroom was stunned. The room was quiet, but an undercurrent of furious whispers ran through the crowd. Could it be? *The guard* was dead? Why was it kept a secret? Who benefitted from not telling the world? When would they have told us? Lisle looked at the men and women who were slowly moving from stunned silence to anger. In her head, she could her Katie squealing with joy at the turn of events. The thought made her smile.

The judge turned to Krang. "I can have you charged for committing perjury for claiming to be Walter Krang, whom the state has determined to be dead."

Krang shrugged his shoulders, bewildered. "Your Honor, I have only spoken the truth. I can do no more than that," he said, staring at Lev.

"Why would this man risk death to claim he was *the guard*?" the judge asked Janos Lev.

"He is suicidal but lacks the courage to try to kill himself. He wishes to force the state to do it for him. Other men rob banks with empty guns. It happens."

"Have you ever tried to kill yourself since the war ended?" the judge asked Krang.

Krang thought for a moment. "Yes, I have," he answered wearily. "In the mountains, when I lost someone I loved, I put a shotgun in my mouth and pulled the trigger, but it would not fire. I walked through some of the heaviest fighting of the war, burying the dead, but I did not ever get hurt myself. I stood on the edge of a mass grave as soldiers shot the men who had dug it in the back of the head, but they skipped me. God has cursed me to live with the truth of who I am, and has refused to let me die."

Belthus looked at Lev. "May I see the report?"

"It is a classified document..."

"If you want it entered as evidence, I must read it. It will not be a part of the court record, but I must ascertain that it says what you claim it says."

Lev approached the bench and handed the portfolio to Belthus. The courtroom hummed with energy as the judge read.

Did you do this Katie? Is this why you left us so peacefully, so that you could save him? Lisle shook her head. You wouldn't leave me for him in life, but did you do it in death? Is that what love is about?

Belthus finished the report, a frown on his face. He nodded for Lev to continue.

"He is clearly a danger to himself and others..." Lev began.

"So you cannot die?" the judge interrupted, turning to Krang.

Krang shook his head. "I have not been able to die. I was sure I was kept alive simply to tell the truth of Sarah's divine act, and that would cost me my life."

"Because you would admit to being Walter Krang."

"Because I would admit to the truth."

"And you believe you are a monster?"

"I believe that I am a divine child of God, as we all are. I also know that I have done terrible things that demand vengeance. I cannot reconcile those truths. That's why I am here."

"So that I can reconcile them?"

Krang nodded. "Yes."

"Did you kill during the war?"

Krang nodded, and wiped a tear from his face. "Yes," he said quietly.

"How many?"

Krang shrugged his shoulders. "Too many to count. I expected them to be here to see this moment. They traveled with me for months until they lost their anger and rested."

The judge was silent for a moment. "You believe the dead traveled with you through the war?"

Krang nodded. "Only their souls. Their bodies were in the pit. They were my witnesses. They watched me bury the dead as I made my way here to the Homeland."

"Perhaps they protected you?"

"I wouldn't think so, your Honor, but I cannot say for sure. They wanted to hear me say publicly what I had done."

Belthus stared at Krang for several minutes. "Since the state has declared that Walter Krang is dead, I cannot hold your claim to be *the guard* as true."

Krang slumped in his chair, defeated.

"However, since the state has also claimed that you are clearly a survivor of the camps, and cannot produce any evidence to show which camp, I cannot uphold their claim that you were not an inmate in the Mountain City camp. I believe that you know the truth of what happened between Sarah Jezek and Walter Krang, and Sarah's subsequent execution. It is my ruling that the state inscribes the name Sarah Jezek on the National monument, and adds a marker acknowledging that she sacrificed her life to honor her faith..."

"Your Honor! I object! You cannot do this..." Janos Lev was red faced with anger.

365

The judge brought his gavel down sharply on the podium. "Be still! I further hold that Mr. Werkamp poses no threat to himself, since he knows that God protects him and will not let him die before his time, and that he poses no threat to society, and shall be freed immediately."

The courtroom erupted into a mixture of shouts, jeers and cheers as the audience began arguing the decision amongst themselves. Lisle was unsure if they supported the decision or not.

"Katie," she whispered, "I don't know how you managed to protect him, but you did."

Lisle knew that she was the only person in the courtroom who knew the truth. She was amazed that Walter had never faltered in his attempt to tell the truth. Katie was right to see something in you, she thought. She saw beyond the obvious and found the better part of you.

"Order! Order!" the bailiff shouted, quieting the crowd.

"Mr. Werkamp," the judge continued, "it is unfortunate, but we have a number of persons in our society who believe it is their right to take judgment into their own hands whenever they disagree with the statements of this court. I would suggest that you plan on leaving the Homeland, for although our nation was conceived in a spirit of hope and peace, to be a place where God's dream for us is realized, in truth it is simply another political state filled with people who are unable to live up to the Ideas and Truths they claim are self-evident and necessary. We are all just like the man you claim to be: divine children of God , but capable of undertaking terrible actions against each other. I must admit our divine experiment is an immense failure in practice. There are many in our land who will want to act against you because of your testimony, and the state is unable to accept the burden of guaranteeing your safety. I encourage you to leave this nation immediately. You are free to go."

Janos Lev stepped forward. "Bailiff, arrest this man..."

Belthus pounded his gavel on the bench. "Ignore that request," he told the Bailiff.

"Your Honor," Lev snapped, "he must be arrested. You heard his testimony."

"Testimony that you proved to be false with your information that Krang was dead."

"Then he must be someone else!"

"Exactly. And that someone is free."

"Your Honor, you misunderstand. He must be a guard from the camp, and he claimed to be Krang to enjoy his notoriety."

"Mr. Prosecutor," Belthus said, "Your own arguments proved that not to be true. You have acknowledged the camp tattoo as real. You have provided an overwhelming array of witnesses who each testified that this man was never at the camp."

"But Bily Guordlet just testified that this man is Krang. We can recall him to the stand now, your Honor..."

Belthus rapped the gavel again. He held up the report in one hand. "We can do nothing of the kind. What we can do is order an investigation into the death of Walter Krang. We can investigate who knew *the guard* was dead, and for how long. This report is from last summer, just a few months after the camp was liberated. We can investigate when this information was going to be made public, and if you were holding it to be released as part of your campaign for Prime Minister..."

"Be careful of what you say," Lev snapped.

Belthus smiled grimly. "I think it is too late to be careful." He nodded to the court stenographer. "The comment is already in the public record. I imagine it will be in the evening paper as well."

"This is political suicide," Lev said. "You will pay for this for years."

"Sarah Jezek was wrongly accused and executed. Her name belongs on that monument. That's all this case was about. You are the one who tried to launch a bid for Prime Minister on the back of an innocent man at the cost of woman's humiliation and death. You are the one who purposefully kept secret a story of great faith and heroism. I have no fear of how all this will look in the papers."

Belthus turned to Krang. "You may step down. You are a free man." He rapped his gavel again, and the crowd erupted. Lisle ignored the pandemonium around her, and kept her eyes on Krang. She could see that he was crying. He sat in the witness seat without moving, except to slowly shake his head. After several minutes the bailiff came up and whispered something into his ear. Krang looked up at the man and Lisle could see the look of despair on his face. He was deflated, a man without hope.

He thinks he has failed, Lisle realized. Katie was right. He was trying to kill himself. He never imagined he could survive testifying, and now he doesn't know what to do. Lisle watched as the bailiff escorted him from the courtroom through a side door, so he wouldn't have to face the crowd.

Lisle found Krang in a narrow hallway in the basement of the courthouse. Two police officers were standing a few feet away from him, smoking. Krang just leaned against the wall and stared at the floor. Lisle breathed a sigh of relief. She had been looking for him for half an hour, and was afraid she had somehow missed him.

Krang was lost in thought, staring at the floor tile. She couldn't see the violence in him, couldn't see the killer who had taken so many lives. But how would you see that, she wondered? Can you really tell evil? Katie had loved him so fiercely. What had she seen in his broken soul?

Katie restored me to life, Lisle thought. I was ready to throw myself from that train when she saw me and through sheer will of being she brought me back to life. Katie must have been much stronger than I realized, to do the same thing for you. Your soul must have been dead, you couldn't recognize anything in common with another human being, and she restored you. This is what she meant when she said you were as scarred on the inside as I on the outside. Lisle remembered that Katie had also said the Krang needed someone like Lisle to love him. She shook her head. I couldn't love a man like Krang, so capable of violence. But why had Katie?

She was a healer. The thought caught Lisle off guard. Katie was a healer. She healed both of us, and restored us to life. Somehow she gave us back our humanity. So why didn't she heal herself?

"Stop, miss." One of the officers dropped his cigarette and raised his hand. "Don't come any closer. Mr. Werkamp is under our protection."

Krang looked up at her. His eyes were so full of pain. He shook his head at the officer and motioned her forward with his hand. Lisle noticed that he steeled himself slightly, as if he worried she might attack him. Or hoped? He looked back at the floor.

Lisle approached Krang slowly, trying to overcome her fear that when he spoke she would realize it was all an act. That he hadn't changed at all. That Katie hadn't healed him, but just been fooled by him. Finally, she found herself just a few feet away.

"Excuse me?"

Krang looked up. His eyes, the lightest shade of blue, took a moment to focus. "Yes?"

"I'm a friend of Katie...." she caught herself, and groaned slightly. "I was a friend of Katie..., you know that she..."

Krang nodded slowly. "Yes," he said gently. "I know."

"She had a baby girl. She wanted you to know." Lisle was on the verge of tears.

Krang nodded again. "Her father said so in his testimony." His voice was flat and emotionless.

Lisle shook her head. I knew this was a mistake she thought. "I'm sorry I bothered you," she said. She turned around and walked down the hall.

Krang watched her go. He wanted to chase after the woman and beg her to tell him more, but he had no right. He had forfeited all of that with his other children. It seemed fitting that the son he had never bothered to go see, born just before the camp fell, would be joined by a half-sister that he would also never see.

He wished he'd been more open to her, but he wasn't able to focus his attention. He still didn't understand what had happened in the courtroom. How had he been freed? He had told the truth, but they refused to listen. Krang shook his head. He had been so sure this was how he was to do his penance for his crimes.... How could they let him go?

Krang looked up from the floor and saw the woman moving slowly away. He watched as she walked away. She was a few years older than Katie. Her shoulders were shaking, as if she were crying. He was glad that Katie had made a friend who mourned her passing, but sorry at the same time for the young woman's pain. Love costs us so much, he thought. Maybe that's why it's so important.

She stopped at the corner of the hall, lingering, then turned around and walked back. Her determination reminded him of Sarah approaching him on the parade ground. Of how she had come and looked, and then walked away, before turning around and marching back into his life.

"Excuse me," Lisle said again. Krang nodded, a faint smile on his lips at her return.

"Your accent," he said, "isn't from around here. You don't look like someone who went through the camps. Are you Montrovian?"

Lisle nodded. "From the western hills. I was sent here because it wasn't safe for me to remain in my village. I met Katie on the train here, a few days after she left you."

Krang nodded, hating the memory.

"She loved you, you know. Right up to the very end, she loved you with all her heart. She couldn't forgive herself for loving you, because she thought she shouldn't. She thought she should hate you. Even when she feared the worst, that you had tormented and killed her family in the camp, a part of her still loved you. The day her mother's letter arrived...." Lisle shook her head. "I thought she would leave that day to find you. I don't know how you managed to get a letter from her mother, but it made Katie so happy."

"It was God. He put Katie's mother in my path. I held her hand while she died. She died fulfilled, knowing Katie was well. Knowing her grandchild was on the way. I promised her I would deliver her letter to Katie. I tried to make sure she couldn't connect it to me."

Lisle shook her head. "She never realized you were here until her father told her about the trial. That was the night before she died..." Lisle's voice trailed off. "The night before the baby was born."

Krang felt as if she had slapped him. It had been his fault, in the end. He always knew she would die because of him.

Lisle must have seen something in his face because she shook her head vehemently. "No," she said. "You misunderstand. She didn't die in childbirth. The doctor said she had a bad heart. She could have died at any time. He said God wanted her back, that was all."

"Why are you here?"

"Katie sent me to find you. I have something for you. I didn't bring it with me today, I'm sorry. We'll have to meet tomorrow. Where can we meet?"

Krang thought for a moment. "We can meet at the monument. Do you know where it is?"

Lisle nodded. "We never went to see it. Katie felt guilty about never being in the camp."

"I know. I told her she was a hero for running away. That what she thought of as her weakness was a measure of her strength. She never really believed me. Shall we meet at nine am?"

Lisle nodded, and then turned to go. She stopped when she was at the end of the hall, and turned back to Krang. "It's a letter that she wrote you," she said. "That's what I have. She wrote it two days ago, just before she died. And I'll introduce you to Sarah, your daughter."

Krang watched her turn the corner and disappear, his heart hammering in his chest. He was sorry he wouldn't be able to keep the appointment.

Chapter Twenty-Six

A gentle breeze washed the top of the cedar trees, making the branches sway. The sun, bright yellow, hung over the ocean opposite a ghostly crescent moon. Lisle held Sarah to her breast, gently rocking the sleeping infant. Jana, the wet nurse, had left that morning to return to her family in a flood of tears, her leaving Sarah intensifying the loss of her son. Lisle had been crying off and on ever since. She felt lost, like a broken down boat adrift on the ocean, blown whichever direction the winds swirled. Lisle looked at the pale sliver of moon, barely visible against the brightness of the day. I was the moon to Katie's sun, Lisle thought, the pale reflection of her light. How will I go on?

Sarah sighed in her arms, stirring gently. Lisle rocked her, smiling to herself. She was less afraid of Sarah today, thanks to Jana, who had forced her to care for the infant all evening. Even at three days, the child was developing a personality. She was bossy, in a way that reminded Lisle of her mother. Lisle still had no idea how she would raise a child on her own, in a strange country, but she knew she would find a way.

Lisle lifted her eyes from the infant to the monument. She wished that she had forced Katie to visit the monument, at least once. Lisle was sure Katie would have loved it. The pond was just large enough that the breeze could force ripples to race across its surface, creating turmoil within its peacefulness. Katie would have loved that idea, Lisle thought, because that's who she was. And she would have loved the eternal flame burning at the very center of the pond, a fountain of flame rather than water. That was Katie in all her relationships, although who was water and who was flame remained a mystery. Was Krang fire to Katie's water and Katie fire to me? Or was I the one who inflamed Katie, but was unwilling to accept that I could cause desire? She shook her head. It didn't matter now.

Lisle had walked the circumference of the pond when she arrived at the monument, studying the thousands of names carved into the marble surface of the retaining wall. She had stopped in front of one panel, reaching out to trace her fingers along one name: Marek Sobek. The name meant nothing to her, but tracing his name with her finger was enough to bring a tear to her eye. Seeing the hundreds of names on that one panel and knowing every panel had as many made her break out in sobs. Lisle had never understood the magnitude of it. Even what she had seen in her own village, even what she had experienced herself, hadn't made her understand.

She eventually made her way to the bench on which she sat, in front of the panel dedicated to the Mountain City camp. No one had repaired the panel yet, apparently keeping it in case they needed it for the trial. Sarah Jezek's name was etched an eighth-of-an-inch deep, in letters four foot high, across the face of the panel. Sarah's name had eaten over the names of the other victims. Many names were completely destroyed. As much as it was a fitting tribute to Sarah's sacrifice, Lisle couldn't believe the woman would have approved. Based on the story she had heard from Krang, she couldn't believe Sarah would have wanted to put herself above the others, not even on a piece of stone.

The bells of a nearby church rang the three-quarters hour and Lisle gave a sigh of relief. Krang was forty-five minutes late; he wasn't coming. She would give him the full hour, and then she would leave. It would be easier on them all if he failed to show up.

Her relief calmed a fear that had been growing in the back of her mind all morning, based on something Katie had said after Sarah was born. She had told Lisle that Walter needed to be loved. That he deserved to be loved. The idea haunted her: Katie thinks I should love him. She sent me here because she expects me to love him. Lisle felt indignant at the thought. Why would Katie think I could ever love this man? Does she think I am so damaged that I have no other options before me?

Lisle shook her head. Katie had never seen me as damaged. She hadn't cared about the scarring, or my fears. She told me, over and over, how beautiful I was, and meant it. She would have been my lover if I had allowed it. So why does she think I should be with Krang?

Unless.... Katie understood that I see myself as damaged, and only worthy of being loved by someone equally damaged. Lisle wiped her eyes with the back of her hand. I don't see myself that way, do I? Do I really think no one will ever love me, simply for these scars? Or for betraying a boy five years ago? Betraying myself really, for allowing fear to keep me from grieving or calling out for justice?

"There was no justice to be had," Lisle heard Katie say, as clear as day, as if she were sitting next to her in the park. And that was the truth. Lisle took a deep breath as the bells tolled ten o'clock. It was time to go.

"Excuse me."

She started, and looked up and there he was, standing shyly to the side of the bench.

Krang saw the fear that flashed across her face and knew that he should have stayed away. He had been watching her for an hour, from a stand of trees about thirty meters from the monument, trying to decide what he should do. Twice he had walked away, only to return a minute later.

"I thought you weren't coming," she said. He thought h heard regret in her voice.

"I wasn't," Krang replied. "I'm still not sure I should have, but I want to see my daughter."

Lisle pulled the blankets back, giving him a clear view of the sleeping infant. She was sleeping peacefully, her head covered in fine hair. Krang studied her, wondering once again why he had never felt this sense of awe with his other children. They had deserved to be loved as wholly as any child ever born, but he hadn't loved them. One more sin on a very long list.

Lisle nodded at the wall of the monument. "That's some statement," she said.

Krang grinned. "It is. I made the solution too strong. I didn't think the acid would eat through the other names. I wasn't trying to erase them. I can't be free of what I did that easily."

Sarah mewed in Lisle's arms, as if she was agreeing with her father.

"May I hold her?" Krang asked.

Lisle stiffened. Krang could see everything she had heard about him flash through her head.

Krang raised his hand gently, trying to calm her. "Never mind."

She stared at him, as if she couldn't decide.

"I have no illusions of taking her. I'm not able to raise a child on my own, and even if I was, I have no right to this child. I gave away my right to be a parent a long time ago. I won't harm her."

Lisle nodded. Krang stepped forward and lifted Sarah from Lisle's arms. The little hair she had was lighter than Katie's had been, but Krang knew it would darken as she grew older. He could see hints of her mother in the child's face. He raised her gently to his face and smelled her. His eyes blurred and tears ran down his cheeks. He had had four chances to do this right and had thrown them away. Only now did he understand what he had missed. After a minute he gave the infant back.

He studied them, woman and child, so that he would never forget either of them. His heart ached for Katie, knowing that she should be here, holding their daughter, but some part of him recognized that these two had already become a family of their own. Lisle was beautiful, her deep blue eyes piercing and clear, and the child just a delight. In some way they belonged together.

Lisle stared up at him, the hint of a smile on her face. He could tell she was afraid, not just of him, but of what lay before her. She wasn't ready for this, he realized. Or at least she didn't think she was. He trusted Katie's instincts. If Katie believed in her, then Krang would as well. It was time to go. Time to let them go.

"Thank you," he said and turned to go.

"Wait," Lisle said. Krang stopped, looking over his shoulder. "You didn't ask what happened. How she died."

Krang shrugged. "It doesn't matter, does it? How she died doesn't change the outcome at all. At some level, all death is unjust. And I have no right to rail at God or anyone for the callousness of this place. I was blessed to know her for a few sweet months..."

"She loved you," Lisle blurted out.

Krang smiled.

"She couldn't forgive herself for loving you."

"Yes, you mentioned it yesterday."

"You don't understand," Lisle said. "She thought it was wrong, somehow. Not that you shouldn't be loved, she thought you should, but that it was wrong for her to love you."

Krang nodded. "Then it was."

Lisle shook her head. "No," she said. "Katie was wrong. Your love sustained her when nothing else could. She would have come around to it, eventually. She wouldn't have been able to look at Sarah and not want you there."

"I loved her, too," Krang said. "I let the fear of what might happen keep me from her. That betrayal is unforgivable." He turned to go.

"Wait," Lisle called out. She grinned nervously when Krang looked back over his shoulder. "I'm not doing this well. I have the letter she wrote you, just after Sarah was born. That's the other reason I'm here. She made me promise to bring it to you." Lisle reached into her coat pocket and pulled out an envelope.

Krang took it from her and slowly opened it, pulling out the letter.

My Dearest Walter,

We have created a daughter today. She is the most beautiful creature imaginable. The moment I held her on my breast I knew that God brought us together for this child. Whether we were good or bad didn't matter, this child mattered. I have taken the liberty of naming her Sarah in recognition of the faith of the woman who gave you your life back, and Katerina, after my mother, who had faith of her own.

I am sorry, Walter, that the three of us will not be able to be a family. I believe that is what God wants of us, but I haven't the strength to go on. Do not blame God for my passing, for I do not. I'm just so tired, each breathe is harder than the last, and I must go. Do not grieve for me, for you brought such love into my life. You believed in me, Walter. You saw me as a person of strength, not as a thing to be used. I will always love you for it.

I am sending you this letter in the hands of my best friend, Lisle, and I am commanding you (such a strong language from someone in my position. I beg you) to take care of her. Lisle is a fragile soul, on the verge of self destruction. She has been through worse than I have, and must be loved or she will eventually take her own life. DO NOT CONFUSE HER PAIN AND DESPAIR AS WEAKNESS! She is every bit my match and kept me alive when I was at my lowest points.

She will not welcome your love, for she thinks herself unlovable. In that way, she is like you. She is beautiful, as you can see, but her body and soul are deeply scarred. You must capture her heart, and then love her body. I know you well enough to know that you will love her, and desire her. You will find her soul delightful, and you will be able to kiss and caress each scar and lift her to ecstasy. I loved her Walter, and I know how her body responds to a kiss. She is afraid of her passion and blames it for the death of her first lover. I was her second. You must be her next, for neither of you can be alone in this world. You need each other. So please, do as I command.

I wish I could have found you and told you that I loved you. You never left my thoughts, not for a moment. So give me this gift that I beg of you.

I will love you forever,

Katie

Krang closed his eyes. He could hear Katie in his head, telling him what she had written on the page. He could see the worry on her face, worry for the both of them. He knew, even as her death approached, that she would have enjoyed playing matchmaker. He understood that even if she hadn't died, she might have tried to push them together, so that she would know the two people she loved had someone who loved them in their lives.

So what do I do now? Krang carried the letter to the nearest waste bin. He struck a match and held it to the paper, letting the letter burn in his hand. He watched the flame catch, eating the paper greedily, while he considered the impossibility of what Katie had asked of him. It would be impossible if Lisle had agreed, but it was clear from the tone of the letter that she had no idea what Katie expected from him. How do I honor her last wish? He kept turning the page so the flames didn't burn him, letting the last bit burn itself out as it fell into the bin. He returned to find Lisle and Sarah.

Lisle stared at him in horror. "How could you burn her letter?"

Krang shrugged. "Some things are best remembered in your heart, and some letters are not meant to be read again." He sat next to Lisle on the bench.

"What will you do? Take her to Woerful?" he asked

Lisle shook her head. "I made a promise to Katie that I wouldn't let her father raise this child. I told her I wasn't ready to raise Sarah on my own, but she wouldn't listen to me. She was adamant that her father not raise her. I can't stay in Corabia, because in a custody hearing the courts would rule in his favor. Katie asked me to take her to America, where her father will not find us."

"America?"

"I've money to buy the passage. Katie had been saving up for some time. There is a ship that leaves at the end of the week."

"And you are comfortable going off to America? You speak English?"

Lisle shook her head. "No. I'm terrified. I don't know anything about America, except when soldiers came through Montrovia during the war in Europe. Did you ever see the American soldiers?"

"They didn't come so far north as Mountain City."

"I was just a child, thirteen or fourteen. The men were so big, and they had chocolate. That's all I know about America. Everyone has chocolate."

Krang laughed. "It must be a wonderful place, then, if everyone has chocolate."

They sat on the bench in silence. A very awkward silence. Krang knew what Katie wanted from him, but was afraid to act. Afraid Lisle might say yes, and afraid she might say no. Aware that Katie had probably given Lisle directions as well, and not sure how he felt about that. Were they being forced into some kind of arranged marriage, on the whims of a seventeen year old who knew nothing of what it took to have a successful relationship? Or were they being saved through the insight of a young woman who had been wise beyond her years? Krang couldn't say anything.

After a few minutes, Krang stood up. "I should be going," he said. "I have been advised to leave the Corabia as soon as possible."

"Yes," Lisle said. "I was there yesterday. I heard what the judge said."

Krang stared at her. He hadn't thought yesterday that she had been at the courthouse all day. "So you heard my testimony?"

Lisle nodded. "It was very difficult to hear. I guess I was the only one there who knew you were telling the truth. I think Katie was watching out for you."

"Why are you here, if you heard what I did?"

"Katie wanted me to be here. You told her that story, but it couldn't keep her from loving you."

"She shouldn't have denied what I was."

"I think Katie would tell you to quit denying who you are. You know who you've been, now it's time to be who you are."

"It sounds so simple," Krang said, "but it isn't simple. I can't let it go."

"You think Katie was a whore?"

"No, but it's not the same."

"No, it's not, but it proves a point. People do what they do, good and bad. That isn't necessarily who they are. You did something horrible, but now you now that's not who you are. You have to let it go. That's what God has asked of you. Let *the guard* go. Become Walter."

Krang shrugged.

"Where will you go?" Lisle asked.

"I haven't got a clue. I can't go home. Europe, I suppose. Or maybe America." He looked at her, at the sleeping infant in her arms. This was the moment to act, he knew. If he was going to try to do what Katie wanted, now was the time. "Maybe I should travel with you, to make sure you are safe, until you reach America. I could disappear then."

A look of … fear? skittered across her face. At least I tried, he thought.

"I don't know," Lisle said. "I'm not sure I'm comfortable with that idea."

Krang nodded. "You are correct, of course. I wish you the best." He stood up and walked away, feeling like he had let Katie down once again. What did she think I could do? I'm not the right person to help heal someone. I've too much healing of my own to do.

Lisle watched Walter walk away. She had realized when he had been talking what had been in the letter. Katie hadn't just spoken to her, she written it all down for him as well. The nerve of that girl! Life wasn't so simple.

As Walter walked past the monument, his left hand brushed the marble, the fingers running across the names of the dead, as if he could read them without even looking. As if he cared for them. The words were out of her mouth before she even realized what she was doing.

"Wait! Just until America? That might make sense."

Lisle shook her head, wondering what she was doing. I can't love him, she thought. I know what you want of me Katie, but I can't do that.

Krang turned around and came back, a shy smile on his lips. "Just until America, then," he said. He stood a few feet away, hesitant.

Lisle studied him. His eyes shined with warmth. He was amused by her discomfort! She wanted to tell him to forget it, but she couldn't. He stood there like a boy at a school dance, afraid of being rejected, afraid of letting Katie down. As she was. It was funny. She laughed, rich and warm and suddenly full of life. She thought she could hear Katie laughing with her.

I don't know how Katie did this, she thought, as she handed Sarah to Krang and gathered her belongings. They left the park walking side by side. Lisle already knew he would never disappear when they got to America.

377